The Ruin of Angels

THE RUIN OF ANGELS

MAX GLADSTONE

A TOM DOHERTY ASSOCIATES BOOK

NEW YORK

THE RUIN OF ANGELS

Cover art by Goñi Montes
Cover design by Christine Foltzer

Edited by Marco Palmieri

A Tor.com Book
Published by Tom Doherty Associates
175 Fifth Avenue
New York, NY 10010

www.tor.com

Tor® is a registered trademark of
Macmillan Publishing Group, LLC.

ISBN 978-0-7653-9588-7 (ebook)
ISBN 978-0-7653-9589-4 (trade paperback)

First Edition: September 2017

To Steph, for everything.
And to Hal, with love, and my apologies, especially for that one
time in Shanghai.

The Ruin of Angels

Chapter One

LEY BUILT HER SANDCASTLE below the tide line.

Kai warned her, of course. What else was an older sister for? When Ley chose her spot and planted her flag, Kai said, "It will drown." That last word tugged at her, as if it left a hook in her lip. She almost apologized, but stopped herself. "Drown" was the right word. You couldn't avoid words just because they hurt.

When Ley sculpted the gaptoothed ramparts of her keep, like castles from the kind of Schwarzwald fairy-tale picture books where kids got eaten, Kai said: "You see, that's the tide line up there, where the seaweed's drying." When Ley carved a curtain wall with a bright blue trowel, packing wet sand between her palms, Kai said: "Your wall's too thin to keep the water out."

"It's not to keep the water out," Ley said. "It's to keep out our enemies."

"You don't have enemies."

Ley shrugged, and dug her moat.

Mom wasn't there to help. Today was a mourning day; she'd gone with her sisters to Kai's father's grave, to paint her face with ashes and sit naked, alone, until the tears came. She had grieved with her children, noble and sharp in mourning white, the day the bearers brought her husband home—she stood chin out, brow high, eyes bright and black, impassive as a Penitent on the outside. Each body holds multitudes, the old songs sang. As a mother, she helped her children mourn their ship-wrecked father. As a wife, as a woman, as someone who had lost a friend, she needed time alone to break.

She left Kai in charge because Kai was older, and because Kai didn't set things on fire just to see what color they burned. But Ley only had the vaguest grasp of the meaning of the phrase "in charge," and Kai knew better than to test her younger sister on this point. She still had bruises from the last time she tried.

So Kai left Ley to work, and climbed the beach to build her own castle clear of the coming waves. The sand was drier here, and did not pack as well, so she brought a halved coconut shell to the surf, filled it with water, and carried it up the beach to moisten the sand. She built a spreading bay city like Kavekana, with a mountain behind it like Kavekana'ai, and studded the shoreline with pebble statue Penitents watching seaward for the return of long-gone gods. Heroes. Fathers.

Each time she went back to the ocean, her sister's city had grown. Ley excavated alleys with her fingertips, and cut decorations on rooftops with a sliver of bamboo. From above, her city looked intricate as a Craftwork diagram or a work of high theology. Ley, kneeling, brooded in her swimsuit, brows low as if to cut off the half of the world that didn't concern her: the beach, the volcano rising inland, her sister. She bit her lower lip as she worked.

"You have to do something," Kai said. She chose her words carefully. That was the joy of words: you could control them when all else failed. "Or the whole thing will fall down."

Up the beach, bigger kids shouted and screamed. A pale-skinned Iskari tourist girl dove to return a volleyball serve and fountained sand where she fell. The sea lay calm to the horizon, but no one swam. The red flag was up today, gallowglass swarming beneath the water with their long stinging tendrils, though they could not be seen from shore. White sails bellied on the bay. Cutters and dinghies and barques wheeled in defiance of the massive container ships moored near West Claw, at the deepwater port.

"You aren't listening."

Ley didn't look up.

Fine. Let Ley build her doomed city. Kai marched back up the beach. She added houses to her island and dug its bay deep, for the tide, rolling in, to fill. Standing, she judged it good. Then she turned back.

Ley's metropolis sprawled on the shore. She'd worked out in a spiral from that central keep, spread townhouses and factories, extended her lanes as she came round to them again. Kai knew the world she had built from sand—but she knew Ley's world, too, though she had never seen it before. Those broad thoroughfares with divided roads and sidewalks were commercial streets—no, processional boulevards down which ancient emperors once marched in triumph, bookended by arches. There were palaces, there high temples, here a factory; to the north, alleys grew so narrow Ley could not have made them with her fingers, must have dredged them with her bamboo strip. She had found a dream city inside them both, and made it real.

And the tide rolled in.

Ley's hands never stopped. The rest of her knelt rigid beside the districts she shaped, while her thin fingers carved and built and stroked sand smooth.

Kai grabbed her coconut shell, ran below Ley's city, and started to build a wall.

She built artlessly, because art was not the point. She did not know why Ley ignored her, why she made this weird familiar city. She did not know why Ley left glittering traces of her soul in the ramparts beneath her fingers. But she suspected. She could have asked Ley, taken her by the shoulders and shaken her and screamed until she stopped and tried to explain. But Ley's face reminded Kai of Mom's in mourning white, and the words she might say if Kai forced her to speak were words Kai knew she could not bear to hear.

So she built the wall. With her hands, she built it, with her own surging shoulders and legs, with Mom's thick fingers and Dad's fierce grit. She gutted the sand with her coconut shell. The sun burned her eyes and warmed her skin and covered her with sweat.

"Boy!" a voice called to her in Iskari from up the beach: the volleyball girl, drunk, in a white bathing suit. "Boy, you can't stop the tide."

Kai ignored the girl, whose friends shushed her and tried to explain. Kai's wall was more of a hill really, with a moat behind it as deep as Kai was tall. She judged the wall's height against the tide line, and started to curve upslope, to guard the outer edges of Ley's city. She sweat and trembled.

There wasn't time. She could not close the eastern wall before the tide rolled in. She knew this, and did not let herself know, because if she knew she would have stopped trying. An audience gathered up the beach, tourists and other monsters drawn by the two girls striving in the sand. A skeleton in a flower-print shirt watched them, rolling a newspaper into a tighter and tighter cylinder between his fingerbones. Kai ignored them, and kept fighting.

The water rose as she built the east wall. Every wash of

surf bore more sand from the wall back out into the deep. Kai wasn't patting her sand down, now, just digging it, tossing it up, hoping. Behind her, a wave splashed into the moat. Wet sand stuck to Kai's feet. She sank. The wall cracked. Salt rivers poured in and soaked Kai to her waist. The north wall sloughed into the water. Kai scrambled to shore it up, but the next rushing wave tore her feet out from under her. She went down in a tangle of limbs and foam.

Waves and crosscurrents tossed her, tumbled her, and she spilled from the moat onto the beach. She spat out salt water and sand, and when she recovered she looked back, expecting disaster.

But Ley's city stood.

The waves covered it, and drained away through carved alleys that should have collapsed like Kai's wall. Ley stared down through the water and the wash, and her city did not die.

Ley's soul shimmered in the sand. She had built herself into this city, mixing soulstuff into the sand with water, and now she stood above this world she'd made and willed it real, against the waves. The sand held its shape. The city sank, but stayed. It would not break while she had breath.

Ley rose like a goddess over her creation as the tide rolled in. She stretched out her hands as if to calm the waves, and for a moment Kai believed they might obey.

Then Ley fell, screaming, into the dirty water. She gasped surf, gagged, choked—disappeared in the wash and foam.

Kai ran into the water, caught her flailing sister around the shoulders, and dragged her to dry sand. Ley coughed up fluid, screamed again though she had no breath. A white phosphorescent thread wound around her leg, menacing and tiny: a gallowglass tendril, torn free and set drifting on the tide in search of a victim. Probably not fatal. Kai gloved her hands in a gob of seaweed and peeled the tendril free. Snot ran from Ley's nose, and her eyes rolled white behind slitted lids. She breathed deep and fast. Venom leaked through Kai's makeshift glove and burned her palm.

With the tendril gone, Ley stopped screaming, but didn't open her eyes. Kai slung her sister's arm over her shoulder, and pushed up with her legs. She took three steps, and stumbled into water. Building the wall had exhausted her: she could not take Ley's weight. She ground her teeth and tried to will herself upright.

She stood, too fast—someone else held Ley's other side. The Iskari girl in the white suit, the one who'd called her—"Boy," she said again, in Iskari. "What was she doing?"

Kai had not expected that question. She didn't think the Iskari expected it either—she was scared of screams, that was all. She didn't know why Ley fell. Easy to see she'd never suffered a gallowglass sting before—a gallowglass would leave a bright red scar on that sharp pale skin. The girl was embarrassed, like tourists sometimes felt when they helped or even noticed locals, and talking to cover her nerves.

"Playing," Kai replied, in the girl's language, and didn't correct her about the other part. The girl helped her carry Ley upslope. The crowd drew back as they approached, clearing space on the boardwalk. They set Ley down carefully, beside a discarded resort brochure. The skeleton watched them both from behind ruby spectacles, newspaper still clutched in his hand. He could have done something, Kai thought—a Craftsman like that, all the power in the world at his beck and call, lightings danced when he crooked his finger, he could have stopped the pain at once.

He adjusted his spectacles instead.

A lifeguard shouldered through the crowd.

The girl asked, "Why did she stay, when the tide rolled in?"

Kai didn't answer. The lifeguard bent low, took a charm from his neck, and applied it to the sting. Blood seeped through torn skin, but at the charm's touch flesh calmed, blood stilled. Ley stopped shaking. She drew her first even breath.

"She wanted to save it," Kai said. Her voice hooked after "save"—speaking Iskari forced her to gender the pronoun, and she was not sure whether she chose right. She remembered Ley's expression, so like Mom's, unwavering and fierce as pallbearers approached their gate. She could have said, save *him*.

Behind her the sun set and the tide rolled up, the ocean at ease as if it had never killed a man. The parapets and pinnacles of Ley's city melted, its arches seeped out into the deep. Salt water filled Kai's model bay, and her tiny Penitents stared out over the flat, poison sea.

"Save what?" the girl asked.

But Kai wasn't sure, and if she knew, she would not say.

Chapter Two

WHO WOULD BREAK INTO a bank to leave something?

The practice is more common than one might think, though practitioners' motives tend to involve eventually removing more than they originally left. You might duck the bank's wards, dodge its construct and revenant and demonic and even, sometimes, living human guards, evade its detection magics, dance across its pressure-plate floor, answer ye its riddles three, and leave a beacon glyph to guide tunnelers, or a mechanism that would disable all that security during a later, more forceful raid. A simple listening device in the right place could yield the intelligence to corner or crash a market, or make a small, substantial killing—literal or metaphorical. But few people would break into a bank *solely* to leave something, and fewer still would break in to leave a letter.

So while the mailroom of Iskari First Imperial in Agdel Lex noticed that the vellum envelope that appeared in their priority delivery box one workday morning, sealed with blood-colored wax and the impression of a wolfsbane flower, lacked the customary sender's marks, the demon on duty believed this merely an administrative assistant's oversight.

Mortals. Honestly.

If the letter needed shipping to the Shining Empire, or west across the sea to Alt Coulumb, or even north to Telomere, the demon would have wasted precious minutes hunting down the relevant admin so as to bill the postage properly—but an envelope for internal delivery needed no postage. Even so, the demon hissed, and pondered taking bloody, demonstrative action. She'd warned the admin pool against using priority flags for internal mail—in-building post went round hourly, and while some market developments did need immediate response, once you let people flag intraoffice mail, even inane check-ins mysteriously ended up marked TRIPLE URGENT. A little bloodshed ought to clarify the situation.

The mail demon consulted the building register and found—odd—the recipient unlisted. Perhaps it was meant for outside delivery after all? With no address, or postage. She closed her many eyes, and replayed in her mind, as her therapist had suggested, a comforting series of human screams, starting with a ten on the pain scale, counting down. That relaxed her enough for work. Then she checked the guest list, and realized her mistake.

Kai Pohala, whoever she was, was only visiting the office for one day; this message's sender could not meet her in person, and wanted to be sure the letter arrived before she left. Sensible. Saved postage, even. No one need die today.

Though you never could tell when a bleak morning at the office might look up.

. . .

Agdel Lex had a shattered beauty from the air, but Kai was too busy trying not to vomit to pay attention. Turbulence got to her—though the flight attendants claimed the dragon had said not to worry, entirely customary for the Agdel Lex route this time of year, well within their gondola's stress tolerance.

Doubtless they would repeat that "nothing to worry about" line until they all went down in flames. No incentive telling anyone to panic. Blood and hells and all the gods, she hated flying.

Not to mention that her godsdamn silver bowl wouldn't hold still on the godsdamn seat-back tray table—there was a depression, yes, a little courtesy carving in the teak inlay meant to hold the tiny cups of horrible coffee the charming attendants served, but it was too far forward and to the right, and much too small, to hold her brand new "fits-anywhere!" folding sacrificial vessel. If she placed the bowl in the tray table's center, it pressed against the back of the seat in front of her, the inhabitant of which seat had, naturally, reclined, and if she moved the bowl toward her, its lip dug into her chest, and either way, given Kai's luck, a sharp bump would spill blood all over everything. She hesitated, frowned, then tapped the four-armed sculpture of knives and glass sitting ahead of her in 14F on one of its shoulders, after she found a spot she felt reasonably sure wouldn't carve her open when she touched it. "Excuse me." Sir, or ma'am? Godsdamn mainlander languages and their godsdamn gender-dependent forms of respectful address. Put it aside. Focus. The sculpture rotated its head independent of the rest of its body, and glared at her with ruby eyes. "Could you raise your seat?"

It answered in a language she didn't understand, that sounded like the death of something beautiful. But it turned back ahead as smoothly as it had turned to face her, and did not raise the seat.

Fine. She wedged the bowl on the wobbly tray. The cabin lurched and swooped and steadied, and for a stomach-churning moment she saw only ocean and wing beyond her

window, no sky at all, before the dragon reared and corrected itself, tossing Kai's insides through another loop. No
percentage in being sick. Get this over with. She took a sacrificial pipette from her inside jacket pocket, peeled open
the paper to reveal the glass, and, in a reprieve between
lurches, stabbed herself in the forefinger. Blood filled the
thin glass tube through the magic of capillary action. The
cabin shook again—you'd think they'd find some halfway
competent ageless lizards to fly these runs—and the pipette
waggled in the meat of her finger. She plucked it out when
their course eased; the pipette was small, and her professional wards closed the wound instantly. Still stung, though.

Kai bent over the bowl, pursed her lips over the pipette, and
blew. Blood spattered and ran down the silver's nonstick coating, following intricate spidery trails she interpreted, in the
back of her mind, using a dozen augural disciplines from six
continents. A bloodreader of the Sanguine Host would warn
of a troubled morning—no surprises there. Aizu humourists
would say, hm, family problems? Unlikely. Maybe she was
reading it wrong. She hadn't been asked to build an Aizu idol
in a while. She flagged that particular theology for review.

Kai returned the pipette to its wrapper. The man in the seat
next to her coughed into his fist, shifted his weight, and said
nothing in a way that said quite a lot.

She slipped the pipette back into her jacket pocket. "Everybody has to pray sometime."

He tried to look as if he had not heard.

"Hey," she said, "do I go to your altar and slap the knife out
of your hand?"

He turned the page of his copy of *The Thaumaturgist,* and
said nothing, in a way that screamed "Camlaander." Kai liked

this about Camlaanders: if you pretended not to notice their radiant discomfort, they'd never clarify, just shut up and wait for a later opportunity to describe your revolting behavior to friends who would agree with them.

Kai's blood pooled in the bowl. She looked into her reflection, but they hit another bump, and the reflection shattered. As good as she could expect, under the circumstances.

She breathed out above the water.

Lady. I'm listening.

There, in the sky, approaching a foreign city beneath the belly of an ancient beast, tossed by winds, stuck in coach because the priesthood didn't think this side trip rated business class, she felt the touch of a cool blue hand upon her brow.

The touch melted against her forehead and rolled down her skin like honey tears, hot and sweet and deep, to bead and tremble on her lips, then slip within. She tasted salt and sand and volcanic rock. Root musk rolled down her tongue into her throat. She burned all over at once, and exhaled the beauty worming through her veins.

Across an ocean, on an island far away, a girl—a young woman now, gods, Izza was sixteen—looked up from her work, and let her gaze unfix, and said, silently, through the goddess that bound them both—*Aren't you landing in an hour?*

There's been a change of plans, Kai prayed. I have to stay abroad a few more days. Everything will keep at home.

For better or worse.

Trouble?

No more than usual. Fixing Penitents is slow, tricky work. If we just change the settings, we don't help their victims. They forced people to be good by one metric—if we force them to be good by another, we're no better. The problem's the force, not the good.

Changing a culture takes time.

You've only had the Penitents for sixty years. You lived without them for three thousand.

Time's like an ocean, she prayed back. People only swim in the top bit.

You said there was a change of plans. What changed?

Kai wished she'd pressed the matter at once. Now she felt like she had been hiding something. Management approved the venture offering, she prayed. We arranged meetings while I finished up in Telomere. I have an overnight in Agdel Lex.

No answer returned through the ecstasy channel.

It's just a quick stopover, she explained. The city has a good startup community—nightmare telegraphics mostly, dreamshaping and fearcraft, high-energy Craftwork. *Nightmare Quarterly* called it "thriving." That kind of investment is risky, but that means more upside—one or two big bets will give us breathing room to divest from Grimwald holdings in the Southern Gleb, and get out of necromantic earths entirely.

Still, silence.

She continued: I fought for budget, I pulled every favor I could, and I got permission to extend a feeler a few months back—but no dice. Total silence. But, while I was in Telomere for the Martello thing, I got a letter from Twilling, you remember, in sales? Turns out Iskari First Imperial has two modes: slow and fast. They want to make a deal, they've put together meetings, and they need me there today. I don't have permission from the board, but I've given myself a speculative budget of a couple million thaums; I'll make the deals we need, go home, present the contracts with signatures already dry. They'll go along. Everything will be fine.

More silence, warier.

She knew she was praying too fast, but she couldn't help herself: it's a peaceful city these days. The fighting's further south, past the Wastes. I'm just going to meet with a bunch of artists, who will probably be glad—the airship shook. No, not the airship. Her shoulder. Her eyes snapped open. Her veins throbbed with the attenuation of pleasure, and she struggled to focus on soft weak reality. The Camlaander sitting beside her was studiously reading his magazine. Who—

A flight attendant stood in the aisle, frowning. "We're landing soon. Please raise your tray and refrain from excessive prayer."

Fine, Kai said, then remembered she had to use her mouth. "Fine." And she closed her eyes again.

Look, I have to go. Trust me. If we want to change Kavekana, to fix the Penitents and everything else without armed revolt, the priesthood needs a surplus—something to wean us off investments in bone oil and necromantic earths. This will help the Blue Lady, and Kavekana, and it will net me a nice bonus check, so we can buy more kids out of debt. Again, her shoulder shook. She ignored the flight attendant, and prayed faster: It's fine. My sister's been sending me postcards from here for the last, like, five years. She's having a disgustingly bohemian time.

You didn't think to ask me.

Because I knew what you'd say.

And your sister? Did you ask her?

Ley? No.

She felt the shame of that answer like an underground tremor, unseen, easily denied to everyone but herself. Venture thaumaturgics weren't Ley's area, and anyway if Kai reached out, she'd have to visit Ley while she was in town, and there wasn't enough time on a short business trip to dig through everything that had piled up between them. All of which stood to reason, but Izza's question still reminded Kai of that accumulated mess and time, and of the postcards she rarely answered, featureless and glib, each containing some charming anecdote about poetry readings or fruit-related confusion in street markets, best wishes to Mom, bloodless. Strange how much you could write without communicating. And that distance was Kai's fault, somehow—at least, Ley probably thought it was.

"Ma'am," the flight attendant repeated, harsher this time. "We're starting our final descent. Please."

"Did it ever occur to you," Kai said, "how overblown that sounds? *Final descent.* Poets take a final descent into the hells. Emperors have a final descent from the throne before someone chops off their heads. We're about to land, which we will presumably survive, to descend again."

"Prayers interfere with navigation."

"Exactly how many navigational instruments does your enormous, basically immortal lizard need to tell which way is down?"

"Agdel Lex airspace presents navigational challenges—"

"For the love of all your blasted gods," the Camlaander said, and Kai noticed for the first time the white-knuckled grip with which he held his magazine, the sweat beaded on his forehead, the sour smell of his fear, "won't you please wait to make your call until we're safely on the ground?"

She prayed again. Have to go. I don't know why you're so hung up on this.

Five years ago, Izza replied, *in Agdel Lex, I saw the Rectifi-*

cation Authority burn out the Gavreaux Junction hunger strikers. Six hundred people. The leaders went into lock-up, and if they ever came out, I didn't hear about it.

That's horrible. But I'm not coming to reinforce the colonial authority, just—

The connection failed. The Blue Lady's honeyed finger slid out from between her lips, and vines of joy unwound from her thorn by thorn. Kai opened her eyes, red, furious. The flight attendant had closed her bowl; the last remnants of blood smoked within, dried to flakes, and Kai smelled acid and copper and burnt iron. She shoved the flight attendant's hand away, and folded the rest of the bowl herself. "You didn't have to do that. I was almost through."

"We're past the cutoff, ma'am."

Gods save us from petty tyrants. "Down is down. Does your dragon have eyes, or not?"

"We're landing in Agdel Lex, ma'am. Down isn't always where you left it, and you can't ever trust your eyes."

Chapter Three

AFTER ALL THAT OMINOUS nonsense, the airport looked like any other airport, with the same landing strip, the same predatorily priced food stalls and coffee shops, even the same people: Craftsfolk in suits and ties, golems bearing vision gems, demonic construct carts toting luggage. An older woman rolled past in a wheelchair while a bag man struggled to keep up under the weight of his suitcases. Ethnically the mix skewed Gleblander, skin darker than Kai's but lighter than Izza's, curly hair, but beyond that she could have been anywhere in the Old World—though she saw fewer locals than she expected. She hadn't thought about that on the flight, since on some level all airships felt the same, but her gondola was filled mostly with Telomeri and Iskari; there were maybe ten Gleblanders, including the young woman across the aisle, a tall slender girl in a bright yellow sweater, reading a textbook, whom Kai had taken for a student.

Time for speculation later. Kai rolled her shoulders, ignored their cracks and pops, took up her suitcase, and beelined for ground transport.

She brushed past the usual tearful hellos at the rope line. The student ran into the open arms of an equally tall thin woman, who was, Gods, weeping; a shorter girl, who looked to be the student's sister, joined their embrace, and they laughed through the tears. Kai turned away.

She scanned the crowd until she saw a round young woman, broad shouldered and broad hipped in a cream-colored suit, holding a sign that bore Kai's name. "Ms. Pohala! Gavvi Fontaine, from IFI. I'm your account manager"—read: saleswoman—"and I'm here to orient you for the day, make certain you have everything you need." Good smile, firm handshake, faint Iskari accent. Fontaine held the handshake a touch long; a small flat tentacle slithered out from under her cuff, then retreated. No surprise that an IFI banker would belong to the Iskari faith, but the symbiont always left Kai unnerved. Fontaine's smile was very wide. "Such a pleasure to meet you. I'm so glad you could make it." With stress on each modifier.

"Thank you for coming in person," Kai said. "I'm sure you understand my need for discretion." The kind of people who prayed to Kavekana's idols liked secrecy. Scanning the crowd, Kai saw no one who looked like a spy, or worse, a journalist, but you never could tell.

"It's an honor to be working with—" Fontaine caught herself just before Kai had to decide whether it would attract more attention to tackle the woman than to let her say "Kavekanese priesthood" out loud. "Well. We're excited. I've lined up a few meetings to offer a sense of the breadth of opportunity the local community offers. I can answer any questions, but we really should dive right in." She reached for Kai's suitcase; Kai clenched it tighter. "Is that your only luggage?"

"I just brought enough for two days. I sent the rest of my stuff on the slow boat home."

"Fantastic." She grinned. "Follow me."

Fontaine had an even, elegant pace—Kai could have balanced half the scripture she owned on the woman's skull. Nice tailored suit, shiny shoes, dressed to impress, and she'd nailed

Kai's name, which most mainlanders didn't on the first try. Young, ambitious, and a quick study. Fontaine turned to face Kai as they neared the doors; the hypothetical scripture stack on her head wouldn't have so much as wobbled. Backward and in heels. Kai was impressed, and tried not to show it. "Welcome," Fontaine said, as the glass doors rolled open behind her, and Kai emerged into Agdel Lex.

And stopped.

The city twisted before her.

At first glance Agdel Lex looked somewhat normal. Boxy plaster houses lined the mountain ridges that cradled the city to east and west. Glancing south she saw the black mound of the wall against the Godwastes, while to the north, spires of crystal, steel, and glass burst skyward, as if some Craftswoman had frozen the spume that climbed sheer cliffs in a storm. At that eruption's heart stood a tower of—no, it couldn't be flesh, it had to be stone or concrete smoothed to seem organic, an enormous squid mantle sinking tentacles the size of city blocks into the soil. Past that, slopes tumbled toward the Shield Sea.

This was what Kai saw at first.

And yet.

The narrow alleys between those plaster houses writhed. At first she took their movement for mirage, like on the north shore rocklands back home on a hot summer day—but, no, the movement was real. Straight lines went jagged. Boulevards shrank, twisted, disappeared. Gaps opened in the city, streets bubbling into markets. Crystal and concrete towers became translucent, shrinking, uncertain, shadows of another time. Even the wind changed. First she'd felt a hot, punishing desert blast pregnant with motor oil and spent lightning, so dry it robbed breath from her lungs, but now it dampened, soothed, gained fragrances of rosewater and anise.

Two cities, then? Stacked, somehow? Fine. Kai was a priestess of many gods; she was used to overlapping realities. Back in training, the older priests had given her a glass of water and asked her to believe it was half-full and half-empty at once. That was a fun week.

But even when she tried to see both cities at once, they still refused to settle. There were further truths hidden behind that pair. She tried to hold everything at once, to see, to know.

The skyline shifted again. The squid tower disappeared altogether, and the sky where it once stood now bled sick light from a fractal wound. Wreckage spread, deep shattered chasms, broken palaces, topless towers, blasted city blocks peopled with statues of ash.

The city became a tomb. Cold wind caught Kai's throat in a fist of knives, and squeezed. Frost spread on her skin, crackled in her mouth, and she could not breathe. The ground wheeled. The sky was sky, and overhead, and she was—

Not falling anymore. Arms held her. Big dark eyes. Pretty. Warmth returned, life, the bustle of airport commerce. "There." Fontaine. Kai followed her voice. Something moved near Kai's chest—a hand feeling in her jacket. She tried to brush the hand away, but her muscles were too busy freezing. Kai felt herself lowered to pavement. People stared. The sky was full of blades. She couldn't stop shaking. Ghosts whispered in her ear. Fontaine stuck the tip of her tongue between her teeth when she was in a hurry. Stupid habit. Bite it off that way. Gods. Breathe. Don't drown in this. Don't let them see you weak. She tried to sit up. Those blades in the sky twisted, curled back on one another, changed shape. Blood dripped and froze.

What was this place?

Fontaine shoved Kai's passport in front of her eyes. The entry stamp's red ink seemed sharper now, the squid-in-a-circle design perfect. Squid arms formed the circle's edge, and embraced Kai's name.

Deeper, deeper still, it drew her.

She gasped, and this time her lungs filled with scorching desert air. She blinked, and ice crystals sublimed off her eyelashes. Fontaine's arm held her close, strong, steady. Shivering, Kai felt the tentacle beneath the woman's jacket sleeve.

But why was Kai shivering, after all? The day was hot and bright, the blue sky free of clouds. The pavement on which she sprawled radiated heat. A few concerned onlookers lingered (a woman with a bird's head, the four-armed statue from her flight), but most drifted on. A young Gleblander in a three-piece suit passed, shooting Kai a look she recognized—the same glare she gave mainlanders recovering from their first palm liquor hangover in a hotel gutter back home on Kavekana.

Tourist.

Her "I'm fine" ended up crushed and mumbled. Fontaine offered a hand, which Kai, politely, refused, standing on her own with difficulty. On review she found no permanent damage: shoes okay, stockings, more or less.

"Lords, I'm so sorry." Fontaine slapped dust off Kai's jacket and skirt without a moment's concern for personal space. "I've never seen someone fall through that quickly. Twilling told me it was a risk, but I had no idea. You must be very good at your job."

"What was that?"

"The God Wars," she said. "Come on. Let's find a cab."

"I heard there was damage, but—" Heat wormed back into her body. She took a breath, and shivered—even her lungs were cold.

Fontaine explained as she shouldered through the crowd; Kai checked her hair, grabbed her suitcase, and followed. "The old city, the one that stood here before Agdel Lex, fell early in the wars. Gerhardt and his students made their first stand against the Gods here, and almost tore the world apart. Broke time itself. They say he's still alive in that wound in the sky, still fighting. The Iskari saved what they could, sealed off the war zone, and built the city where we live. Sometimes, though, people fall through. The Rectification Authority keeps things stable, but there are holes."

"What happens if I . . . fall through . . . again?"

"Get your passport, look at it, and remind yourself: you're in Agdel Lex. The Iskari city." She spread her hands, taking in the skyline, the sun, the decidedly living metropolis and the line of cabs, a driver seated on each one's bench. "You shouldn't have to worry about it much. The world's very thick, downtown. Now, let's move. We're already late."

Kai glared at the cabs, suspicious. "No driverless carriages?"

"Too risky. Without someone to navigate, you might fall through. Hey!" Fontaine's voice deepened when she called to the driver, and she shifted into a Talbeg dialect Kai couldn't follow, sharp, demonstrative, likely invective laden. Fontaine's body language when she spoke Iskari enveloped, all roundness and fullness; speaking Talbeg, she became a fist. The driver put down his novel and reached for the reins. His metal horse pawed the cobblestones, drawing sparks. Fontaine offered Kai a hand into the carriage, and this time Kai let her help. She still felt unsteady, and the jostling as the carriage veered into traffic made the sickness worse. "My apologies," Fontaine said. "I'll have IFI's private service drive you back to the airport tomorrow."

Right. She'd come here for a reason. Fontaine seemed eager to move on to another subject—any other subject save, perhaps, the one Kai had in mind. "But you didn't want to use the service today. Because you don't want to attract attention."

"I, ah." Fontaine touched her temple, and frowned. "I'm not certain I understand."

"Your letter set a rapid timeline, suggesting urgency, but you came to meet me yourself rather than sending an admin, and we're using a public cab. Ms. Fontaine, do your bosses know about our meeting?"

To Fontaine's credit, she kept it honest. "Management," she admitted, "has low visibility into this deal. You haven't had much success approaching IFI until now, because in your case we find ourselves in an ouroboral situation: without a commitment of funds, IFI can only share so much. But you can't invest without information. Where others see an obstacle, I see opportunity."

"You want to set up a deal, sprinkle on some glitter, and present me with a pretty ribbon to your supervisors: a nice, rich blue sky opportunity. Play it right and you'll get a big bonus out of that, a new office. A few underlings of your own. Not bad for a local woman in an Iskari bank."

Fontaine's smile gained a nervous edge. "I must say, I find your forthrightness bracing."

"I'm leaving tomorrow. I don't have time for bullshit. Am I right?"

"Would it be a problem if you were?"

"Not at all. I just want to know where we stand." In short:

screwed, though not necessarily in a bad way. Fontaine wanted a foreign princess to ride in on a magic horse bringing riches beyond the dreams of avarice. Kai needed IFI's stability and reputation to make a case before the High Priests back home. Look, even IFI thinks these dreamcrafters are a solid investment! *Ouroboral.* Hells. But she could still make this work. She would make this work. "I have two questions. I'd like direct answers to both."

Fontaine took a slim silver box from her inside jacket pocket, opened it, and pondered a selection of pills inside. "Go ahead."

"Do you think we can make a good deal here?"

Fontaine chose a translucent green pill, and held it to the light. "We can make *fortunes.*" She tasted that word like expensive liquor. Then she dry-swallowed the pill.

"Second question. Are you high right now?"

"Ms. Pohala, I'm a dreamcraft banker. I'm high constantly." She offered the pill case. "Would you like some?" Before Kai could say no, she rolled on. "Oh! That reminds me. A letter came for you this morning. Internal post, quite urgent. Did you tell anyone else about your trip?"

"No. But the drugs—"

"Here you go."

"I said I don't—" But Fontaine wasn't offering the pills. She offered an envelope bearing Kai's name in a hand she recognized, sealed, on the back, with her sister's wolfsbane ring.

Godsdammit. Ley.

"I only ask because, if you've mentioned your trip to anyone at IFI, that might prompt a territorial squabble over your business, which I"—Fontaine shuddered with, Kai thought, mostly chemical ecstasy—"would not relish."

"No. Nothing like that."

"Fantastic. Excellent. Wonderful. Now, Kai, can I call you Kai? Are you certain about the drugs? If you want to invest in dreamcraft, you should cultivate familiarity with the platform."

Chapter Four

MY DEAREST SISTER—

Kai spent the rest of the day trying to put the letter from her mind. There wasn't much of it, but what there was, stuck. During pitch meetings she toyed with the envelope, ran her finger down the thick creamy paper. Between meetings she excused herself, reread her sister's words in a bathroom stall, and let the rage flow through her again. Coffee shocked the system awake, but nothing concentrated like fury.

And she needed concentration. Fontaine, true to her word, had filled her day with meetings, two representatives from each Concern, mostly thin kids in flannels who couldn't have looked less professional if they'd tried. Perhaps they had tried: they adhered to a fashion lockstep strict as any uniform code. One young woman kept picking at her pants leg; Kai wondered if she ever wore trousers when she wasn't trying to look like . . . whatever these people wanted to seem.

They had practiced their pitches, though. Oh, yes.

"Two things are happening at once. Global investment is increasingly important for individuals and Concerns looking to maximize returns in a competitive market. But the vehicles for that investment are more complicated than ever. Without expert support, people just don't know what's out there—and most people can't afford a real expert." Kai's clients could, but she didn't interrupt this young man, though he needed an appointment with a razor so badly that Kai considered offering him the one she used on her legs. Besides, he wasn't wrong. He was, however, seeing things: ghosts beside her head, to judge from his darting eyes. He tapped the desk, and the glow-worms on the wall behind him wriggled and reassembled to form a bubbly logo. His partner took over: "Theolog wraps our dreamers into low-involvement Concerns, and connects those Concerns with qualified investment managers. We guide dreamers through scenarios designed to judge their risk toler-ance, moral positioning, and time horizon, on a preconscious level. We know more about our participants than they know about themselves."

Heard you might be in town. Sorry for reaching out this way. Been a while since we caught up.

How in the hells had she heard? And, "caught up"; Ley hadn't been home in years, no dreams even, just occasional postcards, the last of which showed up just after Kai got out of the hospital last year, and which didn't mention her injuries at all. Sorry for reaching out, not even "I'm sorry," just the desul-tory not-quite apology. Gods.

"Two things," said a woman with thick braids and a rich Gleblander accent, who shopped for her flannels in the same store as the guy from Theolog, "are happening at once. We live in an age of global diaspora. During the God Wars, in-ternational migration was largely driven by fear and pro- or anti-religious sentiment: people scattered to places they thought were safe. Now things have stabilized—" Kai tried not to let disbelief show, stabilized, really, the last six years, ser-pents over Dresediel Lex and an outbreak in Alt Coulumb, bond crises, stable? Hells, just a hundred miles south past the Wastes, the Northern Gleb was a hothouse of warring Gods and Craftsmen using one another as catspaws: *stable* was a sick joke. For the five decades immediately after the wars, maybe—three generations had been too dead, tired, or scared to rock the boat. But now, no, never mind, listen to the nice woman who wants you to make her rich. "—Migration has been driven by employment opportunities and the loss of farm jobs due to agricultural automation. At the same time, even in Camlaan and the Iskari Demesne, fewer people describe themselves as more than moderately religious than at any point for which we have data." Which interval was the last century and a half or so, hardly a reliable indicator of broad historical trends given what had happened in those hundred fifty years, might as well try to describe rivers by looking at waterfalls—no, focus. "As people move more, they're tied less than ever by gods, and as divine states become increasingly territorial, traveling coreligionists are less likely to find priests to carry messages. The nightmare telegraph is too harrowing for most to use without assistance, and current telegraph office deployment is borderline inhumane, so: How will this mobile population stay in contact?" She tapped the table, the glow-worms assembled into another bubbly logo, and her partner, an Iskari woman who looked too young for the streaks of gray in her hair, stepped forward. "Enter Auditor."

You're only here for a day, it seems, dear sister. And I need to see you.

How did she know Kai's schedule? How had she snuck the letter into IFI's internal post? Fontaine had whisked Kai into the smoked glass heart of the oddly corkscrew banking tower, bypassing most security, but even so she, Fontaine, had to vouch for Kai to three different guards, pass her through three security circles; Kai'd given blood and spoken her name into a glass box, walked between two crackling ebon stanchions the blank-faced Iskari security guards called a "scanner," and, at the last, passed through a mirror of cascading water that showed, Fontaine claimed, only truth. (Kai tensed when they approached the mirror, wondering what truth, how overzealous fairy-tale Iskari security would react to her, but the mirror reflected her accurately—a Kavekanese woman overcaffeinated, exhausted, and past done with the poking and prodding.)

And that "I need to see you," perfunctory, a queen's dictate, as if of course Kai would have no other pressing demands during her overnight business trip. No, that wasn't right. Ley wasn't thoughtless—anything but. She just thought other people should share her priorities.

A man with nose-pinching glasses, who should have known better than to wear that brimmed hat with that untucked short-sleeved button down: "Two things are happening at once." Gods, had they all read the same book? "Around the world, factory-finished goods have displaced, or are displacing, artisan handcrafts. People joke about this being a developed-society issue, but in fact we're seeing it everywhere, as manufacturers race to capture markets." Betting that, as the global thaumaturgical framework remained stable, those parts of the world still reeling from the God Wars, or the resource conflicts, proxy battles, and zombie plagues that rippled from the wars themselves, would recover to join Dresediel Lex and Agdel and Alt Coulumb and Iskar and the Shining Empire and Camlaan in the light of modernity. Betting the system could support a world where everyone was on top. Which wasn't nearly so maniacally optimistic a wager as it might seem, though the odds were still long. If development, whatever that meant, indeed progressed forever into an impossible bright future, the bet paid off. If it didn't, if the world collapsed in fire and demons tore our guts out, who gave a shit whether share price declined this quarter? "At the same time, around the world, Deathless Kings, High Priests, let's call them the thaumaturgical class, are growing used to power and the resources that accompany it. They form a distinct, large pool of exacting consumers of durable bespoke luxury goods. A person who's functionally immortal expects her crockery to last as long as she does. Highly skilled artisans with enormous experience, literally the best in the world at what they do, struggle to feed themselves even though people across the globe would willingly spend whole souls on their products." His partner, tall, thin, gaunt-cheeked, tapped the tabletop glyph, and the glow-worms did their dance. "Use determines what people with soulstuff to burn want, in their heart of hearts; it passes that inspiration to a growing community of artisans who have the skills, but lack market access."

Meet me at Sauga's, tonight at eight thirty. You'll like the place. Whatever squid you're working with can tell you how to get there. Come alone.

No clue what kind of "place" Sauga's might be. Dive bar? Sex club? When Kai last visited Ley, back when her sister was studying in Southern Iskar, she'd brought her to a fish market straight from the airport, saying it's a nice place to talk.

Kai found Fontaine in the hall between meetings, arguing in Talbeg with someone who, so far as Kai could see, wasn't there. "Are all these people on drugs?"

"Okay," Fontaine said to the air. "Good. We'll pick this up after CoB. Thank you." She blinked, and color returned to the whites of her eyes. "Come on, I'm starving." Over a plate of fries in the palatial cafeteria, all beechwood and mother-of-pearl inlay, Fontaine explained: "Art works through dreams and desires. Most people expose themselves, take a nap, have a nightmare or three, and wake up. The drugs are only important for people who need constant contact. There are downsides, of course."

Kai stole a fry.

"The drugs saturate your normal dreams. You don't sleep well. It's, let's say, inimical to the kind of high concentration required for Craftwork. Or art, awkwardly. But the value's there." She reached for more fries; halfway to the plate, her hand stopped, and her face flushed green. "Gods. Ah. Excuse me, please." When she returned ten minutes later, Kai had eaten most of the fries. They had worked through lunch. "Sorry."

"Nausea?"

"Hallucinations." Fontaine straightened her jacket. "Controlled intoxication blurs the line between sleeping and waking." She tipped the fries into the garbage before Kai could eat more. "It's worth the compromises."

"And your..." She pointed to Fontaine's arm. "Partner doesn't mind?"

"The Good Lords understand the balance of sobriety and opportunity," she said. "Though they get loopy with exposure. I confess regularly to compensate. Meanwhile, there's a whole world at my fingertips."

"A world of two things happening at once. My priesthood invests in girders, Ms. Fontaine. This feels like filigree. It's all so small."

"Most things people need really are. People don't want to save, I don't know, everything, or break it. They want to stay in touch with their families. They want to sell things they've made with their hands, or buy things someone else has made with theirs. They want work. They want to get along. They want minor conveniences, or a few minutes' escape. People get rich off those desires. Where's the harm?"

And anyway, Kai asked herself, wasn't small the point? Get away from the big resource bets, from necromantic earths, from "exploratory missions" one step short of wholesale slaughter, from revenant labor firms that could always, always prove, with flawless paperwork, their debt-zombies were ethically sourced, with repayment schemes that met Craftwork standards. Leave all that behind, bet small, and find something to change the world slightly—maybe for the better.

"To make it happen," said the unshaven man in the flannel shirt, "we're asking for two million thaums."

"To make it happen," said the woman with the braids, "we're asking for two point seven million thaums."

"To make it happen," said the man with the unfortunate hat, "we're asking for three point one million thaums."

The conference room windows faced inward: rooftop mirrors reflected sunlight down the skyscraper's hollow core, and crystal prisms split that sun to light the IFI offices from within. Kai couldn't see sunset, but the conference room blushed rose. Glowworms glowed on the wall. Fontaine rocked in her chair, humming, while Kai made notes, summarizing goals, growth potential, commitment, and poor fashion choices. Her watch, on the table, read: seven.

I need you.

—Ley

Two things are happening at once.

"Fontaine. Fontaine. Fontaine." The name worked on her third try.

"Hmmm?" She knuckled sleep from the corners of her eyes. "Sorry. Just catching up on my prophecies."

"I have to take a meeting after work. Late notice, personal thing. Place called Sauga's. Think I can get there without slipping into some kind of apocalypse?"

Fontaine tried, and failed, to keep herself from laughing.

Chapter Five

ZEDDIG FELL INTO THE dead city.

She landed with a crouch in the wrecked library. Frost iced her ruby lenses. She flipped a switch on her goggles and the frost receded, and she could see again. Beneath and before her, past the enormous jagged gap in the wall, spread streets splashed with ice crystal blood, where metal spiders the size of houses had frozen while grappling with winged statues of glorious flame. Enormous crystal worms stitched and knotted in the sky, tearing one another with their teeth. Books lay splayed on the checkerboard floor, revealing Talbeg script and stark blackletter. Knife-wind flipped the pages. Ash drifted past her, drawn north toward the Wound.

She checked her watch. A Craftwork circle burned around the watch's outer edge, sealed with the same wards as her suit. Blue, now. The light would fade, then blush red; when it died altogether she'd have ten seconds before her suit wards failed, before the death that had claimed her city claimed her, too.

A voice that did not belong whispered in her ear. "Ms. Hala, we have visitors."

She cursed. "Wreckers?"

"Baseline humans, judging from heartbeat and tread. Local security, I should think. Armed, poorly." Gal's elegant accent hid contempt well.

"Raymet said we had a half hour after shift change."

"She may have been mistaken. Perhaps this is an unscheduled patrol." Gal's voice grew contemplative. "There's only three of them. If you wish—"

"No," she interrupted. The last thing they needed was for Gal to leave a trail of bodies. Probably just guards looking for a place to smoke. "How long do I have?"

"They're climbing the stairs."

"Lock the door. Make noise."

"That seems contrary to our plan."

Gods. "Throw some furniture around. Move a desk in rhythm. Groan once in a while. Stall. I have a table at Sauga's tonight—if I miss my rez because I'm in jail, they'll never let me live it down." Not to mention that she'd be chained to a wall in the Rectification Authority tower, with open windows so the birds could get at her after the Wreckers finished.

Her watch circle had paled from midnight blue to the color of the sky at noon. Minutes left at best. This was as close a delve as she'd ever taken to the Wound; she had drowned in preparations. She stood on the third floor of the Circuit Library of Mercy and Light University, Seaside Two Seven, Alikand, and through that door, past the ice-covered skeletons of two men (she thought) who had spent their last living moments making love, lay the treasure she'd come to save.

The door splintered beneath her boot.

The reading room beyond was breathtaking, even ruined: black-and-white geometric lattices climbed the walls, patterns and patterns entwined, a High Scholastic masterpiece. Steady, strong hands in workshops long since burned had shaped these broken chairs and planed these tables. Gold fixtures glinted in the never-light that drifted through the shattered roof. You couldn't buy this craftsmanship for love or money, since the wars.

An angel lay on the floor, dying.

Zeddig did not look at the angel. You never looked at them. Some beauty was too bright to bear, even as it failed. But she had trained herself to see without looking: as she tiptoed past tendrils of gossamer wings, as she climbed over the mound of a fallen wrist without touching the glittering ebon skin, her own breath loud within her mask, she observed the half-flayed chest, the crystal ribs glittering within, the almost-heart made of light that still beat, slowly, the thin trails of rainbow blood. Its eyes were slits, neither closed nor open, like a woman's in intense pain, no iris visible, milky white from lid to lid. The angel's glory caught Zeddig, nested in her soul, and she knew she would scream it out tonight, and writhe, and curse in dreams. She would sleep with a leather strip between her teeth, to keep from biting off her tongue.

"Ms. Hala, they're almost here."

Her watch was the color of sunset pink on desert cliffs. "I see it." The book lay open in its display case beside the angel's outstretched finger. The world had changed, but the glass remained unbroken. She drew her picks and tools. The work was complicated and fine; she had bound the motions she needed to memories, which she summoned by recollection. A kiss in the hollow at the base of the neck. A line of poetry Ley once whispered in her sleep: *howl, bound world.* A fever so deep you begged, not knowing what for. The lock slipped, the case opened. She hefted the book. Classic Late Occupation binding. She read the title on the spine, in Old Telomeri letters: *On Comedy*.

She weighed the book in her hand, reviewed its silver spiderweb fixtures, the tanned drakeskin, the jewels. Just as the records claimed. Except for the silver family library marker on the spine.

"Ms. Hala," Gal whispered from worlds away, "they are banging on the door. I'm making noise, as you said, but they won't leave. Are you certain I shouldn't just kill them?"

"I have it," she said, too loud. The angel shifted, breaking floor tiles in agony. Shit. She ran back around the corpse, book clutched to her chest, watch ticking rose pink—jumped a wrist, ducked a spasming razor-edged wing.

"I really think it'll be easier. Don't worry about the bodies. I can—"

Zeddig leaped a chasm that opened in the library floor. The angel screamed music that bowed her, knelt her weeping with its beauty, but she fell through the door, pulled her legs clear, and fumbled in her suit's breast pocket until she found her passport, thumbed it open, stared, desperately, at the stamp on the first page, the squid-mark of the Rectification Authority of Agdel Lex, cradling her in its arms. Hala'Zeddig, that's my name, and I belong to Agdel Lex.

Take me home.

There was light, and heat, too much of either and not enough. Her jacket steamed. She dropped the passport on tile and clawed with gloved hands at the collar of her suit. Dew beaded inside the goggles. Her fingers moved too slowly. She demanded their obedience. Okay, there's the latch, and pull, and gasp, fill your lungs with the searing air of this city where you're supposed to live, where light hammers down from a merciless sun, where curling winds bear dust and sand, this city that's not, more's the pity, dead.

"Open up!" the guards shouted outside. Iskari accents. Get

up. Yes, your body wants to kneel on this disgusting gray industrial tile, in this closet with its unfinished plaster walls and broken slat blinds and gray metal filing cabinets—but you didn't get this far by listening to your body. Rise, and remember: there, against your chest, you cradle a book lost for more than a hundred years. That's real. And if you don't move now, they'll take it from you, and put it somewhere it will never be seen again.

Don't worry about the library mark just yet.

Get up.

"Ms. Hala?"

Zeddig blinked ice crystals from her eyes, looked up, and saw Gal wreathed in rainbows. The woman still wore the janitor's jumpsuit they'd used to sneak into the library, but even Zeddig, who planned the delve, had to admit the limits of her disguise. The jumpsuit hid Gal like a gemstone filter hid a flame: even covered, she shined through, sharp and glittering as ever, the whole blond, slick, otter-muscled length of her, a deadly curve bent against the room's sole desk, waiting for an excuse to spring.

The guards outside tried to open the door, which stuck against the chair Gal had wedged beneath the knob.

Gal indicated the door with her chin and a raised eyebrow. Her hand drifted to her heart, and tattoos there glowed with golden light. Zeddig heard a distant sound like a horsehead fiddle, but deeper: the music of Gal's sword.

Because of course murder was the ideal solution to any inconvenience.

Gal was an excellent ally, but the people who had raised and trained her left her with odd priorities.

Zeddig tore off her suit, burst snaps and buttons, tugged

hoses free of their mounts, and dumped the whole pile of equipment on the floor with a groan and a grunt. Boots—off! Wriggling out of the trousers, she gained her feet, clad only in thermal underwear, which, before Gal could respond, she removed, and before she could escape, caught her friend in her arms, tore open her shirt, and kissed her.

Gal's eyes went wide and she twisted away, not recognizing the plan. Subterfuge wasn't exactly the point of Gal. Zeddig hooked her neck with her arm, kissed her, and thought about someone else. The guards rammed the door again, and the chair slipped. Someone, peering through, saw her, saw Gal, and swore in Iskari; Zeddig turned, snatched up her discarded jumpsuit, covered her body, and cursed, in Talbeg first, then Iskari, so they knew what to make of her.

The men were university staff, thank Gods, not real Iskers—two guards and a young fellow with a mustache thin as the lines on his gray suit, a Lordly tentacle visible near his neck. "What are you doing here? This section is off-limits." Pencil mustache spoke first, and wanted to sound stern, but his deep rosy blush and averted gaze rubbed the edge off his authority.

"So sorry," she said, "my girlfriend," faking the thick accent and verb-free grammar Iskari mystery play actors used when they impersonated Talbeg people. This kid looked straight from the Education Ministry, usual do-gooder type, didn't think of himself as evil. "Nobody comes here. I thought. Very very sorry." The apology and accent tasted like wadded socks, but Gal was the other option, and she was a limited instrument. Beautiful, but limited.

"Ah," mustache said, still not looking up. "Well. I most certainly would not expect." He didn't finish the sentence. He seemed the type to *most certainly not expect* first, and decide what he most certainly did not expect later. "That is, your supervisor should be—"

"Sir," said the older guard, a sunburned man with considerable paunch about the midsection, "perhaps we could show you the primary tier filing structure, and come back in, say, fifteen minutes?" Switching into bad Talbeg, tenses and formalities mangled: "And whence come we back, both you fucking ass gone, yes?" In Iskari, his tone of voice would read as charming.

She nodded, and tried to look grateful.

"Come on, sir," paunch said, and as he led mustache and the other guard away, continued: "As we were saying, sir, in Agdel Lex it's helpful to maintain a leniency of policy considering day-to-day affairs. Laxity in such cases may seem, admittedly, self-defeating, but the pair of docks of it is, constant maintenance of rigid standards leaves you without a goad to apply when discipline really matters, if you take my meaning. And on a daily basis we must learn to accept different cultural standards of, well, as you see . . ."

Zeddig closed the door, turned around, and legged into her jumpsuit. "Assholes. Let's get out of here."

Gal hadn't moved. She touched her lips with the tips of her fingers, and looked at them, as if she expected to see a mark.

"I'm sorry," she said. "But: a lie, a kiss, and we're free to go without a drop of blood shed. Isn't that better than the alternative?"

Gal buttoned her shirt, and zipped her jumpsuit up to her collar. "It's wrong to lie."

"It's wrong to kill people, too."

"Not always."

"Three bodies for one book is a high price," Zeddig said. "Even for this book."

Rather than responding, Gal touched the knuckle of her left thumb to her heart, and breathed out a prayer. Zeddig watched her: Frozen angels in the dead city looked so still and full of motion.

By the time Gal was done praying, Zeddig had donned her disguise, packed the suit in Gal's duffle bag, and the book in her own.

"Ready?"

"As ever, Ms. Hala."

"Good." Zeddig ran her thumb over the library marker on the *Comedy*'s spine. Genuine. Damn.

Ideal getaways, and Zeddig flattered herself that theirs was nearly ideal, felt boring. No running required. No hiding, even: Why hide if no one was hunting you? Delving had this advantage over normal theft: the victims, using the term loosely, never knew they had been robbed. In a certain sense, they hadn't been. Zeddig and Gal bore their prizes through the Postal Tax Authority's ill-lit gray halls, maintenance personnel burdened with the tools of their profession, invisible.

The only excitement came when they emerged into the oven-hot sandy noontime city, descended the front steps of a building that was once a palace, and passed a Wrecker climbing the stairs.

The woman was robed head to foot to shade her many Lords from the sun. Zeddig only saw the thin curling tentacles that gloved her hands, and a trace of wetness on the cheek beneath the hood. Space around her thickened and callused, and the air dried—the Iskari city, Agdel Lex, strongest in its agents' presence.

Zeddig did not look at Gal. She trusted her friend not to draw.

She hoped that trust was well placed.

The Wrecker hesitated behind them on the steps, and Zeddig's skin prickled, as when the air tensed before lightning. The Wrecker smelled the dead city. But of course: that's why she came. The taint of Zeddig's delve filled the Postal Authority, and the building had to be cleansed. Wreckers' priorities were simple: protect the environment, heal any trace of breach, so as to remove the risk of noncompliance.

Do your job, she willed the woman inside the monster. Follow procedure.

The Wrecker continued up the stairs, and Zeddig did not exhale in relief.

Now she just had to tell Gal the bad news.

• • •

All things considered, Zeddig felt good—at least until sunset, when Raymet caught up with her on narrow, steep, cobbled Coronation Street, crisscrossed with clotheslines, neighbors shouting to neighbors out narrow windows, old women reclining on fire escapes to fan themselves and smoke. Zeddig carried *On Comedy* in her satchel, and breathed heavy as she climbed. Her sweat didn't dry instantly on her skin. Coronation Street wound halfway out of Agdel Lex, and the air felt better here—more real.

"Zeddig," Raymet said, "give me the book."

She kept climbing.

Raymet sprinted in front of her, stopped, and spread her arms to block Zeddig's path. As a barricade, Raymet left much to be desired: her close-shorn head barely reached Zeddig's nose, and she had the build of a woman whose notion of heavy lifting involved stacks of books. Her shoulders were heaving after the brief run, and Zeddig could gauge her pulse from perturbations in her throat. They had been graduate students together, but Raymet still dressed like one. Her nails were painted sparkly black, and she was as angry as Zeddig had ever seen her.

Zeddig let herself be stopped anyway. "I asked Gal not to tell you."

"You know she can't lie."

Zeddig tried to step around her. Raymet lunged for the satchel's shoulder strap, but Zeddig pulled out of reach, and Raymet stumbled into a trash pile. She made a sick face and kicked her thick boots free of muck. "Don't grab my things," Zeddig said. "We've talked about that."

"I'm—you're—Z, we have to get paid for this job. It took us months to track down the *Comedy*, and most of that work was mine, climbing through archives—"

"You love archives."

"I also love to eat. Some of us don't have rich families to sponge off."

That stung. Zeddig paid her own way, and "rich" wasn't the right word for the Hala these days—they were still on the Roll of Fifty, but under Iskari rule the roll was just a list of potential troublemakers. Raymet's family had been outsiders even before the Iskari came. On the one hand, they weren't anyone; on the other, nobody cared what they once were. "We'll get paid."

"My collector's waiting on this, Z. Public research, deep pockets, soulstuff to burn, near the end of a budget cycle, and she was holding a chunk of that budget for us."

"You're sleeping with her."

"That's not the point! She had budget, and now she'll have to scramble to spend what's left before the close of the quarter or she'll lose it, and trust me, she'll remember this mess next time I go to her when we have to unload something in a hurry. Relationships don't just appear, Z, you have to nurture them—or, at least, I have to nurture them. We've found the only surviving volume of the *Comedy* in the world, and you just want to give it away?"

"I'm not giving it away," she said. "I'm returning it."

"To a private collection."

"It's a family library." She glanced up and down the narrow street, drew close to Raymet, and tried to keep her voice level. "The wars broke up libraries families spent centuries building. What wasn't looted fell into the dead city—my family's books, the Ko's, all the old collections."

"I know that."

"But you don't live it. I know every book in the Hala collection. I feel the ones we've lost—like missing teeth. This matters. This is heritage." The anger burst from nowhere, all her solid moral conviction suddenly expanding and aflame. She only recognized it for anger once it passed and left her raw, in the alley, returning Raymet's wide-eyed stare like a kid caught sneaking out after dark, with that same futile hope the parent will say nothing and let the infraction, without comment, be undone.

"This is about Ley, isn't it."

Zeddig checked her satchel to be sure the book was still there. "It's not about Ley."

"It is! Gods. Zeddig." Raymet paced between Zeddig and

the front steps; her hand clawed at air as if she could scrape it away and find the right words. "Look. Breakups hurt. They do! Fine, you felt betrayed. A woman learns from you, sleeps with you, loves you, and turns and uses that in a way you don't like, that sucks. But it's been two years, and we're not talking about exploiting the dead city." She realized, too late, that this line of argument was going nowhere fast, and dismissed it with a frown. "We need to eat. You like eating, right? Food? Hells, even if you don't, we need to pay to set up our next delve."

"I like to eat," Zeddig said. "But we need to do the right thing."

She slipped around Raymet, climbed three steps, and knocked on the door. Raymet grabbed for Zeddig's bag again, but Zeddig glared at her and she slowed, stepped back, hands up. "Fine."

A girl in a dusty smock opened the door, and looked at Zeddig as if waiting for the answer to a question no one had asked.

"Is this the Ko household?" Zeddig pronounced the words slowly and clearly, with respect. She did not use the old formulas often. All the more reason to use them well.

The girl nodded.

"I am Hala'Zeddig, Hala Acquisitor. Is your archivist receiving guests?"

The girl weighed them with her eyes. "Yes."

She led them both—Raymet, behind Zeddig, swearing in Iskari about stairs and humidity and the outside world in general, which for Raymet meant anything beyond the walls of her subbasement apartment— up a winding stair. Zeddig climbed with one hand on the railing, feeling the good wood under bad paint. The lower three floors of this building held four families these days, to judge from the names on post boxes and the toys cluttering up the landings, with eight children, on a range of Iskari assimilations—pink and blue toys on the third floor landing, green and yellow and black on the rest. The stairwell smelled of cinnamon and roast peppers, goat and beef and lemon peel. Chipped plaster revealed a vine mosaic. Zeddig grazed the tiles with her knuckle and judged their age, the soulstuff generations of onlookers had planted so deep not even need could tear it out.

Raymet stuffed her hands into her pockets and hunched her shoulders to her ears and didn't look anywhere save the worn toes of her boots.

The building's top floor was a single dark room, empty save for an old woman in a wicker chair, wrapped in a quilt of black on black, pondering a blank wall.

The girl ran to the old woman, bent to her ear, and whispered.

The woman raised her head, but did not turn.

"You're really doing this?" Raymet whispered in Iskari, but Zeddig silenced her with a look.

"How may I call you?" Zeddig asked.

The old woman nodded, still without looking, and the girl answered, "Grandmother."

Fair enough. "Grandmother Librarian. I am Hala Acquisitor, and I have come to return a volume."

She drew *On Comedy* from the satchel, with reverence. The first time Zeddig saw Gal draw her blade, she'd been shocked to recognize that attitude of prayer. Yes, Gal's sword was pretty, true heart's pledge to her undead queen and so forth, but it was still a sword. What could it do for the world save cut?

The room tightened and grew small. With measured, slow

steps, she approached the old woman, knelt, and placed the book in her lap.

Grandmother Librarian stroked the book's face, the silver trimmings and tanned drakeskin and the small jewels embedded in the cover. Her mouth cracked open. Thin white hairs on her upper lip drifted with her breath. She caressed the binding, curled her fingers around the edge, and guided its covers open.

She read the ancient Talbeg script with her fingertips, mouthing words. Zeddig lacked Raymet's languages; she could pronounce old script but the grammar didn't always jive in her head, so she didn't know what made the old woman's face split into a smile.

Grandmother Librarian closed the book, felt—without urgency, knowing what she would find—along the spine, traced the silver library mark.

"Thank you."

Her voice was old as the edges of the world. Zeddig, still kneeling, thought of her own grandmother, and the dead city and the ice. She could not breathe without weeping.

Grandmother Librarian folded her quilt aside, and drew herself from her chair, *On Comedy* clutched in one hand, the other extended, clawed. The girl slid her shoulder beneath the old woman's searching palm. Grandmother Librarian walked as if ice covered the floor. Her left knee buckled, and the girl took the extra weight.

When she was near enough to touch the wall, she spoke, quiet words, ground by wars and gods and passing ages of the world. "The Ko of Alikand take care," Zeddig might render it in Kathic or Iskari, poorly—"take care," for example, was a single verb. Preserve? Protect? Defend? Await? "Remember" might be the word, if Kathic or Iskari let memory be a physical act.

Grandmother Librarian took her hand from the girl's shoulder, held the book before her, and reached toward the blank wall. Raymet made a small high sound, and started forward, but Zeddig stopped her with a glare.

The wall was not empty anymore. White plaster rippled and melted away, and behind the wall, or in place of it, rested broad, tall cedar shelves canted back like music stands, carved with silver scrollwork prayers. Each shelf held a book, cover out, waiting to be read.

The change spread through the room: shelves bloomed from all four walls, and the labyrinth tiles beneath Zeddig's feet gleamed gray and white marble. She squinted at the sun, which streamed through a skylight that had not existed moments ago.

Zeddig still smelled goat and spices and preserved lemon, and heard the shouted gossip on the street outside. They had not left that city, exactly. But Grandmother Librarian kept another city hidden here, a city where some palaces never fell, a library curled safe as rose petals at nightfall, waiting for dawn.

She set *On Comedy* on a waiting shelf, stood back, and let dusk fall again. The room emptied, and the sunlight failed.

Raymet didn't talk until they reached the street.

"You've seen all that before," Zeddig said.

"Yeah." Raymet didn't sound convinced.

When Zeddig entered the dead city, she wore protective gear: the suit and lenses. She'd die without them, of course, but she was grateful for them, too, because it hurt to see, to touch, what they had lost.

"Here." She took the purse the girl had given them, and shook its contents into her palm: a silver medallion with a lapis inside. "A library marker. Not much use these days, but maybe your contact would be interested—people collect them."

"I can't take this, Z."

"Of course you can."

"What about you?"

"Don't worry about me."

"My collector wanted the *Comedy*, Zeddig. These things, they're beautiful, but they're not her area. Keep it."

"Don't make me beg."

Raymet walked the silver through her fingers, and tested it with her teeth. She breathed a trace of the soulstuff inside the marker, and when she opened her eyes, Zeddig did not remark on their wet gleam. The medallion vanished into Raymet's vest pocket. "Okay," she said. "Hey. We'll get another hit soon."

"You said that months ago."

"Patience is a virtue. Come on." She slapped Zeddig's shoulder, then stepped back, hands raised, apologetic, though Zeddig had not moved or altered her expression. "We'll be fine. We've always been fine."

"Fine," Zeddig echoed. "Have a good night, Raymet."

Raymet caught the bus at the corner. Zeddig walked north. Her stomach growled. She had a few hundred thaums left, mounting debts, and she'd needed that *Comedy* payday. So long, table at Sauga's. So long, stuffed bacon-wrapped dates and planche salmon and weird cheeses from farmers whose names she couldn't pronounce. She could survive, though, and Gal was Gal, and Raymet in her basement apartment with her student loans and her bottle of pills a day needed more than both of them.

You should think bigger, Ley whispered in her ear. *Not just scavenging bits and pieces. Think making fortunes, saving worlds.*

Ley had thought bigger. But she left. So.

Zeddig needed to get laid. She needed soulstuff. She needed a big meal and a mug of strong tea, followed by something stronger.

Those were easy.

Self-respect was harder.

As she reached the Iskari boulevards, the air dried and warmed. She flipped an ancient fertility sign at the Rectification Authority tower, then jogged downhill, north, toward the sea and the bars.

Chapter Six

A NEEDLE OF LIGHT rose from the Shield Sea.

Kai did the math as her carriage rocked downslope toward the ocean. Hard to get a good read on scale from this distance, but the needle was tall as a skyspire, growing from the waves. One more mystery in a city with too many.

Nothing but postcards from her sister in two years, then this. The silence wasn't strange, exactly. There had been no great falling out—Kai just gave herself to the priesthood, while Ley left for the mainland, for Iskar, for the University at Chartegnon. The closest they came to a fight was the night before Ley moved out, while drunk at Mako's: "I don't know why you're leaving," met with "I don't know how you can bear to stay. We're just fooling ourselves, here." But Ley wouldn't explain what she meant, and then she was gone.

In the years since, Kai had rooted out a church conspiracy, defeated it, and joined a silent, slow movement to fix the island. Ley didn't know about any of that, but then, Kai knew little about her sister's life, either. In Chartegnon, Ley studied art and nightmare telegraphics; her postcards from Agdel Lex suggested professional success. At least, she never asked for funds.

Kai had visited Ley at university, once. They hugged, they laughed, they spent the week eating street skewers from disreputable food carts in the brokedown converted warehouse parts of town, drinking in bars that swept the patrons out the front door with the sawdust at closing time, and communicated house rules through crude handpainted signs, ALL PATRONS CHECK WEAPONS WITH BARKEEP ON PAIN OF DISMEMBERMENT (MEMBER OF OUR CHOICE). Ley's fellow students spent their extracurricular time on more curriculum, with occasional forays to licensed burlesques, but Ley claimed she thought best with the background of a fistfight. Even those of Ley's friends who hailed from Iskari High Families cultivated an air of poverty; Kai, freshly ordained and not yet bonus-eligible, still made more than any four of them put together, and picked up checks when she could. They wandered tipsy down alleys hand in hand, dodged gangs of werewolves high on moonshine; Ley tried to get Kai to smoke, and when that failed, set her up with a very attractive and far too earnest young man—but Ley kept her heart to herself, hidden in a secret place she'd never show.

At any rate, that experience left Kai without high hopes for Sauga's.

But to her surprise, the carriage did not turn down any disreputable alleys. It followed broad, main boulevards, well lit by gaslamp. Iskari streetcorner signage locked the city in a grid of heroes' names and lauded concepts, Verity Boulevard and Responsibility Place, though Kai did spot a few odd words she guessed were Iskari approximations of old Talbeg names. The skyline didn't shift here. The road held a constant width. She tried to see the other city, the meandering alleys thin as cracks on glass, but it hid from her.

The closer they drew to the sea, the more up-rent the architecture and attendant businesses: a Muerte Coffee franchise, its grinning skull logo tasteful and understated. A golem show-room. Hells, Kai hadn't imagined Corvid's would even have storefronts outside Iskar proper, and certainly not one so lav-ish—its plate glass windows displayed a wealth of mannequins (she hoped they were mannequins) draped in gowns of spider silk and suits of woven cloud. Painted pupils (she hoped they were painted) followed her. The tourists resembled the Kavekanese variety, Iskari mainlanders in suits or Rectification Authority uniforms, Camlaanders, a few Craftsfolk, citizens of everywhere and nowhere. The locals dressed Iskari, for the most part, even walked like them.

Gods, Kai, listen to yourself. You sound like some mainlan-der come to Kavekana for an overnight, all let down everyone's not running around shirtless in a grass skirt.

She didn't like this part of town. Good thing she wasn't staying long. Any minute now, the carriage would turn left, abandon the well-lit streets for some sewage-sinking side alley where, no, seriously, Kai, you trust me, this place has the best lamb skewers in the city, how do I know, well, I conducted a double blind study, but don't worry, the guy I blinded, he got better, you'd be surprised what they can do with synthetic eye-balls these days.

Of course I'm kidding. Come on, sis. Try some. Trust me.

Any minute now.

The carriage stopped at the beach. Stone steps led down the white sand to the water's edge, where a jeweled garden lay a hundred feet out upon the sea.

It was a small garden, and opulent, ringed with a silver colonnade twined with green vines that glowed softly from within. Guests lingered on the veranda: men in suits that ate the light or robes of brilliant blue, women in gowns jeweled with actual stars. Elegant voices drifted over the waves, words too faint to make out at this distance. Only the rise and fall remained. Somewhere, a string quartet played. Past the columns and phosphorescent vines, diners sat around tables, and at the garden's heart, behind a low wall, chefs worked with flame.

"This can't be the place," she told the cabbie.

"Lady, you ask for Sauga's, you get Sauga's. You want some other place, I can take you there."

"I've never—" she said, then, "I mean, how do I get out there? Are there boats?"

"If you think I ever eat there, lady, I got disappointing news for you about tippers in this town."

She took the hint, and descended the beach steps, pondering. No wonder Fontaine laughed: the world was thick and stable here. Kai had dressed for business, not for a place this fancy. She owned gowns back on Kavekana that would suit—a Corvid number, even, that she'd got on layaway, black with star sapphires down the sides, with a plunging back that showed her scars and the muscles of her shoulders—but since the Martello business hadn't included red carpets or seduction, she hadn't taken the trouble to pack the thing. Even the laughter at Sauga's sounded expensive. Up and down the shore, luxury hotels shimmered with ghostlight; bamboo torches marked off stretches of private beach. She knew those places, or places like them, back home. They were embassies, of a sort. They didn't belong to the same world as Kai.

It worked like this everywhere, she supposed.

She stepped onto the water, and the toe of her black pump dipped through the waves.

Kai would have fallen, if she had not expected this sort of fuckery. Exclusive place, huh? She stood on shore, and stared across the water at the maître d's station, where a thin woman with impossibly pale skin reviewed a guest registry, tapping lacquered fingernails on lacquered wood. She did a fantastic impression of someone who had not noticed Kai.

No doubt Kai had stumbled into some elaborate hierarchy—probably, knowing the Iskari, a hierarchy with real live hierophants. But Kavekana was not an Iskari protectorate, Kai did not pray to Iskari gods, and there was no harm in showing off.

So she reached to her jacket's third inside pocket, produced a slim black book, and thumbed to the proper page. Yes, she'd remembered right—Yavimal was the name, an idol she'd built for a clan of everstorm explorers to protect the fruits of their life-threatening labors on the borders of other worlds. Yavimal had simple prohibitions; Kai hadn't drunk any alcohol yet tonight, wasn't on her period (a mystifying ban, but you worked with the materials your pilgrims gave you). Golden. She chanted three lines of prayer to Yavimal Tideshifter in a Delta dialect, pictured the three-headed crocodile goddess squatting in her palace cave, and as ever these days, felt behind the dread toothsome Lady Yavimal the cool rapture of another, higher Lady, enormous and blue.

She stepped onto the water, and the water bore her up.

The maître d' paid attention then, oh yes.

Kai gave her the most polite *pick a hell and burn there* smile she'd yet devised, and strode across the water to the veranda. The cool fingers that had cupped her cheek faded when she set foot on solid ground. The maître d' kept goggling, which surprised Kai; Craftswomen must dine here from time to time, and she doubted *they* would bother jumping through Sauga's hoops. Though perhaps there were wards against Craftwork interference, or if not that, then at least customs, often stronger than any ward or magic. "A table for two, please. My guest will join me soon."

The maître d' jumped back on-script, and cobbled together a cutting smile. "Do you have a reservation?"

"No."

"I'm so terribly sorry," she said. "But we have no room for walk-ins."

Turn on the charm. "I'm so sorry. This was all very last minute. Can I make a reservation now?"

"Our next opening is"—she paged through the registry—"three months from now—it's a lunch. Will that work?"

What kind of place was this, anyway? But Ley had been specific. "I can't wait that long."

"No." And now the maître d' regained solid ground, her awe replaced by a weapons-grade smirk. Good for her. "I'm quite sorry."

"Maybe my sister made a reservation. The name's Pohala? Ley?" The woman paled, which, considering her skin, was an achievement. Kai tried to crane her neck and examine the maître d's book, but the woman covered the list of names with her hand.

"Please," the maître d' said, "I'll call a cab to take you—wherever." Nice light touch, sliding the knife in. Her bright red nails trailed to a summoning circle beside the desk. "Where are you staying?"

Kai opened her mouth, mind racing to form another argument— but someone else spoke first.

"Marian, I've never known you to turn away a friend."

A hand settled at the small of Kai's back.

Kai recognized her sister's voice: a low, rich alto, like honey and turned soil. She recognized the maître d's blush: Ley had that effect on women. But the tone was different. As a kid, Ley hated the arrogant tourists, criminals, and clients who wandered Kavekana's shores. She watched them all, and later, in private, by cant of shoulder or toss of chin, evoked each one and made them seem ridiculous, the pretense of a Deathless Queen, an Iskari bishop's upturned nose. She could never keep it up long. Sooner or later all that fake pomposity crumbled to a self-deprecating smile, a giggle unfurled into a laugh.

Ley's voice dripped with all the swagger and command she'd ever mocked, but now the joke was gone.

Before Kai could turn to face her sister, Ley revolved into view: slick and sharp-jawed with close-clipped hair, a vector in a plum suit, wearing brogues, Iskari cuffs, a smile. She caught Kai in an embrace too tight for breath. By the time Kai, stunned, moved to hug her back, Ley had slipped away, to lean against the maître d's—Marian's—station. "Marian, you've never met my sister. She leaves home once a never, steady as a monument, guards Kavekana's gods and clients against all enemies, and for all the postcards I've sent enticing her to Agdel Lex, she only just surprised me with a visit. I'm ecstatic."

Marian flushed deeper, though so far as Kai could tell Ley hadn't said anything blushworthy. Maybe you had to be on the receiving end of her smile to get the full effect. "You shouldn't be here," Marian said. "You made a scene last time. I should call the kraken."

"A lover's quarrel, Marian. My fault." And the half smile and declination of head that, on Ley, meant: I was wrong. Me! Yes, I know, a surprise to us all. "A misunderstanding with Zeddig. I've eaten my share of, ah, my own words over it all. Trust me."

Marian turned an impressive shade of scarlet—one more

downside of that paper-white skin. She must burn easily. "I can't seat you without a reservation." Her fingers played with the menus stacked behind the stand; she leaned in, matching Ley's posture. Marian had very curly hair, and Ley had always been fascinated with curls, as with anything she couldn't have.

"Fortunately I have all that sorted." Ley slid her finger under the napkin Marian used to cover the reservation book, looked into Miriam's eyes, and slid the napkin aside. Her finger (nail lacquered purple to match the suit) trailed down the list until she found a name written in cursive Kai couldn't read. "We only learned Kai was in town yesterday, so Zeddig gave me her reservation. I know it's not for another half hour, but the table's turned already, hasn't it? Kai has an early flight tomorrow. Look at her." Ley's arm was longer than it looked. She took Kai by the shoulder. "Long day of meetings. She needs a glass of bright and bubbly."

"I'm fine," Kai said. "We can go somewhere else, if it's a problem." She knew what she was supposed to say. Ley's act drew her in, creating its own good cop. Kai didn't care whether they ate here or at some oyster bar down the water; Ley knew that, and still trusted her to play along. All this—the suit, the nails, the suave exterior—was a game.

"It's no trouble," Ley replied. "Is it?"

Marian spent all her willpower to break Ley's gaze, and once she did, she snapped on-script. "Follow me, please." The smile polished, the voice sweet, the physiognomy welcoming and distant at once—easier to be the maître d' than Marian, with Ley in the room. She selected menus from the stack, and led them, dancer-graceful, beneath the softly glowing ivy and into the restaurant.

When Marian turned her back, Kai saw, thanks to the low

cut of the maître d's sharp red dress, that a section of her spine was made of glyph-carved titanium.

A server seated them, introduced himself, passed menus, poured sparkling wine, retreated. Ley raised her glass. "Carriage accident," she said.

"What?"

"Marian. Four years ago. Hence the—" Ley gestured toward her back, a motion anyone watching could have mistaken for Kai's sister brushing lint off the shoulder of her suit, if Ley's suit ever accumulated lint. "The apparatus. A shame: she's a great poet, and before the accident she'd just completed the first draft of an epic. She should be out building something grand—scrounge through years of eighty-hour days, hook up with the right people, find funding, and she'd be able to buy and sell any of these clowns twice over. But she's not Iskari, so she needs private insurance for the spinal apparatus, and, well, she's lucky Sauga's came through. Maybe when her friends strike it rich, they'll remember her, and sweep her away from all this. That happens sometimes. Not often. Life moves fast. People are good at forgetting who gave them the advice they needed, when they needed it—who fixed their scansion the last instant before a big pitch. Memories fail, with fortunes involved."

In the kitchen, a cook with an iguana's face made a mystic gesture over a pan, or maybe added spice; either way, a column of blue fire blossomed. A girl drew a cleaver from a block, tossed it into the air, caught the handle without looking, and laid into a joint. Tuxedoed waiters danced between tables covered in creamy silk. Craft circles surrounded each table, rubbed the neighboring conversations into an incomprehensible stage murmur more welcoming than the eerie silence

Craftwork wards often wrought. "What are you doing, Ley?"

"I'm treating my sister, who I haven't seen in years, to a meal at the best restaurant in the city." Ley raised her glass, Kai parried with her own, and the result looked almost like a toast. Ley knocked back half her wine in a single pull. She only seemed to take pleasure in the act at its end, granting herself a thin grin. "I've come up in the world, since Chartegnon."

Kai tasted hers, hesitant, patient: peaches without sweetness, a fluttering inside her mouth like a hummingbird trying to escape. She swallowed. "The Chatelenne family are clients of mine. I like their work as much as the next girl, but this is a hundred-thaum bottle. I'm glad you're doing well, Ley, but, come on. You don't have to impress me. Somehow you found out I was coming, and somehow you got into the bank to send me that letter. Play poor Marian if you like, but don't play me."

Ley's fingers stroked the stem of her champagne flute. "How are you, sis?"

"Fine, aside from your avoiding the question."

"You know, I had two letters from Mom in the last year: one to tell me you were in hospital"—without the definite article; she really had been spending too much time in the Old World—"and another, a day later, to tell me you were out."

Kai set the glass down. "Mom didn't know I was in, either, until I woke up and told her. By then, I was out of critical. It wasn't bad—soul loss, deep cuts, broken bones, but treatable. My guidelines for care told them not to tell Mom unless there was a chance I wouldn't make it."

"Or me?" Her free hand waved off Kai's objection. She looked down into the bubbles in her glass. "I was afraid when I heard, but, gods, I can't believe I'm saying this, those letters were a relief. It was nice to have proof you were human."

"What do you mean?"

Ley's eyes, when she opened them, were large and dark as Kai's own. "You remember that footrace—I was six? You tripped, and split your forehead on a conch shell? And I didn't notice, I was sprinting along, so happy to be winning for once, and when I turned back I saw you stagger across the line with your face covered in blood."

"I was fine." Of course Ley had run ahead, unthinking, eager to win. Kai needed stitches. "I kept the scar when I went into the pool." She tapped her forehead, near the hair line.

"I'm glad."

"Why did you break into a bank to send me a letter?"

"Who says I broke in?"

"I asked Fontaine to trace the letter. It appeared this morning, mysteriously."

Ley waved the implied question off. "I wanted to talk with you. I needed a place that was personal and secure."

"So secure you didn't put either of our names on the reservation."

She shrugged.

"How did you know I was coming?"

"I have friends in the bank, and the arts community. Your visit raised a fuss."

"Fontaine wanted to keep things secret."

"It's a small berg, sis."

"Doesn't seem small to me."

"That depends on your angle." Ley sculpted the shore behind them with a wave of her hand. Kai followed the gesture: Agdel Lex rose up the cliffs like a wave, ghostlit offices, skyscrapers, sprawling residential blocks, and the Iskari squid tower. The air wavered with reradiated heat. The frozen horrorscape Kai had glimpsed in that first broken moment of arrival was nowhere to be seen from Sauga's. "There were many cities here even before Gerhardt came, and they've multiplied since—the dead city, the Iskari colony with its squiddy bureaucrats, the nameless city where old Alikanders hide, the refugee city, the criminal city, the city of dockworkers and freight. My city's small, but we do big things." She turned from Agdel Lex, to face the spire out at sea.

"What is that, anyway?" Kai's earlier curiosity overwhelmed, for a moment, her certainty that this was just another artful dodge. "Hotel? Military base?"

"Our great success. How did your meetings go?"

That sharp pivot broke the illusion. Kai felt so tired of all this staggering glib self-possession. Maybe this was nothing more than Ley being Ley, uncomfortable, like the rest of their family, around pain, always ready to flee uncertainty by diving into some new project, or unrelated abstract argument about ship rigging or the cost of trade, police organization or the dynamics of faith. Politics, religion, business, these were all easier than human meat, in the Pohala household. There was love—without love, who could bear so many arguments?—but it clothed itself in other words and ways. "What do you want, Ley?" Their waiter approached, but drew back without need for a signal. Good service here.

"Your meetings—what did you think of them?"

"Good Concerns," she said. "Interesting projects."

"Interesting?" Ley always could hear the words behind her words.

"They felt small."

"They are. Dreamcraft and nightmare implementation have limitless potential, but so much of this data-crunching mind-to-mind work just scratches the surface. Amusements. Cheap tricks. Altus, the Concern that built that spire—they want something different. They'll take the same models, the same spirit, to the stars."

"Bullshit," Kai said, and Ley laughed.

"Swearing already? You've barely touched your wine." She finished hers. "They have financing. The technology's tested. And they have their first big client: an Iskari government launch goes up this week." Ley frowned, shook her head, pressed on. "For Altus, the Iskari are just a stepping stone. Imagine it: Craftsmen drink starlight for power, and warp the darkness. What if they could walk among the stars themselves? What if they wielded the deepest darkness imaginable?"

Kai ignored the hypothetical. "So—you heard about me through your friends."

"It's a tight-knit community, a few thousand at most, all striving for fortune and glory. We come from all over the world, and we scramble, and we live visibly. Every project and verse passes around under a friend-d-a, but everybody's everybody else's friend. I heard you were here, tricked my way into IFI, and now, well." She folded one leg over the other, and looked down into the toe of her shoe as if the reflection might offer her clues as to how she might proceed. "I need help."

There it was: the meat within the shell. *I need help.* Kai tried to remember when she'd last heard those words. When this brilliant sharp woman before her broke her ankle falling out of a palm tree, age seven, she'd not asked for help; she'd propped herself on a branch and tried to limp home, choking off her sobs, and when Kai offered Ley her arm, Ley shrugged her off. Kai had shoved herself under Ley's arm anyway. "Anything."

"Two things are happening at once."

Kai felt her frown form. "Really."

Ley raised one hand. "Let me explain."

"You brought me here to pitch me."

"It's a solid pitch."

"This was a setup."

"No." Ley pinched her nose. "Kai. Come on. I don't have much time."

"You don't have much time? I thought we were here for dinner."

"There's a lot going on," Ley said.

"Uh-huh."

"Sis, listen to me. This is important. I'm involved in a project." She drew a small black envelope from her pocket, unfolded it, and unfolded it again, until she held a large black envelope that never appeared to have been folded. A black wax seal glistened on the flap: wolfsbane. She slid it face down across the table to Kai, who didn't pick it up. "It's a big deal. But the funding's drawn us in a bad direction, and if you were to buy out their stake, we could pivot away. What we're trying to do is—"

"What do you need?"

"Sixteen million thaums," she said. "Tonight."

Kai tensed, remembered Mom and sandcastles, and said, "No."

"Kai."

"Don't." She raised one hand. "You're asking me to spend eight thousand souls—"

"Not spend, invest—in me, in the Concern. There's limitless growth potential. We're going to change the world."

"If you're such a good investment, why do you need sixteen million thaums tonight? Go to a bank."

"The bank's not my sister."

"And it won't give you sixteen million thaums sight unseen, either."

"What do you want from me, Kai?" Even with the sound-dulling ward, Ley's raised voice drew glances from neighboring tables; an Iskari matron pointedly returned her attention to her foie gras, and a Talbeg gentleman reached for his partner's hand. "You want me to kneel? To kiss the ring? You're not even letting me explain. It was hard to write that letter."

"Not hard enough," Kai said, primly as she could manage, and stood, and folded her napkin. She left the wine unfinished on the table, and the folder untouched. "I have to go. I can't sit here anymore."

Ley caught Kai's wrist. Kai looked at Lei's hand. Her sister's knuckles paled with the force of her grip. She looked open, and raw, and scared.

No one around them was even pretending to eat anymore.

Kai said: "Let me go."

Ley did. She stepped back, wooden and slow.

Kai smoothed the cuff of her jacket. She closed her eyes for the length of a blessing. When she opened them again, Ley remained. "I'm sorry for embarrassing you in front of your restaurant friends. The next time I see you, I'll forget we had this conversation."

She crossed the ward, so she did not hear the word Ley said next. But she could read her sister's lips just fine.

Chapter Seven

KAI MARCHED UP THE cliffs of Agdel Lex to pray.

She owed a dozen small gods obeisance, in a dozen different languages, and none of those were right. The moon cast one shadow from her, and the ghostlight lamps another, and she minded neither. The road grew steep as it left the harbor. She leaned against a coffee-seller's stall to switch from sensible heels to the more sensible flats in her purse, and kept climbing, and still couldn't bear to pray the prayers she needed.

Gods save us from our sisters. Sisters know us before we know to hide our secrets, before we learn to guard the latches that close our soul, to hide the chinks in the diamonds that become our armor as we recline upon our hoard. And sisters remember.

She was not being fair. Whatever Ley wanted, however audacious the request—sixteen million thaums, twice Kai's investment budget, enough to support a couple hundred families for a year anywhere in the world, a vast fortune mentioned with an offhand ease that suggested she thought it negligible—there must have been a better way to handle that conversation than just charging out.

Kai left the bright tourist districts behind, joining main arteries of commerce and shipping. Streets meant for cart and horse zigzagged upslope. Kai was the only pedestrian she could see. Behind a high fence, enormous conveyor platforms bore corrugated steel containers downslope toward a shipping depot, where golems and night shift stevedores loaded the containers onto carts they dragged to port.

She climbed as they descended, and thought of salmon swimming upstream, and of the fear she'd read in Ley's grip, in her eyes, the need her sister could not speak.

Kai knew she was wrong to blame sisterhood as a concept, sisters in the abstract. This wasn't a universal problem. She'd just never been able to shake the sense that Ley knew her better than she knew herself, just like Ley knew everything, drew secrets and held them, captured, with perfect gravity.

The desert dried Kai's sweat to salt scales. She bought water from an open convenience store. The man behind the counter had a full beard, was reading a book on mathematics when Kai entered, wore a loose white tunic; if he thought Kai out of place he said nothing and accepted her coin—two thaums without the bottle deposit. Kai did not twitch as the soul left her. Izza'd described being so low on soulstuff a thaum for a scrap of bread left you reeling. There was so much Kai didn't understand. Life was short, and learning took so long.

"Thank you," she told the man, in what she hoped passed for decent Talbeg. He offered her a betel nut from the open bag on the counter, and she shook her head.

When she reached the top of the hill, she found herself panting and exhausted before an enormous train station. The conveyor behind the fence ran through a toothed gate in a curtain wall studded with guard towers; behind the wall, an engine five stories tall surged to a stop. Beetle-black iron hissed and popped and spouted steam. Guards marched atop the train cars, watchful. One sang a war song in Talbeg Kai couldn't follow. Demon ice melted and steamed from the train, and tortured metal creaked. One car hadn't made the journey intact: an enormous claw had torn its side open, and greenish fluid leaked from within. Blood and dried rainbows streaked the steel. Station hands swarmed the train, tossing nets of grounding wire over the hulk, binding it back into this world after its journey through another.

Kai turned back to the ocean and the Altus Spire. Behind her the Iskari tower rose, red and tumescent.

This wasn't her place. She'd leave tomorrow. But she had duties.

She removed her prayer mat from her purse, spread it on the cobblestones, and knelt back on her calves. Eyes closed, she reviewed the litanies come due, and eyes open, she spoke them. Where sacrifices were required, she offered them, in abbreviated form. Some idols lapped blood, others ate the ash of burnt hair. Others sought only poetry, attention. People who didn't understand the role of a Kavekanese priest sometimes asked why she'd ever build an idol whose sacrifice inconvenienced her—bloodletting, say, or sexual abstinence. But while faith, in general, had the same dynamics no matter its object, gods and idols were works of art, and begged thematic consistency. A blood-thirsty God would not eat offerings of grass. Though that would be an interesting challenge: to construct a warrior Goddess whose rituals revolved around unlikely combinations and forms of worship. Sex, say, either orgiastic intoxication in the manner of an Ebon Sea cult, or else some peculiar sort of denial. Meditation handbooks from Sheer Peaks monasteries advised the practitioner to envision herself midcopulation with a sensory lushness from which even an Iskari romance might shrink—and then to envision one's partner undergoing the many stages of death and decomposition, until one lay in congress with a skeleton.

Which proved, to Kai's mind, that monks were a lot kinkier than most people gave them credit.

Neither the bloodletting nor the incense nor the mental progression through the logics of sex—and certainly not the stink of burnt hair—calmed her, but the idols back home appreciated her attention. She felt their light kind touches: a chill hand across her cheek, a flush in her belly, the smell of lavender, adoration returned, like when Maya's cats rubbed against her leg when she arrived to feed them. Inside of fifteen minutes, she was in turn the high priestess Ourakos-who-killed, of Yavimal-who-walks-on-water, of Iara-who-summons, of Komoros-healer-of-small-cuts-and-bruises. (She'd tried to convince the Zurish clients who proposed Komoros that she could build something larger, fuller, and more interesting, but they were a family of limited vision.)

She left the Blue Lady for last, because the Blue Lady scared her.

Lady, guide my steps.

Lead me from Smiling Jack and the bag of knives.

Make me smart, and make me fast.

Catch me in Your hand when I fall.

Bind me to my brothers and my sisters.

(Kai stumbled over the last word. Litany: you often forgot what you were about to say until you said it.)

Unlock the doors that bar.

Help me make others free.

A small prayer, she'd thought at first, when Izza proposed it: a thief's credo. But when she spoke it every night, she realized how much those words could mean if you let them grow.

The Lady wound through her.

She thought about Ley.

For all her years of experience building small idols, semi-conscious almost-gods tailored to fit her clients' needs, Kai was still growing used to a Goddess who talked back. The Blue Lady didn't argue, or tease. She picked the locks of your heart. She stole into your mind. If She wanted you to know She was there, She gave you a taste of Her glory. Often, She just slid out, leaving a thought you could ignore if you wished. A memory, an obsession, which might have been your own all along.

Dammit.

Ley wanted to do everything herself. She was smart and brave and she didn't need other people often. Everything was her responsibility: she could hold it together, tie up her own problems, just get off her case. What would make someone like that ask her sister for sixteen million thaums?

When Kai first read the letter, she'd felt a stab of fear. What could Ley need? Soured by a day of meetings with people begging soulstuff to feed petty projects, Kai had decided without asking: Ley was greedy. Of course she could never be in real trouble.

But maybe she was. Maybe Kai, for all her good intentions, could not hear.

She gathered her ritual apparatus, her fetishes and knife and bowl and lighter, into her purse, stood, shook the prayer mat free of dust, folded it, and returned it to her purse. Golem engines ground behind her; torn metal screamed. A crane lifted the damaged container. Streetlights lit the nameplate on the station wall: Gavreaux Junction.

A smell of ice and broken gods wafted to her from the dead city deep underfoot.

Be careful, Izza had said.

Shit.

Kai shouldered her bag, and walked fast, looking for a cab.

Chapter Eight

A ZOMBIE IN A sharkskin suit and a small red hat found Zeddig at the Cavern Diver, when she was already four drinks into the night and the stars—no, those weren't stars, just lights, little recessed fake diamond motherfuckers constellating the ceiling, which Marygray thought added to the ambiance, though her sense of the Cavern Diver's ambiance always having been a bit left of center of the clientele's—well anyway the starlike light things twinkled. The zombie set a hand on Zeddig's shoulder, and his touch chilled her, though not so much as the dead city had. "You owe me, Zeddig."

Burn and tear. Some people lacked the decency to let a woman stew after doing the right thing. "Vogel." She slammed sorghum whiskey and slid her shot glass across the bar for another pour. Shouldn't be drinking now, here, but it had been a long day. "Is that how you say hi to all your business partners?"

"Business partners!" Vogel's face could convey a great deal of surprise, given that the right half of it wasn't there anymore. He'd paid someone to wire his jaw together with gold to keep it from falling off, but his wormy left side was still too stiff for human expressions. Some people let themselves die when their time came. Some grappled to a reasonable facsimile of life, sustained by insurance contracts, phylacteric trusts, and premortem exercises. Others were Vogel. He just died, decayed, and stuck around. "Business partner, boys, you hear that?" The boys in question chuckled, two big dockhand types; one wore a Zurish mask, the other bore crude mining colony glyphs, like someone had remodeled him with a cleaver. "Business partners"—he still hadn't let go of Zeddig's shoulder—"work together. They don't run out on jobs. They pay back loans."

She'd expected this—but had hoped for a night's grace to get good and drunk before the shark smelled blood. "We got a bad tip. There was a library marker."

"You confuse me for someone who cares. I advanced you funds for the job. You were supposed to do the damn thing, get paid, and pay me back, not run around playing Reynardine." She tried to turn back to her drink, but Vogel spun her on her barstool to face him. She wanted to sit up, to take this situation seriously. Unfortunately, slamming four shots in under an hour seemed to have increased local gravity. Maybe someone smarter or more sober could have explained. Zeddig stayed slumped, and Vogel looked sideways and furious.

She pushed herself almost vertical, which fixed the sideways, if not the furious. "We just need coverage until the next job, that's all."

"There's no score big enough," he said. "Not in Agdel Lex."

"Alikand," she said, automatically, because she was drunk.

"Agdel Lex," he repeated through teeth his wires didn't leave him any choice but to clench. "You won't work your way out of this by delving on your own. But there's another option."

"No."

"Come work for me. You got skills I need. One train job will cancel out the debt." He patted her shoulder and to her surprise, no doubt because she was very, very drunk, she did not hit him.

"Delvers you hire for big jobs have a nasty tendency to turn up dead, or stuck in a squid. Wonder why that might be."

"No idea," he said. "Wouldn't have anything to do with the fact you people seem to think I'm the kind of punk you can screw with."

"Aw, Vogel. We know exactly what kind of punk you are." She grinned, sloppy. "Now, let go of my shoulder."

He released her, leaving wet tracks on her skin.

"I'm good for it," she said. "Give me a week."

"A week? I can do a week." He slid one hand into his shark-skin suit, and withdrew a vial traced with gold wire, a drop of blood inside. Zeddig's gut clenched. She'd known this was coming, but that didn't help. "Let's talk about interest."

"Ahem," Gal said.

Gal hadn't cleared her throat. She actually said, "Ahem." Not loud, either—but her tone of voice made the bar go quiet. Gal hadn't drawn her sword. She just stood behind Vogel and his bully-boys, arms loose at her sides. Fake starlight caught in her golden hair, and her eyes glittered their weird alien blue, utterly calm.

That calm didn't break when Zur-boy and Cleaverface spun around, Zur with a knife, Cleaverface leveling a crossbow at Gal's forehead.

She smiled, like he'd told a bad joke. "Try."

"I don't want trouble," Marygray said from behind the bar. Zeddig glanced right. Easy to mistake Marygray. She looked like, because she was, one of those crunchy antiestablishment foreign types who drifted Alikand way, seeking a place outside their empires: pale and soft even after two decades of Glebland sun, gray hair dyed psychedelic neon stripes. But she kept a blasting rod behind the bar, and spent every weekend at the range. Dear heart, she said when Zeddig needled her about the contradiction: ask any imperialist. It's best to speak softly and carry a small stick that makes people's bones explode.

Zur-boy drew a rod of his own, but before he could point it toward Marygray, chairs ground against floorboards and a disquieting number of the dockfolk who frequented the Cavern Diver rose to their feet.

With all the wire holding Vogel's face together, Zeddig couldn't tell whether his smile was placating, nervous, or triumphant. "No need to get excited. You say a week, Zeddig, I can let you have a week. I'm a generous guy. But I need a down payment. Half a soul."

"I can't afford that."

"Not a problem," he said. "I'll take it in pain. Right here."

Gal met Zeddig's gaze, as if nobody else in the bar held weapons, as if there weren't two pointed at her, as if Zeddig's choice here was all that mattered. "Ms. Hala?"

"It's fine," she said to Gal, and then, to Vogel, "Go ahead."

He touched the vial.

Zeddig felt a knife enter her arm and peel slowly up.

She twitched. She kept her feet. She watched him. She did not puke.

Then it really started.

• • •

Gal cleaned her up and walked her home down narrow dark alleys up to the Wings. Laundry lines crisscrossed the starless sky. Their path wound into *her* city, the city where she was born; streets narrowed and colors brightened, the air grew wet and soft. Iskari street signs disappeared. "I don't need," she said, pushed off Gal's arm, tried to stand on her own, then stumbled into a trash can.

"Of course you don't." Gal took her arm anyway. Zeddig felt the other woman's shoulders—soft, supple, smooth. No knots, no clicks, no unnecessary tension. Gal cared for her body like a weapon, because it was. "Why did you borrow from Vogel?"

She'd gargled three times in the alley behind the Cavern Diver, but her teeth still felt gritty with vomit. "He limited my debt. No matter how much I owe him, he can't touch my family, can't touch their library. The Wreckers work with banks these days—each loan's a chance to get their claws on the collection."

"Surely there were other options."

"We needed the soulstuff." Idiot. "And—a full *On Comedy*? We could have paid off Vogel with room to spare. Seemed like a good idea at the time. Besides, he's a pushover. By loan shark standards."

"Ah."

"I didn't beg," she said. "And I only screamed that once."

"I wish you had let me intervene."

"It's just a debt."

"You should have told us."

"You would have told me it was a bad idea. And if I told you, you would have told Raymet, and the two of you would have found some way to stop me. It was a big score. I took a risk."

"You have a week to pay him back."

She nodded. Far up, a father sang a lullaby to his baby at an open window.

"You don't have the soulstuff."

"I'll figure out something."

"I could kill him."

"You could," she said. "But you don't want Raymet to see you as a killer."

Gal blinked. "I have no idea what you mean."

"Oh, come on."

"You are changing the subject."

"Damn right."

They walked together in silence for a while. Zeddig noticed how much she was leaning against Gal, and didn't stop. At last, after a sort of leftish right and a rightish left, they reached a three-story house with a baked tile roof and a thick wooden door carved with vines. Home. Gal helped her up the steps, and knocked.

The door opened, and Zeddig tried her best smile, which had, admittedly, seen better days. "Hi, Grandma."

Chapter Nine

THE CAB LET KAI off three blocks from Ley's apartment. "I'll get you close as I can," he'd said when she showed him the return address on the letter she brought from home: Ley's last note, three smeared lines congratulating Kai on her promotion—the ink must have been wet when she folded the paper into the envelope. "Downtown streets, you know."

She didn't argue, but neither did she understand until she saw. Hearing "downtown," she pictured the kind of swank foreigner enclave she'd never deign visit in Kavekana, home to the kind of people Ley wanted her to think she was. But as the carriage climbed away from Gavreaux Junction, they left ghostlight modernity behind. Unfinished plaster buildings flanked dusty alleys cluttered with garbage and broken furniture. Billowing cursive script rippled on the walls, pulling at the eye in quarterlight. The art made the world less stable.

Kai tensed with fear and reached for her passport, expecting that cold sharp snap of the dead city—but though the city changed as they left Iskari streets behind, it did not die. Air moistened, tensed with ozone and orange. Out of the corner of her eye, Kai saw narrow streets between the shops and homes, people milling there: three old men played music on drums and something like a banjo, while a girl kicked a shuttlecock with the insides of her feet, tap, tap, tap. When Kai tried to look at them directly, they vanished.

The cabbie let her off at "East Wind Lane," which existed even when she looked at it head-on. "Up there," he said, "and in."

"What if I get lost?"

"Ask for directions."

She didn't have to. Gathering heels and purse and assembling her jacket into a reasonable approximation of professional order, she proceeded uphill, ignoring the protests of legs and calves. Scar tissue bunched in her back.

The mind makes distance weird. The three-mile walk from Kai's house to the Priesthood's offices back home passed in an unconscious blur; she'd climbed the dormant volcano of Kavekana'ai so many times she'd built a callus against the sky and distant tang of surf and the touch of small gods. But three blocks down a side street in Agdel Lex felt raw.

Four women played cards on a folding table. A storyteller at a fountain square worked a crowd of young men and women drinking dark beer. A baby cried through an open window and a cat, yowling, answered from a rooftop. Crowded coffee bars glowed beside shuttered groceries. A dense crowd watched a masked poetry slam:

> *flit feint fierce*
> *a tongue trials down*
> *to crease a joint*
> *of leg and hip*

and in the audience a man hooted and the crowd caught the laugh from him and the masked poet raised her hand, flourishing diaphanous silk sleeves, to grip that laugh by the throat until silence returned.

Observations on her own observation: the unfamiliar drew her eye, so she noticed life-ways she didn't know, this story-teller, that blue wine, the mask, that unrecognizable card game like a sort of four-way solitaire. She didn't note samenesses: fathers and children, boys holding hands, a kiss in shadows. Some part of her kept insisting this was a dirty place, but it wasn't, any more than any given Kavekana side street.

Most of the foreigners here, if foreigners they were, looked young, wearing garish checks and stripes, hair unkempt. Some sported mustaches Kai had only ever seen on old cigarette ads. A pre-wars Zurish flag draped over a fourth-floor balcony; she smelled weed-skunk and sour beer as she passed beneath. Not all foreigners came to Agdel Lex for crystal towers. Were these castaways Ley's people?

Kai passed her sister's building on the first try. In her de-fense, the numbers were noncontiguous, and mostly con-cealed by decoration. Whoever designed Ley's door hid her 117 in a carved bird's nest in a wooden tree whose branches advertised the bookshop underneath. The bookshop's name translated to "Tale Forest," punning on a trick of Talbeg gram-mar in which the word for "forest" meant what "horde" or "swarm" might in Kathic, say—a terrifyingly large assembly, so many of a thing one suspected evil influence.

Yes, fine, she was putting things off, pondering the meaning of bookshop names. Yes, she'd lingered. Years of separation, the first meeting goes horribly, and now what? Just climb the stairs and apologize?

Easier to leave, forget this ever happened, and get on with her life. Ley could sort out her problems, and the next time their paths crossed they could handle each other civilly. They did just fine alone.

But she'd come this far. And the fourth-floor lights were on. Gods.

Kai opened the door, and climbed.

Music pulsed in the stairwell. Men laughed. Two women fought. Another woman, who Kai hoped (for her own sanity's sake) was not her sister, shrieked toward orgasm.

First floor: bookshop. Second floor: astronomers who drank too much, judging from the broken telescope stand and beer bottle pyramid on the landing. (The music loudest here.) Third floor: either several painters, or a single painter with a style that encompassed abstract soul-gouging shapes, impressionist sunrises, and stunningly beautiful naked young men. (The climax came. Cheers from the astronomers below.) And the fourth floor.

Nothing on the landing. The door, simple dark wood.

Behind that door, the argument.

"—your godsdamn hidebound pathetic loyalism to the same bullshit sentimentality that's strangling this planet—" Imperious soprano, precise, clipped, a slight Camlaander accent.

"—no idea what the fuck you've done—" Ley.

"—will be good for us, good for the city, you lack imagination—"

"—almost fixed everything—"

"—ruining us all—"

Kai raised her hand. Gods. Knock, or leave?

She knocked.

"Lady and Lords." Ley again. "You brought backup. Not enough to steal—"

"Steal? We're partners, dammit. If anything, *you* stole from *us*. And we're moving forward. One way or another."

A muffled word. A curse? A promise?

She heard flesh strike flesh. A cry. Wood broke.

The bottom dropped out of Kai's stomach.

"Ley!" She tried the doorknob. Locked. Slammed her shoulder into the wood, which didn't budge. That bruise would hurt come morning. A roar from the other side: anger, pain, adrenaline released. Her sister's voice. More wood shattered, and glass.

Kai fumbled in her jacket pocket for a fresh needle, her hands shook, there wasn't time. She tore the paper, jabbed the needle into her finger, blood welled, a scream, the Lady burst through her

Unlock the doors that bar

The door popped open.

Kai stumbled into Ley's room, and saw:

Her sister first. (Center of the room, center of everything, the still and panicked core around which the rest revolved, staring everywhere at once, at Kai, at the door, holding—)

The knife. (More the outline of a knife, a ray-traced prism of mottled red-blue-green roiling light, wound in silver, wet with—)

Blood. (Which did not drip, but rolled from the blade's flat to its edge and slid inside somehow, into the roil, while more blood pooled on the floor, gushing from—)

The body. (Gods, the body, a golden dancer's frame, a face some Lowlands master might have painted, haughty, shocked, dead, a crimson stain spreading over her gray blouse and skirt, her eyes glassy, her face slack, one hand groping at her wound, for the knife, for—)

Ley, again, first last and forever. Ley holding the knife, which dripped blood. Ley, stepping back.

"Kai," she said.

Words, yes, words happened sometimes. "Ley. What are you—what is—what—"

Ley drew back another step, keeping her hand between them, the knife away. The window behind her stood open. Wind billowed the curtains.

"This isn't what it looks like."

"Ley. Put the knife down. Come here. I can fix this." Fucking *how,* she didn't know. She'd work it out. There would be, okay, they'd need to find a Craftswoman, get something on that wound before the woman bled out, maybe (hah!) if they could settle the whole thing fast there wouldn't be a murder charge, and depending on who this woman was, she might not see death as an inconvenience. Maybe she had insurance, or a trust. Young for that, but maybe. "We can save her."

And Ley laughed. Laughed! Not hysterically—as if Kai'd made some accidental joke, a slip of the tongue. "I already have."

"It doesn't look that way." Her voice shook. She made it stop. "I don't know what's going on here. Put that knife down and let me help you."

"You can't," she said. "I asked you earlier. It's too late." She took another step toward the window. Four stories up. "I'll do what I can myself."

"Listen to me!"

Ley shook her head. Tears glittered on her cheeks. Kai hadn't realized she was crying. Her voice sounded so steady.

She caught Ley before she could dive out the window. Kai had always been faster, even in heels. Ley lurched back through the curtains onto the balcony, keeping the knife away from Kai, who clutched her sister's other wrist with both hands.

Stars spread over them and the city beneath, and the Authority tower cast the dark in sunset rose. Light glinted off Ley's teeth. "Let me go!"

"No."

Ley tugged against Kai's thumbs, but she wasn't fast or strong enough to break her sister's grip. She gave up and moved inside, trying to bury her elbow in Kai's stomach, but Kai pulled back, tripped her, scrambled on top. She clawed for the knife. Ley writhed and growled, but couldn't pull away.

A hissing pillow full of knives hit Kai in the side of the face, and she fell, screaming. The cat landed on the floor, skidded, bundled for another leap.

Ley regained her feet. Kai lunged for her again, and caught her sister's arm. Their gazes met, and she saw Ley afraid—but distant, as if a cloud had passed between them. She held tighter.

Cold wind struck her like a fist. She couldn't breathe. Frost stung her wet eyes. Razors carved bright tracks in a sky from which starlight bled. Great screaming bodies of ice towered over a pitted city. Angels writhed, impaled on aurora thorns. The streets crawled with armies of spiders made from corpses and metal. The squid tower was gone: in its place sprawled palaces torn in half, exploded gardens, and a summit of crystal and marble breaking, always breaking, as it pulled the dead city toward itself, as it pulled Kai toward itself, and the world grayed and she staggered and her hand

slipped

and Ley drew back, supple still, strong, as if the cold could not touch her, and said, I'm sorry,

as Kai clutched, freezing, for her passport, flipped it to the squid page, and let those words drag her back to

Agdel Lex. Where she knelt, shivered, wept, on a balcony in a desert city, steaming with sublimed ice, pulling breath and heat into her, while a cat hissed and, nearby, the woman her sister stabbed stopped bleeding.

Chapter Ten

AFTER SURVIVING THREE REBELLIONS and one revolution, the emigration of two sons, rest them in text, and the birth of seven children, Hala'Aman had long since satisfied whatever responsibility she might once have felt she had to take shit from anyone. Her children and grandchildren still had time for that sort of thing, and since they were where most shit came from in the first place (especially the grandchildren), the least they could do was sort out the sewage on their own. Aman was old and dark as the powdered star onyx she added to her tea to aid her digestion and to her tobacco to give her prophetic dreams, and when she was a girl, she'd lifted a fallen freight cart off a young man so neatly and easily he hadn't even had to lose the leg.

So when she helped Zeddig down the front hall, Zeddig didn't even consider excusing herself, even though she was exhausted as well as drunk.

Aman made an anise tisane in the shoebox kitchen with the mosaic tilework, and added star onyx from a bottle she kept in her belt pouch. Aman didn't look at much of anything straight on. She saw in spots and splotches and memories now: there was too much world inside her head to see the one in front of her eyes clear. It happened to every Archivist sooner or later. You lived for Alikand, and slowly you lost sight of Agdel Lex, until you had no more to give, and passed the city on to a daughter who could give more.

When Aman passed Zeddig a mug, she took it, and drank, and Aman drank her own. The anise soothed and the onyx sparked in her mouth—it wasn't onyx at all, really, but the hardened sap of some Southern Glebland tree, but when the first Iskari explorers found it they thought it looked like onyx, so that was the name markets sold it by these days. "Heard Vogel was looking for you."

How Aman heard, Zeddig didn't bother asking. She played cards with friends who played cards with friends who played cards with friends, and everyone was someone's aunt or uncle or grandmother or cousin. Even a rat like Vogel couldn't dig through the underworld without Aman feeling the vibrations. "It's not a problem. One good job and my debt's clear."

"You should have come to us before you went to him. We would help you."

How, exactly? Yes, there were old alliances to call, old debts to cash, but this wasn't a favors for favors situation. Raymet needed soulstuff to pay off the Rectification Authority sources from whom she pulled her leads, and to delay Wreckers long enough for Zeddig to escape. And Tell's tuition cost too much to settle by passing a hat. But those were Zeddig's problems. Aman had saved the family enough for one life. "Of course, Aman."

Aman sipped her tea in silent satisfaction.

"I saw the Ko library today," Zeddig said. "We found a book with their mark, so I brought it back." She breathed anise steam and saw again the shelves lined with books waiting to be read: jokes and histories (they were the same, if you had a dark sense of humor), maps and tragedies, diaries and diagrams, passed down, waiting. "A treasury of spices, a fragrant flood and flow, untold riches, deepest warmth."

"Unending warmth," Aman said, correcting the vowel. When Mother corrected her, no matter how gently, Zeddig bristled, but Aman had a different art: each slip a stroke along her granddaughter's jaw. Or maybe that was not Aman's art of guiding, but Zeddig's of accepting—easier to take her grandmother's guidance than her mom's. "I thought of Tabar too, when I first saw the Ko library. Stones that anchor time / Opening to space / musk and scratch between the world's thighs. Tabar at her most hyperbolic. I'm jealous of how much of Adal's collection survives, though I wish she'd get out more." She drank her tea. "This is a long fight, Zeddig. Your family needs you. You take too many risks."

You don't see it, Zeddig did not say. You don't feel it like I do. We're losing. The dead city grows colder every day, and the Authority more certain. Most delvers don't care who owned what back when. They sift history for gold. Back in your day, you could delve into Alikand for a half hour at a time; I lasted three minutes today, rescued one book, and almost died. We need to take risks while we can—before the past slides out of reach.

She sat still as a fixed star. She finished her tea, and while it sparked inside her mouth she said, "Of course, Aman," stood, and kissed her on the forehead, which Aman liked. Aman's arm circled her waist, thick and heavy, and clinched, but let her go.

Zeddig climbed the stairs past Tell's empty room; Father and Mother were long since asleep, and her sisters and brothers, only Aman awake now. The walls spun, and vines in the paintings writhed as star onyx introduced itself to the sorghum whiskey still buzzing in Zeddig's blood, and made friends.

Zeddig stumbled into her dark bedchamber, tiny and

cramped with bookcases and a desk; she lit a candle with a match, opened the window, and sat on her bed facing the door, elbows on her thighs, head sloping over piled books.

She needed a job, faster than Raymet could pull one together. Vogel's train theft? No. She didn't want to give that creep any more hold over her, and besides, people had a nasty tendency to come back from his jobs dead. Maybe dead wasn't a big deal for Vogel, but Zeddig liked living, and she had so little saved that if she passed she'd be lucky to end up a dockside revenant, hauling freight 'til her limbs gave out. So. Something else. Something, sorry Aman, risky.

Now she just had to decide what.

Night wind cooled the bare skin of her arms.

She heard a footstep on her windowsill.

Her jaw tightened. Wreckers would not bother sneaking up on her. Not Vogel, either. The sharkskin zombie had made his threat—he wouldn't move on her before she had time to sit and stew, and miss another payment. A rival? Maybe the Agravaines finally figured out who screwed them, wanted revenge. Death came cheap in Agdel Lex, if you knew the market and weren't afraid to comparison shop.

Zeddig pictured water in a clear glass cup, then poured that water out in a slow smooth motion. She turned.

The lurker on her windowsill wasn't fast enough. Zeddig caught them by their belt, hauled them through the window, and with a twist of hip dropped them on her bed. Springs creaked and her stalker's skull thunked against the headboard, and she swore, and as Zeddig's hand found the attacker's throat, she recognized the voice.

Time runs at its own pace, and always in the same direction, mostly to give philosophers and thaumaturgists something to argue about. Sometimes, it stands still.

"Moving a little fast, aren't we?" Ley said, one eyebrow raised, as if she didn't notice Zeddig's hand around her throat. "Though I admit, I missed this." She twisted her lips in a way that wasn't quite smiling. She placed her hand over Zeddig's on her throat, not to fight her, just to squeeze. Her hand was caked with dried blood.

Zeddig recoiled, as if she'd touched a stove, and let her go. "What the hells are you doing here?" She looked down at her hand, too shocked to feel anything yet. Ice crystals glittered on her palm, steaming off in the dry heat of Agdel Lex. "You came from the dead city."

"It's far too lively for my taste. One of those corpse-spiders clawed through my jacket." She stuck her hand through the tear to demonstrate.

"You're bleeding."

"I'm not—" She looked down at the hole in her shirt beneath the jacket. "Sorry. Didn't notice. Most of this belongs to someone else, though. I'll explain later."

"Not a godsdamn word from you in months, and you show up on my window and— Fuck that. Explain now."

"I have a proposition." She sat up on the bed, adjusted the lapels of her charred and lacerated jacket, and slicked hair back from her forehead with her bloody right hand. "If you want to hear it, we'll have to move quickly."

"What do you mean?" Zeddig felt the Wreckers, then: a wave of nausea, the queasy pressure of inhuman minds, a cello bow rasped across her spinal column. "Tell me you surfaced a district over. Tell me you've been reciting street signs for the last mile to clear your scent. Tell me you didn't just lead Wreckers to my house."

Ley shrugged as if removing a coat. "I promised never to lie to you. Remember?" She stretched out her legs and, deliberately, crossed them, staring straight through Zeddig's eyes into her brain.

The Wreckers closed in, and Zeddig glowered. "Gods. What kind of trouble are you in?"

With a laugh, Ley's stillness became motion; she was up and around in a second, one foot on the windowsill, one hand on the wall outside. "I need a partner for the biggest delve in history. I need a team. You're the best. And you've never screwed me over."

"You did more than enough of that for both of us."

"Cast me as a devil if you like. I can dig up a blue dress if you want me to look the part. But I don't have the time. As you so perspicaciously observed, the Wreckers are after me. If you're curious, follow. If not, have a nice life."

And she was gone.

Godsdammit.

Zeddig stood slack-jawed and alone in her room. Time started again. How long had Ley been here? Seconds? Ley was the shortest distance between any two points in Zeddig's heart. She had never bothered waiting, not from the first moment they met in that burning library, nor on the docks two years past when Zeddig asked her the final question.

The Wrecker-call echoed up the alley.

Blood and ink.

Zeddig climbed the windowsill, turned, jumped, caught the trellis overhead one-handed, swung her leg around a drain-pipe, pulled with the leg, swept her left hand up to the roof's edge, found a toehold in the lattice, strained for a good grip—

Ley grabbed her, fingers sticky with blood, and pulled Zeddig up. If Zeddig trusted Ley with her full weight, they would have both fallen—the other woman was wiry as ever, made of skin-wrapped snakes—but Zeddig knew how much she could bear, and used her for balance as she scrambled to the rooftop. Ley grinned as Zeddig found her feet. "Glad to have you on board."

Zeddig ignored her, and searched for their enemy.

Moonlit rooftops spread for miles, cascading downslope toward the Wrecker Tower and the bay. Stillness, cabs, waves—and there, to the south, movement. Dark figures leapt from roof to roof. Their robes fluttered like wings at the apex of every leap; one lashed out with a tentacle to catch a water tower spar. By night the city could be an overgrown ruin, a human jungle, a labyrinth replete with minotaurs, a haven and a hell at once, but the Wreckers left a trail of certainty where they passed: the streets beneath them met at right angles, and never could have been other than they were.

"Three of them," she counted. "What the hells did you do?"

"You know," Ley said. "The usual." And she ran.

They didn't have to discuss strategy. You never ran from Wreckers unless you had to, but if you did, you kept to rooftops first, following Authority streets, steeping yourself in approved visions of the world, until the taint of other, different cities faded. So they ran, and Zeddig locked herself into Agdel Lex.

To escape, she recited the official narrative she'd learned in school: After the God Wars, the Iskari revitalized commercial districts by rationalizing the street plan and inflicting—sorry, clarifying—zoning. (Leap after Ley across an alley, follow her onto a balcony ledge, jump to the next ledge, lungs working hard, Zeddig never had patience for this cliff running bullshit.) Once a clear trade structure was in place, thaumaturgical ties to the Iskari Demesne and to the Deathless Kings of the Northern Gleb soon followed, based primarily (clatter down a fire escape) on raw material exports. During the midcentury post-wars period Agdelic textiles enjoyed brief popularity in Telomeri fashion, but thaumaturgy still depends on necromantic earths (glance back—no distortion surrounds the Wreckers, congratulations, you've matched their vision of the world), along with the dreamdust trade. Local industrial development lags global standards (see Ley snatch a sand-colored overcoat from a laundry line and don it over her suit), but a burgeoning dreamcraft community, drawn by depressed local rents and the Rectification Authority's extensive infrastructure developments (don't call them Wreckers even in your own mind, not until you know you've lost them) may finally shift the city to from a resource hub to knowledge and service industries.

They emerged onto broad, brilliant Regency Boulevard, a street that might have been cut from Chartegnon and grafted here, ringing trolleys and spacious sidewalks lined with cafe tables, continental fashions in the windows. Save for a slight edge of garlic and lemon wafting from the restaurants, they might not have been in Agdel Lex at all.

Ley jogged to a trolley stop, stuck her right hand into her pocket, and raised her left, which was not bloody so far as Zeddig could see. Trolley doors rolled back, and she tossed a two-thaum coin into the bin, then waved Zeddig up the steps. "My treat."

A mustachioed man with a newspaper gave up his seat so they could sit together. Zeddig leaned against the window, and thought about sacrifice and registry forms. Ley slumped against her, both hands in the pockets of her stolen coat, smiling softly. She'd slowed her breathing, but could not control her heartbeat. Zeddig felt a pulse like hummingbird wings beneath Ley's skin.

The trolley pulled away.

The Wreckers—sorry, Rectification Authority agents—reached the Regency rooftops. One spread her cloak and fell. Tentacles slithered out from the fluttering hem to spring-cushion her landing. The Rectifier searched the street, and Zeddig felt the pressure of her sight. But she and Ley were nothing special, on this trolley—just two tired women, not even women, citizens merely, bound for home and bed.

They could have been anyone.

They weren't.

"Wasn't that fun?" Ley asked—her half smile a perfect mask, as if she had not been afraid, as if they had not almost died four times on that run, desperate, as always, that Zeddig think she was the woman she dreamed of being: inviolate, strong, secure. "I've missed that."

Zeddig wanted to kiss her, and didn't. "What do you want to steal?"

"Everything."

Chapter Eleven

THE COPS COMFORTED KAI.

Not, to be clear, that the cops were actively comforting, that they offered even the trappings of compassion, nor that they displayed any consideration that might be due someone who had just seen her sister, basically, so far as Kai could tell, though she was no expert on such matters, kill someone. No, the cops were cops, and Kai had dated enough of those (sample size one) to understand the breed.

But there was a murder, so of course there would be cops. This was a thing that happened. And since Kai's evening so far had involved her sister *killing* someone, which was emphatically not a thing that happened, being surrounded by things that did happen offered her some comfort.

She'd spent the fifteen minutes as she waited for the cops trying to keep Ley's cat from eating the woman on the floor. After triggering the household summoning circle, she'd collapsed against the kitchen island, staring at the body but seeing nothing. That was good, she told herself, as she breathed in wet little gasps. Get through the messy stuff before the cops get here. Not the blood, of course. Don't disturb the evidence. Just. She rubbed her eyes with the heels of her hands Just the stuff about her that was messy.

She laughed, and looked up, which was when she saw the cat nibbling at the body's fingertips.

"Kitty!" Don't shout at cats, Maya had told her once—makes them nervous, and when they get nervous they get defensive. But, fuck, how were you supposed to respond when a cat started eating a dead woman's fingers—"Kitty?" The cat looked over at her, lowered its head, and tried another nibble.

The cat didn't seem perturbed when Kai scooped it—him—up. After the attack on the balcony, she'd expected more fight—but bygones seemed to be bygones. When Kai didn't pet the cat at once, though, it yawned, flicked its tongue between its teeth, poured itself from her arms, and approached the corpse again.

She grabbed it before it could take another bite, and tried to pet it this time. The beast's collar read "Behemoth" in Kathic and old Archipelagic script. Ley must have had a hard time finding someone to engrave those letters here. Maybe she did it herself.

Kai slumped to the ground. Behemoth settled, and let her pet him, though he didn't start to purr. He was angry. Maybe he remembered her wrestling with Ley on the balcony, before Ley slipped into the dying city.

Kai realized she was bleeding. Must have scraped a rock or something on the balcony. She let the blood drip onto the floor. She watched it, and prayed.

Izza.

The Lady spread through her veins, cold as an injection. Far away, she felt a young woman tear herself from something violent—or sex. *What?*

Izza, I'm in trouble. Ley's in trouble. I think she's killed—someone.

The echoed heart rate jumped, sweat cooled, sheets shifted

over someone else's skin. A hand caught Izza's arm and she sloughed the whoever off. *You're serious.*

Of course. I just don't. She's gone, she ran, and there's this cat, and there's a body.

The blood smoked and hissed on the floorboards, almost gone.

You have to get out of there, the answer came at last. *You don't know these people. Don't give them your sister's name. Don't give them your name. Just—wipe down the apartment, anything you've touched, and go. Someone will find the body.*

I called the cops already.

A shadow fell between them, reddish and sharp-tinged. Kai felt blood vessels tighten.

You saw your sister kill this person.

I did.

Don't tell them. They'll bring you in, and they will not let you go.

I can't do that. You didn't see her, Izza. There was a knife.

Kai, don't—

The blood snapped and hissed and left a stain of ash. She felt the Lady's chill outside her mind, but she could not bear to be told what to do, not now. She shut out Izza's answering prayer, refused the grace, and clutched the cat, who wriggled in her arms but settled at last, draped paws over her arm.

That's how the cops found Kai when they arrived: sitting with legs folded and Behemoth in her arms, staring into the open blue eyes of the corpse.

A man took her by the elbow, escorted her to the sofa. (There was a sofa. That was nice.) Set her there. They asked her name, and her sister's, and she told them both. Cops circled the body with tape. Cops picked through the purse near the body's feet. (There was a purse near the body's feet.) Cops spoke her sister's name. Cops examined the balcony. Cops said another name—Vane, or something like it. She remembered her sister saying "Allie." Cops discussed weapons, motives, the weather. Cops spoke on the balcony with seven-foot-tall robed beings who landed and perched on the balustrade, tentacular shadows writhing in the darkness beneath their cowls, before they leapt off into the night.

Comforting.

A woman swept into the room a few minutes after the cops: Iskari, square and strong, wearing a suit and a ratty overcoat, sunglasses folded in the breast pocket. The cop who'd talked to Kai ran to her, one hand raised, but the woman flashed a badge and brushed past him to the body.

"Ma'am—"

"Lieutenant," she said. "Bescond, Authority. How much time has passed?"

"Call came at ten thirteen—"

"Who's that?"

Pointing at Kai, or Behemoth.

"Witness. Pohala's sister."

"When did this happen? Exactly."

"Two past ten."

"Fuck." She checked her watch again. "Fuck." The second time her accent slipped. It had been full Chartegnon before, nasal as a knife's edge and dripping class. The second fuck broadened, Agdelic. Born here, educated abroad? Or the other way around? "Rectifiers?"

"Dispatched already. Haven't heard back yet."

Kai stroked Behemoth's head; the cat nipped her finger, and she pulled her hand back, and wondered if being bitten by a cat who'd just tried to eat a (fresh, admittedly) corpse was more dangerous, infection-wise, than being bitten by a cat who hadn't.

The Craftswoman, when she showed up, was less comforting than the cops. Kai heard raised voices in the hall and the beginnings of a struggle, before a burst of moonlight-flashed shadow roiled out into the room. (There was only one room, not counting the closet and bathroom, and few furnishings: sofa, standing lamp, kitchen island, two chairs at the island.) Behemoth yowled and dug claws into Kai's arm. The shadow failed and a Craftswoman emerged: dark skinned with curly black hair, glyphs shining on her arms, wearing a glower and a charcoal suit.

"Out of my way." Her Iskari had a distinct Kathic accent, which shocked Kai at first, before she wondered if that was racist.

"Abernathy," Bescond said. "We called you as soon as we could."

"I flew halfway across town. Your air traffic control is down in the lobby waiting to arrest me. Get them off my back, and give me space." She paused, considered. "Please."

Bescond did not leave. She gestured to the cops, who went—scuttled, edging around the room to stay as far from Abernathy as possible. From the hallway, Kai heard moans.

The Craftswoman knelt over the body. She checked the breath with a silver mirror, and took four different pulses; she snapped her fingers and killed the lights, then snapped her fingers again and the corpse glowed from within, as if someone had laced it with the phosphorescent algae that grew in closed harbors. When the lights returned, Abernathy looked even less happy than before.

"Well?" Bescond asked, but if the Craftswoman heard, she didn't answer. She drew a piece of silver chalk from her inside pocket, closed her eyes, and let it fall. Glyph rings burned beneath the skin of her outstretched hand, and the chalk swept around her, drawing a swift arcing diagram lined with glyphs. Kai recognized a Craft circle, but she'd never seen one formed so fast. Abernathy's hand did not shake, but her mouth tightened. The chalk flew back to her hand.

The cops were gone.

"Bescond," Abernathy said. "I need your soul."

Bescond stepped back, and touched her breastbone, offended. Something wriggled beneath her shirt, out of sight.

Abernathy shook her head. "I won't take much, your partner won't feel a thing, and we don't have time to argue."

"Take mine." Kai stood, spilling the cat from her lap. She approached the body, but did not cross the circle. Abernathy reviewed her: not the usual hair-to-ankles sweep, but a single glance focused on the mouth that took in the rest of her, a gaze too broad to avoid. The Craftswoman offered her hand, and Kai took it: Abernathy's skin was warm, and her palm bore shovel calluses and small, well-healed bloodletting scars.

The Craftswoman's glyphs took light. Shadows rolled from her skin, or the world's colors deepened, or both, as her power unfurled. Thought came labored, like movement underwater. The woman asked before she took: Kai felt the request at her soul's edge, a need she could ignore.

She did not.

"Yes," she breathed, and that yes pulled a plug in the basin of her soul: she rushed into Abernathy. Color drained from the world, and joy and panic together surged out into the Craftswoman, a few hundred thaums consumed in an instant. Kai saw by castoffs, by the shed skin of atoms; her every touch, every kiss, each lover's hand on her face, was only like repelling like. The shock of that cold vision knelt her. She did not, at least, collapse.

"Sorry, Lady," Abernathy said, but Kai did not think she was talking to her.

A blade of moon and lightning burned in Abernathy's grip. It opened, then, into a sharp flower Abernathy placed against the dead woman's chest; the world tightened. The woman's—Vane's?—lungs filled. Muscles spasmed. Her mouth moved. She exhaled, a wet gargling inhuman sound. Abernathy frowned, and chanted a formula in a language Kai didn't know, and suspected might not, exactly, exist. Vane's eyes snapped open like a doll's. Sparks danced in their inhuman blue, but only sparks. No soul remained.

The corpse fell silent. Light slunk back from its hiding spots in the recessed ceiling ghostlamps.

Abernathy sat back on her thighs. She watched the corpse for a long minute, then remembered Kai existed. Her smile looked genuine, if distant. "Thank you."

Bescond had drawn back behind the kitchen island, and wore her sunglasses.

Abernathy stood, and offered Kai her hand for a different purpose. Kai appreciated the help; her legs wobbled as she rose, and her knees refused to lock. The Craftswoman released Kai's hand, and Kai's fingers tingled as warm air reminded them to feel. Behemoth's head struck the back of her calf.

Abernathy glared down at the corpse.

"Too late?" Bescond removed her sunglasses, trying to act cool, though her voice did not cooperate.

"It shouldn't be," Abernathy said. "Not yet."

"What do you mean?"

"I mean," she said, "even after an hour, even without a trust, even if she'd never done a trace of premortem prep, there should be enough left of Ms. Vane to question. The organs are all in place, and there's no decay—less than you'd expect over a half hour. Ms. Vane's just not there. You're saying her partner did this?"

"That's what the witness said."

"Witness." Abernathy revolved. Her head clocked five minutes to one side. She had a hawk's way of watching.

Don't tell them anything, Izza had prayed.

"I'm her sister," Kai said, answering a question the Craftswoman hadn't asked. "Not hers." Pointing to the woman on the floor. "Kai Pohala."

"Tara Abernathy," the Craftswoman said, then blinked. "You're Kavekanese."

"You noticed."

"A priestess."

"You deduce that from, what, my shoes, the faint smell of incense?" Loud voices in the back of Kai's head warned her against fucking with this woman, but so much of the rest of her was screaming that she didn't listen.

"I guessed," Abernathy said. "Small world."

"What?"

"You met a friend of mine, briefly. A little over a year back."

"I meet a lot of people."

"She had silver wings."

Kai remembered fountains of flame, explosions, remembered falling from a gruesome height clasped in arms stronger than steel, beneath wings that warped reflected stars. All that was too much to fit out her mouth at once, so what she said was, "Oh." And then, as names and memory connected: "You work in Alt Coulumb, don't you?"

"You could say that."

"What are you doing here?"

"Leaving," she said. "At least, that's what I planned. Looks like I'll have to delay my flight."

Bescond cleared her throat. "Ms. Pohala. Would you come with us? I have a few questions to ask."

"I talked to the cops already."

"Different branch," Bescond said. "They're metro police; I'm Rectification Authority."

Kai turned from Tara. "Do I have a choice?"

Bescond shrugged.

"Can I bring the cat?"

Chapter Twelve

"EXPLAIN," ZEDDIG said as they slipped through the night market.

"Later."

They'd lost the Wreckers, drowning the dead city's taint in living Agdel Lex, in Iskari street names, squiddy temples, tentacular flags, in newsstands that sold guidebooks and tourist maps for three thaums each. Ley and Zeddig were model citizens, weren't they, two women walking side by side past stalls where Talbeg men and women in garish approximations of traditional dress offered fig cakes for sale. Zeddig even bought a scorpion skewer.

But cops flooded the roads, badges gleaming at streetcorners, consulting small sketches that looked an awful lot like Ley. Zeddig guided them away from a checkpoint down a side street that seemed to double back on itself, but in fact connected Regency with Probity. Maybe there—but no. More cops waited at Probity and Temperance, tentacles pulsing by their thick necks. Zeddig snatched Ley's arm and turned her to face the window of a nearby toy shop. Cops searched the street in plate glass reflection, and marionettes grinned grimly.

"Whose blood is on your hand?" Zeddig asked.

"You don't need to worry about her."

"That what you'll say about me after the knife goes in?"

"Zeddig!" Shocked. But laughing, too, as if Zeddig had

made a scandalous joke. "I'd never stab you." With emphasis on the penultimate word. Which, as reassurances went, didn't.

They traced the cordon. Checkpoints bounded the Reine market north and south, east and west. Grumbling lines formed: shoppers smoking with bags of clothing piled at their feet. Street acrobats, faces painted rainbow colors, set up beside the lines and performed patter interspersed with handsprings. They passed an herbalist shaking down two tourists over an exorbitantly priced cup of tea they'd thought was a sample; Ley shouted, "It's wheatgrass," and Zeddig tugged her along before anyone could get a clear look at her face.

Wreckers circled the Reine, their attention forcing streets into their supposedly proper shape.

"At least tell me what they want you for."

"Murder. Obviously."

"Did you do it?"

"Have you ever known me to do anything without reason?"

"That's not an answer."

"Do you want me to say more?"

"No," she said. "Look. I have friends in the port, people I trust. They won't have any trouble slipping you past customs. We can get you back to the Archipelago."

"I can't leave," she said. Those words burned away the fog of her sly levity. "Not now."

"Why? What's happening?"

Ley didn't answer. She shoved her hands into her pockets, and walked raw by Zeddig's side.

"If we're going to work together," Zeddig said, "you'll have to trust me."

The shell closed again, with a cold laugh and an easy shrug, and once more Ley was flawless. "You trust too easily. You tell people, and those people tell people, and pretty soon everyone knows everything. I'll play this close to my chest."

Zeddig stopped, turned, and shoved Ley against a tree.

"I'd planned to take our reunion slower," Ley said. "But I can be flexible."

Zeddig smelled her, sweat, cinnamon, and smoke. She almost—she almost a lot of things. She didn't. She'd known Ley too long not to know the game, the slight dig as she withdrew, like a retreating boxer's jabs. "You're in trouble. I get that. But you're scared, and it's making you dumb. Give me something. Half the city's looking for a woman who looks like you."

"And you found me."

"Shut up." She did, which was a surprise, but then, Ley could say more with a raised eyebrow than most people could with words. "Two years gone, and you show up on my windowsill, wearing a fancy suit over your tattoos, with blood on your hands."

"I'm in trouble. I have a job for you. What more do you need?"

"The truth. Or I walk."

Ley's lips tightened. "I was working on a project. My partner and I had a difference of opinion. I hoped—what I hoped doesn't matter now. What matters is what I can do for you." They were too close for her to touch Zeddig's chest, so she touched her side instead, long fingers curling around Zeddig's flank, and godsdamn but she remembered that, and what came after. "And what you can do for me." Those long fingers trailing up to touch her, just below the neck. "You're not asking the right questions."

"You're not answering."

"Ask where I slipped into the dead city."

People were watching. Dammit. She needed this finished, fast. "Where." She ground the word between her teeth.

"My apartment, in 'Kander's Cliffs."

Three miles away. Zeddig's grip loosened on her shoulder.

"And I came back to Agdel Lex a few blocks from your roof. I tried to lose the Wreckers, but the taint was stronger than I expected."

"That's—" She tried to wrap her mind around that notion, and couldn't. So much time in the dead city's soul-shearing cold. The best suits anyone could rig lasted ten minutes at the outside. "Where's your gear?"

"No gear. No wards."

"You delved for an hour, in that suit. You should be dead."

"That's my offer," she said. "I can keep you in the city longer than either of us ever dreamed. But I don't have your skills, and I don't have a crew, and everyone on the scene hates me."

"Which is your fault."

"I don't disagree. Now. Kiss me."

"What?"

"People are watching," she said, as if the explanation were written on her face in ten-foot-tall letters. She often used that tone of voice when they were together: scornful, teasing. She knew precisely what effect it had on Zeddig. But there was another edge Zeddig had taken longer to detect, a gentle self-mockery. Look how absurd we are, you for offering me this power, and me for accepting, as if my acceptance didn't place me in your power, too. "They need a story to tell themselves about us that won't strain their tiny minds."

Oh, but this was a trap Zeddig had never been able to resist, Ley's self-assurance sheer and cold as stained glass. Was Zeddig a fist, to smash that glass, or a ray of light, to strike and tumble through bewildered into colors? Had Ley come to her to be illuminated? Shattered? Both?

She kissed her anyway.

This, too, Zeddig remembered.

"Come on," she said, and led Ley to a used bookshop in the Reine's heart, beside a diamond fountain. The owner had cleared merchandise for Zeddig before, mostly icons and badges of gods dead long before the Telomeri first stretched their claws south across the Shield Sea. In the shop's basement, behind a—hand to gods—bookcase on hidden hinges (Ley: "Seriously?" But Zeddig didn't answer), stood a door marked on no Authority map, that led to an even narrower winding stair (Zeddig had to proceed sideways and even that required breath control), which led, in turn, to narrow musty tunnels lined with copper pipes claimed by verdigris. Zeddig draped a cloth over her nose and mouth for spores, offered Ley one in turn, and, in the ghostlight of hand torches, they moved through the wreckage beneath the city. Half-metal insects scuttled away down the tunnel; a trapdoor lasher roped Ley in its legs—newbie delvers called them tentacles, but they were legs, really, long and whiplike like the legs of house centipedes—and tried to drag her up into its ceiling lair, so Zeddig climbed into the pipes, fought through the barbed wire web, and stabbed through the lasher's ear into the closest thing the critter owned to a brain. Ley hadn't taken too much poison—"I'm fine," she said, tried to stand, then slumped against the tunnel wall, but she could still walk if she leaned on Zeddig.

Zeddig counted turns. After three miles, one stare-down with a nest of wolf rats (green multifaceted eyes glittering), and a great deal of not talking, they reached a ladder. Zeddig climbed—"Stay here"—and knocked three times, then twice, then once again on a hatch set into the brick.

She waited, hanging in the dripping dark, as footsteps neared. Far down, Ley leaned against the pipes, and bled.

The hatch swung open. Zeddig's pupils schooled themselves to the flood of light.

Raymet stood behind the hatch, wearing sweatpants, a T-shirt with some comic book logo, and fuzzy pink slippers. She held a bowl roughly the size of her head that contained a sickening quantity of ice cream, she smelled not-so-faintly of weed, and she sounded like someone who had not anticipated using her voice to communicate for the next few days. "Z? What —" And then, because Raymet stoned was sharper than most folks sober: "What the hells is she doing here?"

"Bleeding," Ley said. "It's a pleasure see you again as well, Raymet."

"Z."

Close friends, Zeddig had found, developed a sort of telepathy. Nothing mystical about it—though a musing Craftswoman might spin you a tale of spiritual entanglement and primitive localized divinity, then charge you a few hundred thaums for the musing. Graybeard coffee-fiend dockside chessmasters could glance at a position and say, mate in twelve, because they knew the game. Friends just learned the game of you.

So when Raymet said Zeddig's name, Zeddig also heard, Zeddig, are you sure about this, and, Zeddig, you remember what she did last time, and, Zeddig, I trust you, but I don't trust her, and I don't trust you *with* her, and, Zeddig, I had blocked off a few days for ice cream and comic books and there better be a damn good reason you're here other than a booty call from the Queen of the Evil Exes.

"We're good," Zeddig said. "But we need a place to spend the night."

Raymet stepped aside. "Come on up."

Chapter Thirteen

THEY BROUGHT KAI AND the cat to the Rectification Authority tower. In the carriage, Bescond sat across from Kai and watched her, or something beyond her, gaze flat and weighing. Abernathy crossed her arms and stared out the window. The Craftswoman reminded Kai of a clock wound until it would wind no more, terrible mainspring pressure straining against the tiny gears built to make that tension useful. Kai did not want to stand nearby when those gears gave and all that violence sprang forth at once, in shards.

The body lay in the carriage's trunk, hovering above a slab, ringed by wards that cast silver light.

Up close, the tower seemed carved from pink marble: Kai's subconscious insisted it was, since nothing so large could possibly live. (Strange, how the subconscious could insist on that point, and accept dragons. A survival tactic, perhaps?) But pink marble did not twitch, and the tower did. Pink marble did not wind and unwind with grotesque slow grace. Light did not shimmer inside pink marble, branching treelike beneath translucent skin, and those blue veins were not veins of ore.

The tower locked the world into place. As they neared it, side streets stopped shifting. The carriage turned onto a four-lane boulevard with a row of acacias in the median, each tree planted four meters from every other. The air dried, and grew hot. She remembered the deep bone-cello sound the faceless cloaked figures made, and wondered why, until she realized she heard that same sound everywhere, so subtle and pervasive she had not noticed. She stood on an immense bridge, strong as ages, and beneath that bridge lay a chasm, and at that chasm's base, a maw.

Behemoth curled in Kai's lap and purred like a jackhammer.

"What is that sound?" Kai said.

Abernathy drummed her fingertips on the windowsill.

Bescond did not answer.

Kai wondered whether asking again would help. Before she could decide, Abernathy spoke. "This used to be the university district, before the wars, when this city had another name."

"I heard the story," she said. "Gerhardt fought the local Gods. The battle left a breach. The tower seals it. But nobody's told me how."

Abernathy paused, searching for the right words, and Bescond took over with the ease of long practice. Kai recognized a sales pitch when she heard one. "The Rectification Authority keeps the city from falling into the wound Gerhardt left in the world when he refused to die. We impose order. We lock the chaos of Agdel Lex into form. This requires constant observation. So our Lords built us a constant observer. She lives, and watches."

"You're not a cop," Kai said.

"No."

"What are you, then?"

Bescond flipped her notebook closed, capped her pen, and slid both into her pocket. "Throughout the world, the Iskari Demesne preserves order, to help humans flourish. Without us, this city—and many others—would collapse. Theological surveys suggest the Wound, untended, would freeze the Shield Sea halfway to Iskar, leaving us with a new Crack in the World. That's the best-case scenario. Police heal ruptures in society—so, no, we are not police. Our role is prior to theirs. We enable society's existence."

Behemoth curled his head under Kai's palm. "So why did they call you in for a murder?"

The tower blocked out the sky. Behind it, somewhere, stretched the bay. Before the wars, the university must have had a beautiful view. Their carriage juddered toward a wall carved in a spiral pattern—or at least, Kai thought it was a carving at first. As they neared, the pattern opened. Tentacles uncurled and spread like arms to welcome them into darkness.

Abernathy stopped drumming on the windowsill. She looked impassive, unimpressed, but Kai had spent enough time selling to see through the poker face. The Craftswoman wanted to look relaxed, but her little finger pressed so hard against the wood that it trembled.

Tentacles wrapped the wall closed behind them, and the darkness turned into a garage.

"Society requires order," Bescond said. "Some crimes strike against that order, as well as against the social fabric."

Bescond led them to a lift like any lift Kai had ever seen, which moved almost the same, though with an unsettling peristaltic rhythm. They climbed. The cat hunkered down in Kai's arms and flattened his ears, glaring at the wall. The lift stopped at the eighteenth floor to admit two robed, hooded figures who smelled of must and ink and fish and departed on floor twenty-two. At the thirtieth floor, Bescond led them down a hall, through a door in a row of doors, into a round room with pearlescent walls, a heavy table, three chairs, a water cooler with paper cups, a filing cabinet, and a painfully fake fern.

"I'd like my own advocate present," Kai said.

The wall rippled as she spoke, and her words took shape near the ceiling, in trailing, organic Iskari script.

"Wow," Kai said, and wow, the wall wrote. "That's not even slightly creepy."

Abernathy sat facing the door. "This isn't an adversarial situation, technically. You're not under suspicion of anything. Bescond and I"—with a slight pause that suggested strange bedfellows—"want to ask a few questions. We need to understand what's happened to Ley, where she might have gone. It's . . ." She leaned back. "Important."

"We understand," Bescond said, "that you spoke with her this evening."

"How do you know that?"

"What did you talk about?" The wall recorded Bescond's words too.

"The weather," Kai said.

The filing cabinet behind Abernathy opened, and a file rose from it and flew to the Craftswoman's hand. Kai recognized the black envelope Ley had tried to offer her. "What's inside the envelope?"

"You haven't opened it?"

"It's sealed," she said. "With impressive wards. If we opened it, it would destroy itself."

Kai sat. Behemoth flowed from her arms to the floor. "Were you watching my sister, or watching me?"

"Your sister is in a dangerous position," Abernathy said. "She may have committed murder. She may have destroyed a soul. Or she may have just . . . borrowed one for a while. It can happen, with the right tools. If we can restore Vane's soul to her body, your sister's no longer a murderer. She'll face a civil suit from Vane, but she'd be safe from the Iskari justice system." Said with a slight hesitation before "justice," unless Kai was very much mistaken; Bescond's face was a study in stoicism. "If you help us, you're helping her."

Kai walked to the water cooler, poured herself a cup, and drank. She hadn't realized how dry she was until she swallowed. She poured another cup. The room thrummed underfoot. She returned to the table, sat opposite Abernathy, and leaned back. "Lieutenant Bescond had that nice speech about the Authority being, what? Prior to police? You're not interested in the murder."

"You told the police—" Bescond started, but Abernathy held out her hand, and she stopped.

"The police arrived suspiciously fast, didn't they?" Kai asked. "Given that those back streets are too narrow for carriages? Almost as if they were holding back, waiting to see if I'd try to leave without reporting the crime. If I had, we'd be having a different conversation, I imagine?"

Abernathy's eyes flicked right, to Bescond, who didn't seem concerned.

"What's Alt Coulumb doing in bed with Iskar, Ms. Abernathy?"

"We are allies," Abernathy said, with a wry smile. "Cooperating for mutual advantage."

Kai pushed back her chair. "I'm leaving now."

"Fine," Abernathy said, just as Bescond said, "No."

The building's heart beat. Far away, lift doors dinged.

"Your sister's accused of reality subversion," Bescond said. "We can detain you for questioning."

"First you want to help my sister, now you say she's a suspect."

"It's a complicated situation," Bescond said. "You're not cleared for the details."

"So clear me." Neither woman spoke. Kai knelt, and gathered Behemoth, who only squirmed a little. "You know who I am. You know more about my sister's business than I do. Are you going to tell me what's going on? Did you ask me here because you want my help? Can I just"—shifting her attention to Abernathy now—"walk out this door?"

She reached for the doorknob, but it wasn't there. The wall curved smooth as an eggshell. Abernathy turned to Bescond; Bescond turned to Kai. The room grew quiet. Shadows flickered beneath the pearl white walls and their trailing blackletter words.

Then the wall burst open, and Fontaine stumbled in. "Ms. Pohala, there you are! I got the room number from the front desk but sometimes these halls, you know, they have minds of their own, hah, not to mention obeying alien geometries no man could possibly, nor woman neither, and so on and so forth. Very fascinating, I'm sure." She laughed, high-pitched and too quick. Her pupils were so dilated only the faintest ring of iris showed, and she actually bowed to Bescond and Abernathy, like they were all on stage, one arm out and the other to her chest. "Madame and Madame. Pardon my interruption. Ms. Pohala is a guest of First Imperial, the papers are all on file, but here's—" She popped her briefcase open on the third try, and dumped a small pile of sealed scrolls onto the table. "You know. Copies and so on."

"This isn't a thaumaturgical matter," Bescond said. The Lieutenant seemed to have swallowed a storm cloud, but when Kai glanced to Abernathy, she saw the Craftswoman's lips twitch upward before her professional mask returned.

"Of course not, oh, of course." Fontaine shook her head rapidly. "I'm sure Ms. Pohala will answer any questions concerning this unpleasantness, during business hours, on IFI premises, as per standard protocol for Official Friends of the Demesne as the Chartegnon Accords stipulate. I've contacted my manager, who's of course happy to liaise with your Knight Cardinal, should you have any concerns."

"Of course," Bescond echoed. She snatched up a scroll, broke its seal, and glowered at the words, as if intimidation might inspire them to rearrange themselves to her liking. "Official Friends protocol." She wrung the scroll shut. "Her visa form suggested this was an exploratory visit."

"Market considerations, you know," Fontaine said. She gathered the scrolls with one hand and made an expansive, cloudy gesture with the other. "Don't inform on peanuts to the elephants. And so on." She slammed her briefcase shut. "Ms. Pohala. We have a carriage waiting, and the meter's running, I'm afraid."

Kai smoothed her blouse, drew her shoulders back, and allowed herself a smile, slighter even than Abernathy's. "Thank you very much, ladies. If you want to continue this at IFI tomorrow, my flight out's scheduled for six."

She saluted them both—two fingers to the temple, like an airman in a mystery play—as she withdrew. Abernathy saluted in answer; Bescond only glared as Fontaine led Kai out.

Chapter Fourteen

"OUT," RAYMET TOLD THE three undergrads playing a dice-and-toy-soldiers game in her book-stuffed living room. "Out," she told the bearded dude with the clockwork arm pruning a warped potted pine tree on her bottle-strewn kitchen table. "Out," she told the person in her bed, whose name Zeddig didn't know, but who complied with a speed of which she, Zeddig, approved. Soon Raymet's three-level basement flat was as empty as you could ever call a space where every wall strained under the weight of shelving, where books, magazines, spare dishes and half-finished mugs of tea covered every horizontal surface, including the bed. Most people Zeddig knew didn't like basement apartments, found them suffocating, but Raymet loved wriggling through tight spaces. Zeddig knocked over three piles of books and one precariously balanced water pipe while she followed Raymet around the house, which was a good average for her visits.

Once the front door was closed and locked, the last protesting gamer on the other side (the person in Raymet's bed put up less of a fight than the ejected hobbyists, though the collar suggested that obedience was at least part of the point of that particular relationship), Raymet collapsed against it, exhaled with her whole body, and said, "This is the dumbest idea any of us have had in at least a year. Certifiably dumb. If the U finds out, I'll need to turn in, like, at least a doctorate."

Zeddig did not disagree.

Raymet finished the last of the ice cream, slammed a shot of bourbon, and offered Zeddig the bottle, which she refused. She needed sleep, not liquor. A pot of coffee stood half-empty on the burner. "How old is this?"

From the other room, Raymet answered: "Anything growing in it?"

She sloshed the liquid against the light. "Not that I can see."

"It's fine."

Zeddig opened the cupboard, which contained no cups, but an impressive array of titration equipment. The next cupboard boasted some sort of blacklit permaculture aquarium situation, translucent fish nibbling the roots of luminescent purple plants. The next cupboard was empty. The mugs on the counter seemed too suspicious, so Zeddig drank from the pot. Sour, too much acid, just like her mood. She mercy-killed the pot down the sink, and threw out the filter. "Okay," she said, realizing that she'd been hesitating, that the coffee and the exhaustion were just excuses for delay. "Let's hear what she has to say."

The under-under-basement held Raymet's office, with its steam tunnel access, its desk (remarkably clean compared to the rest of the apartment), its shelves of rare or illegal books, and, currently, Ley, snoozing in Raymet's desk chair, shoes off and feet up. She didn't snore, but when she slept heavily, she hissed on the out breath. Gods, she looked good asleep, the blade of her gone loose, the teeth bare between the lips. What could have ever come between them?

"If you two have seen enough," she said, without opening her eyes, and without a twitch to betray her shift from sleep to waking, "I'm ready to talk business."

Oh, right.

Raymet perched on the desk, caught Ley's legs by the ankle, lifted them off, and let them drop. Ley came upright. "Zeddig told me what you told her. Woolly and imprecise. I have questions."

Ley cracked her neck, then cracked it again in the opposite direction, then stretched her arms over her head until her elbows popped, which sinuous arching of back triggered (as she of course would know) a great many memories in Zeddig, who looked away. "Ask away."

"How long can you last in the dead city?"

"Controlling for other factors, and given that the chill falls off on an inverse cube law away from the Wound—you could last for at least twenty-four hours outside the university district. Two days in the Wastes, maybe more."

"Bullshit," Raymet said.

"You haven't heard the best part yet." She laced her fingers behind her head, and leaned back. "The system fails faster close to the Wound. But not that fast. I can get you as far as the sixth floor of the Anaxmander Stacks."

Feelings don't strike turn by turn: they well up stepwise with slow reaction rates, as an alchemist would say, causes transforming into effects even as traces of cause remain. Human features, no matter how expressive, are too slow and simple to convey this welling conflict, and tend to freeze in some awkward intermediate position while the process works out. Zeddig knew Raymet felt skepticism and hope and terror and avarice, all shifting into one another, not because she could read her friend's features, but because she knew her, and because she felt that same roil in herself.

Upon the roof of the Anaxmander Stacks, Maestre Gerhardt slew the gods and angels set against him, and upon that roof he remained, dying and refusing to die, unwilling to lose, within the Wound that killed the dead city. The Stacks: full of volumes lost to history, texts heretical and heterodox, untranslatable and plain weird, manuscripts, archives, histories dating back to the wars against Telomere Across the Waves. A public glory, a treasure trove forever out of reach. The most advanced wards lasted minutes in the university district, seconds near the Stacks. "What do you want?"

She hurt when Ley smiled, and she wondered if knowing that would make Ley smile less. "I need you to help me raid the Altus facility in the Wastes."

Zeddig waited for Raymet to respond, but Raymet was sputtering too much to form proper words.

"Four years back, the Iskari tried to extend the wards around the Gleb Line train, hoping they could use the Wastes for high-energy Craftwork research and development, because reality's weaker out there. Rules are flexible. Altus built their first launch facility there; when the wards collapsed, the Wastes swallowed the whole thing in an instant. The people are all long dead, but the systems should still be there—just inaccessible. I need to get inside. It won't be a problem."

"A problem." Raymet had finally recovered. "A god-haunted ruin infested with monsters and ordnance. In the middle of the Wastes."

"It won't be a problem," she repeated, calm as ever, "for the right team. You get me to Altus. I get you to the Stacks. We go our separate ways."

Raymet wasn't done: you haven't given us one single reason to trust you, you're on the run from the Wreckers, there's blood on your hands, and you're swanning in as if we're the ones who need your help. You ran with us while it was fun, then turned tail. We're not toys. We're not, fuck, I don't even know what you play with back where you came from, we're not dolls you can toss aside and pick back up as you fancy.

Ley watched Raymet rant, and Zeddig watched her in turn, watched her jaw twitch at "dolls" and "toss aside" as Ley fought her instincts to cut back—watched Ley need this in a way she had never needed anything. Even naked and sweating, Ley did not let herself want, simply, visibly. She was muscle tensed to guard an injured nerve.

"It's your choice," Ley said when Raymet was done. She faked carelessness so well even Zeddig almost believed her.

"Raymet." Zeddig took her by the shoulder. "Outside, please."

Raymet resisted, but let herself be guided back out of the office, let Zeddig toe the door shut behind them. "Z, this business stinks."

"I think we should do it."

"She fucked you over and left, and you want to go into the Wastes with her?"

"She thinks we can make it."

"How can you trust her?"

Good question. She deflected. "Think about the Anaxmander Stacks. You know what's in there."

"Heritage," Raymet said, sourly.

"Heritage," Zeddig agreed, "and a fortune. The Stacks don't belong to a House Library. Selling the duplicates alone would set all three of us up for life."

"Unless she leaves us to die once she has what she wants."

The hard part about arguing with people at least as smart as you, Zeddig had found, was that sometimes they were right. "She won't."

"She did before."

Zeddig remembered the courtyard of the Hanged Man the night she and Ley broke up—no, "broke up" wasn't the right term—the night their six months' war grew too hot. Dreamdust addicts sprawled on couches, mewling in their stupor as drums and bass pulsed from the dance hall upstairs. She reached for Ley's arm, but Ley always could slide away when she wanted. "She didn't leave us to die." Just me. And not to die: just to live my life without her. "She just left."

"She stole our work and ran off to make her fortune, and if that suit's any sign, she did well. She's not Talbeg. She's not even local. She's in trouble? She can just leave."

"It's a risky job. We've taken risks before."

"What will you do when she goes?"

That question should not have caught Zeddig by surprise. She should have an answer. It hadn't even occurred to her. To Ley, she was all levers and buttons and dials: a system to be pressed and turned at will. She should have thought further ahead, so she could give Raymet an answer more honest than: "I'll be fine." And: "You're telling me you don't want it? Fortune, glory, and our history all in one blow? You don't want to give a middle finger to those fuckers in the tower?"

Ley wasn't the only one who knew levers and buttons and dials.

The reaction bubbled on behind Raymet's eyes. She stared at Zeddig, fiercely, not because she was certain, but (Zeddig thought) because the opposite: everything inside her moved, and her gaze could at least be still. Zeddig saw the decision form, though regret remained in solution. "I'm in," she said, "if Gal is."

Zeddig opened the door. Ley leaned against the bookcases

that lined the office's far wall, scanning a two-thousand-year-old clay tablet. She raised one eyebrow, and waited for Zeddig's question.

"Why did you come to us?" Zeddig asked.

"Because you're the best."

She was lying. Or she was scared. Or she was on the run, hiding in her ex-girlfriend's business partner's basement, and she could not bear the weakness of her position, and presented this cool front to keep things . . . professional. Or she was what she seemed. Zeddig wondered which truth would hurt her more.

"We have one more partner. Convince her, and you're in."

"Fantastic." Ley turned away quickly, replaced the tablet on its shelf—and in the instant she turned away Zeddig thought she saw Ley's facade crack, revealing relief below. Or else she'd imagined it. Or else the crack was meant to soften Zeddig for the next request. "I have to do one small task first. A loose end. And I need your help."

"Of course," Raymet said.

"It's nothing serious. I just need to spend a few minutes as a maid."

Chapter Fifteen

IN THE CARRIAGE BETWEEN the Authority tower and Kai's hotel, the cat discovered Fontaine was allergic.

"We could open a window," Kai suggested as she pulled Behemoth back into her lap.

"I'll be fine." Fontaine sneezed into a handkerchief. "Once the beast is somewhere else. I must say, Ms. Pohala, you have an odd sense of how to maintain a low profile."

"Most people don't get arrested on the first day?"

"You weren't—" She sneezed again, and wiped her tears with her wrist. Behemoth tried to writhe from Kai's arms. "Arrested, quite. The Authority detains, but it's not the same, technically. It's all a bit sordid, to be honest, but for the best. Roughly speaking. The Rectifiers fulfill a vital function—without them, we'd all fall into the Wound. But such mechanisms have a range of, oh, unfortunate associated tangles. Once a well-meaning, even compliant, individual gets caught in the system, extraction can prove difficult. It doesn't happen nearly so often as the radical press make it out, but, you know, it does, ah, happen."

Unfortunate associated tangles. Kai remembered her own "mixup" back on Kavekana—Penitent stone closing around her limbs, crystal spears piercing her flesh, the splintering pain of superhuman strength and speed. She remembered her mind forced to think and her body forced to move, and suppressed a shudder at the word "compliant." But no sense mentioning all that to Fontaine now. "What do they do with people who get caught?"

"Depends on the nature of the offense. Nothing for you to worry about." He smile was wide, from an earnest desire to change the topic, or from pills, or both. "Your Mr. Twilling contacted me through the nightmare telegraph, and he sounded, let's say, concerned you might be in trouble with our Rectifiers. I said, certainly not, she was bound for a restaurant and then her hotel, and he said, check, and when the hotel confirmed that you never checked in—they almost cancelled your reservation, would you believe—I started for the Authority tower at once." Behemoth sank claws into Kai's arm, pulled free, and jumped to Fontaine's lap; Kai caught him by the scruff of the neck and pulled him back. How would Twilling have known about any of this?

"Thank you," Kai said. "Whatever they get up to in that tower, I want no part of it. Clever thinking, too—getting me out like that."

"You may not think so when you see the bill."

Kai blinked.

"Well, you see. Ah." Fontaine blew her nose again. "Official Friend status is reserved for financial partners of the Demesne responsible for at least ten million thaums of foreign direct investment." Kai thought she displayed remarkable self-control under the circumstances. She didn't scream, for example. Fontaine, teary from cat and bloodshot from drugs, opened her briefcase and sorted through the forms. "I postdated the paperwork—there's no direct transfer of funds required at this time to maintain status, but a calendar-year commitment is standard, I'm afraid. It's a good thing our meetings today were so productive!"

"I," Kai said, forcing herself to breathe deeply, "thought you had faked the paperwork."

Fontaine gasped.

"I mean, ten million thaums is a big commitment for an exploratory mission."

"Of course," Fontaine said, "I understand. But—at the risk of besmirching the Rectification Authority's reputation for probity—Lieutenant Bescond has a slight personal tendency toward, shall we say, obstinacy and vengeance. IFI's records office is closed for the night, so her queries won't be answered before the market opens tomorrow. But when she does query, if she discovers you have not been granted Official Friend status, you may find yourself regrettably, and this time unavoidably, detained. If you take my meaning. The bureaucracy is an enormous many-legged beast, and we control it with flimsy reins. So: I've prepared the paperwork. Your options, as I see them, are the following: sign a formal commitment of funds, or get yourself on the next flight from Agdel Lex, before our records office opens. The six-twenty should still have first class seats available."

Kai glanced up from the paper. "You get a commission on this, I assume."

"That's not the point." Fontaine looked hurt, but when Kai didn't speak, she gave in. "Well. Yes." The carriage jerked to a stop before a sprawling mansion. Fontaine opened the door with a smile. "Have a pleasant evening, Ms. Pohala. I suggest a swim: the Arms has a brilliant pool."

Kai took the contract with her, and the cat.

No doubt travelers' guide writers lavished mellifluent descriptions on the Alikand Arms, highlighting for the discerning tourist its sculptural fountains and panoramic views of the port city (with roofs sloped to obscure the uncomfortable hulk of the Rectification Authority), as well as the hotel's restaurants, its swim-up bar and morning all-ages calisthenics classes, and the massage parlor. Kai, who'd asked IFI to put her in a business hotel, glowered through check-in, especially when she wrote the glyphs for the Priesthood travel account on the bill and imagined the argument she'd have with Accounting to justify the expense. Behemoth yowled. Kai asked the regulation-smiley desk clerk for a saucer of milk (cats liked milk, didn't they?) and a litter box to be delivered to her room, and received a nonplussed expression and some nonsense about the Arms's no-pets policy, which she answered with a glare, and: "Saucer. Milk. Litter box." Then she snatched the key and staggered toward the lift, looking godsdamn fabulous in heels, in spite of, well. Everything.

Room: spacious, opulent. Carpet: thick. View: the travel writer Kai wasn't would have gushed ink. Cat: toilet trained, which Kai had not realized was a thing. Kai, herself: exhausted.

She closed the door with her back, and slid down the wood, until she sat with the palatial suite in front of her, and the whole world at her back.

Bescond, in the heart of that fucking pulsing tower. Abernathy, uncomfortable with the Authority, uncomfortable with the entire mess, but still, there. The Craftswoman might have stopped Bescond before things got ugly. That had been Kai's play, her edge: lean into the hairline fracture between the two. And if that didn't work? If Abernathy decided her business with Ley, or this Vane person, justified extraordinary measures? Unfortunate associated tangles. The Penitent shell closing around her again. The voices, and the pain.

And, somewhere beneath all that, she was still wrestling

with Ley, gods, bloodslick Ley, knife in hand, on her balcony, as the body cooled. She remembered her sister's face as she slid free. "I'm sorry." Kai'd seen that expression before, on a dying goddess, reaching toward the light. That was the look of a woman who saw her last chance breaking.

Desperation like that didn't grow in hours. It must have lurked there, hidden, through their conversation at Sauga's. Whatever trouble Ley was in, she'd thought investment could help. But failing that, she reached for a knife.

If Kai had listened to her—if she hadn't assumed, if she asked, if she hadn't been so fucking tired and so certain in her judgment—

Ley needed her, and she didn't listen, and now they were both alone in a broken, breaking city. Because whoever Ley found to help her, she wouldn't bring them close, wouldn't let them in. Ever since they were kids, if Ley was in trouble, she had to get out herself. She couldn't reach for people. That was her big sister's job: to see when she needed help, and reach for her instead.

Kai realized she crying. Tears felt good. Breath came to her by the grace of some power too meat-deep to call anything but a god. She sobbed. She couldn't do this in public, not ever, could barely cry with even just one other person watching. Too proud.

A cold nose touched the back of her hand. Behemoth rubbed against her stockings and purred. She'd drawn her knees up to her chest; he topped them with a pounce, and slid down into the hollow, warm fur against her belly.

She heard, and ignored, a knock on the door.

Six twenty, the flight out. She couldn't stay. Ten million thaums—the High Priests would kill her.

Behemoth rumbled. Kai stood, slowly, with the aid of the wall, and felt like a much older woman. Scar tissue pulled in her back and legs. She opened the door.

Saucer of milk. Litter box (unnecessary, thank gods). And a slip of paper under the milk. A bill? They should have just billed it to the room. She picked up the paper, and turned it over.

Then she started to run, barestockinged, down the hall.

The elevators weren't moving. The near stair was empty, up and down. So too was the farther stair. No fire alarms sounded that she could hear. She shoved through the "Service Personnel Only" door into a closet where three janitors played poker, a razor-toothed goddess flickering above their table. She ran five floors down to the lobby, still shoeless, and saw milling crowds, and no sister.

When she returned, Behemoth raised his head, having finished the saucer of milk, and regarded her with mild interest.

The unsigned note read, in Ley's hand:

I'm fine.

I'm glad they let you go.

Leave the city.

You're not safe while I'm here.

And, more terrifying than all the rest:

I love you.

The cat asked a question Kai could not answer.

She grabbed Fontaine's contract off the floor, slammed it against the wall, drew a pen from her purse, and signed her name.

Chapter Sixteen

LEY CHANGED OUT OF her disguise in Raymet's carriage, while Aleph the spider-golem clunked them down narrow side streets. She ditched the wig onto the bench seat, and unbuttoned the uniform blouse—Zeddig turned her back too late to avoid seeing a flash of skin. "I'm glad you had these uniforms, but I always wondered why. The Arms wasn't built over anything important."

"Not anything recently important," Raymet corrected from the driver's seat, apparently unconcerned with Ley's undress. "There was a Telomeri villa on that site two thousand years back, during the occupation, and those assholes keep archives in basements—mystery cult nonsense, for the most part, but we found an *Elements* in the steam tunnels once, guarded by half-living geometry. We don't go back often these days, because Zeddig doesn't like being a maid."

"The uniforms are scratchy," Zeddig said.

"Also, you tend to punch people while you're wearing them."

Aleph juddered over a gap in the cobblestones. "I'm decent," Ley said, "more or less." When Zeddig turned around, she was: her shirt done up to the button below the collarbone, sleeves rolled, hair still a pointy mess from the wig. "And now shall we our darkest deeds darkly do," which Zeddig thought was Cawleigh; she groped to cap the line.

"Like slugs we'll paint the world our greenish hue."

"Shimm'ring hue," Ley corrected without superiority: just the care of artist for work, like a potter smoothing a vase lip straight. She grinned, and looked up through the strands of hair that had escaped her fingers' comb, and for a moment they were almost them again, damn distance and time.

They climbed. The Arms's colonial gables set behind a horizon of sun-dried plaster and laundry lines. Stars glistened. A dragon flew overhead, twisting against the confused currents of the city's sky. A coffee seller hawked his wares in a high warbling cant unchanged since the wars. "What did you need back there, anyway?"

"I had to be sure of something," she said. "That's all."

Zeddig asked, "What?" Meaning, among other things, "Who."

But the shutters behind Ley's eyes closed, and she said nothing else on their ride back.

Raymet spread a sheet over the couch for Ley, next to the living room table covered with dice and armored miniatures, and brought her a pillow cased in a T-shirt screen printed with the flower logo of an old friend's band. Raymet sniffed the blanket draped over the love seat, made a face, dumped the blanket into a hamper, and fetched a fresh, if dusty, quilt. "Don't suppose either of you brought a toothbrush?"

"I was running for my life," Ley said. "Must have slipped my mind."

"What she said."

Raymet dug in the cabinet beneath her sink and produced a few bamboo models, sealed in wax paper. "Good night." And she stormed downstairs to her own bed, before Ley or Zeddig could respond.

Zeddig followed, and found Raymet hanging in her room. She'd slung a thick rope over a hook in her ceiling, and dangled from that hook now, shoulders flared. Cords stood out on her forearms, but her hands did not shake. Her grip seemed effortless. Zeddig knew how much effort Raymet used to sell that lie.

"We can do this," Zeddig said.

Raymet rolled her shoulders, and pointed her toes toward the clothes on her floor. "Go to bed, Zeddig."

She went to the pallet Raymet had laid out in her office, and lay in the dark, watching the ceiling.

Raymet would be fine. They'd known each other since the block school Aman ran to teach local kids history. Raymet learned for control. If she knew the right answers, the other students would listen to her, and maybe they'd stop trying to beat her up after class. Some kids thought the girl with her thick glasses would make a good target. She learned to fight by doing, liked the taste of her own blood and its slickness against her teeth.

That need for control didn't go away. Raymet went to university not to learn foreign ways because they were better, but because you had to know squid words to control the squids. She delved to control the dead city, and the horror of history.

Zeddig's eyes burned when she closed them. She rolled, and shifted, and could not sleep. She rose from bed, felt joints pop, and shuffled barefoot from the office to find a drink, guiding herself by memory and dim light from the glow-in-the-dark skulls Raymet pasted above her baseboards.

As she passed Raymet's room, she heard Ley's voice upstairs.

"—not any business of yours."

Was she talking with Raymet? Zeddig felt, and tried to un-feel, a stab of jealousy. But no voice interrupted the silence be-fore Ley spoke again.

"Oh, yes, I'm sure you'd like me to explain my plan in serial villain style. Should I grow a mustache for proper twirling?"

The glow-in-the-dark skulls were not the stairwell's only source of light: a soft blue-white glow issued from the living room. Zeddig crept upstairs—tested each step with the ball of her foot. She moved as if she were climbing over a fallen angel.

Soundless, she crested the stairs.

She could only see Ley's arm, propping a glowing knife tip-first on Raymet's coffee table, a fat triangular blade with a carved handle, almost a Nyongtho design, only uncarved: the knife was a ray-traced outline, and a cloud of blood whirled within. And in that blood, did she see—features? A face, in miniature?

"Sentiment, of course," Ley said, and Zeddig stopped breathing. "And utility." She stretched on the couch: the knife wobbled, and its tip dug a groove in the table between a toy centaur and a tank. Cushions shifted. "Oh, come now. Was I ever more than that to you?"

Zeddig watched the face in the blood, and wished she could read the movement of the lips.

"That's what I thought. Good night, Allie. Sweet dreams—if you can dream in there."

The knife fell, hit the table, and rung not entirely unlike dropped crystal. The light died.

Zeddig could get a glass of water just as well from the bath-room sink. She crept downstairs.

Deep down, she hoped Gal would say no.

Chapter Seventeen

KAI DOUBLED IN DREAMS.

She wrestled Ley on the apartment balcony, breath shallow in her chest, hand slick with the blood that slicked her sister's hands, I can help you, let me help you, and at the same time she paced the room, perfectly composed in heels and a checked camelhair skirt, around the body circled in blood, tapping her chin with one bent knuckle. Somewhere, Behemoth yowled.

The body belonged to a woman named Alethea Vane, and Alethea Vane was beautiful.

To Kai's mind "beautiful" was the most useless adjective ever minted. Most people were beautiful, in one way or another, and line up ten beautiful people and search for common factors and you'd come up blank. In school she'd read aesthetic philosophers who argued some formal unity behind the angle of a gymnast's bicep and the curve of a dancer's thigh, some common thread binding the lean long climber's arms to the soft smile of a reader delighted in repose, but unity, symmetry, crumbled in the mouth like bad cake. Beauty varied too much from person to person, from one island to the next, let alone from continent to continent and era to era, for the word to mean anything at all. In the Harmonious Empire that preceded the Shining by a few dynasties, poets wrote paeans to their lovers' black teeth.

Move past beauty to useful questions. Who was Allie Vane, to have come here, to have become this body on the floor?

Focus.

Seafoam eyes that matched her suit, those said something. The precise architecture of the face didn't matter, only fools tried to read personality in the splay of cheekbones, though skin quality said something about nutrition, and sometimes there were scars. Sclera slightly yellowed, overwork and determination in the corners of that full mouth. (Ley's type? Absolutely.) Soft hands, calluses on the fingertips: a string player. She should have gone through Vane's purse before the cops arrived.

"You need help," Izza said behind her.

Kai hadn't felt her dreamspace ripple when the girl entered. "Is this something we can do to each other now? Just—slide in and out? I thought the nightmare telegraph needs choice. I didn't open a door to you."

She heard Izza's footsteps as the girl orbited the corpse. "This room has a door. I picked the lock."

Kai looked up.

Once again, beautiful, the useless descriptor. She remembered the first time she and Izza met, a year and a half ago: the girl's knife pressed to her throat, her eyes shining with rage and sorrow. Back then Izza was a street kid hiding from Penitents in Kavekana alleys, worshipping her secret goddess, who had become Kai's secret goddess too. Izza had grown. She ate better now, like all her orphan crew. She still kept her hair in tight braids, she still wore battered slacks and a ragged shirt, but she no longer looked so brittle.

"I'm fine."

Izza looked over her shoulder, toward the balcony. "Who's

the lady with the red right hand?"

"My sister."

"You're not fine."

"I'm just reviewing options," Kai said. "The Authority won't let me near the crime scene, but I can use my memories."

"You're remembering all this?" Izza shook her head. "Impossible."

Kai straightened. "This is my job. Pilgrims ask me to build their idols and keep their secrets. We make records, naturally, but what I'm told in confidence stays here." She tapped her temple. "Along with all the various myths and observances, the sacred mysteries. If I had to carry full rites documentation everywhere I go, I'd only visit airports that offer complimentary forklifts in baggage claim. Priests have good memories, and tools to navigate them."

"You didn't remember the soles of this woman's shoes," Izza said, kneeling, peering at the bottom of the sole. "They're fuzzy."

"Good, I said. Not perfect." Pacing the room, she reviewed its emptiness. The couch could fold out into a bed. There was no proper bedroom. The kitchen looked seldom used. She hadn't thought to check the icebox; the presence or absence of milk, and its condition, would have told her so much. She toed grooves in the laminated pale wood floor. "Ley didn't live here. She must have, once. I have the return address. But this place is too neat. You should have seen her room in Chartegnon. She puts herself together before she goes out, always presents a sharp front, but she lives in a nest. So she was living somewhere else, perhaps even with someone else, and kept this—what? As a retreat?"

"Or she cleaned tonight for a particular reason." Izza circled the dream shadows of Kai and Ley, fighting on the balcony. She touched that Kai's shoulder, and the Kai searching for clues in the next room felt the echo of that touch. "Or she's changed."

"You didn't grow up with her." Even she heard the false certainty in her voice. Once more she crouched, and watched Vane's face. "Ley came to me for help, but painted it as investment. Whatever was wrong, she thought sixteen million thaums could fix it. When I didn't help her, this was her only option." The blood reflected Kai's face. "So that's the avenue. Trace Vane, and Ley, and their business. Learn what brought them here."

This time, the hand on her shoulder wasn't an echo.

The girl stood over her, tall and thin and impossibly steady, a ship's mast firm against a storm. "You want to find her before the Iskari."

"I want to help her. She's in trouble. Obviously. I mean, she doesn't usually go around stabbing people."

Izza looked skeptical. "She killed someone."

"The Craftswoman thinks 'kill' is the wrong word. If I find Vane, I can patch up whatever this is, make sure Ley's safe, and move on."

"Kai, you barely know this city."

"So, tell me."

"This isn't something I can just tell you. It's a dangerous place."

Kai rose, and stepped away from Izza. The girl—woman—just wanted to help, was the damnable thing. "This won't be like before. I don't know Agdel Lex like I know home—but I won't make the same mistakes." Sometimes, angry or afraid, Kai still smelled the Penitent around her: glass and sun-baked rock and fear-sweat. She buried all that beneath more comfortable nightmares. "I don't think the Authority's on my side. Ley came to me for help; I didn't understand. I was a fool. But I have to fix this. She's my sister." She only realized how angry she'd become when the rage broke. She dropped her hands. "Even if I am bad at sistering."

"She's your sister," Izza said. "And I'm your friend."

Lava, flowing into the sea, cools with an eruption of steam, leaving arches, bridges, structures that endure when the heat's gone. Lava wasn't often sentient, and volcanoes didn't talk much, but Kai wondered, sometimes, if they ever felt embarrassed by the visible aftermath of their eruption.

She turned back. Izza was still there. "You weren't trying to warn me off."

"You don't know this place," Izza said. "I do."

"No." Kai raised her hands. "No. No, and no."

"I lived here, Kai. Fought here. And you owe me: I got you away from the Iskari."

"Fontaine said that was Twilling."

"How do you think he knew to call?"

"Oh," she said. And: "Thank you. But I don't want your help."

"Name one reason I shouldn't come."

"Do you have a criminal record in Agdel Lex?"

Izza's hands plumbed the depths of her pockets, and she developed a sudden interest in the bare wall behind Ley's couch. "Doesn't everyone?"

Kai took a moment, palm to brow, to control her breath, and her voice. "Even if you could get through customs—"

"I have papers, we took care of that—"

"—then we'd both be here, in danger—"

"I don't think that's fair—"

"—with the congregation abandoned on Kavekana—"

"It's not like the kids don't know the ritual, and anyway, the congregation's not just kids anymore. They can handle things on their own for a week or two, might even be good for them, there's some weird cult of personality shit going on, which, I mean, it gets me laid, so that's nice, but—"

"Izza."

No silence weighs quite like the silence of your own dream. Izza froze mid-pace. Kai reached for her arm, and Izza didn't pull away.

"I don't know what's happening here," Kai said. "You're right. I barely speak the language. The dead city, the broken sky—I've never seen anything like this. My sister's in the middle of it all, doing Lady alone knows what, Lady alone knows why. I can't let her go. Whatever's caught her, I have to steal her back. I'm not fucking—" Her voice slipped out of control, and in a moment of panic she found her reins. That didn't bother her. She'd spent years before ordination, before she remade herself into herself, managing her voice. "I'm not naive. I know the risks. Some of them, at least, and the rest I can guess. I can't drag you into this. You're too important."

"And you aren't?"

"You have other contacts in the priesthood. Twilling—"

"Isn't you."

"No." She smiled, sadly. "And I'll be back soon. But for now—I have to do this alone."

"Kai."

But she'd fought hard enough already. She let the room go;

the nightmare petaled beneath her and she fell, screaming, into blue crystal jaws that pierced and ground her, into an oubliette of knives, and far away there was a door with no lock for Izza to pick, a wall too high and smooth for her to scale, and in those depths, alone in pain, Kai slept.

Chapter Eighteen

GAL WAS RAYMET'S LAST hope.

Raymet knew better than to trust her own judgment about this job. She'd grown up poor, educated by charity and libraries and mistreated in Iskari public schools, chasing scholars around the university at age twelve to ask about proper conjugation of the highly irregular old Talbeg verb *la'at,* which depending on modifiers and attendant grammar might mean to be, to read, to know, to have sex with, or to change. She'd always been an outsider. She used her hunger like fuel. Most of the old High Family kids she came to know in college grew up in certainty. They took fewer risks, because they had more to lose. When you're playing short stack poker, a gambler Raymet slept with had told her once, you bide your time, and when you see your golden hand, you go all in.

But you choose that moment carefully. Don't play every big pot, don't fall for a pair of queens. And care was Raymet's weakness. Climb her family tree and you'd find generations of hungry men and women, desperate for the big score, overplaying hands on the verge of triumph.

So, with a prize like this before her—the Anaxmander Stacks, wealth beyond the dreams of avarice, and academic fame in the bargain—she knew better than to trust her judgment.

But she couldn't trust Zeddig's, either. Ley was a good

pitchwoman, and she didn't have to be with Zeddig. Raymet had known them both separately at school, before they knew each other: each indomitable in her own idiom, guarded by layers of detachment and strength. Their relationship had been a sort of experiment—a Quechal standoff, each one's blade to the other's throat, waiting to see who would cut first. When Ley betrayed them and left, Raymet felt furious, but relieved. At least that was over with.

So: she couldn't trust herself, and she couldn't trust Zeddig.

That left Gal. Raymet's hope. Her moral compass, sitting cross-legged and radiant in the room she kept, unfurnished save for a mattress on the floor, eyes closed, listening to Ley's pitch as she might a sermon—Gal, light in her hair, pure as a statue, gorgeous and simple as a blade.

Gal could not be tempted. Gal would know what to do.

Raymet had never visited Camlaan, and she loathed the Camlaander expat community in Agdel Lex, bunch of priggish drunken isolates, most of whom worked in necromantic geology for the big drilling Concerns south of the Wastes. Their homeland was a barbaric mess of stereotype and myth: undead queens, land-bonding, fertility rituals of the bloodier sort, sickles, wicker, and flame, grails and other theological cutlery. Raymet grew up, like everyone, on stories of Camlaan's Knights, questing, determined, anointed sons and daughters of the realm sent by the Crown's will to smite monsters foreign and domestic. They had been ginned up in a war by some divine monarch or other two thousand years back, and pledged oaths to succor the innocent and help all those in need, though in practice they had a selective sense of what constituted need, or innocence. Monsters had a convenient tendency to live on land that would be valuable if not for the monsters living there; the innocent had a convenient tendency to be oppressed by wicked kings and queens who ruled territory coveted by Camlaan's Crown.

Knights these days tilted against the Golden Horde; Knights faced Zurish Champions in Schwarzwald nightclubs; Knights ventured south into what the *Thaumaturgist* described as "the sectarian madness of the Northern Gleb," drew shining swords and took up the armor of their faith and slaughtered in the name of truth, freedom, and so on, until their priggish drunken isolate compatriots could safely lease mineral rights to that no-longer-quite-so-monster-haunted wilderness.

And so on until empire.

The Knights were a myth wrapped around naked bloody power: a neat clean story to justify destruction. Gross. If you wanted to make people bow before you, to conquer their homes and break them to your will, just do it and have done. Don't lie to yourself that you mean all this for their own good.

But Gal lived the myth.

She never lied and rarely swore. She cared for her friends. She worked hard without complaint. Strong, immensely strong, she used that strength gently save in battle. She sweat and bled like any woman. Someone else had made her a weapon, but she made herself kind.

Her calm, her patience, reminded Raymet of those High Family kids, holding back, waiting for a sure bet. But that wasn't Gal at all. Not when she fought.

Raymet had first seen Gal in the Blood Brawls, in one of the foreigner drum-and-bass-and-gladiator-arena clubs she avoided like she used to avoid her thesis advisor. She'd only come with Zeddig, and Zeddig only came because she'd been dating someone—not Ley—who later proved to be evil.

(Zeddig had a problem with exes.)

The Brawl had simple rules: one point for each limb taken, three points to victory, decapitation or bisection an immediate win. According to Zeddig's soon-to-be-ex, the current champion was a woman without insurance or phylacteric trust, no safety net of any kind. If she died, she died. Yet she'd won eight nights running, and each night staked her winnings on herself and let them ride.

That was Gal.

Everyone knew she'd die eventually, and odds were on tonight, which was why Zeddig's soon-to-be-ex demanded they attend. A mantis-centaur thing had tagged Gal's arm in her last fight with a serrated blade: Gal's first major injury. She'd fall tonight, or tomorrow. Odds against were celestial. Raymet wasn't a bloodsport kind of girl, ask anyone—she'd come to give Zeddig moral support with the evil soon-to-be-ex—but cheers and bar smoke tension woke something in her chest that turned and yawned and bared sharp claws.

Drums built. The crowd roared.

A shining woman stepped onto the sand.

Gal seemed alien under spotlights. Even angels didn't look so sure, though perhaps Raymet only thought that because she tended to see them dying. She stared at the surreal gold of her, the cornsilk hair and cornflower eyes, the bare strong limbs, one marred by a cotton bandage. Not all the first editions in the world could have made her look away.

Chains lifted the gate, and something skinless shambled through: a gorilla skull nestled in a tangle of muscle Raymet's brain interpreted as a chest, despite its lack of ribs, and the skull had gems for eyes, and when it opened its jaw to roar, no sound emerged. The rest of the thing was wriggling flesh and metal rods bunched into limbs. Blood circled by hydraulic pump. When the creature walked, it splashed.

Nobody knew what the skinless thing was; it fought under the ring handle "Oscar." It began with four limbs, but those limbs peeled from one another as needed, and were flexible as whips. The fight, to judge from the crowd's hush, should have been one-sided.

It wasn't.

Gal fought defensively. She circled, sought openings. She danced around Oscar's brutal gouging blows, supple and smooth, as if her bandage was a joke, as if she had come for some purpose more noble than a fight. She drew her blade, but only parried. Oscar pressed its advantage. Gal bled, and bled again. The crowd roared. She smiled at their fury, and, Raymet thought, at the prospect of her own demise.

Raymet's hands tightened on the rail.

That thing in Raymet's chest dug its brilliant claws into the meat between her lungs. That shining woman could not die here. Not like this. Whatever drove her wasn't worth it. Nothing could be. Yet Raymet stood watching, powerless as she'd ever been, once more a broke kid on the street. What could she do? Cry out? Force them to stop the fight? How?

She saw it then: jump into the pit. Ruin the odds, at least, spoil the match. Distract the monster. And, quite likely, die. Raymet could handle herself in a street fight, but Oscar looked like it ate streets.

It was a bad gamble. She might just trip the other woman up—spoil her rhythm, die trying. She held cards unsuited, no connectors, a sucker's hand.

Gal slowed. Her bandage was a mess of blood. Her teeth were perfect.

She had to do it.

Raymet gathered herself to jump, and glanced, at the last instant, to Zeddig, for reassurance or out of hope Zeddig might stop her.

But Zeddig wasn't there. Because, of course, she had already jumped into the pit.

(That was when Zeddig's soon-to-be became her ex.)

Raymet watched, horrified, sick, and ashamed she hadn't jumped first. Why hadn't she? She almost followed—but it all happened so fast. Oscar swept Gal's legs out from under her and writhed toward Zeddig. Its torso inverted so the jewel-eyed skull faced out from where the spine should be, and it pinned Zeddig with a glare; a meat-limb whipped out to snare her throat, and missed, but another caught her arm—

And then Gal stood between them, wreathed in light.

She had not seemed slow before, but she moved faster now.

The fight ended soon.

There was blood everywhere.

After the promoter screamed at them and had them thrown out of the club by bouncers who were very polite, for obvious reasons, Raymet caught Zeddig in the alley, furious in her shame, what the hell were you doing, you almost got yourself killed, but she stopped when she saw Gal standing in shadow by Zeddig's side. The woman so ready to die back in the ring seemed resigned to life instead. Not excited, relieved, triumphant. Just—tired. What will you do? Zeddig asked. And Gal said, I'll find another way. Zeddig didn't know how to answer that. But Raymet, her mouth dry, cursing herself on the inside for a fool, said: Are you looking for dangerous work?

And that was how it started.

They needed muscle for delves. The dead city was dangerous. Gal knew little about Agdel Lex—the Knights were not historically trained, their masters thought context unhelpful on their missions—and she couldn't read modern Talbeg, let alone Old High, or Telomeri, any of the languages necessary for their work. Hells, she could barely read Kathic. But then, neither Zeddig nor Raymet could wrestle angels.

So they worked together, fought together, caroused when they won, and endured failure. Time and again, Gal saved them, and each time Raymet remembered that shame, of not running fast enough to Gal's defense. If she ever mentioned it, Gal would have waved the whole thing off—even if Raymet was a fighter, that was not her fight—which made things worse.

And now, as they gathered in her cell, and Raymet hoped she'd save them once more.

They called Gal's one-room flat above Madhin's Tea Shop a cell not because Gal was confined there, but because it looked like a monk's chamber: in six years the Camlaander had never furnished the place beyond a cheap straw mattress with sheets so poor she must have imported them—no cotton vendor in Agdel Lex would sell a weave that rough. Raymet didn't know how Gal spent her take of their missions: most people stored their souls in homes and things, soulstuff sloughing into tapestries and furniture, art and books and cookware, or deposited what they could into a bank to earn interest. Gal probably believed banking and interest were sins. But people couldn't hold more than a few thousand thaums without going strange.

Then again, with Gal, how would you tell?

Ley made her pitch.

Gal listened. Golden light haloed her short hair. The room's one arrowslit window cast light on the bed, not Gal, so the light must have come from inside her. Raymet watched her, and remembered the ring of sand, and the smile. They'd known each other for years, and she still felt those bright claws sink into the meat between her lungs. "That's the deal," Ley said. "You get me into the Altus facility. I get you into the Stacks. No questions asked, none answered."

You see the golden hand, you go all in. Don't pass this up.

But it was still a bad job.

So Raymet watched Gal like she would watch a lighthouse, hoping for guidance through the storm.

Gal's eyes were blue, and light, and there was light inside them.

"Yes," she said. "But I want to see your tools at work."

Chapter Nineteen

KAI FOUND FONTAINE IN her office the next morning, cocked back in her desk chair, feet propped on a filing cabinet, chin raised, right eyelid pried open by her left thumb and forefinger while her right pinched a tiny neon lizard over the wet dome of her cornea. The lizard hissed and squirmed, but Fontaine did not let herself blink.

"I can come back later," Kai said.

"Not at all, Ms. Pohala, come in, come in." Fontaine adjusted the lizard. "*Amodosia* are a pain in the posterior, to be honest, hard to make the glands express at this size. The price we pay to stay current. Nothing goes to the optic nerve quite like these babies, even if you have to—ow." A flailing rear claw drew a line of blood from her thumb. "Come in, please."

Kai sidled in, quietly. She'd never been comfortable with drugs. Kavekanese artists who took them tended to be desperate, poets and painters who'd so worn out their capacity for dream that they could see visions no other way. But if Fontaine spent her life in meetings like the kind Kai had yesterday, no wonder she'd grown callous to nightmares. "I signed your paper."

"Wonderful!" Fontaine found the spot she sought in the hissing lizard's jaw, and pushed her thumbnail into the scales. The lizard gagged; a drop of oily rainbowed liquid fell from its mouth into Fontaine's eye. She snapped her eyes shut, then, and doubled over, shuddering. She made a sound like she'd been caught in the fist of some other enormous being, held pendant over its eye, and squeezed. "There" was her first word after, drawn like a dispatch from the grave. Her second "There" was shorter, chipped, chirpy. Fontaine hopped to her feet, head raised as if ready to be crowned. She grinned rapture, and, without looking, tossed the lizard into a glass terrarium that stood, top open, near her desk. Then she closed the top.

When she opened her eyes, the paper-thin ring of iris visible around her left pupil remained the usual brown, but the ring around her right was the blue of ice in gin.

"Brilliant! I'm so glad we can work together." Fontaine snatched the contract and unfolded it, crumpling the paper in her fingers. "We can build a profitable relationship without a doubt, Ms. Pohala, and since you're extending your stay, along with your investment horizon, let's expand the range and depth of our interviews to compensate, as I really don't think you"—she opened her desk drawer and dropped the paper inside—"appreciated the depth and growth potential of the Concerns we saw yesterday—and our broader time frame lets us focus on a fuller"—she laughed at a joke Kai hadn't understood, and locked the drawer—"range of associations, thematic and structural relationships we glossed over given yesterday's focus on short-term growth potential, why, depending on your interest there are a number of incubators and co-op programs we could—"

"I'd like to discuss Alethea Vane," Kai said, and sat.

The next time Fontaine blinked, her right eye was a deeper blue, about the color mainland poets said robins' eggs were. There weren't robins on Kavekana—traders tried to introduce them, once, but the trees kept eating them. "Ms. Vane."

"And Ley Pohala, if you recognize that name."

"I think," Fontaine said, lowering herself to her chair, "Dreamspinner is well past your investment horizon." Another blink. Desert sky. "Pohala? Any relation?"

"My sister." Interesting. So: the murder hadn't made the news. Or Fontaine didn't read the news—did she even have to read? Perhaps drugs just dropped news into her brain. Someone in Zur was probably dreaming to her about oil prices as they spoke.

"You're related? No sense talking about Dreamspinner then, conflict of interest issues there—we could build a structure that wouldn't attract Court attention, but it doesn't matter since they're not on the funding market—"

Interesting. Then why was Ley hunting for funding last night? "I don't want to invest in them," Kai said. "I want to learn about their industry. I want an unvarnished opinion of their stability, current positioning, and growth prospects."

"Unvarnished, you say." Fontaine chuckled. "Sorry." She laughed some more, realized she was laughing, and tried to stop the laugh with her fist, without success. Kai waited. "Okay," she said after a while. "This is good. We're good. *Good* is a funny word in Kathic, isn't it?" They were speaking Iskari, which Kai didn't mention. "I have just the person, think I can set up a meeting this afternoon, and meanwhile—" She stretched toward a filing cabinet in the room's far corner; Kai was about to get up and open it for her, but a long thin tendril wriggled out from beneath Fontaine's cuff, arrowed across the room, tugged open the drawer, slithered into the files, pinched a particularly thick folder, and drew it out—tried to lift it, but settled for dropping the folder to the floor and dragging it toward Fontaine's chair, where the woman bent to pick it up. Kai didn't blame the tentacle. She'd read theological regulations thinner than that file. "So you want to learn about infrastructure and defense."

"Do you need to make an appointment? With the person you want me to talk to? I could find an admin—"

"No, hardly, I mean, I've already done it, you see." She tapped her still-blue eye. "Now!" Fontaine opened the folder, and grinned at the contents. "Infrastructure! Or, would you like a snack first?"

. . .

After two and a half hours, punctuated by a trip to the canteen for a plate of fries smothered in chili sauce, and a second trip forty-five minutes later to one of Fontaine's colleagues' desks to ransack her secret cookie stash (vividly colored cardboard boxes, "she gets them from some weird foreign paramilitary evangelist front, can't find 'em anywhere in Agdel Lex but the necro-G people sponsor a troop and she does their financing, which is why she's away right now, conference in Dhisthra, so"), Kai understood more than she ever expected to know about Iskari defense contracting and military appropriations. She was overjoyed when Fontaine's admin knocked to interrupt, and said, in Talbeg, "There's a woman here for Ms. Pohala."

Which Fontaine translated for Kai, who still hadn't let on that she spoke Talbeg, even if she didn't quite have a handle on the local dialect yet. "So popular!"

Kai excused herself and followed the admin. He left her at the conference room, where Ms. Abernathy waited.

The Craftswoman stood against the city, looking down. From the twenty-third floor of the IFI building, Agdel Lex looked like a mosaic of crystal and plaster, roads the gaps between colored tiles. The sun beat down from a desert blue sky, and glistened off the faintly pulsing walls of the Authority tower nearby.

"You're never supposed to stand with your back to a door," Kai said, approaching.

Abernathy didn't look back. "That's from Hebenon, isn't it?"

"I forget. I never read the book; my ex was a fan, and he used to say that all the time."

"Do you think I should be worried about assassination?"

Kai sat on the table, and crossed her legs. "You tell me."

"The funny thing about never sitting with your back to the door is that it leaves you with your back to the window." She turned to face Kai, and leaned against the window glass. Kai's heart and stomach swapped places; the glass was so clear as to seem nonexistent. Deep in Kai's brain a vestigial monkey insisted Abernathy was about to fall. "Do you expect greater danger from within, or without?"

"You're being cryptic, Ms. Abernathy." Then again, Kai did not know who else might be listening.

"We're on the same side here." Abernathy snapped her fingers. Shadow rolled from the glyphs cut into her skin. The world grayed, quaked, stabilized. She'd inked, Kai saw now, thin Craft circles on the conference room's walls, ceiling, and floor, each design bridged by an arc of moonlight. "Or at least, on similar sides. We can speak freely. The squids may notice they can't listen in, but if they break the ward, I'll know."

"Nice trick." Kai tapped her nails on the table. "In what sense are we on the same side?"

"You want your sister safe. You want to know what's going on here. So do I."

"You'll forgive my skepticism, Ms. Abernathy."

"Call me Tara."

Kai waited, and so did the Craftswoman. "Tara," she said, in the end. "You're working with Bescond, but you don't trust her. You're not from around here, and you're not certain you can rein Bescond in if she does—whatever she wanted to do to me last night before Fontaine showed up."

The Craftswoman's hand tensed on her jacket sleeve. Watching her, Kai remembered the overwound watch and the straining mainspring, and thought about traveler's tales of still mountain mornings after heavy snow, when a song could break white cliffs to avalanche. "I can't say much."

"Likewise."

"Alt Coulumb is collaborating with the Iskari Demesne. We"—she smiled in self-mockery when she said that word, and Kai felt a stab of affection for her for that—"have our differences, but we've been allies. We reached out to the Iskari for help with an important project; they were working on something similar, and offered to bring us on board if we helped them with financing. I just came to town a couple weeks back to observe the final stages. But the project can't move forward without the woman your sister, let's say, stole. This"—she pointed over her shoulder with her thumb at the cracked city and the throbbing tower—"is new to me. I want Vane back, alive, soon. I don't care whether your sister's brought to justice. Bescond's a loyal officer with a limited vision, and she wants Ley caught. But we might be able to work together—you and I, I mean."

"You just told me you don't care what happens to my sister."

"I told you," Abernathy said, "I don't care whether she's brought to justice." That word, too, seemed to amuse her. "I don't know your sister well, though, having met Vane, I sympathize with a desire to stab her. You want your sister safe. I want Vane. I think we can cooperate."

"Can I trust you? You didn't speak up for me last night."

"If I put Bescond on the spot, she would have doubled down. I would have freed you somehow. But you don't have proof of that, so for now, I can only say: I'm sorry."

"And you can't tell me why you're here," she said. "Maybe we're not necessarily on opposite sides, but we're not on the same side, either. I need to find my sister and get her out of this mess. Your project, her Concern, this city—none of that matters to me. The way I see it, my best play is to thank you for your time and walk out that door." She stood. "Are we done?"

Abernathy pushed herself off the window, and Kai's stomach lurched again. The Craftswoman moved, and stood, like a woman who was not afraid to fall. She held a business card she hadn't held before. Had she produced it with Craftwork, or sleight of hand?

Sometimes Kai wondered about the difference between the two.

Kai drew back. "No way. I've worked with Craftswomen before. I take that, and you can listen in on my conversations, or track me, or gods know what."

Tara laughed. "Not my plan." The card disappeared anyway. "But I'd rather not make you nervous. If you change your mind, find me. I room at the Temple of All Gods, Eastridge, near the Cleft. Cascade Street. I'm there most nights after ten, and mornings before seven. The longer you wait, the less I can help."

"I'll take that risk," Kai said, and left.

Chapter Twenty

ZEDDIG LED THEM THROUGH the slough tunnels into Gavreaux Junction, dodging scavenger lice, and they waited in the high ductwork for their chance. The eleven-thirty freight from Garde du Leon arrived on time—vents opened and supercooled toxic slush flooded in. The blue-green liquid gurgled below, extruding pseudopods that lashed tunnel walls but found no grip on the laminated stone. Clinging to hydraulic tubes twenty feet above the rushing current, Zeddig and Ley and Gal and Raymet breathed through masks.

When the vents cycled open, Zeddig led the way—slid out between the enormous blades, spaced just wide enough for an athletic woman to squeeze through if she didn't breathe too deep, and, squinting against the light, reached back to help Ley and Raymet along. Ley didn't need help; Raymet's leg caught in a cable, and she cursed—the sludge rush tailed off to a trickle before she could work her foot clear. She rolled through just as the vents snapped shut. Gal offered Raymet a hand up, and she almost accepted, then pulled back, looked away and stood, slapping dust off her overalls, embarrassed.

Freight arrival at the Junction was a glorious screaming mess, as union men and women in brown jumpsuits (just like those Raymet had found for the crew) swarmed over colossal freight cars. Enormous winches pulled the train forward car by car, and car by car each slick black lozenge split, petaled open, and vented its insulation into the slough tunnels. Cranes swung into position, unloading containers onto waiting flatbeds. Everyone had a job in that first half hour of arrival, every job required everyone's full attention, and a few delvers (with client) could sneak through if they walked fast and looked like they meant business. Zeddig, playing foreman, shoved Gal in the shoulder. Raymet approximated a scurry. "Come on, come on." She almost pushed Ley, but Ley glared back over her shoulder and Zeddig thought better of it.

Overhead was the only place one could linger while the trains unloaded, so Zeddig led them to the arch houses—massive jawed structures built over the track, from which high-speed pulleys could unload each flatbed from the top while lesser cranes and liftsuits worked from the side. Fifteen stories up the arch house made for a lot of ladder to climb, but you got one hell of a view: the Junction an anthill kicked over, brown jumpsuited ants and their machines carrying cargo containers rather than eggs to market rather than to safety. North of the Junction's fortress walls, flatbed elevators bore cargo downhill to port, where the Treasure Fleet waited to fill its wrong-angled holds with the bounty of the Gleb.

This had been a good run, by Waste freight standards: only one car missing, only one container breached. Two million thaums of necromantic earths gone forever—maybe more. Prices were up this week.

At the end of the climb Zeddig collapsed in the sunlight on the arch house roof. Shadow passed over her: Ley, staring down on the city, taut as drumskin. Zeddig sat up, and looked for Gal—she lay beside the ladder, one hand down, helping Raymet up the last few rungs. Raymet stumbled onto the roof, and slipped—but Gal caught her, and lowered her onto the roof, where she sprawled, breathing fast. Gal sat back on her calves, smooth, sweatless, watching Raymet with an angel's concern; she touched her side.

"I'm okay," Raymet said, eyes still screwed shut. "There's just too much here out here."

The *here* spread north and downslope to the port and the beachfront resorts, and south past the airport to the shield wall, warded and silvery-black.

"Would you like water?" Gal asked, as if offering high tea.

Raymet groped in the vague direction of her legs. Gal unslung the water skin from her shoulder; Raymet took a small sip, then forced herself, not quite upright, but to her knees at least. "Okay," she said. Gal offered her hand again; this time Raymet let the other woman draw her to her feet.

"Don't look at the city," Gal said. "Focus on the floor. Or on me."

Raymet kept her eye on their meshed hands, as Gal led her to Zeddig's side. "I hope this demonstration's worth it."

Ley must have heard the accusation there, but she shrugged it off. "We could have tried this in the steam tunnels. Or in your house."

"You can lead the Wreckers to your own house, if you like." Raymet glared at Ley. "I don't mind a field trip. But if we did all this for nothing . . ."

"Not nothing." Ley reached into her jumpsuit, and drew her knife. Its blue outlines shone through her hand, as if she held a fire.

Raymet drew back. Zeddig sat up and watched, wary. Gal didn't move. One eyebrow twitched up, at most.

"Ley," Zeddig said.

"Do you trust me?"

Zeddig wished she knew.

Ley gripped one of the blade's three edges between thumb and forefinger, bit her lower lip—Zeddig's breath caught like it always had when she made that face, not quite worried, groping around the edges of a problem or an orgasm—and peeled the knife apart. She did the same with each of the blade's three edges, until she held the knife by the handle alone—and then she let the handle go. The rings and rays that had been the handle extended and realigned, forming a shape Zeddig lacked the math to call its proper name, an ever-branching spiderweb—each ray spread small sharp twigs and leaves, only each leaf's edge was somehow the whole spiderweb itself, spinning spinning spinning further down to the center, where a wet red sphere glistened. The web hovered between them, growing, until its furthest substrands bloomed about a meter out from the blood.

It was beautiful. Terrible. Terrifying. Sexy. Scary. No single word in Talbeg, Kathic, or Iskari did it justice. "What is that?" She reached for the thing, and where her hand approached, the blue lines burned gold.

"Art," Ley said.

"What does it do?"

"Pull you in," she said. "Touch it. Just—don't, really don't, stroke the lines, or press against them. They're very . . . thin? Sharp?"

Zeddig did. Raymet, brow furrowed, followed suit. Gal pinched one of the web-leaves. Ley took hold of an inner ring.

Gold spread from their fingers through the web. The design did not move, or else it had never stopped moving—spreading, turning, wheels within wheels spun against one another to spread even more filigree of wheels within wheels within wheels, and she—

slipped

—and was smaller than she should have been, her heart racing against the iron bars of her ribs, every muscle tight, crushed on all sides by the enormity of the horizon—

—and was still, and large, and calm, and, wondering, heard her own voice say, "keep still"—

—and was—something—she slid through, unable to find purchase, furious—

—and returned, gasping, unsteady, to her self.

"What?" was the first word she found, and the second.

Ley, across from her, adjusted the innermost ring of the web. "Sorry, overdid it—there. You can let go now."

She did. And she shivered.

The dead city spread below them.

They stood on a suggestion, a ghost of solid air, the memory of a warehouse that never existed here. Below them lay Alikand, torn, shattered, frozen, bleeding light. Gods screamed in the sky. Armies wrestled freezing armies in the streets. Bloody clouds spiraled overhead, drawing ever inward like a cyclone toward the Wound, toward the library she could barely stand to behold, where, in a frozen instant of time, Maestre Gerhardt stood dying. There were cracks in the clouds, and many-faceted eyes stared through.

This was her great-grandmother's city, in ruins. No one living had seen it whole, not even Aman, though Aman learned her art from those who had. Alikand, the wonder of the world, who sheltered infant Craftsmen and was broken in return. That blackened crater where a skeleton in an enormous metal suit had thrust her fist through an angel's chest to tear free its crystal heart, that was Kisbey Market, where chefs in training cooked for the poor, and the university laid feasts on cross-quarter days. The seven-winged mansion there on the western ridge, that should be the Ko family estate, the libraries licked with frozen flames. These icy ruins were museums. Those, schools. That, a hospital.

She wept.

She had seen all this before, but always with a mission: some volume or artifact to rescue, some death to record. This was a crime confronting did not expunge.

She wept, but her tears did not freeze.

Zeddig shivered in her jumpsuit. Her fingers numbed against the gold web. But she should not be merely cold—she should be dying. Yet her breath barely steamed.

"What is this?"

Ley wasn't even looking at the city. She grinned, as unforced an expression as Zeddig had ever seen on her face. "When you delve, you reject one city, and embrace another—binding yourself by its rules. Stands to reason you could create a different community, a different city, with different rules. That's where art comes in: an audience is a community based around the art. Once I learned delving, thanks to you, I could build a work to bring viewers into a community that interacted with the dead city, without entering it. Identity slippage is a side effect—sorry. It's not perfect, but here we are. You get me into Altus, and I'll give you the blade."

Fierce amber wheels turned in Ley's eyes.

"Stop it," Zeddig said.

"Seen enough?"

Zeddig's throat was too tight, and she couldn't breathe, and a red layer overlay the city. Her city. The city that should have been hers. Below, in a train station that didn't exist, a woman screamed. "Stop it, damn you."

The web snapped shut, the world inverted, and they stood above Gavreaux Junction and the Authority tower rose obscene to the north and east where the Library had once been, and Ley reached for her, that kicked-puppy expression on her face, what did I do wrong. Zeddig pulled back. Ice crystals melted on her skin. Below, winches worked and the kicked ant farm writhed and foul almost-living gunk gushed through pipes, and scavenger lice lurked and waited to eat. The sun burned—not *her* sun, no, the sun some Iskari motherfuckers thought should shine here, because this was the Gleb, wasn't it, this was a desert, that's where these people lived—curses caught in her throat and Ley needed answers and Zeddig had none to give.

"Zeddig—"

She'd turned away, so she didn't see whether Gal or Raymet stopped Ley from saying more. But it was Raymet who told the big lie. "It's okay."

Chapter Twenty-one

KAI CREPT INTO THE stained glass warehouse.

She did not fear discovery. She had an appointment. The address Fontaine gave her led to a dangerously hip foreigner enclave west of Sauga's, the kind of place where twenty-year-old guidebooks would have cautioned visitors against walking alone at night, but which had since embraced a coffee shop– and performance space–based economy. From outside, the warehouse looked abandoned by the west waterfront's enhippening, windows broken, sign defaced with graffiti, an investment property whose investors had not yet cashed in. But when she passed through the empty front office—a wolf spider scuttled across the secretary's desk—and stared into the bare open space beyond, she did not announce herself. She entered softly, because she did not want to disturb the colors.

High dirty windows begrudged sunlight entrance to a warehouse bare of shelves and forklifts and hand carts. The chamber should have been dim, but wasn't. Mirrors and prisms, some mounted, others pendant from thin steel cables that crisscrossed the vastness, broke and bent the light to majesties.

Some of the stained glass was new. Kai had only seen the stuff antique, in Iskari or Telomeri churches, dragons and star kraken and mountain-sized spiders formed pane by monochrome pane. Fresh, it dazzled. Shards hung, some meters on a side, others no larger than Kai's smallest fingernail, recasting the light in stark panels of overlapping color. Curved mirrors reflected the world back weird, warping those colors into a riot, a cataclysm, a liberation of form, or a transformation of form into something . . . else.

Kai had felt this way before.

There was a pool in the center of the sacred mountain of Kavekana'ai, and in that pool gods lived, and dreamed, and built the world. Form slipped there, and changed. Ideas mattered more than matter.

At the chamber's heart, broken colors overlapped in a circle of blinding white. As Kai approached, the vastness rippled, transforming with each footstep. Recognizable forms emerged: half-glimpsed beasts that, when she turned face to them, were not there at all.

She neared the circle of light. Warmth pressed against her face like a lover's hand. She reached for it—

"I wouldn't," said a voice of crushed glass. "If I were you."

She pulled her hand back, and whirled, searching the colors and shadows for a face. The rainbow reflected her skewed, foreshortened, pared, immense.

She did not see the demon until it landed in front of her.

It glittered in the light: mantis-like but with a spider's legs, sharp mandibles, all planes and edges of black glass save for multifaceted red eyes. It reared, and cocked its head to the side like a confused dog. With one great sickle-claw it stroked the underside of its mandible. "You wanted to enter the circle," it said. "Would you please tell me why?"

"Ah." All her words had scurried off to hide under some sofa of her mind. "It's not, that is . . ." Nothing terrible, just a demon, you've seen them before, this guy's not even particularly large as they go, just three meters or so at the shoulder. She looked for binding marks, and found none. "What would have happened if I did?"

The demon scraped a chunk of cement off the floor as easily as Kai might have scooped a handful of sand, and threw it into the light. The cement stuck in midair, vibrated—no, not vibrated, vibranted instead, every shadow and curve and peculiarity visible in stark relief—then exploded and imploded at once. Kai flinched, felt a wash of heat, and when she turned back there was nothing left in the circle, not even ash.

"Why the hells," she said, only too conscious of the irony, "would you build something like that?"

"It's an interesting problem," the demon said. "What is this thing we call form, and to what extent do we comprehend our own forms? I have a form, surely, as do you, and let us grant that we're both conscious even though certain philosophers would argue that assertion—fortunately they're not here. So! Both conscious. But we have imperfect knowledge of our own forms, let alone our own selves—consider the human man, his last self-image formed at the age of twenty-five, surprised by wrinkles on his forehead as he looks in the bathroom mirror. Deathless Kings' residual physicalities endure long after they've become skeletons—and they perform premortem exercises to stem mental fragmentation. You'd be surprised how frequently and how widely mental image and physical form differ."

"I really wouldn't," Kai said.

She'd meant that to come off as wry, or at least free of pain or resentment—no sense getting into personal stuff on a professional call—but the demon's flood of enthusiasm froze, and it bowed its head.

"I did not mean to cause offense," it said, "and I apologize if I have. How's this: I am frequently surprised by the range of difference. Not least because I am not native to your physical frame of reference. Everything works ... differently where I come from. The distinctions I describe aren't only physical-mental—as if the two were different." It laughed a rolling of wind chimes. "Rather, let us include differences in perception and conception. We are not complete in ourselves without others, without a world to complement our self-conception—and were we to become so complete, we could not bear it! The fullness of ourselves would break us. We burn. The point of Figment/Fragment/Filament"—claws spread to encompass the whole warehouse space—"is to reflect, refract the beauty of physical form, the glorious futility of our quest for complete knowledge, mastery, or independence. Yet every time a human visits, without fail you gawk a bit at the pretty lights, then make a beeline for the center, and reach for the circle! As I'm sure you can imagine, immolating the guests would put a dampener on an otherwise successful installation opening. So—why?"

"Have you considered," Kai said, "putting a rope around the pretty glowing circle of murder light?"

The demon turned from her, to the light, and back. Kai hadn't thought those eyes capable of narrowing, but they grew sharper. She pondered the distance to the exit. The demon had more legs than she did, and she was wearing heels.

Then the demon doubled over, chittering. One sickle arm slapped the concrete, and left a deep gouge.

"Are you R'ok?" Kai guessed. Fontaine had said "Rock," leaving off the epiglottal fricative, which had left Kai expecting—she wasn't precisely sure, but it wasn't this. "Ms. Fontaine sent me."

"Of course, pleased to meet you. Kai, isn't it? I'm glad you did not immolate yourself. Would you like tea? This great new place just opened down the street."

R'ok locked the door behind him with some sort of extruded ebon glass in place of a key, and led Kai three blocks west past several tea shops that seemed perfectly passable, to a small cart with a long line in front. "Before you ask anything," R'ok said, "I have to say that I'm very limited in what I can discuss about Dreamspinner."

"You're not with the Concern anymore."

"Not for eight months. Your sister recruited me. You shouldn't act so surprised—there are not terribly many Archipelagese in Agdel Lex, Pohala is not a common surname, and she spoke highly of you."

Kai felt something twist in her stomach. "Were you and Ley close?"

"We never slept together, if that's what you mean," R'ok said.

"Is that even—I'm sorry, I didn't mean to—"

"Quite all right. It is possible, if one is willing to be patient and respect the range and diversity of . . . apparatus. But, no. We collaborated. We were friends, though your sister is a guarded person. We met working on an exhibit; a sculpture of mine came to life and made matters awkward for the exhibitor. The exhibit hall burnt down, and the two of us went out for drinks. She was dating Zeddig at the time, I believe."

Kai blinked. "Dating?"

"Well. Yes. They were together for, it must have been two years? It ended, as such things do. A shame—they were good for one another. Ley showed up on my doorstep drunk after their breakup; she stayed with me in varying degrees of intoxication for a month afterward. She never told me what went wrong between the two of them. Spent her time making small sculptures to crystallize human dreams, then destroying each dream from within. It was a bleak period."

"Do you know Alethea Vane?"

R'ok coughed. They'd reached the front of the line; he bought two mint teas from the heavyset woman who tended the cart, who recognized him and slapped his exoskeleton by way of greeting. R'ok paid before Kai could, and passed her the tea. "I'm not at liberty to discuss my relationship with Ms. Vane."

"What about Ley's?"

He sipped the tea, or did something similar, which process involved a number of small sharp fingerlike protrusions between his mandibles. Kai breathed rich mint steam. "I believe that is not covered by my nondisclosure agreement. Allie Vane and Ley were both active on the artistic scene at about the same time—Vane's work and your sister's pushed in opposite directions from my own. Vane is a genius of scale: she goes big, or not at all, and her work turned around conceptual lock-in, the experience of audience arrest. You're familiar with Zeybach's Syndrome, in which visitors to old Telomeri cities are overcome by aesthetic response? Like that. Meanwhile, Ley focused on audience *dynamics*: community formation and dramatic presentations. They couldn't stand one another, but there was a pheromonal mix at work—I mean. I'm no human expert, but, wow. Vane grew frustrated with the limited social impact of conceptual art, jumped into application, founded Dreamspinner, but funding lay thin on the ground until she joined forces with your sister. Then—well. They received an immense Sternum Series from a fund that, the most open secret in town is their capital comes from the Iskari Defense

Ministry. I should never have gotten involved. But your sister came to me saying, R'ok, it's great, R'ok, I understand your ideological objections, but, R'ok, the funding, the scale of the work, R'ok, come on. Against my better judgment, I joined. Which, the sudden burning pressure around my heart indicates, is where my nondisclosure agreement cuts in." He finished the tea, and ate the cup. "I hope that helps."

Kai nodded, mute.

"You haven't tried your tea."

She did. It tasted clear and bright. She breathed out. "You mentioned my sister's ex."

"Hala'Zeddig," R'ok said. "Yes. Vivid person. As is your sister, of course. They were . . . an interesting pair."

"Do you know where she lives?"

Chapter Twenty-two

VOGEL HAD NO FIXED business address. He wriggled ratlike through the city's alleys and avenues, collecting his dues, and retreated by night to corner booths in the restaurants he offered protection at rates he claimed were reasonable. Vogel had come to the city back during reconstruction, one more refugee from the war-torn Ebonwald-Zurish front where so many millions died, and built a cut-rate empire offering cut-rate services to those who fled here after him. Old habits died harder than the old man himself: though the wars were long over, and most of his refugee client-victims these days came huddled in passenger trains from the Gleb beyond the Wastes, he still visited the wharves at night to watch the sand where, as Zeddig had heard the story, he once huddled beneath the knit blanket that was all he could salvage from the wreck of his home. The wars had been thorough on Vogel.

So she went to the wharves to find him, with Gal at her side.

"This is a bad idea," Gal said as they climbed metal stairs to the public walkway overlooking the Kadah port: sea walls angels built between offshore islands two thousand years ago, creating the best harbor west of Apophis. The waterfront felt more Agdel Lex than anywhere: the punishing sun, the air a dry lash against her skin, and everywhere the scent of cinnamon. The Wreckers were hard at work. "Vogel is a thug, Ms. Hala, and he owns your marker. He is vindictive, unsanitary, backbiting, and grotesque."

"That's why we need him."

"I see." Gal sounded unconvinced, to put it mildly.

"We'll need supplies for the Altus run, and we can't gather those without him hearing about it. If he thinks we're trying to cut him out, he'll come after us, or turn us in. We can head that off at the pass, and cancel my debt at the same time. Get him on our side from the start."

"Vogel humiliated you in public."

She waved it off. "He gave me a stomachache."

"You were screaming."

"It hurt."

"You are not helping your case, Ms. Hala."

"Look, he may be vindictive, unsanitary, backbiting, and—what was the last one?"

"Grotesque."

"But he's not that bad once you get to know him," Zeddig said, at which point they reached the top of the stairs, turned left, and saw Vogel dangling a boy, maybe fifteen, over the railing by his ankles.

Vogel wasn't doing the dangling personally, of course. His big Zurish associate, the maskorovik, Ivan, actually held the kid; Ivan's wrists were thicker than the kid's ankles, which was backhandedly reassuring under the circumstances. But Vogel's men were Vogel's arms, and if Vogel had done the dangling himself, he wouldn't have his hands free to cut, and smoke, a cigar.

The walkway was scrupulously empty aside from the crooks. It wasn't a popular couples spot, but normally at least a few kids with a fetish for heavy machinery would be necking by the container ships. But everyone knew to give Vogel space to work.

Ivan shook the kid again, and loose bits of paper floated down from his pockets. He screamed and cursed and begged in heavily accented Talbeg, and Ivan laughed.

Zeddig ran toward the kid; Josep, Vogel's other bodyguard, blocked her, but she dipped under his arm and past. "Ivan!" Cables worked in the Zurish man's forearms.

"I'd recommend against asking Ivan to 'put him down,' if I were you, Zeddig." Vogel sounded pleased with himself. "He might listen."

"What the hell." The kid was babbling—no, praying. She recognized a Kaj family chant, one of the collateral branches. There were tears, but he hadn't pissed himself yet. "Vogel. What did he do?"

"He told me he would do a job," Vogel said. "Something small. But he failed, and tried to hide. Failure, I forgive. But it's so hard to find loyal help in this city. People assume that because you give everyone a chance, you're a nice guy, someone they can walk all over. It's worse, begging your pardon, and you're very much the exception here, Zeddig, with locals. My local partners tend to assume they can hide: those shifting back alleys of yours, the not-quite-there parts of the city that keep you safe from cops and Wreckers. But you're never safe from me."

"Whatever he did to you, it's not worth this."

"Zeddig." He blew a smoke ring that split and twisted back through itself. "If you're not here to talk business, I really must return to mine."

Josep caught her arm in his coconut-sized fist, her shoulder in his other, and wrenched her arm behind her back. Before the joint could crinkle beneath the pressure, she was free. "Gal, don't —" But she wasn't fast enough. She heard a crack, and a scream. Josep lay on the ground with white bone protruding jagged through the skin of his forearm. Gal hadn't even drawn her blade.

Ivan whirled around; he'd forgotten that he held the kid, who smacked against the rail of the observation deck, and screamed again. Josep groaned.

Vogel rolled the one eye that still worked. "Josep. Get ahold of yourself. What's broken, we can fix." Josep bit his lip between his teeth; he lay on the ground, sweat-beaded, cradling his arm.

"I wanted to talk about my debt," Zeddig said.

"I'm listening."

"You mentioned a train job."

"It's a job," Vogel said. "There's a train involved. The rest is somewhat negotiable."

"I'll work the train. I'll bring my crew along. We time the hit, and make our way home on our own."

"Through the Wastes? Have you acquired a suicidal streak?"

"Something like that," Zeddig said.

"I'll need a second crew just to get my score back."

"Which means you can bring twice as much home. A few more heads, but more than twice the payday."

Vogel took the cigar from between his teeth and tipped ash over the bannister.

"In exchange," Zeddig continued, "you cancel my marker—before we go out, not after. And you let him go."

"What's this number-runner to you?"

She could have said, a cousin, could have said, a countryman, could have said, someone who doesn't deserve to die today, but instead she said, "Nothing."

"What do I gain from canceling your marker before the job?"

"Same."

"Eh." He scratched the skinless meat of his left cheek, found something small burrowing there, ate it, and returned to his cigar. "I drop the kid, and cancel your marker in advance. Now, in fact." He drew the vial from his jacket pocket. Sunset cast its shadow red on the ground. She felt the air grow thick, as if he held her, rather than the glass. "Or I free the kid, and cancel your marker when the job's done."

"Fuck you."

"I never fraternize with business partners." He pressed his thumb against the glass. Zeddig's ribs creaked, but she tried not to let the pain show. "Ivan—"

"It's a deal," Zeddig said. "Save him."

"Lovely." Vogel pointed with the cigar. Ivan lifted the kid without apparent effort, and lowered him to the observation deck. At the port, cranes loaded and unloaded container ships with that same precise motion, and as little apparent effort. "Pleasure doing business with you, Zeddig. Don't worry about Josep, he'll be hale and hearty soon. Now. Get this kid out of my sight, before I stop feeling so generous."

Zeddig draped the boy's arm over her shoulder and lifted him; Gal took his other side, and most of the weight. When they reached the road, he muttered thanks, and ran off without looking at either of them.

"That went better than I expected," Gal said, "actually."

Zeddig wondered what she'd expected, and decided she didn't want to know. "Let's go share the good news."

Chapter Twenty-three

KAI VISITED DREAMSPINNER AFTER sunset. The offices looked innocuous enough from the street: a smart but unobtrusive gray building high on the slope, about a half-mile's walk downhill from the Authority tower. Small black windows faced out and down. Nothing about the place seemed even slightly extraordinary.

At least, that was Kai's first impression. But when she decided there would be no harm trying to sneak in, play the embarrassed guest routine, so sorry, didn't mean to bother you, I was just looking for the bathroom, she circled the building three times without identifying an entrance.

She parked herself in a Muerte Coffee two doors down and across the road and drank burnt espresso while watching the building. A prim Dhisthran woman in a black-and-gold robe appeared on the sidewalk in front of the Dreamspinner offices while Kai's attention had flicked away from the street, drawn by, well, no sense denying it, the barista, stretching his hands over his head, his shirt riding up to bare a belly just rounded with muscle—anyway. The woman seemed to have appeared from nowhere, carrying a briefcase. Kai forsook all baristas and baristos (did gender actually inflect that word?), and watched as if it were a religious obligation, until she saw three young men, reedy bearded thick-glasses types, one Gleblander and two tanned Iskari, all wearing ill-fitting tunics blazoned with glyphs Kai imagined were supposed to be funny if one understood their references, emerge from the building—literally. A white stucco wall bulged as if budding the young men from its substance. They walked on without breaking stride.

Craftwork security, of course. If you were the right person, the door existed; if you weren't, the door did not. The key might be anything: a talisman, an employment contract, a glyph inked on the skin. The last option was rare these days, since access credentials in tattoo form were hard to revoke, though Kai had known Craftswomen who wouldn't shrink from subjecting soon-to-be-ex-employees to a little unelective surgery. She thought about Tara Abernathy, and about her business card.

Kai did worship a goddess of creative larceny, but she'd always regarded those aspects of the litany as more symbolic. Breaking and entering were not her strong suit. You can't do this alone, Izza had told Kai in her nightmares. Let me help.

And Kai had said as much to Ley, before she vanished.

No sense wallowing. She could learn from Dreamspinner, even if she couldn't get inside.

Night fell, and office lights clicked on, clearing windows opaque by day. Kai breathed her coffee's acrid fumes. The road choked with pedestrians and commuters, men and women casting off the broad-brimmed hats and robes that hid them from the sun by day. Trolleys winched up the steep hill. Overhead, a few choked stars resisted the city's ghostlight and fire.

Dreamspinner's interior, revealed by its nighttime lighting, seemed cut from the same cloth as the priesthood offices back on Kavekana. Standing desks interspersed with the normal variety, filing cabinets, desk toys. A Talbeg man with a shaved head reviewed paperwork in one window; an Imperial woman poured herself a glass of iced coffee from a jug in an office fridge, then paced, chewing a pencil; a worker with a squid stuck to the back of his skull vacuumed on the second floor. The Talbeg man finished his paperwork, tapped his folders against the desk to make a regular stack, and left. The vacuum squid disappeared, reappeared on the third floor. The Imperial woman left her office, pencil behind one ear, and turned out the door. Two floors up and over, a Talbeg man with a shaved head entered another office, a different office, opened a folder, uncapped a pen, and reviewed paperwork; two floors up and over in the other direction, an Imperial woman poured herself a glass of iced coffee from a jug in an office fridge, then paced, chewing a pencil.

Wait a second.

Once she saw the pattern, she saw it repeating everywhere, with a few preprogrammed variations: the redhead with the freckles might do two pull-ups on a doorjamb pull-up bar, or three. The graybeard with the staff paced as he harangued his assistant, or he stood in place performing the oratorical theatrics young initiates back home described as "milking the great Sky-Cow."

Dreamspinner: an artistic Concern sponsored, almost entirely, by the Iskari Defense Ministry, so secure they didn't merely opaque their windows, they projected a fake office upon them. Good thing she hadn't followed through with the bumbling tourist routine. People with this sort of security might not be kind to poor, lost tourists.

She'd expected a tight ship, with one cofounder a fugitive and the other slightly deceased, but this wasn't the kind of security you threw together in an emergency. Dreamspinner had been built impregnable.

Gods, Ley, what did you get yourself into?

Kai rose from her counter seat, turned to go, and ran into Lieutenant Bescond.

"Oh," Kai said, and, "well," and, after suppressing a number of curses in an impressive range of languages, finished with, "I didn't expect to see you here, Lieutenant."

"I wish I could say the same, Ms. Pohala."

"Just taking in the neighborhood." Kai, focused on the Lieutenant, hadn't noticed the hooded and cloaked figure behind her. Beneath the cowl, the figure's face glistened smooth and wet where there should have been lips, or a nose. Blue eyes shone from the shadows there, also wet. Tears? No: joy. "I don't believe I've met your friend. I saw her last night, though—or her twin sister."

"My friend," Bescond said, "is an Initiate of the Mysteries of Rectification."

"How nice," generally filled space while waiting for someone to explain.

"The city, Ms. Pohala, does not care for herself. We care for her. The Rectifiers watch the world into shape, and hold the dead city at bay. It's quite straightforward, really."

"I see."

"Can I offer you an escort back to your hotel?"

Kai shouldered her purse. "It's a long walk. I wouldn't want to trouble you."

"I have a golem cart down the block."

"I prefer to walk," she said, brushing past. "I want to get to know the city." But the cloaked figure moved— flowed—slithered—it wasn't walking, whatever it was—to block the door. Kai glanced around for help. Muerte Coffee's three other inhabitants, and the staff, even the cute baristo, were doing their best impressions of walls and furniture. *Thanks, guys.*

"All the more reason to have someone who knows it show it to you." Bescond had an easy smile. "Honestly, Ms. Pohala. I understand some hesitation. We met under bad circumstances. I'm not trying to make your life difficult—though I wish you would extend me that same courtesy."

"How have I made your life difficult?" Kai placed a special emphasis on *I* and *your*.

"As I'm sure you can imagine, the last few days have produced a lot of paperwork," she said. "None of which gets done if I have to leave the office to explain things to people who should know better. Now: can I give you a lift?"

Kai decided not to argue with that. "My mother told me never to get in cars with strange women."

"I'm not strange."

"Your friend looks pretty strange to me."

Bescond laughed. "I promise: we'll drive you back to the Arms, by the most direct route, and let you out when we arrive. An Authority cruiser is the fastest, safest cab in town. On the way, you can ask me questions, and I'll give you what answers I can."

"What's in this for you?"

"Company, and the chance to make up for a bad first impression."

Agdel Lex cooled quickly after sunset. Kai shivered under her demijacket; Bescond swept off her coat and draped it over Kai's shoulders without asking. "I'm fine," Kai said, and passed the jacket back. "Really." A man in a tower sang a high warbling song. This street, with its bright offices, clear signs, and utter absence of life, had seemed stable when Kai walked it earlier that afternoon—but stable like a ship's deck in calm water. Pacing beside the Rectifier, Kai strode on bedrock. The skyline never twitched, and the writhing streets did not rewrite themselves.

The Rectifier drove; Kai and Bescond settled in the rear. Good shocks and rubber tires made the ride eerily smooth. They descended toward the bay; out on the water, the Altus Spire was a pillar of light. Bescond crossed her legs ankle-on-knee, removed her sunglasses, and polished them with her jacket lining. "I'd hoped I wouldn't find you here."

"There's no law against Muerte Coffee," Kai said, "though sometimes I think there should be."

Bescond did not quite scoff. "It's more the neighborhood that I object to. Fontaine plays her cards well. Official Friend status covers many sins, but it's been abused more than I'd care to admit as cover for espionage."

"I'm just a priestess," Kai said.

"I believe you." Bescond raised her hands, a calming gesture, though Kai didn't feel upset. Not yet. Perhaps she should. "I do. But in a city like Agdel Lex, well. The wars to the south have a religious character, and the apocalypse is always a heartbeat away. Unsanctioned priests make people nervous. And, espionage being espionage, individual officers get a lot of leeway in the interpretation of evidence."

"I asked Fontaine for investment opportunities. She pointed me here." Bescond started to interrupt, but Kai decided to roll over the Lieutenant for a change. "I know my sister founded Dreamspinner. I just want to understand the threat I face, staying here. I'd be mad to ignore what happened yesterday."

"Madness," Bescond said, "is not a word taken lightly in Agdel Lex."

"Good. I've never liked it when people called me crazy."

"I don't think you understand. Here, sanity is a security issue. Deranged perceptions, including conspiracy theories, can breach consensus reality, and let the dead city in. That's why the Rectification program exists." She touched her breastbone. "We all doubt, sometimes. We doubt ourselves, our worlds, our truths. It can happen to anyone. Even to people of faith. When we can no longer bear the work, we seek refuge in a clearer mind."

"Wrap them in squid to fix them, is that it," Kai said, then showed Bescond her teeth. "Punish them sane. I've been through worse."

"You don't understand." Bescond smiled, easy and smooth. "The Lords do not punish. They offer bliss."

They rode the rest of the way in silence, and stopped before the Arms.

"This is great," Kai said. "I keep getting rides home. Certainly helps stretch the old expense account."

"You have two options, as I see it," Bescond replied. "Help our investigation, or stay away."

"I'm not here to investigate." Kai wrenched the door open, and stepped out. "I'm here to invest. Thanks for the lift."

She didn't let herself shiver until she closed her hotel room door, but even that wasn't so bad, and besides, she had Behemoth to keep her company.

Chapter Twenty-four

LEY NEEDED TOOLS. She wrote Zeddig and Raymet and Gal shopping lists in a disguised, sharply slanting hand: lists of texts, lengths of wire, pickled organs of various exotic lizards, moonlight caught in a crystal vial on the seashore. Raymet had most of the books already, but the rest—

Zeddig glowered at a request for "cold pressed renal gland extract." "Why do you want all this stuff?"

"I," Ley replied, shifting cards on her game of solitaire, "am taking precautions. If all goes well, they'll be unnecessary." She moved the seven of spiders onto the eight of cups. "The chance of all going well, I'll leave to your own capacious imagination."

The tools accumulated over a few days. Books colonized Raymet's coffee table, beakers bubbled over gas burners, boards held insects pinned and painstakingly dissected. For all the clutter, Ley left little mess. Each time Zeddig returned, Raymet's house was slightly cleaner than she left it. Lost in thought, Ley's fingertips explored Raymet's rooms, and order spread from their touch. She paced, drank coffee, and talked to herself. At least, Zeddig thought she was talking to herself.

One night Zeddig returned with a tiny packet of night hazel, worth more per ounce than gold. "I've never heard of this stuff before. Neither had the clerk; she had to ask the old chemist they keep chained to the wall upstairs." She meant it as a joke.

"It's rare," Ley said. "There's an isle in the Ebon Sea most maps don't feature, a place people last frequented back when they still called islands isles. Women carved from rock by storm waves tend gardens of night hazel there; they sun themselves on the beach to tempt sailors, who steer their ships into the shoals and die. Their blood feeds the gardens. The women trade cuttings from their crop for memories: memories of touch, mostly, since stone doesn't feel the world like flesh. Night hazel helps with journeys to the underworld, but the supply's limited: the isle in question only exists on intercalary days."

"Are we going to the underworld?"

"Don't be silly." She snatched the envelope from Zeddig's fingers, opened the flap, and inhaled. She almost smiled, then. "Nothing like that exists, in the way you mean. Faithful leave deep impressions on their gods and subcreations; cause and effect applies, so obviously the dead linger in some form. But—layered chambers for departed souls? Souls that obviously don't go anywhere, but reenter the market? Please."

"If there's no underworld, why do you need this stuff?"

"I need it," Ley said, "because nobody remembered to tell the underworld it didn't exist. Thank you."

And she returned to her book.

Zeddig stormed out. Ley of course didn't notice.

After their rooftop chase Zeddig had felt something between them. Not love, but—openness. She'd seen Ley scared, exhilarated, happy. Her friend, her onetime lover, let the mask of control slip, and for a moment Zeddig remembered what it felt like for Ley to trust her. But that passed, and now she felt like she had at the bloody end: they were two perfect spheres trapped in mutual orbit, bound, but unable to touch.

Raymet had more practical issues with Ley's presence. "I

need my space. Did you see what she did to my library?" Raymet's place was so thick with bookcases Zeddig wasn't certain which room she meant. "All the papers off the shelves, in neat stacks on the floor, with sticky notes indicating how she'd sorted them. I had a system! And I swear she's been watering my plants."

"Your plants were looking dry," Zeddig said, diplomatically.

"Yesterday she saw me reading Cawleigh and interrupted to talk to me about the gender ratios of the people murdered in those books, and dammit, I don't care if she's being friendly, I need her out of my house for an afternoon. Just one afternoon to, I don't know, run around and pee on the furniture."

"She's a wanted woman."

"And I want her somewhere else."

Zeddig broached the subject with Ley the next morning, when she returned with the moonlight vial. "Disappointing. I expected her to last longer." Ley poured the contents of one test tube into another, and both sublimed, which the slight adjustment of Ley's eyebrows suggested had been an unexpected, but desirable, result. It hurt to be able to read her so well. "She's more tense than I remember. Has she really not made a move on Gal in all this time?"

Zeddig glanced over her shoulder in case either of them had heard. "That's not the point."

"Fortunately, I anticipated just such an emergency. Let's take a walk."

"With half the city looking for you?"

She held out one hand, meaning pause, settled the empty test tube carefully in a clamp, and sealed the tube with wax. Then she reached into her inside jacket pocket and produced a mask.

Zeddig went cold all over. "Ley, what the hells is that?"

"Zurish 'clave mask, more or less."

"You're a maskorovik?"

"Hardly. This is counterfeit."

"I thought the whole point of those was—"

"You're not *supposed* to be able to counterfeit them. But copy protection is tricky magic, and, as I believe I mentioned, I've made a close study of community formation. The maskorovim are a novel approach—really neat, setting aside the organized crime theatrics. The Zurish mask-lords' system pairs anonymity with authentication, but they haven't actually settled on a god, so far as anyone can tell. Of course, they still rely on a top-down organizational model, supplemented with occasional kneecap breaking—well, anyway, I've avoided replicating the mask's higher functions, but it should serve for a shopping trip." She stood, took the mask in both hands, applied it to her face, and swept her hands back over her hair, which brightened from black to red, lengthened, and wove itself into a plait. "How do I look?"

"I like you the other way."

"Sadly, so do the Wreckers." She shook her head to test the braid's weight. With a frown, she tugged on the elaborate weave. "Impractical, but it'll do." She glanced at her suit, which several days' wear and laboratory work, along with their rooftop chase and a considerable quantity of blood, had left in a sorry state. "Hold on." She descended into the depths of Raymet's apartment—prompting a squawk and cascade of curses from the owner when Ley opened her bedroom door.

Ley returned minutes later, unsinged by the invective, bearing a few armfuls of fabric. She shucked her jacket, and began to unbutton her shirt. Zeddig about-faced, fast. "Warning next time, maybe?"

"There's nothing here you haven't seen before."

She stared at a stain on the wallpaper roughly the shape of Southern Kath. "That's not the point."

"What is, then? I don't care, and you have an excellent memory—there's no sense standing there looking ridiculous and faking interest in Raymet's failed attempts at home maintenance. No one's harmed."

"Maybe that's what bothers me," Zeddig said, before she realized what she was saying. "Nobody's harmed. Whatever we were is so far gone you think there's no harm in my seeing you naked."

"Harm," Ley said, softly, "was never the operative word between us."

"What was?"

"Love was in the running, I thought."

"Not utility?"

"I learned from you," Ley said. "I don't deny that. That's one of the things love is. I learned from you, and you learned from me. Don't try to paint me with the seductress-who-stole-my-secrets brush. It's beneath you."

Zeddig scraped the stain with her fingernail, and the wallpaper around it came off. "You learned from me. And you left."

"We made other mistakes in between, if you'll remember. If you really want to rehash our every old half-dressed bedroom argument, you might as well turn around and remove your pants to complete the picture."

"I showed you my city, and you . . . You used it."

"I made art. Yes. That's what I do."

"And you're still doing it. That knife—"

"Agdel Lex is a special place," she said. "I understand your sentimental attachment, but if I stumbled upon some cache of perfectly preserved High Telomeri porn in a cave during a sordid kidnapping episode, I guarantee that once my tears were dried et cetera, you'd ask me to show you the cache."

"You're comparing a hypothetical with my real life. With my city." She tried to press the torn wallpaper back, but it curled up. "You made a sculpture out of me, and sold it."

"That's fair," Ley said, after a silence. "And we fought, and I left. I tried to help, and I fucked up, and you hated me for it. And you're still angry."

"You could have stayed. Listened. Apologized."

"I didn't say you were wrong to be angry. I wish things had gone a different way. They didn't. But we can work together now."

"That settles that, then," Zeddig said, sour. "Fine. Good talk."

"I'm happy to drop the issue, or talk more. But either way, there's no sense in your staring at the wall."

"I'm not going to look."

"I've changed."

Zeddig turned.

The dress was very blue, and full of light and air. It showed off her shoulders, which did not need the help. Zeddig watched the thumbprint shadow at the V of Ley's collarbone, and tried not to feel . . . anything, really. The heels were high, and changed the architecture of her legs. She looked brilliant, and deeply wrong. This wasn't her.

That was the point.

"The leggings don't fit with the dress and heels," Zeddig said, once she got her breath back.

"I haven't shaved in a week, and I'm not about to do so now just because Raymet has a hangup about having sex while I'm in the house. I'll cover with attitude." She smiled.

"You look like you want to cut someone."

"That's the idea." She extended her hand. "Let's."

Zeddig took the hint, and took her arm.

Chapter Twenty-five

KAI SUFFERED THREE DAYS of meetings before her next excursion.

The meetings went as well as could be expected. Entirely too many things were happening at once: increasing volatility in the Kathic housing market, demand for quality experiences (whatever those were), unequal access to equity resulting from a high barrier to entry on derivatives trade, shifting tastes in wine, shrinking arable land and water supply due to the demands high-energy Craftwork placed on soil, concerns about dwindling supplies of everything from alchemical silver and necromantic earths to coal and iron. "Is anything not falling apart?" she asked Fontaine after a grim meeting about water futures.

"And you wonder why I spend so much time high," Fontaine said.

"I had no idea the water table in Dresediel Lex was so low."

"And that's a comparatively rich, thaumaturgically strong area. You want depressing figures, look at Northwest Dhisthra sometime. They don't have a Deathless King, or a convenient rain god. Hells, you don't have to go that far afield—my family were small-time holy folks for a village out beyond what's now the Wastes, before the God Wars started. The Wastes suck up water and simple soulstuff for miles beyond the blast zone—even now, you can barely herd out there, let alone grow crops. So my great-great-grand-so-ons marched around the Wastes to the safe zone, and we've been here ever since."

"I knew the equity part, and the theological derivatives, but hearing them in this context—a lot of Craftspeople are getting richer than gods, the market has become so complicated nobody understands more than a shade of it, and people optimize local outcomes without concern for global consequences. We're walking a razor's edge without even considering actual bad actors—and there's no shortage of those, either."

"Yup," Fontaine said. "I mean, you wanted to hear about the big stuff."

"I did. I just didn't expect it all to be so big, or so connected."

"You know what's the problem?"

Kai cracked a smile. "The world," she said, quoting one of their more hapless presenters, "is becoming increasingly global?"

"The world," Fontaine intoned, "is becoming increasingly global."

All of which was—"fun" wasn't the right word exactly, more: instructive. But she was also killing time, buying her freedom with midnights and meetings and cups of coffee. The first day, five hooded Rectifiers followed her from rooftops, waited outside her hotel in the morning. The second day, the five reduced to three. The third day, the two reduced to one. On the fourth day, she half-decided, half-hoped she'd lulled them into a false sense of security.

She'd taken the trolley to work three days in a row, even though her strained expense account would have covered a cab. (She'd received a nightmare telegraph from Kavekana the night before, Twilling's carefully worded message boiling down to "What the fuck are you doing, come home at once." She ignored it.) In her morning commute upslope she studied the thousand villages knit together to make Agdel Lex: R'ok lived in the Iron Band; east of the Iron Band ran the Iskari Concession, east of that the port, and south of all those, upslope, the Wings, Talbeg neighborhoods whose property values rose as you climbed the cliffs, with windows that were carefully aimed to offer views of everything in the city except the Authority tower.

The Wings and the Iron Band held the best restaurants and nightlife, so at 7 P.M. on a Fifthday night, the evening commute downslope was a packed, sweaty, jovial riot, drunks calling to other, presumably acquainted, drunks over the heads of those few wage earners not yet drunk themselves. (Not all drank, of course. Certainly some wanted to go home and see their families. They just didn't talk so much, or so loud.)

Even half-squid cop monsters would have trouble tracking Kai through that booze-slicked mess.

She pulled all the tricks she ever read about in spy novels, changing trolleys at the last second, or seeming to, only to dive back onto the trolley she just left; she hailed a cab and paid it to drive to a random address while she stepped out its opposite door. She folded her jacket into her purse. She'd worn a white flower in her hair, and planted that flower in the hair of a woman about her height and build on a bar street in the Wings, as that woman cheered a bare-knuckle boxing match. The further Kai fled, the more natural she felt. She encountered fewer broad Iskari boulevards, and fewer signs. A bicycle rickshaw offered her a lift; when she gave the peddler Zeddig's address, he said, "I know a shortcut."

Shortcut didn't do his path justice. Kai had studied the city's layout in her hotel, nudging Behemoth aside when he settled on the map, and their route was impossible. The driver should have had to cross two tank-broad Iskari boulevards to reach the Hala district, but somehow he stitched together a route that crossed neither Mandate nor Regency. They wove down narrow streets past wicker tables where old women played cards. Crossed laundry lines flew underwear prayer flags. The rickshaw driver's calves surged and bulged. Kai watched planes of muscle swell, round, and stretch smooth: alchemy at work in that body, in the curve of his shoulders and his rigid arms. Kai knew big men, strong men, back home, but this was a different kind of strength, and she felt guilty for using it, yoking him. And yet, the transformations that strength worked on distance! Buildings closed out the sky overhead, and perhaps they entered a tunnel—but they emerged before the terror of confinement seized her.

"Here you are," he said, in Talbeg. "Hala's Fell."

They'd stopped in a small five-sided square with a fountain in the center, a faceless goddess, or perhaps an angel—they had those here, once. The air felt soft, and did not smell at all of salt or cinnamon. Vine-grown wicker arches crisscrossed the square, and cast patterns of shadow around fountain and angel alike. Beyond them, the sky seemed deeper than it did from her hotel window.

"Thank you," she said, which did not seem enough. "How can I find the Hala family?"

"Ask around," he answered.

She paid him, which did not seem enough either, and tipped well. If she wanted to be a good spy, she shouldn't draw attention to herself; cabbies remembered a big tipper. But he had pedaled her uphill into a dream, so she paid him what she thought his service worth, even if the expense made her head swim for a second. She rested on the fountainside, one hand in the water, until color returned to her world.

Kai wandered through Hala's Fell, feeling foolish and alone. The buildings looked indistinguishable, to her, from others in the local style: white plaster and squared roofs with small windows, functional for the climate. Decorations, where she found them, were geometric or natural—patterned flat mosaics of tiny tiles that bloomed three-dimensional forms from their walls, neon floral explosions that might have been graffiti or art. A woman in a high window sang a high song, accompanying herself on a banjo-adjacent instrument. Children joined in for the chorus. Someone cooked with preserved lemon and coriander and a hint of chile. This was a different city than the city of the Arms. Kai did not belong here.

Not that there were many Archipelagese anywhere in Agdel Lex, but downslope, in the foreigner districts, the mix of peoples reminded her of portside life back home. She hadn't seen anyone since reaching Hala's Fell who wasn't Talbeg—hadn't seen many people at all, in fact: a woman in a pencil skirt returning barefoot from work, carrying her heels over her shoulder; an old man whittling a piece of rosewood on a stoop; two kids beating a rug. They had their own lives. They were not here for her.

Of course they weren't. If Fontaine ever came to Kavekana, and sobered up enough to wander upslope from the Godsdistrikt and the foreigner enclaves, she would feel the same—people she didn't know, who spoke her language haltingly if at all, and cooked food she recognized from restaurants if that (and at best barely—most mainland Archipelagic food was sickly sweet Kova cuisine, since Kovans had a larger diaspora after the wars). Kai was a stranger here, not an enemy.

But she thought about the tower invisible behind these tall square rooftops, and the boulevards her rickshaw driver pedaled her around, beneath, or past, and the rubbery Rectifiers and the dead city, and it occurred to her that Kavekana and Agdel Lex had reason to feel differently about strangers.

Oh, hells. She could wander in circles, obsessing and second-guessing all night. But she didn't have the time.

She marched back to the man carving rosewood and asked him, in Talbeg pitched as politely as she could manage (considering that she'd practiced the language back home with a street rat and sneak thief), "Excuse me. Could you tell me how to get to the Hala house? My name is Kai"—always name yourself, Izza'd stressed, it's rude not to—"and I'm looking for Hala'Zeddig."

The man folded his knife one-handed. He was carving, she saw, a mermaid. "What do you want?"

"She—" She rifled through her mental files; old Alikand had no hang-ups about same-sex relationships, but Iskar was a department store of weird taboos, and modern Agdel Lex was an alloy of those metals and a hundred others from across the Northern Gleb. Best not risk it. "She knows my sister, and I'm looking for her."

"Of course," the man said. "My name is Hala'Saim, and I can lead, if you follow me."

She did, down the road and up an alley she had passed without recognizing it was a through street, to another road and then a cul de sac. The buildings here seemed older—the plaster more set, the wooden accents and ornaments more ornate. Lemon trees grew in the cul-de-sac's center. Saim knocked three times on a door, then twice, then three times, waited for a moment, shrugged, knocked three times again, then twice, at which point the door opened and an old white-eyed woman frowned at him: "Saim, the finest watchmakers have not yet made an instrument so sensitive as to determine the length of your patience."

"Aunt, astronomers have not yet invented a unit of measurement sufficiently vast to describe my joy at seeing you. I bring you a mermaid, and a guest."

She accepted the carving. "Your knife work leaves something to be desired." But the carving man grinned when she said that, and Kai suspected that from this woman, that counted as a compliment. "Who have you brought?"

"Ah," Kai said, surprised by the force of those clouded eyes. This woman wasn't Mako, she told herself. She probably wasn't even a god. But she had a habit of authority. "My name is Kai Pohala. I'm looking for your, I guess, daughter?"

"Pohala." The name had weight in the old woman's mouth. Above, the sky deepened to the color of a fresh plum.

"Your daughter Zeddig knows my sister, Ley."

"You may call me Aman," the old woman said. "Please come inside."

Chapter Twenty-six

LEY SWANNED INTO THE Iron Band apothecary, hips swishing, chin high, every inch a furious Zurish crime-world aristocrat. Ley was so deep into character that Zeddig, following, slipped deeper into her own, less complicated ruse: walking as if she held invisible suitcases, faking surly, glaring at the wall hangings with open contempt. (That part she didn't have to fake. They were imitation Imperial floating world prints, with an inauthentic color palette, and a pouting tits-out pose on the models she'd only ever seen in erotic art from north of the Shield Sea.)

Ley arrived at the counter like a warship arrived in a foreign port, and rapped her fingertips against the unvarnished wood. The apothecary's apprentice seemed occupied by a hallucination that involved punching flying fruit. When Ley cleared her throat, he fell back into his chair, and shook himself awake. "Anatoly sent me," Ley said, in a thick Zurish accent, each syllable lubricated with scorn. "He requires fifty grams of aged ground dragonheart. Presently."

"Ah," the apprentice said, living up to Zeddig's estimation of him. "We only, I mean, that is, ah, sorry. It's, um. We only have, er." He gaped at Ley, shook his head, staggered out from behind the counter, flipped the sign on the door to closed. "'That . . . I mean, if we had any, which, like, obviously we don't, because you're talking military grade here, we'd only have it by special arrangement, right? Like, there'd be a list, and I'd know if you were on the list, and you're, um." The next word took effort, but he managed to say it. "Not?"

"I am not on list," Ley said, "nor is Anatoly. It is not good for Anatoly to be on . . . lists. But he has made an arrangement with your master, and compensation has been settled. Is it not so?"

"Yes, I mean, no? I don't, um." His eyes darted, and Zeddig wondered if he was still suffering the fruit hallucination. "I can't help you. Anatoly, maybe he can, um, come himself? Or we could wait until my boss gets back?"

"Our schedule does not permit delay," Ley said. "And do you expect Anatoly would enter such an establishment? You deal with me, or you deal with Nadezhda." Zeddig recognized her cue to look threatening, and turned from the least biologically improbable of the wall hangings, moving as a ponderous unit, as if her shoulders and hips were a fused bulk of muscle. She gave him the look she wanted to give Ley.

"Fine," the clerk squeaked. "Fine!" He raised his hands more, and bowed his head. "Okay. Just a second." He retreated behind the counter, donned heavy rubber gloves, opened a door that hadn't existed seconds before, and withdrew a lead-lined box. Inside, nestled in packing immaterial, lay a small bottle of reddish sand. The clerk set up a balance and weights, lifted the bottle using tongs, and poured a precise amount into a velvet bag until it hung even with the weights. Sweat rolled down his forehead. "There it is," he said, quickly, when the scales evened out. "Now, I don't know what you planned to pay—"

"Not payment," Ley said. "Forgiveness of a debt. This is a start." She took the bag, and walked out of the store. Zeddig followed, flipping the closed sign to open before she left.

Two blocks down, she noticed Ley was grinning.

"You scared that kid half to death."

"He deserved it."

"They'll sack him. If he's lucky."

"Ah, he'll be fine. That store owner does have an enormous debt to Anatoly, and Anatoly does need dragonheart powder—"

"Wait a second. Anatoly's real?"

"Of course he's real, Z. If you want to conjure, you need names to conjure with."

"What happens when he comes for his powder?"

"Violence, likely. Soon enough, though, he'll discover that even though I currently resemble one of his associates—"

"You're impersonating a specific mobster. Have you lost your mind?"

"I modeled the mask on that of another 'clave, Anatoly's home country rivals who don't, so far as he knows, have a presence in the Gleb. So! Anatoly shifts his attentions homeward, life in the Zurish underworld becomes exciting, and Agdel Lex endures a brief respite. In the future, if he wants powdered dragonheart, he may seek a different channel. There's an off chance you may enter the conversation, in which case you could claim to have been earning a few thaums as hired muscle—but our drug-addled young friend will find it difficult to give a precise description."

Zeddig realized she was smiling with half her mouth. She covered that smile with a frown, and a shake of her head.

"What?"

"It's too complicated, is what. What if Anatoly's angrier than you think? What if he doesn't blame his rival?"

"He'd be stupid not to. People expect problems that fit contexts they understand. Anatoly expects his enemies, so he'll see them; he doesn't expect us. I hope they won't blame the apothecary. Even if his choice in wall hangings leaves something to be desired. Frozen yogurt? This place has great toppings."

They stopped in. Ley covered a pineapple frozen yogurt in marshmallow topping and graham crackers. Zeddig stuck with fruit and sour. After, they walked down toward the beach as yogurt melted in their paper cups.

"You have something on your mind," Zeddig said. "Tell me."

"It's not important."

"I could use some of that right now."

"My sister," Ley said, then cut herself off.

"Go ahead."

"My sister hates this stuff. She has a thing about how these stores pop up everywhere back home, three on a block. At least they used to." Ley never talked much about home, even when they were together. Zeddig was surprised by the pain she heard. "Tasty, though." The Shield Sea stretched north, pierced by the Altus Spire; the sea smelled of seaweed and fish and salt and green, but the spire, Zeddig imagined, would have no smell at all. The first time they'd walked this beach together, there had been no spire, no promise of the stars—just two women side by side, hand in hand. Their hands were occupied, now, not to mention sticky. "I can't, Z."

"I didn't ask you anything."

"You are. You want me to talk. I wish I could. But I don't want you hurt."

"You brought me into this damn thing." There wasn't any weight in the curse—the word only there to pad a rhythm, like a wave after a wave.

"You're doing a job for me. I'm paying you. When they come looking, that's all they need to know. They might not believe it at first, but they will, in the end. When they ask, tell them you hated me for leaving, tell them my voice sounded like the world's sharpest nails on the world's grittiest chalkboard, tell them I was paper cuts and lime, but you stuck with it because I paid you."

"I did hate you," Zeddig said, "for leaving. I still do, a little."

"I know," she said. "That's why I hope they'll believe you."

"You think this is important."

"Yes."

"And you're not telling me, because if we're caught—"

"I can't let them take you."

"You're not keeping me in the dark because I might try to stop you?"

"Zeddig," she said. "No. I don't—I hope you wouldn't. I don't think you would."

She sounded lonely, uncertain, more naked than Zeddig had ever known her. Zeddig wondered if she could only talk this way because she wore the mask.

"I love you," Zeddig said, meaning, fine, I'll let it drop, meaning, I don't like this but I will go with you, meaning, I hear you, meaning, for the sake of any gods you care to name let yourself break for once, let yourself crack, let yourself bleed, don't stand there so damn silent and stubborn—meaning, beneath all the rest, I love you, and knowing those words would only complicate things between them.

But some things needed complication.

"Thank you," Ley said, as the sun set.

Chapter Twenty-seven

AMAN LED KAI DOWN a dark hall past a flight of stairs, through a door that might have been invisible in the shadows, or might have sidled into existence as the old woman reached for the knob.

They emerged into a narrow courtyard. Ivy climbed high white walls, and the sun's last light glinted off a black-and-white mosaic under the green. Soft air embraced her, and the sky seemed so close Kai could have reached into the deepening purple and plucked stars free. Aman set her feet carefully on the world. She moved differently from Mako, Kai's blind friend back home—more intent, more certain, more comfortable with her degree of sight. But she recognized Kai by her voice.

"Like your sister's." The old woman sat in a wicker chair beside a glass-topped table upon which she'd spread a chess board, mid-game. "You bite words the same way. You share intonation, rhythm. Do you play chess?"

"Never well."

Aman poured tea.

Kai examined the position. "Who are you playing?"

"A person six hundred years dead." Aman took a book from the pocket of her long sweater: a battered Zurish paperback, bold strange letters Kai could pronounce but not interpret, and an improbably foreshortened chessboard. "A person lack-

ing figure, subtlety, or grace. Chess was not a game of principle, then, but of tricks and flourishes. Games change, even
if the rules do not: their place in culture, their form of play,
the language of their players. Modern chess is played by different people, in different ways, than its counterpart six centuries
past, and victory and defeat have different meanings."

"I want to find my sister," Kai said. The tea filled her with
licorice and mint and longing. "I heard she was close to
Zeddig—your granddaughter?"

"They love one another," Aman said.

Kai blinked. "I heard they broke up."

"They fought, and they stopped sleeping together, and living together. Love lasts longer than either party to that love
might want." Aman pondered the chessboard queen with her
fingertips. "You told me your real name. Thank you. But if you
tried to lie, I would have known."

"By my voice, you said."

"Not only that." The old woman let the white queen settle
on her white square. "Ley," and Kai had not expected the shock
of hearing her sister's name in Aman's mouth, "has your same
habit of knowledge. She knew what she had to know, and pursued that knowledge fiercely. Have you ever owned a *beagle*?"
She framed the word in italics, the way tourists overpro-
nounced Kavekanese words for palm liquor or dance hall.

"Only the one in the comic strips."

Aman's laugh was rich and wet. "When I was younger, I
knew a man who had a beagle, and the man and the dog were
the same kind of fool. A beagle scents a deer, and the dog must
give chase—without thought to home or safety. You come to
my house, and you ask after your sister, because that is what
you decided to ask, and you give no thought to other ques-

tions. I tell you, you are safe here. This is my house. I am Hala Archivist, and keep my treasures well. What else would you like to ask?"

"That chess book," Kai said. "How can you read it?"

"Since it is not printed in dots?" Aman flipped pages in the book without glancing down. "I do not see Agdel Lex. I barely see you. But the book belongs to my city, and so I see it. Ask me another question."

Kai crossed her legs. "We passed through a door to get here. Did the door exist before you reached for it?"

"Inhale."

She did: cedar smoke, roasting lamb, cardamom, dust, and the promise of rain.

"Is this the air of Agdel Lex you are breathing now?"

"No," she said. "It's too . . . wet."

Aman refilled her own tea. "No city is one city, as no one mind is altogether and only itself. A woman is many women, a man is many men, a city is many cities—not in sequence, but all at once. In Alikand Gerhardt broke the world, and the Iskari only saved what they knew how to see. Your forebears cut us, and we bled."

"Not my forebears. They weren't part of this."

"Your forebears of spirit," Aman said. "Gerhardt, forever dying in the center of the Wound—his Craft made you possible."

"I'm no Craftswoman," Kai said. "I'm no child of his."

Aman spread her hands. "As I said. One woman is many women."

"So we're not in Agdel Lex. But we're not in the dead city, either."

Aman's laugh now was colder, and made Kai wonder what she had seen, and where, and how deeply it scarred her. She pictured Aman, younger, stronger, staring upon the city's frozen husk. "The Hala mansion in the dead city burned and froze long ago. Our vaults, our archives—sayings of prophets, diaries of Blood-mad soldiers, scripture that came west from the Shining Empire before the Golden Horde, records of births and deaths, dreams saved for future generations, diagrams of structures we cannot build with current tools—they perished, and monsters nest among their ruins. My daughter went there once, and would have died there, paralyzed and devoured from within by wasp-brood, had not your sister saved her. No," she said, "this is not the dead city."

"Where, then?"

"We are in my garden, in a city with a name we rarely whisper—a city that threads itself around the world of iron words the Iskari forged. We are not angels anymore. We do not take on shapes of righteous truth. But we build, though the Wreckers think our building a subversion."

"Is my sister in this city, now? This place without a name?"

"That," said a new voice, "is not your business. Leave our house."

Kai stood and turned too fast to hold her balance. Her bad leg twisted under her. She leaned on the back of the chair. "Zeddig?"

The woman was strong, her dark skin darkened further with sun, and she had short thick braids and wore a sleeveless shirt and loose trousers tucked into her boots and was not in a mood to talk to Kai. She marched across the courtyard. "I am," she said, "and it's time for you to leave."

"I'm Kai," she said. "I was just here to ask questions."

"And you've asked them. Aman should have known better than to answer."

Aman sipped her tea, unconcerned. "I'll answer what others ask, or what's an archivist for?"

"I'm trying to help her," Kai said. "I'm not with the Rectifiers. I just want to know she's safe."

"I'm asking you, politely, to leave my family's house. If you don't, I will ask you less politely."

"I let her down. This is all my fault. I want to help, if I can."

Zeddig's eyes were fierce and dark and Kai wished she knew what coiled behind them.

She turned to thank Aman for the tea, but Zeddig caught her arm and tugged her from the garden down the dark hall to the front door, which she opened with such force its slam echoed in the empty street. "You want to help? Then leave."

Kai put her hand on Zeddig's wrist, and tried to push her off. The woman's grip tightened, and for a heartbeat Kai wondered if they were about to fight. Then Zeddig let go, turned her back on Kai, and placed one hand against the wall. Hard lines stood out on the blade of her shoulders beneath the fabric of her shirt. She was a monument. Kai could not read her inscription. "You know where she is."

"Get out of here."

"I want to help."

"She told me about you—working with priesthoods, flying high. You stink of Agdel Lex. You bring their dryness and sand. The Wreckers are watching you."

"I lost them."

Her laugh was not so kind as her grandmother's. "You think that. But they'll just find you again, and pry what they need from your mind. If they don't buy it outright."

"I'm not selling," Kai said. "Look, I get it. You're afraid. You put your family in danger by helping her."

Zeddig looked over her shoulder, and Kai stopped talking. A wagon rolled down the street. She smelled lamb close to burning.

Zeddig's next words, cool and level: "Who said I was helping her?"

"You don't know the trouble she's in."

"I do."

"Really?" Kai dropped her voice to a whisper. "She killed someone—stole their soul, put it in a knife. A woman, her colleague, someone important to the Iskari. The Rectifiers want her back. Did she tell you any of this?"

Zeddig's body gave the answer she tried to keep from her face.

"I can help," she said, "if you tell me what's going on."

"Stay away from us." She didn't clarify that "us." Her voice was cold, and she was large, and Kai saw what drew Ley to this woman: the commitment, the sheer force of personality, a vector around which Ley could twine. She was a wall, she was a woman. This was going all wrong. "Go, now."

"The Iskari want that soul," Kai said. "They would trade for it: her freedom, yours. Protection. Immunity. Think it over."

That was the wrong thing to say. The deal, proposed, made her a dealer. Zeddig's whole body closed. She held the door open and ushered Kai out, grim and formal. "Leave."

So she did.

Chapter Twenty-eight

ZEDDIG FOUGHT WITH AMAN in the courtyard after Kai left. Ley's sister was unknown, suspect, tied to the Iskari, to the banks, and she didn't know how far deep she was, how little control she could summon, how great was the danger. And knowing this, Aman still brought Kai into the courtyard, and told her secrets.

Aman scoffed at Zeddig's fury. Secrets? What secrets did I tell her? She learned no hidden knowledge from me. The Authority will not let us speak of certain things in public—so we speak in private. This woman wants to help her sister. She should know the dangers. And, daughter of my daughter, she was right: your helping Ley endangers us. You do what you must—but don't blame Kai Pohala for that.

Aman drank tea, and consulted her book, and moved her chess piece, and was right, so Zeddig let the conversation drop.

She slept in Raymet's house that night. Ley had set up glassware and burners in the living room, and was titrating a solution of dragonheart powder. "Isn't that dangerous?"

"Everything's dangerous in sufficient quantities, or with prolonged exposure. Life itself is invariably fatal. Though I'd advise against inhaling in the next ten seconds."

Those ten seconds, as the smoke cleared, gave Zeddig time to think. "I saw your sister today."

Ley's hand twitched as she poured the titrated solution into a test tube. A drop of burgundy liquid struck the table and started eating through the wood. "What did you tell her?"

"Nothing. She barely knows her way around the city, but she's ready to jump into the hells for you. I tried to warn her off."

Ley frowned. "Let me tell you about my sister."

"Shouldn't you deal with the acid?" The solution hissed into the table, leaving a worm-smooth hole in the rich dark wood.

"I'm getting to that." She finished pouring. "Once, because Kai said something I thought was mean, I waited for a day we didn't have school, set her alarm clock for the time we usually woke up, and changed her bedside calendar to a school day. She woke with the alarm, saw the clock and calendar, and went about her business. She woke our mother up, insisting it was a school day. She woke me up, saying I'd slept through my alarm. She marched me halfway to school before she saw the date on the newspapers." Ley took white leather gloves from her purse, donned them, and held the test tube with the dragonheart titration under the table. The spilled mixture hissed through the tabletop at last, and dripped into the tube, which she capped at once. "Kai's a freight train in human form. Once you get her on a track, she'll remake the world to fit that track. The hardest thing she's ever had to do in life is admit she's wrong."

"Reminds me of someone I know."

"You do have a stubborn streak."

Zeddig boggled. "Me?"

Ley replaced the test tube next to the other vials in her caustic rainbow. "I rarely mention it, because you work so hard resist that tendency. But determination can be a handicap."

"Have you ever looked in a mirror?"

"I try not to. Things stare back at me." Ley returned the gloves to her purse, dusted off her hands, and stood. "Well. You saw my infuriating sister, she professed her good intentions, and you decided, wisely, not to trust her. Was that all?"

"She said you stole something when you . . . left."

"I stole many things, or nothing at all, depending on what definitions of 'stole' and 'thing' you employ."

"Apparently there's one in particular they want back. A mind."

Ley grabbed a beaker that contained an amber liquid. "The Iskari Rectification Authority admits its mindlessness. Well, that's a first. Here's to honesty, however belated." She toasted with the beaker.

"Ley, don't—"

"It's whiskey," she said.

"That's a dumb place to put whiskey."

"Near to hand?" When Zeddig didn't answer at once: "The day I forget which beaker contains the poison and which whiskey, I'll deserve my fate."

"Fine," Zeddig said. "Have it your way. But I think you're taking the wrong lesson from that story."

"Oh?"

"Seems to me your sister's not a woman we want on the wrong track."

Zeddig went out for drinks with Raymet and Gal that night—Raymet radiant after an afternoon's isolation, and eager to discuss, in hushed voices in the corner of a smoke-filled room while a mustachioed kid played syrinx, the potential upside of their arrangement. "There's nothing of interest, I mean, real interest, in Altus, though I imagine we could move some high-priced equipment if we trek it out.

But Anaxmander—we only have incomplete catalog data, and just look at this stuff." Her voice got louder when she was excited. She pinned the scroll open with two beer glasses, and stabbed the list with her forefinger. "First edition. First edition. Ananke of Oreskos, only fragments survived the Occupation—this looks like extensive contemporary scholarship, on parchment, Zeddig. Parchment!" When the waitress came by with the next round, Raymet covered the scroll with her arms, and craned her neck up like a tiny small dragon to smile, too broadly to seem nonchalant, at the waitress, who smiled back.

They meandered home, Raymet leaning on Gal's shoulder; she was in such a good, or at least tipsy, mood that when they found Ley working a chess problem at the kitchen table, Raymet challenged her to drunken guillotine blitz. "Five minutes time control each, winner takes a shot and a minute off the clock." Gal cautioned—"You've drunk quite a bit already"—but Raymet waved her off, and sat down to play. She won the first four games before the first shots metabolized, lost the next four, won the last one, and spent the rest of the night protesting how fine she was through the closed bathroom door, in between vomiting sessions, while Gal fetched her water. When Zeddig and Gal helped her into bed—she hadn't removed the manacles from the bed frame—Raymet sat bolt upright, caught Gal's shoulder said, "Zzzgood," laughed, fell back, and started to snore.

Gal remained half bent over the bed; she watched Raymet sleep with the same expression Ley had when pondering her chess problem. "I should stay," she said. "You're both drunk, and Ms. Pohala's bed is far from this room. She might not hear if Raymet has trouble. I can keep vigil as easily here as anywhere." Keeping vigil was what Gal did when others would sleep.

"She'll be fine." Zeddig lurched to the door. "Raymet's been here before."

"That," Gal said, "is what worries me. She pushes herself hard—to keep pace with you, I think." Soft reproach in that voice. "I worry about her."

"You really think I'm the one she wants to keep pace with?"

Gal blinked. "I don't know what you mean."

"Come on." She breathed out. "Let's go. She'll be fine."

Zeddig escorted Gal to the street and watched her go, hands in pockets, head back, staring up into the stars that lingered behind the clouds: Gal, pale gold and alien and at full ease, as if the night held no terrors, which of course it did not, for her. Morons, Zeddig thought, as she closed the door. Both of them. Beautiful morons.

Her fingers slipped twice on the lock before she managed to close it. She leaned against the closed door and closed her eyes and leaned into the post-intoxicated fuzz she liked more than drunkenness itself, that time when colors unclenched and nobody expected much of anything. She thought about Gal, and Raymet. After everything she'd put them through, with a chain of others before, at last, with Ley, she'd long since given up any high ground. She deprived herself of the sturdy front door and proceeded through the kitchen, testing the steadiness of the wall with her right hand in case of secret passages, to the living room, to check on Ley.

Ley slept on the cracked leather couch. Hot with drink, she'd unbuttoned her shirt and tossed it onto the jacket already heaped on the chair beside the couch, and sprawled in tank top and trousers with one arm over her face and the other hugging her stomach. Little bumps stood up on her arm, and she grumbled when Zeddig passed between her and the light, but didn't wake up. Zeddig had averted her eyes that morning, but Ley asleep felt less dangerous. She looked like a person.

Zeddig took a blanket from the closet and draped it over Ley, and breathed in, not intentionally, just breathed like people breathe, but when she did she smelled her, and that hurt, so she turned away.

The knife glowed on the bedside table.

She shouldn't. Absolutely not. There were dumb ideas and dumb ideas, and this would be the latter. She'd told Ley she wouldn't pry, even if she hadn't exactly promised. Her silence at least suggested she respected Ley's judgment as to what she could say and what not, her attempt to protect Zeddig from whatever she'd gotten herself into. Whatever absurdity she'd gotten herself into. Whatever godsforsaken madness. Whatever.

And yet.

The knife glowed on the bedside table. Its blue outlines cast weird shadows from glassware.

She hadn't exactly promised. And if Ley wanted to protect Zeddig, shouldn't Zeddig want to protect Ley? There was a mutual obligation at work, an if-you-love-something-let-it-go sort of thing. Protecting Ley meant understanding what sort of trouble she was in. Was Kai right? Would the Iskari and their servants get off Ley's back, and by principle of extension off Zeddig's, if Ley returned what she'd stolen?

And yet.

The knife glowed on the bedside table. Its blue outlines cast weird shadows from glassware. A red sphere revolved at its heart.

Zeddig lifted the knife. It weighed nothing in her hand, which did not surprise her. This was not a blade. It was an idea.

"Aren't you a puzzle," the knife said.

Zeddig did not drop it. She'd expected—not this exactly, but something. The knife had no voice, but the blood inside it pulsed, and she heard a voice in her head.

"I can't read your mind, just so you know. I can't even see you—not the you you think of when you hear the word 'see.' It's dark in here, and lonely. Good for meditation. I've developed an ingenious method of prime factorization, but there's not enough space in this marginal existence to write it down. But I can see so many versions of you: a self in shards, different women for different worlds, different names. Tell me which one I should use. Speak, and I'll hear."

Zeddig retreated to the kitchen, with the knife, but didn't answer.

"Come, now. If you want to be rude—I'll bet it's Hala'Zeddig, right? Ley's ex. The delver. Naturally she'd run to you. You'd help her hide, even from the Wreckers, and she knows just how to make you dance. She'll keep you in the dark, because telling you doesn't suit her. Am I warm? Burning up, I imagine, though I doubt this form's flammable."

"I don't have to tell you my name," Zeddig said. "You haven't told me yours."

"Vane," the knife replied. "Alethea Vane. The woman you're trying to protect stabbed me, stole my life's work."

"Why?"

"I had something she wanted." When she spoke, the surface of the blood-sphere within the knife dimpled and pitted, sprouted mountains that collapsed to valleys. When she was silent, the sphere might have been a large, oddly colored pearl. "You know what that feels like, I imagine. She betrayed you for the same reason."

"You don't know anything about that," Zeddig said.

"Of course I do. She told me. We were partners, after all. I know her, inside and out. I've shaped her work and made it . . . perfect." A gross pause ensued. The wind elemental trapped in Raymet's air-conditioning system groaned behind the ducts. "She took your methods and ideas, and used them, and she took my methods and ideas, and she's using them. She has her own goals, as always. She'll step on anyone in her path to reach them. And she won't tell you what she wants, or why, because that would give you leverage over her. It's a familiar story. She says she's protecting you, but she's only protecting herself."

"Why should I listen to a pissy knife?"

"Because she's used us both," Vane said. "In her own way, and for her own reasons, and the only difference between us is, you still have a body to do something about it. You know she's using you, and you're ignoring it. Please do let me know how that works out. For me, it ended with my body on ice at the tower."

"If you know so much," Zeddig said.

"I do."

"What isn't she telling me?"

"Let's trade."

The knife felt warm in her hand. "What do you want? What *can* you want? Sharpening?"

"Tell me everything she's asked you to do for her."

"No deal."

"I can't tell you her plan if I don't have details."

Zeddig did not like the hunger in the knife's voice. The surface of the blood sharpened. "Ask something else."

"What could I want but knowledge? A bath? Bourbon? A massage, for fuck's sake?"

"We're done here."

"This is your last chance."

"I can find you again."

"I'm surprised she let you find me once, sweetie. Don't count on a repeat engagement."

"I don't need you."

"Not now," the knife said. "But soon she'll leave again, and you'll wish you'd listened. Or you'll turn your back at the wrong moment and end up in here with—"

Zeddig dropped the knife before Vane could say "me." It stuck in Raymet's kitchen table, point down beside the chess board, and quivered. She picked the knife up with a kitchen towel, and returned it to the living room. The whites of Ley's eyes showed in the gap through her slitted lids. She did not snore, but she breathed heavily.

Zeddig left her there in the glow of the blade.

Chapter Twenty-nine

KAI LED HER TAIL through a night carnival in the Wings.

Jugglers spun fire poi, acrobats balanced on chairs balanced on plates balanced on brooms balanced on rubber balls, singers performed arias from operas Kai had never heard, and people milled, drinking beer from absurdly tall glasses, eating fried squid out of paper cones. (Kai wondered if that was some sort of political protest.) Four middle-aged women cheered as the acrobat bent atop her precarious column, shifted weight, and lifted her feet from the serving tray, uncurling to a perfect handstand; the acrobat canted to one side, unsteady—and lifted one hand from the handstand, propped on her fingertips above a tilting world. Kai thought the audience might topple her with the force of their applause. Drummers drummed and people laughed and barkers barked.

And Kai was being followed.

Her shadow was a large man, square-jawed and clad in grays that might have been blues or greens. He wore a hat, and he had the kind of arms that required work or Crafty augmentation to maintain. He never looked at her directly. Whenever Kai looked back, he was always turning to some new distraction: bare skin, fire, ice cream. She rarely saw him approach her. By the time she had found him in a crowd, he'd already changed direction, or stopped. But he kept a constant distance, and never let her leave his sight.

She'd first noticed him on an empty street outside Hala's Fell. He ambled a block back, chewing gristle from a lamb skewer. She'd walked faster, and he let her draw ahead. She cut into the Wings, through a bar street with a name she didn't yet know, and thought she lost him, but there he was, in the crowd—waving, apparently, to a friend who did not wave back.

He had to have noticed her noticing him, but he made no move to close the distance, which Kai doubted meant anything good. The shadow was playing her. He planned for her to make him.

Tail, shadow, make. She knew those spy words because she'd read about people who knew how to handle this sort of thing, who clumped problems like this into jargon the way Kai sorted different gods by type. Using those words, Kai engaged in a bit of magical thinking—as if knowing the right word would make her the spy she had to be to get out of this mess.

Oh, hells. She just had to lose someone in a crowd. How hard could that be? This man might be a professional, but even professionals screwed up. So: she cut a hard left into a bar, ducked under a waiter's raised tray of drinks, pushed between too-close tables, accidentally elbowed a young man who seemed to be in mid–marriage proposal in the temple, made an apologetic face at the samite-clad singer onstage, and pushed out the serving exit into a narrow, fish-stinking, and grossly puddled back alley parallel to the carnival's main drag. So far, so good. She just had to double back, get behind her tail, then cut downslope—the tail would assume she was heading in the same direction, run to outpace her, and realize too late that she'd taken another path. She'd handled worse.

She ran (cursing her heels, which were the practical sort, but every time she ran in them she felt like some mystery play gangster's moll) past leaking garbage bins and shop doors toward the burst of color, light, incense, and (as a fire-eater exhaled) flame at the alley's mouth.

A man in silhouette stepped out to block her path.

He was too broad, too short, for her tail.

Of course, she reflected, one man could only do so much. If someone wanted to tail her so she stayed tailed, they probably wouldn't use only one man, who, in retrospect, had obviously let her see him.

Fuck.

She turned, and ran into a man behind her. Tall, with a narrow-brimmed cap. "Ma'am, you look lost." An accent more mainland Iskari than Talbeg.

"I'm not," she said.

"We can help you." The big man behind her approached. He had forearms about the size of Kai's neck, and the way he moved told her a great deal, including that he held a thin metal pipe flush against his arm, which he didn't want her to see.

Okay. Just another big night in the hard city. Hard night in the big city? Whatever. She shifted so her back was to the wall, and used the voice she'd use on a dog that kept jumping up. "No. Thank you. I'm leaving." And she sidled along the wall, thinking, this was a shit idea, and, they're awfully professional for crooks, and, don't move until the big guy shifts his weight.

Which he did, to his back foot, before he swung at her with the pipe. She sidled into the swing, caught his wrist on her arm, hit him in the throat with the blade of her hand, and ran when he staggered back, thinking, self-defense classes, worth it, stupid pilgrims who pray to idols of martial prowess, worth it, I'll send wine later. Narrow-brim snagged her purse strap; she let the purse slide off over her arm, and he stumbled. A few more feet to the alley, and—

Someone stepped into the alley mouth.

Then it all went black.

Unconsciousness, she thought at first, then realized (thanks, adrenaline) that you probably couldn't *think* when you were unconscious. This was the darkness of closed eyes in a black room and darker, darkness with texture, darkness of a lover's hand over your face, and she heard cries and curses and ran, somehow finding her footing despite the gross slick pavement and the absent light. She did not know the way, yet, running in the dark, she did not trip, did not strike a garbage bin or a wall.

She burst from the inky black into carnival firelight and noise, and kept running. People moved aside, and she ran past them into the blue-tinged night.

A woman shouted, "Hey, wait!" but she did not slow down. She ran from the carnival to the teeming Iskari boulevards, crossed the road with a pack of revelers, and stopped, breathing hard, cursing seventy-seven gods and as many hells, at a trolley stop. An old Talbeg man glanced at her and shrugged, and returned to his comic book.

"Lady," said a voice nearby, a voice she recognized—"you run fast in those heels."

She should have placed the voice back at the carnival, but she had never expected to hear it in Agdel Lex, awake. Hearing it now, as the trolley bells approached and the few stars burned overhead, she felt as if the record of her life had skipped, its needle darting to an unexpected song.

But there Izza stood, on the Regency Boulevard sidewalk,

wearing tan slacks and sandals and a loose white hooded tunic, Kai's purse over her shoulder. She looked young and happy, flush with a run that hadn't winded her nearly as much as it winded Kai. "I thought I'd save you a trip to the purse shop."

Kai wanted to hug her, and scream, and cry, but she started with: "What the hells are you doing here?"

"You need help," Izza said, and plopped beside her on the bench. "And friends don't wait for friends to ask."

Chapter Thirty

KAI SHUT HER HOTEL room door and tried and failed, again, to wrap her mind around the situation. Izza pirouetted through the hotel room, touching dresser and walls and sheets and drapes. "Kitty!" She tried to scoop up Behemoth, who hissed and launched himself from Izza's arms to the floor, to a chair, to the dresser, to the top of the squid-and-torch idol there. Izza reached for the cat again. Behemoth swiped at her. "Some place you've got here."

Kai picked up the pieces in her mind: Izza's presence, her attack in the alley, Aman, Zeddig, Ley. Okay, her plans were in shambles. Make new plans. She marched to the bathroom, poured herself a glass of water from the tap, drank the water, poured a second, drank that. Almost better. "You need to leave."

"I just got here." The cat hissed. Izza was shadow-boxing with him, sliding her hand through the clawed perimeter to tap Behemoth on the head before the cat could scratch her. She won twice for each exchange she lost. "You need my help."

"The alley situation could have gone better," Kai admitted.

"You don't even know what happened back there."

"Some thugs tried to jump me. I look like a tourist."

Izza worried her lower lip between her teeth, and stared into Behemoth's eyes. She stilled into the faraway focus she had when praying: the world might fall away piece by piece unnoticed, until at last the thing on which she'd fixed herself fell too and left Izza drifting in empty space, staring into nothing at all.

Her hand slipped out, faster than Kai could follow, and tapped Behemoth on the forehead. "Boop!" The cat snatched for Izza's hand, but lost his balance and ended up in a corkscrew sideways roll to the floor. "There was a Wrecker Lieutenant around the corner with a few of those squid boys, waiting to ride to the rescue. Suit pressed, armor spic-and-span. She'd have made an impression, saving you. I almost wanted to watch."

"You're saying it was a setup?" Kai set down the glass. Her hands were wet. Was she shaking when she poured the water? She dried herself with a towel.

The cat tried to swipe Izza, but Izza drew out of reach.

"Describe the Lieutenant," Kai said.

"Short, dark hair, square jaw, scars here and here. Iskari."

"Bescond. She was trying to warn me off the investigation."

"She wanted to give you the works. You shouldn't be out after dark, miss. Not alone. Foreigners come to bad ends in Agdel Lex if they're not careful." Izza made a pitch-perfect mockery of the Iskari accent. "They wouldn't have let their men in the alley rough you up much, but us priestesses have to watch out for one another."

"You have to leave."

"Excuse me?" Izza leaned back against the dresser, and crossed her arms. "You barely know this city. The Wreckers are after you. You keep poking around and they'll stop trying to scare you."

This was the bit where Kai was supposed to say, that doesn't sound too bad, and Izza would reply, they'll stop scaring you because they'll start hurting you. Kai didn't want to fight that battle. She didn't want to fight anything. She wasn't in this to stop the Iskari, she didn't want revolution. Her sister was in trouble. Zeddig had told her to get lost. So had Ley. Maybe she should. But when she thought about leaving, she saw a girl by the seashore as the tide rolled in, holding a city in her mind until pain broke her and she fell. "I know what you think."

Izza raised one eyebrow.

"That I don't understand the danger. I believe the Iskari won't hurt a Kavekanese priestess, I don't know how easy it would be for me to disappear in some back alley—how many people disappear in Agdel Lex every day. I know." She looked up through loose strands of hair. "I got locked in a Penitent last time I tried something like this. That won't happen again."

Behemoth had steadied himself on the idol and turned, crouched to pounce, eyeing the back of Izza's head with the same predatory expression Izza had fixed on him earlier. Kai thought about warning Izza, and decided against it.

"Fine," Izza said. "But you still need my help."

The tail twitched. "Why?"

"Your sister's gone underground with Zeddig. The Iskari know you're looking for her. Bescond could stop you—or follow you, wait until you find her, and snatch her first. You need someone on your side who isn't a known quantity. Someone who has enough cred to figure out what your sister's planning, while you use your status with the Iskari to find a way to get her out of trouble."

Behemoth's nose wrinkled. His tail stilled.

"I can't let you do that," Kai said, as Behemoth pounced.

But instead of sinking claws into Izza's skull, the cat landed on her shoulder, slithered down into her waiting arms, and curled there, purring. Izza stroked him as if she hadn't noticed the change. The cat, now uninterested, poured from her arms to the floor.

"Why?"

You're a kid, was the wrong thing to say. Izza had saved Kai from the Penitents—sort of—and lived here when she was ten. She could handle herself. "The congregation back home isn't strong enough without us yet. We can't risk you on something this . . ." It hurt more than she wanted to admit to say, "Inconsequential."

Izza walked to Kai. She, and the kids with which she'd grown, darting down Kavekanese back streets, stealing, telling tales, moved like no one else Kai knew. They walked as if the world might give way at any time—their steps that light, their bodies that tense, their eyes that open. Izza had the purpose of an arrow.

She reached for Kai's hands. Kai looked down. Unthinking, she had curled her hand towel into a rope, and started strangling the rope. Izza's fingers, callused, thin, strong, slid into the knot of Kai's grip, and Kai had to choose—her hands had to choose—between fighting Izza and letting go.

She let go.

Izza held the towel rope, and Kai held Izza's hands.

"The Lady," Izza said, slowly, still so unused to talking about goddesses and gods, "is bigger than that. Because She has to be, and so do we. If we're not, we're lost."

But we are lost, Izza. You don't know that yet. We cast about in the darkness, drowning offshore, like Dad, and we can't count on any rope, we can't count on each other, because we're all in the ocean together. You can only rescue a drowning woman from safety, and nowhere's safe. You've lived harder, but I've lived longer. I've seen people reach the end of the certainty you still have, and bend, and learn to marshal their conviction, to sacrifice some truths for the sake of others.

It would be sick to say that to a woman who had lived the life Izza lived, who fought like she fought, without the safety of the lies Kai grew up swaddled in. But Kai felt that way, and maybe she was right.

Izza stood there, waiting.

So easy to look out at the world through warped glass and think the world was warped itself. Easy, too, to live in a warped world and forget that, with effort, you could make crooked lines straight.

"Say we work together," Kai said.

One corner of Izza's mouth quirked up. "Say."

"What's next?"

"We have two groups circling each other—the Iskari, and Zeddig. We need to find our way into both. I can get us a lead on the delvers. Bescond, though—"

"I'll handle her."

Chapter Thirty-one

TOO MANY PEOPLE CAME to Vogel's meeting.

Zeddig and Raymet and Gal reached the taproom on time, and Ley, too, masked, her fake coppery hair braided in a high coil atop her head. Ley marched imperious past the rattling roulette wheel and the torn velvet craps table where drunk pierced men rolled dice and screamed at one another, and the young man passed out in a puddle of what Zeddig hoped was beer, as the tap master guided them downstairs to the pool hall where they'd arranged to meet Vogel and his hand-picked hoodlums.

When the tapmaster opened the door and thirty heads turned toward her, lizards' heads and maskorovim and steel shields of warmade men, clattering mandibles, eye patches, and, at the far end of the room, Vogel, Zeddig realized that she should have expected this sort of bullshit. "Pleasure to see you, ladies," Vogel said, one hand raised, his teeth yellow in the lamplight. "Now we're all here, let's get down to business."

"Vogel," Zeddig said. "Can we talk outside?"

The meat-mounds seated on and around the billiards tables grumbled. Knuckles cracked. It was hard to drink beer menacingly, but these guys had practice. Raymet stepped back. Gal didn't step forward. She just smiled.

"Absolutely," Vogel said. "Is the stairwell private enough?"

Ley followed, and closed the door behind herself. Zeddig

felt a moment's concern for Raymet and Gal, then remembered Gal's smile, and saved her concern for Vogel's muscle.

Vogel examined the nail of his forefinger, which was peeling away from the nail bed. "Who are you?" he asked Ley.

"The talent," Ley replied. "I thought this was supposed to be a small operation."

"Exigencies, my dear Talent," Vogel said. He pressed the loose nail against his thumb, and it peeled back. Something wriggled underneath. "So you're the one who convinced Zeddig to dirty her hands? I owe you a favor."

"I'm the one," Ley said, "who wants to make sure this job goes smoothly, and no micromanaging loan shark fucks everything up."

Vogel left his nail alone, and went still.

"Let's all calm down," Zeddig said. "Okay? Vogel, this is a larger group than we expected. That's all."

The crowd behind the closed door cheered. The cheers didn't sound violent, so Zeddig kept her attention on Vogel. "I'm sure these are nice guys. Trustworthy. But it doesn't take a traitor to fuck up a plan. We only need one talkative drunk."

"I vouch for them." Vogel raised one hand to Ley, open, palm up, at the level of her jaw. He might have tried to cup her chin, if he hadn't been worried Ley might break his hand. "As I'm sure you vouch for her."

"You brought thirty strangers into this job," Ley said, "just to start."

"It's a question of profit margin." Vogel returned his attention to the nail. Zeddig knew him just well enough to tell the difference between Vogel bored and Vogel faking boredom because he didn't want to meet your gaze. "You're only taking my people halfway, you said. So I hired Klieg's crew to guide the retrieval team."

"Klieg's a butcher." In Agdel Lex, there were delvers and then there were delvers—some born here, some came for the history, or to see traces of the God Wars firsthand. Some, like Klieg, came for the souls they could earn selling history on the black market.

"Precisely why I wanted you on this job, dear Zeddig. But I need someone to escort my cargo home. And, as long as I'm hiring Klieg *and* you, we can bring even more personnel and equipment. Which will, in turn, allow us to recover more cargo than I'd otherwise dare. You called the dance. I'm just figuring out how to play the tune." Boots stomped in fierce, excited rhythm behind the closed door. "Do we understand each other?"

"The Iskari will notice a job this big," Ley said.

"Certainly. They've baked their fingers into oh so many pies." He peeled off the nail, dropped it to the floor, and crushed it with his heel. Zeddig didn't let herself feel nauseous. "But I mentioned greasing palms before: the added cargo will more than cover the added protection money. Don't worry. Everything will come out fine." There was a question in his face, if not his voice, as he looked first at Ley, then Zeddig. The boot-stomp rhythm behind them quickened. Men screamed: numbers, bets, a name. Someone enormous roared, and there was a loud crack, and cheers, and the sort of whimper a mountain might have.

"Fine," Zeddig said. Ley said nothing.

"Excellent. Now, if that's all!"

Back in the billiards room, the crowd had gathered in a U around a small table near the far wall. They broke, unevenly, as

Zeddig approached, big men and living weapons alike chuck-
ling or dismayed. Raymet moved among them, grinning, collecting coins in her hat. Gal sat at the table across from an
enormous armor-plated man with cat slit eyes, who wept lava
tears. Gal's hands glowed, faint but noticeable in the dim
room, as she smoothed the armor-plated man's ulna back into
place, melding his snapped bone. She'd rolled up her sleeves,
and looked radiant with triumph.

"Would you care to try for best two out of three?" she asked.

• • •

"We can't trust him," Ley said, later, in a bar, over whiskey
Raymet had bought with the proceeds from her turn as bookie
for Gal's arm wrestling match. "He will betray us. We have to
be ready."

"If you have any ideas," Raymet said, around a chicken
wing, "go ahead."

Gal did not exactly hide her skepticism as she raised her
shot of whiskey, but when she drank, her eyes popped open.
She sagged back into her chair with a distant, glazed
expression.

Raymet grinned. "Good, right?"

"Raymet, is this some sort of solvent?"

"A drop of water opens up the taste a little."

"He's not unknowable," Zeddig said. "He has ideas and
goals. He just plays his cards close to his chest. That doesn't
sound like anyone I know."

Ley smiled a cheerful fuck-you sort of smile.

"We cut and run," Zeddig said, "once he has the cargo."

"He has your marker."

"Let me worry about that."

"We're all in this together." Ley slammed back the whiskey, ignoring Raymet's wince. "I'll handle it."

"You don't know this guy."

"And he doesn't know me. So he won't know what to expect," Ley said. "Now. Cigars?"

Chapter Thirty-two

AFTER THREE DAYS IN Agdel Lex, Kai was not surprised when Tara's address proved more vague than the word "address" might suggest. The cab driver dropped them off on a sidewalk before sunrise, but his directions wrinkled even Izza's forehead. He buzzed his tongue to his horse and drove away as soon as Kai paid him, before she had time to ask for another pass, slower this time, with compassion for foreigners whose grasp of the language fell short of colloquial. She raised her hand to call him back, but Izza caught her wrist. "I know where we're going." Izza's determined expression did not reassure—she knew where she was doing, what need for determination?—and marched into the alley.

The sun wasn't yet up, but the district lived. Kids hung laundry from lines. Dough hissed and eggs scrambled in the frying pans of sidewalk chefs. Men and women dressed for business downtown, wearing Iskari cuffs and dark gray suits, they poured themselves earthenware mugs of thick sweet milky tea and leaned against walls near food carts waiting for their breakfast to clear the pan. Kai followed Izza through the streets. Izza turned, glowered, turned again, doubled back. At last, she shrugged. "Can I borrow a few thaums?" Kai passed them to her; she walked up to a coffee seller, and returned with a small cup of dark bitter coffee and directions. "See? No problem."

Kai memorized turns: a left and a right, followed by a slight right down that side street that looked like a dead end, followed by a hairpin-tight turn, but she suspected that if she retraced her steps she'd find herself somewhere else entirely. Izza's stops for directions seemed to matter more than the cross streets. So Kai recorded the path that way instead: straight on past the coffee, right at a flaky butter pastry sweetened with honey and sesame seeds, left at a thin pancake folded around a fried cracker and eggs and sprigs of something almost vegetable. "Is it like you remember?"

"Mostly," Izza said, and "too much."

"You seem at home."

"I speak the language," she said around bites of pancake. "But this isn't home. It never was. And I left."

"Because of Gavreaux Junction?"

"That. And—look. The people who grew up here, who've been here hundreds of years, all these folk—" She waved vaguely at the kids in the upstairs windows, at the women and men shuffling downhill toward the boulevards. "They keep their secrets, because they have to. They live with that big red Iskari dick on the horizon, so they close up. All these handshakes, the streets with names that change, the shifting map, they're walls. On the one hand, keeps the Wreckers out. On the other hand, when half the Gleb's at war, and people run from that and end up here, they don't know the handshakes. They're stuck in the Iskari city, which has no place for them, because as far as the Iskari are concerned, refugees bring the war along. The locals and the squids carry on their cold war, and there's little room left for us."

"Charity?"

"A few groups help out. Not enough, though, and the Iskari

run most of those, so it's hard to get help if you don't want a squid in your head." She shook her head. "It's crime or the streets, and when the Iskari make it a crime to sleep on the streets, it's easy to prove people like me are menaces to society." She finished the pancake and licked her fingers. "Good food here, though."

"Gods." Kai made herself walk with the weight of that.

"There were charities," she said, almost embarrassed. "The temple was one of the less shit, because our people founded it—priests from down south mostly, last faithful of dying gods and goddesses. They ran a soup kitchen by the docks, healing those as needed. I broke my leg in a riot when I was ten, and I made it up here in the middle of the night, with a stick for a crutch. If not for them, I'd still have a limp." She wadded the wax paper that had held the pancake, and tossed it into a trash bin. "Should be around this next corner. You'll like the place. It's not posh like you're used to, they gave away all the grace they could spare, but they made it comfy. Kept it up. Tended gardens. Nice wall hangings, good wood, good leather. Beats me why Abernathy's staying with them. Maybe some sort of show of good faith from Alt Coulumb."

Then they rounded the corner and found the ruin.

They'd been climbing the ridge for a while. Roads cut back and forth to disguise the slope, while houses grew narrower and streets wider. The Temple took up an entire block, squat, whitewashed, glass broken and narrow windows boarded up. Vines loving hands once tended now curtained the wall and widened cracks in plaster that bared abandoned rooms to scourging wind and rain. The front gate leaned, off its hinges, against the arch.

"Looks nice," Kai said, then realized that was cruel.

Izza didn't have words.

Kai waited in the sunlight. When she thought Izza was ready, she took her arm and, feeling no resistance, led her through.

They passed beneath the monochrome mosaic tiles that covered the arch, and emerged in a courtyard that once was beautiful. Vines strangled columns. Weeds choked flower beds. There had been—was still—a fountain in the courtyard's center, a woman, seated, hands cupped above her head. Kai had seen this kind of fountain before: built not to vomit water, but to slick the statue glistening and transform stone to nobler substance. There was no water now, only soft green.

Tara Abernathy knelt in a plot of weeded earth, planting. She wore leather gloves, thick denim trousers, a sleeveless shirt, and a thin coating of sweat. The scars of her Craftwork glyphs barely showed. She worked, unhurried, seeds in one hand, spade in the other, folding each into the earth.

Kai hesitated. She did not want to interrupt. She recognized the way Abernathy moved, in the looseness of her shoulders. Whether the woman realized it or not, she was close to peace.

Abernathy sat back on her calves, wiped sweat from her eyes, and reached for a bottle of water wedged into the dirt. When she saw Kai, her movement hitched. She stood, leaving the water, and dusted off her hands. "Ms. Pohala. Good to see you. Sorry for my . . ." She gestured down. Kai saw nothing to apologize for.

"I didn't see you as the gardening type," she said.

"I'm not. I hated it growing up, whenever Ma made me help. We had so many fights about weeding and planting, planting and weeding. Have you ever gardened?"

"No."

Abernathy removed her gloves from the fingertips, like a surgeon. "Start with a prepared plot, and you're golden. Start with grass, like we did, and you're in for a heavy summer, weeding and more weeding, and more weeding after. Soil's wild. It does not care what you want. This is in between, a once-tended plot gone to seed. The owners are putting me up; the least I can do is help them recover. I hated this so much when I was a kid, but now it's almost restful."

"Almost" sold the feeling short, Kai could tell, but then, there was probably only so much Abernathy could admit she liked weeding. "This place has owners?"

"It did," Abernathy said. "Ran into credit trouble a couple years back. We're helping get them on their feet. I didn't expect to put in this much elbow grease, but I should spend more time in the gym anyway. Now. Why are you here?"

Kai glanced to her side, to introduce Izza—but the girl was gone. Of course. Sapphire laughter rolled from deep pools in the caverns of her mind. Izza had brought her this far. The rest was up to Kai. "I don't want to know your secrets. I don't care about Bescond's project. I want to keep my sister safe." And keep an eye on you. Until I come up with a better idea.

"I can work with that." Abernathy extended her hand.

Kai, uncertain, shook. Abernathy's hands were strong, and her fingers and thumb callused smooth where they would grip a knife.

Chapter Thirty-three

IZZA WANDERED THE WRECKAGE of the Temple of All Gods.

She had disappeared to let Kai talk with Abernathy in private, and to preserve her anonymity—the less she had to do with the squids and their allies the better. But the ruined temple raised questions. Yes, the world's glories passed, as the opera said, even such shabby glories as the Temple of All Gods once possessed. But this was too much passing, too fast. So she slid away, stepped softly, and trusted the Lady to guide her feet.

The stairs beside the front door bore her weight. Dust and mold had claimed the second level, the walkway that ringed the courtyard. Izza crept along the balcony, crouched low in case Abernathy should look up, or Kai. She haunted the temple like a proper ghost.

She hadn't told Kai the whole story.

After Gavreaux Junction, ten years old and stinking of burnt meat, Izza had forced herself, limping on improvised crutch, crawling sometimes, up these alleys, past blind shuttered windows, to this courtyard, under a sky city lights boiled free of stars. Cots lined the temple's garden rows. Burnt men and women screamed. The crutch broke a block away; she remembered falling, the white of bone through her shin, remembered a calm face and a healing touch.

The Blue Lady's little church—she still felt weird when she used that word—was growing now, on Kavekana. Street kids told Lady stories to other kids. They came to Izza sometimes, asking which story was right and which wrong, and she, scared by what saying "wrong" would make her, guided the stories that did not fit her goddess into ones that did. She made new rituals and upheld the old. Two years had passed since they last mourned a god. They rescued kids from Penitents. Someday it would end, of course, in fire, or a knife across her throat, or with Craftsmen's demon chariots in the sky. She didn't have any illusions about what the world did to people who tried what she was trying. But she might as well build with passion, and enjoy the building while it lasted. What other choice did she have? Shivering in some godsforsaken corner until the world tore itself to shreds anyway? Because doom came. It found you wherever you ran. She knew that as well as anyone.

In the back of her mind she had always hoped that before the fall, before the world ended in fire, she might come back here to the temple, thank its priests, and apologize.

Hard to thank rotted sheets and walls purpling with fungus.

But as she worked around to the courtyard, the building's condition improved. Someone had swept this wing, polished this bannister. This was more work than Abernathy could do alone and Craftless in the early morning hours before she sidled off to whatever Iskari office she was hot-desking—and she had used little Craft here. Sorcery would have killed the garden.

Izza smelled incense, and crept faster.

In those hungry painful nights, there had been a room atop the stairs in the rear of the courtyard, private to the priests for prayer and whatever little shines they kept for their gods. Half-starved and desperate, Izza had dreamed of that room: tapestries in cloth of gold and silver, candelabras everywhere, lush velvet furniture, statues of gods carved in ivory and dragon-bone and lapis. Wealth she longed to steal.

Be honest with yourself, Izza: wealth you tried to steal.

The night after old Hasim healed her leg, she woke from fever dreams around three in the morning. She lay between a stand of squash and a bed of improbably large sunflowers, next to an enormous man who groaned in his sleep and tossed against the gentle bonds that held him down, opening new cracks in the salve-slathered ruin of his skin. She'd tiptoed through the maze of wounded, testing the strength of her re-grown leg, marveling at the speed with which her traitor memory papered over the pants-pissing pain of bone splinters worming back through muscle to their proper place, of muscles reweaving and skin becoming skin again. How strange that, after just a few hours, she could revisit those memories without vomiting.

Still she could not trust her healed leg, so she had leaned against the wall to climb to the second floor, and limped to where they kept the treasures.

It didn't look fancy from outside: just a door no one could enter without a god or goddess at their back. But Izza knew how to steal by then, even from churches. She had learned her tricks against the Iskari, and tried them that night. The door wouldn't open.

She believed—she tried to believe—in something, the way she'd believed in the pain of her leg. It didn't matter what. That was the trick of lockpicking: you let the lock teach you. You became what it needed, whatever would get you inside, so you could grab what you needed In turn and run, farther than any-one ever ran before.

On that choked smoky night the lock unlocked at last, and

young Izza felt a stab of streetwise triumph—only to fall forward into the robe of the tall man who'd opened the door. She looked up, and up, and saw Doctor Hasim: the same thin face that had soothed her in the screaming depths of healing. Hasim, confused. Disappointed.

She fled, on the new leg he'd given her.

Now, older, a priestess in her own right, she approached the door. The balcony was clean. Someone had swept the stair. Here the sandalwood smell was strongest.

She set a hand to the door, and called on the Lady. Something cool and strong slid from her into the wood, and the door opened.

The room within did not glitter.

She saw no cloth of gold, no statues, no scriptures illuminated in ink of crushed jewels, no sign anything so rich ever occupied this dark spare space. She had conjured the temple's treasures from dark corners of her own mind. She saw a low table, two men seated, a bowl in the table's center, water in the bowl, and flame dancing on the surface of the water. The man facing her was enormous and tawny and muscled, hair short, beard dark; when she opened the door his eyes opened too, and she almost fled. But before she could, and before the big man could move, the other raised one hand, and said, "Umar," and the big man steadied.

She recognized that voice. She recognized the man now standing, slowly, with the table's aid and consideration for his knees, though he'd grown older in seven years than seemed possible. There was gray in his beard, which he wore short now. "Come in," he said. "We are not what once we were, but we offer what shelter we can. I am Doctor Hasim. This is Umar. What are you called?" The eyes at least had not changed: dark and keen and kind. He did not remember her. "Would you like to pray with us?"

She held herself on the step. Was that memory she'd carried with her all these years real, or a fever dream? How did you apologize to someone who did not know your fault? "I don't share your gods."

"No one does," Hasim replied, softly. "Such is our calling. But you are welcome nonetheless."

Chapter Thirty-four

KAI AND ABERNATHY RODE the peristaltic lift to the fortieth floor of the Rectification Authority tower. From within, the lift looked like any machine: metal doors, walls that did their best impression of anything that wasn't a coffin, illuminated numbers ticking up. Simple, boring, normal. The muscular contractions that replaced cables, winches, and engines were so smooth Kai almost forgot she was being swallowed into the sky.

Abernathy stood beside her, calm, cool, collected, perfect image of a Craftswoman. The Tara Abernathy of the temple courtyard seemed impossible now—how human she had looked in undershirt and gardening gloves with sweat on her skin in the morning light, how made of blood and meat. Kai knew better than anyone that armor and office bound as they empowered: Penitents back home, Blacksuits in Abernathy's own city, the Wreckers here, and of course the old Camlaander Knights, ecstatic in their servitude. Magic helped make people inhuman, but a shower and a change of clothes could have the same effect. Dressed like this, Abernathy was a being of edge and purpose. All that was soft, she hid.

"You told me you could save Ley," Kai had said in the courtyard, in the morning, projecting earnestness and desperation. She was saleswoman enough for that. "How?"

Abernathy responded at once. Kai felt almost guilty for

leading the woman like this, but then, she hadn't yet lied. "Bescond's not interested in compromise," Tara said. "She's out for blood. But if we get Vane back, I can talk Bescond down."

"You're sure."

"She'll listen to me. Bescond's bosses value their relationship with Alt Coulumb—which gives me leverage. Get me Vane, and your sister goes free. There's only one hitch."

"Just one?" Hitches seemed to grow by threes in this city.

"Bescond thinks you're dangerous now. Before we move any further, you have to eat crow."

"I never liked that expression," Kai said. "Crows have long memories."

"So does Bescond."

The lift's convulsive rhythm stopped, and with a chirp—not a golemetric recording or a phonograph, but an actual bird chirp produced by vocal cords somewhere—the doors rolled back to reveal a hall that reminded Kai of the hall down which she'd been marched the night of the not-quite-murder, a hall of white rooms whose doors did not exist when closed.

The tower's flesh and blood and bowels spoke to Kai's in a tongue of dread, of vibrations too large and deep to be heard. She walked inside a living being. She felt the change in the air, the change in space, the weight of body heat masked by air conditioning. The softness of Hala's Fell back streets was gone. The Iskari city was hard and smooth as an eggshell.

Less brittle, though, she hoped.

Abernathy opened a door around which the wall blushed violet.

The room beyond had dropped all pretense of normality. The pill-like calcium shell was gone, leaving a pocket of pale rubbery flesh, a floor firm as a tensed thigh. Kai smelled salt and inhuman blood. A man hung from the far wall, limbs wrapped in octopoid arms, mouth and neck covered with a creature like a slick gray hand. His one visible eye darted to Kai, away, around the room, chasing phantoms. He breathed high in his chest, and fast as a mouse.

Bescond paced in front of him, crooked finger on her chin, considering. She hadn't looked up when the door opened, but she turned when Abernathy said, "Evangeline."

Bescond started and turned to them, as if there were no man panting and shaking on the wall. "Tara. And—" She smiled with what Kai hoped were the usual number of teeth. "A guest! Ms. Pohala, I confess I didn't expect to see you here under your own power." Kai did her best to ignore the implications. "What changed your mind? Are you under compulsion? Not, of course, that you could tell me if you were."

The man moaned. Kai would have felt more comfortable if she had been certain that was a moan of pain. "I want to cooperate. I just had to think things through first."

"Good," she said. "Good. One of my patrols reported that a woman fitting your description was almost mugged in the Wings last night. I hoped it wasn't you. This is a grotesque city, in places. The Iskari sectors are wholesome—we guard our people. But the warrens, the back streets, well. People come from struggles down south, rebels and disaffected mercenaries and the poor, and while we do our best to enter them on the city rolls, we rarely know who they are, what they want, how to control them. So they make mischief, and some fall into the dead city, which weakens our hold on reality further, brings us all closer to chaos. The fear of freezing terrifies those who remain—and they will to do anything to appease the unscrupulous souls who shelter them. I love my city, but anything can happen in its alleys. I'm glad to see you safe."

"Yes," Kai said. "I wouldn't want to end up chained to a wall and tortured, or anything."

The corner of Abernathy's mouth twitched up—though she covered well and instantly. Kai might have to work with Bescond, but she would do it on her terms. She knew the Lieutenant's type. She ran into them often enough back home.

Bescond let the room's heart pulse twice before she made herself laugh. "Ms. Pohala! This must look so odd, given your cultural baggage—I investigated your Penitents, of course, and if you don't mind a foreigner's confusion: couldn't you have found a better way?"

To Kai's surprise, the first three replies her brain supplied were all nativist defenses: the Penitents worked, they were effective deterrents, island nations don't have enough people or space to stick human beings in cages until they get better, and the Penitents, for all their horror, have a near-perfect rehabilitation record. Her stomach would not let any of those answers escape her mouth. Gods and demons. Her own old teacher had stuck her inside one of those fucking things. She'd felt it break her, she had heard the crystal voices whisper in her ears, she shook and wept and bled and ground in its grip, and some nights she woke in terror thinking everything since the rock snapped shut was just a dream and she still stood on the seashore, on the verge of her final surrender. But she'd grown up with stories of the Penitents' virtue, and, caught unawares, her reflex answer was a Kavekana schoolkid's catechism.

The Penitents had warped her, in her way, before she was ever stuck inside.

"We should have found a better way," she said, honestly.

"What you see here," Bescond said, "is entirely consensual."

The man thrashed against the tentacles that held him. His arms strained. A vein in his pale forehead pulsed. His nails dragged troughs in the room's flesh, but the room did not seem to mind.

"Really."

"Pain," Bescond said, "and compulsion, don't work. Not for long. That's, and you'll excuse me, Ms. Abernathy, the problem with the Craft—you don't care for the long game. Your Deathless Kings profess immortality, but their oldest member is barely a century and a half; we have yet to see how that experiment will turn out."

"Seems to be going strong so far," Tara said, "but don't let that interrupt your monologue."

Bescond smiled to Tara, then to Kai. "She's right, you know. I'm theory trash—I think about all this nonsense far too much. Pain works on individuals, but as the foundation of a society? Please. Break one woman and her children will grow up hating you. And no God or King or army, no sorcery, no wall however thick, is proof against a generation of children who grow up hating. You may defeat them, kill or cow them, but the hatred will only grow. Far better to offer joy: elevate behavior you prefer, celebrate actions and service that leads to the results you desire. Gretancourt," she approached the man on the wall and placed a gentle hand on his chest, "is a Sergeant in Rectification, of excellent record and high standing. Union with God is affirmation, pleasure, glory. It supports us in an uncertain world—especially uncertain in this uncertain city. I see you're skeptical. Fine. Let me show you." She peeled the gray hand back from Gretancourt's mouth.

Kai heard him whisper: "don't stop don't stop not yet put it back put it back put it back"

Bescond replaced the creature, and Gretancourt thrashed once more against his bonds. Bescond wiped her hand with a handkerchief. "I'm sorry for the digression. I am glad you've seen this. I didn't realize the depth of your misapprehension. No wonder you felt anxious for your sister's safety! I'm so glad that's cleared up, so we can work together. Let's compare notes."

"Yes," Kai said. "Let's." She didn't throw up until later.

Chapter Thirty-five

IZZA HIT THE STREET.

She stole an orange from a fruit stand, by reflex and for old time's sake, skinned it with a thumbnail twist, and prayed to her Lady as she climbed a drainpipe to the rooftops. The pipe creaked under her weight. That was new. She'd grown since she met Kai, grown more since she left Agdel Lex.

Or else someone had shrunk the city.

Keep it simple. She crouched on the rooftop edge to scan the writhing alleys and geometric boulevards. Note how streets shifted, where they didn't. Once you learned to tell apart the desert blue Iskari thought should sky the city from the deeper, wetter indigo over old Alikand, you could read the skyline like sailors read wind from ripples on a sea. And by shadows on that the surface, you could tell where sharks gathered.

There were forty Wreckers on patrol, thickest in Hala's Fell and around the Junction. In the old days they didn't need so many.

Izza burned the orange peel on the rooftop, and prayed to the Lady, breathing thick bitter smoke.

Mission: simple. Reclaim the city. Make it dance. You're both in danger now.

Dockside gambling rats had warned her doubling down was bad for business. You doubled down because you thought your lucky number due, because you drank too much, because you wanted to impress that monte dealer who knew his patter and had that slight shy smile the good ones know how to look like they can't quite hide. You doubled down when you had no choice.

So why had Izza leaned on her customs converts to sneak her on a fast ship to a city where she'd sworn never to return?

Kai, was the one-word answer. The priestess was brave enough to fight for her sister, smart enough to get into trouble, and strong enough to break herself trying to get free. Losing Kai, the Blue Lady would lose Her link to the Kavekanese priesthood. And, losing Kai, Izza would lose a friend. She'd once thought she didn't need friends—and few friendships started with one party holding a knife to the other's throat. With faithful coming to her constantly for advice, for blessing, it didn't seem right that she should feel lonely. But then, even the Lady's oldest faithful back home—how weird was that, to call Kavekana "home"—the kids she'd grown up alongside and fought to keep safe, watched her with awe and expectation.

Kai didn't.

So she crossed rooftops down into the city.

She knew Agdel Lex once, like a tick knew the dog it fed on. She crawled through its hair, bit its flesh, wriggled, sucked. As a refugee fresh from the Gleb, emerging from a smuggler's container after days' sweaty stinking ride through the Wastes with no light save the ghostlamps the kids pitched in to kindle, after days spent learning songs sung by kids from other villages that no longer existed either, after coughing up dust and crying in her sleep, she collapsed on the beach in Agdel Lex.

She looked upon the jeweled skyline, the spreading streets,

more people than she had ever thought to see, and gasped. Izza had snuck into a palace.

And, like any palace, this one was trapped. Wreckers wanted to catch you, and cops, and the men with nets (visible and in-, Craftwork and mundane) who dropped the kids too slow to run in the High Sisters' care. You crept, you learned the way, and you learned the people. You found out where to get small jobs and who to ask for help. The locals had their Alikand, the city whose name they'd never speak, the secret architecture that kept them safe. Izza found hers.

Now she sought it again.

But cities changed over time.

She combed East Ridge first. The old roulette cafes must have closed years ago. That kid lingering on the corner had the marks of a dreamdust dealer's spotter, but she wasn't looking for dreamdust. She wanted delvers. She wanted the big time.

She rode a trolley downslope to the Iron Shore and found the old warehouse district choked with artists and people who wanted to look like artists; she wandered the docks, but cops kept streets here cleaner than in her day.

Come noon she felt down, and lost. Seven years was a long time to leave a place. Good crooks kept moving. The landscape, hell, even the slang must have changed by now.

She ate chicken and preserved lemon and pickled veggies in a pita on the boardwalk overlooking the port. Off-duty construction workers, shirtless, drank stiff tea from ceramic thermoses. One spread his arms on the bench back and let his head loll, and moaned about his hangover. Two Iskari tourists passing arm in arm glared at the man; the one in the dark dress guided her partner away, and the one in the white dress hid her smile behind her hand. The construction worker's arms lay behind the two men who sat to his either side. Kavekanese would read that as a forward, courting gesture, playful; in Iskar, it was one step from an ownership claim. In Agdel Lex, not so much.

More tourists lingered on the boardwalk than Izza remembered, and fewer street kids: one boy tried to sell flowers to the Iskari women, while two more sat kicking their legs over the boardwalk's edge, bouquets abandoned by their side. The boy selling had a half-moon scar on his cheek. Izza's hand rose to her own cheek, where the scar would have been. He must have jumped too slow to dodge the men with nets.

That brought her up short.

Of course the men with nets still existed. Of course kids still sold flowers on the boardwalk to pay down laughably enormous debt. The city changed—buildings changed, streets changed, languages changed—but people adapted, and endured. She just had to find them.

She finished her pita, tossed the wax paper wrapping into the trash, and walked toward the stairs.

The boy with the flowers blocked her path. His eyes were big and wet and needy, and that need ran deeper than the sale. The scar on his cheek drank sunlight. He offered her a flower.

Izza produced a flat disk of blue stone from thin air, but actually from her sleeve. There was a hole at one end; she'd drilled it special, with a stolen augur, telling herself stories to pass time as she worked.

The kid stiffened, as if he recognized the token, which made no sense. Izza'd handed out the first one on Kavekana, a year ago and an ocean away. But he took the disk anyway, from that grabby reflex Izza still couldn't shake, the skepticism of the prey animal: doubt gifts first, then clutch them fast in case they're taken back.

As the kid grabbed the token, Izza looked into him with eyes of faith. There was a hook in his heart, a loan of soulstuff at interest no bank would dare offer, taken from an old orphan master to pay for flowers and clothes and gruel—debt that would grow and grow. He might always be two months' good luck from paying it off, but two months' good luck never came at once. Need was the trap and debt its teeth.

She let the Lady pass into him and slide the hook free. He staggered, half-kneeling, and cursed in Talbeg with a high clear voice and an eastern accent. "What was that?"

On his face, she saw that old edge of awe.

"I didn't do anything," she said. "She did." Gods, but she missed speaking Talbeg. Kathic, and even Kavekanese, you had to signify the capital letter with your accent. Talbeg had a proper, what did you call it, case, for gods.

"What's the catch?"

"No catch."

He looked down at the flowers, and up at her.

"I do have questions, though. Names. Friends I haven't seen in years. I don't want to get anyone in any trouble." When he stepped back, wary: "Kid, do I look like a cop?"

He shook his head.

"I haven't been here in a while. I'm just looking for old friends."

He hadn't left, yet. She had been that young—still hardening, still learning to survive, sussing who was kind and who would hit you if you crossed them, or for no reason at all. She would have left. But that awe lingered behind his eyes, in his back; he did not know whether to throw himself at her or run away or kneel. The Lady's touch had that effect. Izza hated it.

"I'll say some names. Tell me if you know them."

No answer.

"Fatine Dubreque? Used to dance at the Netted Maid?" Nothing. "Slapback Dietrich?" Nothing. "Zhang Three-eyes?"

"He's dead."

That hit her in the stomach. "No shit."

"They say he killed a Wrecker and fell through into the dead city and then he died but I didn't see it myself but Ahn says . . ." The kid stopped himself from talking.

Zhang had been a hard old bastard, a first-story man, a bonebreaker. She would have bet on him against the world, every time. But then, she knew as well as anyone that people who fought didn't always last. It hurt to imagine him going out—even in a blaze of glory, with a Wrecker's blood on his hands. Her other absent friends she could imagine escaped, gone on to better lives. But so few got out. That was why she left. That was one of many reasons why she left.

It all hurt.

"Ous Hana?"

This time when the kid shook his head, she could not lie to herself—saw Hana bleeding out in a back alley, alone, reaching for the friends who might have stood by her side, who might have stopped the blow before it came—Hana, too kind to be that sharp, too sharp to be that kind.

This was a bad idea. She should never have come. But she'd risk one more name, the hardest to speak. "Isaak Bonventure?"

The kid's eyes widened in shock. He'd given up almost as much hope as she. "He plays chess?"

"Yes." Relief felt almost as good as the Lady's hand. "He plays chess. Do you know where?"

The kid gave her directions, and she thanked him, and rose

to go, but he still blocked her path. "I can't take this." Holding out the blue stone. "This is special."

"You keep it," she said. "If you have extra, send Her a share of what you steal. Help people out of jams when you can. She'll be there when you need Her."

She hoped, as she walked away, she hadn't traded his old hook for a new one.

Even with the distraction of the kid and the flowers, she made it across town in half an hour. The bus schedules hadn't changed, and the public transit stink symphony called her straight back to childhood. People sweat and smelled on Kavekana, of course, but new spices changed the savor. The bus dropped her off in the Bite, and she climbed three blocks to a dusty park where old men played chess on public tables.

The tables were full, but only half hosted games, the other half featuring a more-or-less usual assortment of Agdel Lex urbanites on lunch hour. A fragrant bum slept on one, head down, drooling into his folded arms. At another, a gaunt woman in gray university robes read a book of poetry, its title rendered in calligraphy Izza couldn't read. Two overmuscled gents and a woman who looked to have been made from those thigh-thick ropes dockhands used to tie off fishing boats traded pull-up sets on multicolored parallel bars. A couple drank tea far from the snoring bum; the woman wore a red gold ring, pledged but available for flings, and the man wore no ring at all, and Izza wondered if they were courting or friends.

Her first sweep disappointed her. No one fit her memory, and she shoved her hands in her pockets and cursed herself for thinking anything would be so easy. People changed. Maybe the kid was wrong. Maybe he lied. Yes, Isaak used to come here to learn from hustlers and work the crowd, yes, he loved chess, made his own set out of rocks and chalk and challenged Izza to game after fucking game, no, he never shut up about checks and mates, sure he'd once, during a break-in uptown, solved a chess problem left out on the house board, but—

Her gaze shifted to an enormous figure seated across from a dreadlocked graybeard.

People changed.

The Isaak she'd known lacked armor plating, had hair, wasn't nearly so massive. But that croc-toothed monster resting his lantern jaw on clawed fingers thick as a good cigar—subtract the back-alley hedge witch mods and the bandage on his right forearm, not to mention seventy pounds of muscle, add a close-cropped frizz of black hair, replace the armor with dark shining skin . . .

He still worked his jaw the same way as he thought.

And the glasses were the same: tortoiseshell frames fixed across the nose with gray tape. He'd replaced the left earpiece with a metal rod. The armor plates had widened his nose, but the glasses still slid down as he thought. He knuckled them into position, another motion that hadn't changed. He worked his sharp teeth across his upper lip, and then, with the same urchin swiftness the boy used to grab Izza's disk, he pushed his rook deep into enemy territory. The graybeard cursed, knocked over his king, passed a silver coin across the table, and retired in disgust.

Izza sat across the table while he reset the board. "Twenty thaums a game," he said, not looking.

"Been a while," Izza replied. "You offer a beginner discount, Isaak?"

"I'll go as low as ten," he said, then glanced over the glasses rims. The whites of his eyes were black now, but the irises the same soft brown, almost gold. "Do I know you?"

"I won our second game," she said. "I lost the first bad, then hustled you up to twenty thaums back when we didn't have twice that much between us, and I caught you in the fool's mate with the queen. Which leaves our record at one to a hundred or so, I think—"

She meant to play it cool, but when he said, "Izza," she grinned, and he was around the board faster than she'd thought possible, catching her in a hug, lifting her against the hard plate in which he'd clad himself—then setting her down as fast, apologizing: "Gods and blood, I can't—Izza. I'm sorry, I mean, I didn't, I—" and she beamed. "I thought—I mean, you jumped ship. You left."

"And you stayed."

"I, uh." He gripped his arms, claws scraping over armor, and stared at her open-mouthed, which expression, given the double rows of teeth, required some imagination to interpret as the gormless surprise she would have read on an unmodified face. "Wasn't anywhere else to go."

She knew how that felt.

He sat, quickly, not looking at her, and gestured across the table to the seat. "Game?"

She opened with pawns to the center and he responded likewise, unconsciously.

"I, gods, tell me everything. Why did you come back?"

"Looking for work," she said. "The islands were a good place for a kid, but I outgrew them."

"Yeah, for sure, I mean, you hear things. Those statues. Shit."

"And you?"

"Oh, man, you know. I just." She developed her pieces; he developed his better. "It's the usual. Heavy lifting and living light between jobs." Was how they put it when she was a kid here: heavy lifting meant muscle, a guy you'd bring in to bend bars that needed bending, smash gates that needed smashing, and scare guards that needed scaring. "You grew up."

"It happens." She traded a bishop for a knight, then remembered that was a dumb idea. "You don't look like the kid I used to know, either."

"Well, one thing leads to another. I got too big for second-story work. Man's got to eat, and everyone's got mods these days, lots of competition—from the Iskari Legion headed south, laid-off mercs headed north, people with serious Craft. And, man, just between us there's no rush like taking a mod. Hurts to all hells when they go in, but afterward, hoo." His smile would have been boyish if not for the blades inside it. "I mean, I definitely went too far. But I'm okay now. Mate on board."

She blinked. "Bullshit."

"Two rooks against pawns. Another game?"

She knocked over the king, taking his word for it. "I am looking for a game," which had its own meaning in the language of their respective not-quite-childhoods. Gods—weird as she found Isaak's remade body, this felt good, to chatter in Talbeg with a friend as if nothing had changed. She felt almost home. She could pretend she'd never been burned and broken, pretend she'd never snuck away, pretend they'd spent seven years playing chess here at lunch and embroiling themselves deeper in an underworld that hadn't yet killed them both. It hurt—the good kind of hurt. "Any leads?"

He reset his pieces. "If you came two weeks ago, I'd have said no chance. It's been a, you know, fallow period. But there's something big brewing. Cost me a broken arm, my own fault."

He gestured to the bandage. "It's fine, woman who did it fixed me nice and straight, but still, a shock, you know! These bones are stress-rated. Anyway, sounds like good game. Risky, but huge upside. If you're interested I'll see if we have room for one more on the crew. You're not quite muscle, I mean, you know what I mean, but I trust you."

"Thanks," she said, and tried something with the bishop's pawn. "Who's involved?"

"Some sort of joint venture. You remember Vogel?"

"That asshole?"

"But he's got the backing. It's a joint venture, anyway, with this serious delver crew, all chicks, I mean, girls, ladies."

"Women, Isaak."

"Women." Knights developed. "Vogel's a risk, known for fuckery, but word on the street is you can trust Zeddig's crew."

"Zeddig?" She didn't let on that she recognized the name.

"Started delving after you left. Takes her time, but delivers. Lady wills, we'll muddle through."

Izza's fingers froze on a bishop. "What did you just say?"

"Lady wills," he said, and looked at her blankly. "You never heard that before? I thought this was an island thing. You must have run into it. Blue Lady shelter us who live in shadows? Guide us free of traps and mazes?" Izza's heart split, rose and sank at once. She chilled in the noon sun, and thanked her Goddess, ironically under the circumstances, that Isaak remained as oblivious as ever. Even so, she almost lost it when he reached for his belt pouch and fished out a blue stone disk. "I never was much for gods. But she's, I mean. You should hear the stories. It's people like us, you know, running, chasing, getting caught, getting free. Rabbit stories, spider stories. I traded for this with a deckhand I know—she says she got it from the Prophet herself."

He looked at her, and she felt pinned. Two rooks to pawns.

Lady. That the stories could have spread so far, so fast—that she should have come here before herself—that all she had to do was tell the truth, open her heart and call on her faith, and her friend would look at her and see a Prophet.

Izza felt sick.

And, thank all gods, not just the one she served, Isaak misread that, too. The disk vanished back into his pouch, and he raised both hands, spread. "Sorry, sorry, I bet that sounds weird. I just get excited. We'll talk religion later. It's so good to see you! I'll chat with the crew, see what we can do, where are you staying? And, um. It's your move?"

So it was. Mute, she pushed a pawn.

Chapter Thirty-six

SHE'S USED US BOTH, the blade told Zeddig, to get what she wants. And you still have a body to do something about it.

Zeddig didn't want to remember those words. She wanted to remember Ley on the Iron Shore, speaking more openly with her mask than she could bear without it. She wanted to remember running over rooftops; she wanted to remember further back, all the way to the beginning.

They had met through grad school friends, before Zeddig cut ties to the Iskari academy. Ley dazzled: quick with a comeback and a laugh, full of undergrad stories about sneaking into Iskari royal balls, dodging guards and breaking hearts and diving out princesses' bedroom windows to escape their fathers.

Zeddig saw at once the root motive for all that dazzle: kaleidoscope beads tossed between mirrors to dazzle and distract. She understood. She guarded herself, too, in different ways, with silence, gym time, books, study. Zeddig and Ley moved through the world wrapped in spiked armor, like Knights in old etchings, Zeddig's thicker and sharper and more forbidding, Ley's so seamless and glossy even light glanced off. So, when Zeddig found Ley alone one night after a party, on a university balcony overlooking the step-roofed jewel garden city, she suggested they play a game.

"What game would that be?"

"Honesty."

Which worked, for a while. They removed their armor piece by piece and handed each other their most vicious knives and stood naked, all gooseflesh with fear, testing game theory kink: they could only survive so long as neither would flinch, and gouge.

Now they had grown too dangerous to one another naked. And Ley could only speak behind a mask.

She's used us both, the blade said.

But Zeddig ignored all that. They had work to do.

Ley wouldn't share her plan to steal back Zeddig's blood. The morning after their chat, Zeddig woke on her pallet in Raymet's office, mouth fuzzy with cigar aftermath, to find Ley seated on the desk, sweaty from exercise, wearing a headband: "I need a detailed list of Vogel's vices." Zeddig groaned, and tossed a pillow, but gave her what she wanted.

The next day, Ley vanished. Zeddig spent the afternoon searching for her, dragging Raymet to the Iron Shore and the Wings and Bite and to every asshole fence's den Ley'd ever expressed interest in, without luck. And when they came back, they found Gal applying an ice pack and a healing touch to the swollen, bruised side of Ley's face. Ley herself stank of blood and sex. "I went," she said, "to the Pits."

"You're fucking kidding me."

"Well," Ley said, "I wasn't kidding you. I wasn't fucking, either, though there was a lot of that nearby. I had to check your list. There are some arts to which the four of us, alas, aren't privy."

"Privy," Zeddig said, "is the word. You look like shit."

Ley grinned through bloody teeth.

That night, when they still weren't speaking—or at least Zeddig wasn't speaking to Ley, but watching her, bent at the kitchen table over vials of reagents: "Does he sleep?"

"Vogel? He's mentioned sleeping."

"Did he mention when?"

"Mornings, I think. He doesn't like sunlight."

"It hurts him?"

"He just doesn't like it."

"Mmm."

"Please don't do that again," Zeddig said. "Disappear, I mean."

She ate a bite of a peanut butter sandwich.

"I was worried about you."

"I had everything under control." The swelling had gone down, and the bruise faded under Gal's touch, but a faint purple lace of ruptured capillaries still colored her cheek. "You always were nervous. Come here." And Zeddig did, was the damnedest thing. Ley did not command—if she had, Zeddig would have slugged her. Ley just assumed Zeddig would do what she asked, and she did.

Without looking up from her work, Ley raised her hand to cup Zeddig's cheek, and Zeddig could not tame the thrill that ran through her, the infuriating rush of skin on skin. The next second lasted longer than a second. Then she felt a sharp pain in her cheek, and pulled back, clapping one hand to the cut. "Fuck!"

Between her first and second finger Ley held a slip of glass, its edge wet with Zeddig's blood. "Perfect. All I need."

"What the rotting hell—"

Ley frowned the glass soft, pinched it. It folded, as if molten, around the blood drop.

Pain faded fast, but anger put down roots. "Don't we want to reduce the amount of my blood in circulation?"

"I need to be sure I have the right vial. Who knows how many other marks he's cornered? I'll destroy it when I'm done." She turned back to her work without saying the implicit: trust me.

After the house was dark and still, Zeddig crept upstairs to the living room, but Ley slept wrapped around the handle of the knife with the blood, with Vane, at its center.

Soon, the crew assembled to walk through checkpoints and loadouts and timing. It was the summer solstice, Monster's Day in Iskar, and children and drunk students filled the streets wearing fanged masks and rot makeup and Craftwork sets of false extra arms: the demonic hosts of deep space and their grotesque auxiliaries, rising to beat back the legions of light. The crew fit right in.

Zeddig stood at the rear of the room by Ley's side, and while Vogel explained rendezvous, insertion, recovery, she memorized the faces present. More women this time around, which reassured her slightly. The hulking armor-plated guy whose arm Gal broke had brought a friend, a lean sharp young woman with tight braids. The job's scale seemed impossible: two delver crews, thirty people. (She'd avoided acknowledging Klieg, because fuck that guy. They might be working together, but she didn't have to like it.) In a crowd this large, someone would be on the Wreckers' pay, or drunk enough to mention the scheme to someone who was. But maybe Vogel had blood or dirt on everyone. At least the crowd clapped at appropriate moments, and listened, and when the meeting ended, they streamed out to the Wings to drink together.

Zeddig and Gal and Raymet, by custom and discomfort, started to head home. Zeddig searched the crowd for Ley, only for Ley's hand to settle on her shoulder from behind. Ley's voice, darkened by the mask, said, "I'm going out. Don't wait up."

She, reached out to catch her, but Ley's arm slid from her grip, and she was gone, red hair into the thrum of the crowd. She started to follow, but Gal stopped her. "I think she wants to be alone."

"You call that alone?" Ley flowed out with the rest of the crooks, laughing, talking too fast, saying nothing.

"Yes."

Klieg shouldered past her on the stairs. "Looking glum, Hala. Couldn't hold on to your date?"

She showed him her middle finger, and he laughed, and vanished into the city.

She's used us both.

She waited for Ley in the kitchen, thinking about the knife, turning an empty glass on the table and watching the use it made of light. When she woke, there was a cushion beneath her cheek on the table, a drool-stain on the cushion, and Ley, still wearing her mask and that high-slit dress, absurd heels kicked off onto the carpet floor, lay asleep on the couch, holding her blade.

Chapter Thirty-seven

"**TELL ME ABOUT THE** two things," Kai said when the precise man settled into his chair across the table. Fontaine, leaning against the wall, tried to hide her grin with the back of her fist.

"Excuse me?"

If Kai tried to paint an aggregate portrait of all the nightmare artists she'd met in the last week, she'd have settled, after faffing about with pigments, on a hairy, twitchy individual of generally male persuasion, flannel-clad, uncomfortable in a bank conference room, phrases and gestures polished but brittle: the social skills of folk who navigated conversations by maps drawn far in advance.

The painting would look very little like Eberhardt Jax.

He was older, for one thing, and darker, and he looked good in a suit. He wore his hair short, a simple, expensive cut, jet black. He laced his fingers in his lap, and when he raised one eyebrow, his skin did not wrinkle. His features flowed to accommodate. "I'm not sure I understand the question." His accent sounded vaguely Schwarzwald, polished smooth, matte and deep as the shoes he wore. "The two things?"

"Everyone I've seen so far," she said, "started with a two-things pitch. Two things are happening at once. More people are eating hazelnuts than ever before, and more people are eating chocolate than ever before, so we've founded ChocoNut to combine hazelnuts and chocolate."

Jax laughed. "I haven't heard that one in a while."

"You have no idea what you're missing."

"I do," he said—so smoothly that, even though he had just contradicted her, she didn't feel contradicted. "These fashions pass every few months, in and out, easy as a knife between the ribs." He mimed with his hand flattened into a blade, lazy and slow, and when he drew the blade-hand out, he inspected his glistening nails as if for blood drawn from the air. "Especially among people who believe themselves ignorant of, or insulated from, fashion. Imagine: five years ago, every job posting for a designer requested a 'design ghultha.'"

Kai blinked. "What do sacred assassins have to do with design?"

Jax opened his arms like an orchestra conductor. "I stopped asking a long time ago. The answer tends to be, 'like, it's cool, man.'" He did a good imitation of a Kathic college kid stoned. The accent disappeared entirely. She liked this guy and hated him at once. "At any rate, I know I'm making a hash of this meeting. I haven't been on the market for funding recently. I'm generally sitting in your seat."

Fontaine giggled this time, though she tried to cover it with a cough afterward.

Was this a practical joke? Jax carried himself like a player, and now Kai was paying attention, she could tell his suit cost more than anyone should ever pay for a suit. Who had Fontaine booked her with?

"It seems," Kai said, suppressing her scramble, "you have me at a disadvantage."

"Not really." Jax, graceful or vicious, let her off the hook. "This isn't how I planned our conversation to go, for which my thanks. Novelty is pleasure. It's been a while. Would you mind if I did pitch you?"

Kai sipped tea, and invited him to start with her free hand.

"Two things are not happening at once," Jax said. "There is only one thing happening. The planet is about to die."

She set her teacup down.

"It's true. The Kavekanese know this as much as anyone. Three record-shattering hurricanes in as many years. Erosion at an all-time high. The God Wars—speaking of knives between the ribs, right? Of course, we could both sing the Craftsman's justification from memory: modern Craft made our world better than ever before in history. Two hundred years ago, ninety-nine percent of people lived in conditions we would view as abject squalor. They suffered and died without knowing why. Do you want mass famines, blood sacrifice, dead children? Craftsmen love children as a rhetorical device. Think of the kids! 'Any god or goddess who allows the suffering of a single child is a goddess or god to whom I'll never bow' is a typical line." He might have been listing the menu for a dinner he'd disliked.

"You don't approve."

"Please." He waved the question of his approval away. "As if the modern system doesn't make children suffer. Yet suffering has decreased, on the whole. This is a better world by most metrics than the one into which our great-grandparents were born. I'd be the last man to reject the advances the last two centuries of pain have brought. I have two children, and I love them dearly. And when I almost died giving birth to my second son, I was glad to have modern doctors with anesthetic to hand. So. Despite culture warriors in the Southern Gleb, bleeding hearts in the Two Serpents Group, various academics suggesting we need a more 'natural' relationship with the world, untainted by modernity —I'm skeptical."

"Huh." The room twisted and inverted around Kai—not the physical space, but the model of the room, and of Jax, she'd built in her mind.

Jax seemed to notice, and frowned. "I understand that during initiation Kavekanese priests and priestesses rebuild themselves around their soul, which allows the smooth and complete correction of many . . . bookkeeping errors. Not all of us have such access, and medical Craft has certain path-dependent limitations: physical transformations of any sort are trivial if you don't mind dying in the process. I happen to enjoy my independence—not to mention my heartbeat. I'm happy to share a moment later, but can we focus on business for now?"

"Of course," Kai said. She did not look at Eberhardt Jax in the brief pause as he lifted his briefcase to the table and spun the wheel locks on its latch. That much she could offer, even in this room, even chained and buttressed by their roles of venture-priest and pitchman. The pool let her rewrite herself from the inside out, but she still felt a stab of anxiety meeting mainlanders who knew: do they see me, or are they looking for something inside me that isn't there at all? Jax must have felt the same. Worse. But they weren't meeting to discuss that.

"There are borderline sustainable models of Craftwork," Jax said, "dependent on starlight and meditation, but despite all the clouds that cover the so-called free cities, we need more power than that methodology allows. We consume necromantic earths and ancient oils. We tax reality to the breaking point, then develop new Craft to tax it further. Vast engines of desire draw ever more value from the physical substrate—which is not, as some envision, a pool to be drained and replenished, but a complex, subtle, interlocking system we attack as if with an ice cream scoop. Soon the system will break. Oceans will burst the walls of the shore. Bond markets will collapse, bankrupting continents, causing a rolling liquidity crisis, tearing souls from the population en masse. The outbreaks we've seen so far, in Dresediel Lex and Alt Coulumb, will seem cute compared to what comes. As I said: the world is dying."

"I thought pitches were supposed to end on an up note," Kai said.

"We're getting there." Jax popped open the briefcase and withdrew a single crystal. It lay flat on his palm. When he blew on its surface, light kindled within, and when he raised his hand, the crystal flew like a wind-caught feather to land in the center of the table. The light built, and built, blinding—and then the crystal shattered.

Kai covered her face by reflex, but no shards pierced her skin. She lowered her arm.

Microscopic crystal lenses hung in space above the table, catching light, reflecting, refracting. At their core, a line of coherent brilliance speared toward the ceiling—only to be caught, shattered, and bent back down by a tiny mirror. Lines of light built a hovering sculpture in midair. A geometric pillar reared over geometric waves and sunk beneath them, anchored to the sea floor. Kai had seen it before, on the horizon.

She did not realize she'd said "Altus" until the name had passed her lips.

"Means high," Eberhardt Jax translated, "or deep, in Old Telomeri. For obvious reasons. It's anchored below the sea floor: we had to drill down far enough to tap the heat of the planet's heart, and to extend our launch tube. Which required inventing new drilling technology and Craft, which we subsequently sublicensed. I made my first fortunes perfecting the nightmare telegraph system your firm, apologies, priesthood, employs today. But this work will save the world."

"You want to leave." Again, the meeting inverted. "Out into the dark." Kai could not picture the blackness so much as feel it: depth beyond depth, like the pool of the gods at the heart of Kavekana'ai. Even the ocean had a floor, but not the sky. There was no end: just falling, forever. Myth after myth told of the dangers of heaven. Monsters waited there, watching, hungry, their webs spun between the stars.

"It's not so dark as all that. And I don't want to leave yet—I want leaving to be an option. At first I want us to reach out and drag some stars home. Mine rare minerals and elements from rocks in the sky. Drink power from the sun. We've fought our little wars on this little world for so long we've used up most of the resources with which we might have saved ourselves. So we need more."

"We'll waste those, too."

"I doubt it. As a species, we are neither infinitely arrogant, nor infinitely blind. We are, however, the children of the children of the children and so forth of dumb apes who spent most of their days worried about avoiding tigers. We'll see the danger eventually. I just want to ensure that, when the danger becomes so obvious even our poor cognitive equipment can grasp it, we still have options. I've invested my own capital in Altus; our primary clients, at the moment, are divine, but we'll expand our services to private Concerns in the future. Our society is largely market-driven, so we will create a market for the technology we need to survive what's coming."

"And you want me to invest."

The image hovered between them, slow revolving geometries of the future.

"No," Jax said.

"I don't understand."

"Your recent interviews have given you a reputation; Fontaine cast a wide net, and fish talk about nets. Most people on your side of the game want a quick payout. You've met ten candidates, so far, who could give you the return you want, in a rapid time frame. You've turned each one aside, because you're looking for something more."

Kai turned from the glitter. Jax stood, clutching the back of his chair, Altus reflected in his eyes. "So you came to show me something I want, but I can't have?"

"I came," he said, "because in ten years I'll be the savior of the world, and the world will pay me for the privilege. I'll have more soulstuff than most major religions. I'm a wealthy man now, but then I'll be, functionally, a God. And I'll want an investment manager. Most priests lack the right perspective. I came to encourage you, and ensure you knew the stakes. I came to tell you not to settle. Because I may need your services."

"Do I pass the test?"

Jax snapped his fingers. The crystal tower collapsed to its gleaming seed, and flew back to his open palm. "You're looking in the right way, Ms. Pohala. Even if you are not looking in the right place."

Chapter Thirty-eight

THE TRAIN JOB STARTED LATE—or early, depending on how you read the clock.

Izza would have said *early*. She woke before Isaak most days, in the room they shared in Westridge that, no matter how clean, still stank from the garbage bins in the alley out back. She prayed with her pin and bowl and blood, her words piercing Kai's dreams as the needle pierced her finger. She kept their conversation short: saw Zeddig tonight with her crew, a Camlaander and a Talbeg woman, and a maskorovik with red hair, about the right height, though the features are wrong. But, of course, that's what the mask is for.

Ley's not a maskorovik, the reply came, sluggish with sleep and grumpy.

She might have joined. She might be faking it.

How? The masks can't be faked.

You said she was a genius.

Kai's exhaustion rolled through the link, and the length of her rolled too, turning against high-thread-count cotton. The Blue Lady bound their minds, faith like a sheet between bare bodies. *Can't you call at a normal hour?*

No, and, after a pause of biting lip, my host and I have religious differences.

She did not elaborate on the nature of those differences.

So, on the morning of the job, when Isaak woke her in the

gross undigested hours before dawn, she groaned, and rolled on the bed he'd abandoned to her on the first night. He claimed not to mind the floor, though there was hardly enough floor in the tiny, barely legal efficiency for Isaak to stretch his bulk: the bed, a couch, a kitchen counter, gas burner, stack of books in one corner, that was the space. Across the street, a family of four shared a room slightly larger. Isaak took up most of the floor lying down. "Izza. The runner just came. It's time."

She rolled up on the bed, slid her feet into sandals, laced them, grabbed her shirt from the wall hook. "Thought we'd have warning," she said, garbled and sleep-furred, but Isaak understood.

"The less warning the less chance someone turns us in." He turned his back as she dressed, as if either of them had ever had the luxury of nakedness taboos. She hooked her shirt closed, swung her arms through easy circles to loosen the bands of muscle across her back, tied her braids back with a thick cord, raised her hood, and turned.

He knelt beside a shallow dish of water, in the center of which floated his thin blue stone.

"Pray with me?"

And this was why she'd woken early each day, for all the hangovers and headaches and exhaustion after days of trailing Isaak on his city rounds. Once a kid who'd pledged himself to no gods at all, who'd fled those motherfuckers across sand that cut like knives, who'd lived horrors he never described to her, just like she never described hers to him, he'd become too devout for her comfort. And devout, somehow, in the service of the Blue Lady, whose only response to Izza's angry wordless inquiries on the subject had been a poker player's smile. Stories spread, yes, and yes the Lady would grow, as Izza preached

Her and taught Her and passed Her along, but this was farther, and faster, than she'd thought possible.

Isaak seemed so content when he prayed. He loved the words, loved his version of the ritual—floating the stone! A perfect symbol of the miracle of theft, of unearned salvation. The stone disk, a nerdy, Kai-ish part of her explained in schoolteachers' drone, had a kind of metonymic significance: the stone was Kavekana, the Lady's birthplace, a rock in the water with a hole bored through. Whatever Isaak's theology, he loved the Lady with the simple faith of a man who spent most of his days beating people up for money. And she still hadn't told him.

When he looked at her, she saw the puppy in the attack dog's face. They'd been kids together, or whatever you were when you were eight and bleeding, smeared with filth in a rail depot in some fucking Camlaander Peace Station where Knights gathered in quest of something that wasn't Empire but sure as all hells wasn't Peace, in a place you barely knew to call the Northern Gleb in the middle of something newspapers were careful not to call a war, clutching a person your age who seemed nearly as fucked as you. That wasn't being a kid, not the way the mainlander birthday cards meant, and after you'd been that you could never be a kid again really, not a birthday card kid. But you were something else, and whatever that was, she and Isaak were that together, after they survived the journey to Agdel Lex. They kept each other company in this broken city, before she left and he stayed. Now, together, they wound time back past the kneecaps he'd learned to break and the lives she'd learned to save and steal.

He wanted to share this Goddess with her, who'd given his life a shred of meaning, this Goddess who happened to be

Izza's. But if he learned she was the Prophet he sought, well, so much for happy memories of not-childhood. The kids on Kavekana never looked at her the same since she took up the mantle. She didn't want to lose this last look, too.

"I thought we were in a hurry," Izza said. "We can pray together later, maybe?"

"You said the same thing yesterday."

"I meant it yesterday. But we have to go, don't we? Half an hour?"

"I'll just be a moment." He bowed his head. "Shelter me, guide my steps, help me help myself." Her words. They weren't great, and she'd given thought to writing others, but for Isaak, they served. The blue stone burned. Izza felt, as much as saw, the Lady pass into him. The sheet of Her pressed against Izza's own mind, only rather than Kai on the other side, she felt Something much larger—the Being she'd sheltered in its infancy, grown great. *Give him what he wants,* She said. *Show him who you really are. What would be the harm?*

Izza kept Her quiet.

He plucked the stone from the water, threaded it around his neck, then grabbed a hooded jacket. "Let's go."

In the dark, running north through Agdel Lex, under balconies where old women slept quilt-wrapped in the midnight cool, through this shrunken dream of the place she'd known a long time gone, they might have been not-quite-kids again. He ran, but she outpaced him, vaulting over trash cans and park benches and drowsing drunks. They used back roads, Isaak correcting her path—"they closed that way," or "the watchtower burned down"—crossing boulevards only when they had to, and then slowly, hands in pockets, heads down, adopting the shuffling tired gait of drunks or late shift workers who didn't much like the homes toward which they stumbled—until they reached the warehouse by the stinking pier. The side door stood open as promised, and they sidled down the unlit hall behind. The Lady added a shine to Izza's eyes, and the dark bloomed with form. Isaak only stumbled once, and they emerged into a stockroom packed with shipping containers, silent and enormous as standing stones.

Two containers near the warehouse's main gate stood open, crews crouched within, grumbling, rubbing their hands. Ivan, Vogel's three-hundred-pound maskorovik errand boy, counted the passengers in each. How he managed to count that high without taking off his shoes, Izza did not know. "You," he said, pointing to Isaak, "in there, and you," to Izza, "there."

"We're together," Isaak said.

"Does it look like I care?"

Isaak folded down his hood. The maskorovik was almost Isaak's height, and broader, but Isaak's eyes were not human anymore. The scales down his neck bristled like a cat's hair. To Izza, in the half light, they looked very sharp. Isaak did a thing like smiling that wasn't. He had many teeth. He made a sound like a purr, deep in his throat: content with coming violence.

"Fine," Ivan said, faking boredom. "Anything else I can do for you? Glass of orange juice? Hand job?"

"Which one's Zeddig's?" Izza asked, long as he was offering.

"You don't want to go with her."

"She seems more dependable."

"Your funeral, kid." Ivan hooked a thumb toward the lead container. His gaze hadn't left Isaak's teeth. "Go on. Some of us got more work to do tonight than sitting in a godsdamn box."

He closed them in before he left, and snapped a padlock shut outside. The container smelled of salt and earth and unwashed flesh, stale tobacco and staler weed. Bodies moved against one another. Someone grumbled. Someone else swore. Someone, later, snored.

Thanks to the Lady, Izza could see, despite the absence of light—the gathered thieves' souls spun in tight self-feeding spirals, Craftwork tools hung at their belts, and small gods drifted between them. But the rest was darkness, and the still air within the container walls. Her heart raced. She sweat. She had not been inside a box like this for years. The memory squeezed her mind.

Light eased the dark. Isaak sat across from her, cross-legged. The stone on his chest shed a pale calm glow to blunt the panic.

"It's not hard to pray," he said. "And it helps me. I won't ask again, if you don't want me to."

He wouldn't, was the killer. He'd stopper this new thing he loved inside, and never mention it again, rather than annoy her.

"Okay." She palmed her needle. "I'll try anything once."

"The Lady," he said, as quiet has he could make his voice, "is the sharpest and fastest of the many gods. She's quick-step and hiding, She slides and evades. And always, behind, comes Smiling Jack with his bag that inside's all teeth."

She listened, and prayed, *Don't get any ideas.*

The vast silence beyond wondered what Izza might mean by such an outrageous accusation.

As Isaak taught Izza her own story, Izza stuck her thumb on the pin, and prayed: *It's time.*

Chapter Thirty-nine

KAI SOUGHT TARA ABERNATHY in nightmares. She'd grown accustomed to the practice since her first chaotic attempts, and knew how to follow the terror down. These days different fears claimed her—she seldom dreamed the cocoon dream, chained to a bed and guarded, cared for, kept from all that might shatter or break. She dreamed, instead, of puppets: she knelt naked onstage before an invisible audience, and worked a marionette kneeling also naked and also, of course, onstage, working a smaller marionette, and so on down, and each marionette looked like her, same haircut, same scars. Only of course the marionette wires were not tied to the puppets' limbs, but hooked through, piercing skin she thought at first was fake, but the puppets bled when she moved them. She tried to let the puppets go, but their guide wires hooked through her fingers and palm. And she tried to rise and flee, only to feel, in her wrists and arms and legs, the bite of still greater wires tying her to something bigger, higher, and as she turned up to look, she saw the other marionettes turn too, seeking her, and through her seeking something too enormous to comprehend, a Her so much larger than Kai that when she tried to understand it the wires that held her up and made her strong all broke.

And she fell.

There followed a tumbling broken interval of pain, Kai's self held by an enormous hand, her body broken. Somewhere in that scream she found a door, and, though she could not move, she knocked.

Tara Abernathy stood on the other side, panting, bloodslick from her elbows down, her own blood mostly. Wounds carved her over and over, on arms and legs and flank, always in the same pattern: four deep parallel cuts and one slightly slant, as if she'd been caressed by hands made of knives. Behind her towered a sharp-toothed shape Kai tried not to think about.

"It's time," Kai said.

Abernathy swallowed her heartbeat, and closed her eyes. When she opened them again, she seemed cool and calm. "Good. I wasn't getting much rest anyway."

They met at Gavreaux Junction in the waking world just before dawn, Tara in a light gray suit, Kai in dark. The freight elevators ran full capacity, one container every five minutes, and behind thick walls capped with barbed wire machines ground and stevedores called to one another in a coarse tradesman's dialect of Talbeg. Kai knew the sounds and smells from the industrial port back home, where deepwater container ships deposited their wares and police reviewed the cargo for smuggled gods and joss. This was bigger, though, and at least some gods were welcome.

"Tickets" was the first waking word Tara spoke. She did not mention the puppet Kai she'd seen in her dream, and Kai said nothing about hands that were knives, or a gray-eyed woman made of glass. And yet Kai realized that for the first time, in her own head, she was calling the other woman by her given name. "This way."

They bought tickets in a bare concrete hall lined with bare concrete pillars, from a drowsing Iskari kid still high from the night before. Kai followed Tara past long benches and patches of floor where families slept on unfolded newspaper, waiting for a train.

"Bound for points south?" Kai nodded toward the families. Tara stopped at a magazine stand, tossed the vendor a coin, and selected an Iskari daily from the rack. "I thought most of these people would be coming from trouble, not going toward it."

Tara opened the newspaper. "I missed these. We don't have them back home." Realizing she hadn't answered Kai's question: "They aren't headed for the troubles. They'll take the costal line east to Apophis, and from there, they can reach Dhisthra, Zur, anywhere on the Ebon Sea, the Shining Empire if they want. People only stay here if they don't mind the Iskari."

"Sounds like there's no love lost between you."

Tara tucked the newspaper under her arm. "The Iskari are a god-fearing people, emphasis on the fearing."

"You work with gods in Alt Coulumb."

"Alt Coulumb is different. And better, though don't tell our esteemed allies I said so."

"Yet you're cooperating."

"Path dependency makes strange bedfellows. Take the two of us, for example."

Whoever designed the Southern Express waiting room had expected it would be the station's focus. Broad concrete steps climbed to a mezzanine for no reason Kai could see, beyond giving the architect an excuse to raise an enormous arch in the shape of an Iskari modernist Lady Progress, broad strong arms spread to embrace the huddled masses below. Progress shed rays of concrete light—or tentacles. This, Kai realized, passing underneath, was the first representation of a human being she'd seen in Agdel Lex. Which sent a different message: this place was not made by, or for, locals.

Fewer people waited in the lounge atop the stairs, and none of those slept on newspapers. Seven tall, knife-thin persons in identical black suits read copies of the same newspaper on the same bench. A woman in a floral print dress checked her wristwatch. The overhead clock chimed six. Pink light seeped through high, smoked station windows. Tara passed their tickets to the golem and led Kai through the turnstile, outside. This was all old hat to her, nothing worth a second glance.

But even Tara stopped when she saw the train.

The stairs they'd climbed seemed to have a purpose after all: raising them above the train's wheel bed. The passenger car curved over them, a dark metal hill glistening in morning light. Kai had seen dragons smaller. To her left bloomed the metal fungus of the locomotive, and to her right, perspective shrank even these enormous cars to a point. A few cars lay open, unhinged like waiting jaws as cranes lowered boxy shipping containers inside. The insects that swarmed the train's surface were, of course, people. Kai watched one freight car snap shut around a shipping container, slow and inevitable, terrifying mass driven by great hidden engines.

"Wow," Kai said.

"Neat, isn't it?" Looking at the train, Kai felt a kind of holy awe: this was a thing beyond any scale human minds evolved to comprehend. She read another emotion in Tara's thrust-back shoulders, in her smile: pride. "Most of those containers are empty—they fill them south of the Wastes. Those double walls hold the insulation that lets them pass through the Wastes unharmed. Otherwise the gods out there, what's left of them, sneak into the cargo, and when they make it to the wider world—" She pinched her fingers together and opened them quickly, like a flower blooming, faster. "It's good to be careful."

"And my sister plans to rob—this."

The Craftswoman shrugged. "It's a rich target."

"Does she have an army? Two? You said those containers were empty."

"Most of them." Hands pocketed, newspaper under one arm, Tara marched to the passenger car. A conductor waited by the open door, navy blue uniform, white cap, shined shoes, military insignia, mustache. He clicked his heels as Tara passed; the Craftswoman did not stop or speak. He clicked his heels for Kai, too, and Kai smiled at him. The conductor's face didn't seem to have moved since the nineties.

As she climbed the long stairway through the passenger car's insulation, Kai thought about cargo, and the depot south of the Waste, in the heart of the Gleb, and the conductor's military bearing, and the thin identical personages in identical black suits. "We're carrying joss, aren't we? Liquid souls, gems, palladium—raw and untraceable. You're not trading with miners. You're trading with warlords."

Tara stopped at the top of the stairs. "Ms. Pohala." Her voice was sharper than the moonlight knife Kai'd seen her wield. The shadows in the stairwell darkened, and glyphs glimmered beneath the other woman's skin. The Blue Lady curled Kai's nerves tight and whispered, run. "I don't trade. My employers' church and Iskar have an old relationship, which has been nothing but trouble since before I started, and if people listened to me around the office, we'd have cut through this knot a long time ago. I came into this mess with a single goal: to see your sister's project through. And, in the midst of your moral indignation, ask yourself what the, sure, call them warlords, do with the fortunes the Iskari toss their way. Might they, just possibly, end up back home on good old Kavekana, funding your bonus?"

Kai stopped on the steps. "I'm trying to change that."

"We're all trying," Tara said. "Whether we're trying hard enough—that's the question. Meanwhile, the joss is likely your sister's target. If she is here."

"She is."

Tara shrugged, and disappeared around the corner.

Designers, decorators, and Craftsmen had molded the passenger car into a perfect illusion of a normal train cabin. Every surface shimmered with inlaid brass and polished wood. Light issued through translucent panels approximating windows. Even Kai, who'd seen no windows outside the enormous smooth plane of the insulation tanks, mistook that light for day at first, so well were the ghostlamps tuned. Compartments bordered the aisle on the left, half occupied, most with single passengers dozing on the lush leather cushions, shades pulled down over the fake windows. By the time Kai caught up with Tara, the Craftswoman was seated in their compartment, reading the paper.

She settled across from her. Tara turned the page. A tea cart rolled down the hall outside. "I'm sorry," Kai said. "It's horrible. I mean. I have a friend who comes from—" She stopped herself. "This is gross."

The page turned. "I agree."

"Do you ever think," Kai asked, looking out the not-window though there was nothing outside to see, "about games?"

"Not often."

"Or sports?"

"No."

She tried anyway. "Good players depend on the rules of the game. Tollan's the best ullamal player in the world, but if she got, I don't know, zapped back in time and to another country, to the Shining Empire, say—would it matter?"

"If mystery plays are to be believed," Tara said, "she would teach the locals to play ullamal, have a series of madcap adventures, overcome her arch-rival in the Shining Empire, find a predictable focus-group-tested romance, and ultimately stay in the past because she found true friendship and love of the game there, as opposed to returning to our crass fast-paced world in which she's rich, universally beloved, and functionally a goddess. Which development would make sense to the audience, for"—she waved her hand vaguely without looking up from the stocks page—"reasons. Probably because it reinforces the carefully packaged narrative that rich people are inherently unhappy, so you poor folks in the provinces should just stay in your seats and buy another ticket."

The tea cart came again, and Kai bought tea with milk and sugar, and wished they had coffee. Tara took her tea black and bitter. "You want power," Kai said, "so you play the game. You learn its rules and use them. But what if the game's wrong?"

The train shuddered. Footsteps padded over the thick hall carpet. Tara glanced over the top of the newspaper and Kai, for a moment, felt herself seen through—not, for once, seen as the person she wasn't, but seen beneath her flesh and past, seen as a soul wrapped in a Lady's web. She felt naked and raw beneath that gaze, and she crossed her legs and clutched the hem of her skirt.

Tara folded the paper, and set it down beside Kai's milky

tea. She looked like she was about to ask a question, or say—something.

The compartment door opened. "We're fine," Kai said, automatically, expecting the tea cart again.

"I would expect nothing less," said Lieutenant Bescond.

Chapter Forty

ZEDDIG'S CREW—and they were Zeddig's crew for this job, she'd made that much clear to Ley before they left, Ley might be the mission specialist but Zeddig gave the orders, which Ley, with slantwise smile, accepted: "You're the boss"—reached the train station before dawn, clad in coveralls and weaponry. Raymet might have been a calliope for all the jangles that followed her as she moved. Ley sported blades at every limb, and others out of sight. Gal bore only a band of twisted blue cord around her arm.

"A shield?" Raymet asked on the way, pointing to the armband. "Or curse? Whip? Lightning garrote?"

"Good luck charm," Gal replied, as if she had not noticed she was wearing it and expected no one else to notice either. "My mother gave it to me. I assumed it was for luck."

"What does it do?" Raymet adjusted her belt, trying to balance the heavy repeating crossbows strapped to her hips.

Gal tilted her arm and examined the braiding. "Looks nice?"

"We're bound into the Wastes, I'm loaded for God, and you've brought a good luck charm."

"I like luck."

Raymet unbelted one of the crossbows and shoved it stock-first at Gal. "Here. You carry this one."

So Gal wore the crossbow and the cord, and carried a duffle

bag large enough to hide a small body. They walked through the service entrance, and Zeddig knocked on thick safety glass. The clerk behind the glass glanced up from yesterday's half-filled crossword. A dictionary lay by her hand. "What?"

Zeddig gestured to her companions. "Four for detail." She drew papers from her coverall, flattened them with gloved hands, passed them through. This wasn't *the* critical moment—there were too many chances for this whole operation to go to shit for Zeddig to call any one critical—but it was *a* critical moment.

"ID?"

Those, too, she had. Stamped and official-looking scrip, sharp as Vogel's pass man could make them, which, Raymet had assured her, was sharp. She could spot the difference, but they'd pass the security checkpoint.

Fighters came to Agdel Lex from the world over, tight landless mercenary groups, each with resumés of villages saved, justice imposed through heroic adversity, and many more tales they did not tell, of other less convenient villages put to the sword or abandoned, of monsters that could speak dispatched. They washed blood off their hands, and got paid. The Northern Gleb was a good market for their skills, and so was the High Steppe, and getting from one to the other required passage through the Waste, and tickets cost more capital than hobo mercs tended to have after they spent their roll on body mods, reagents, and weapons. Fortunately—though Craftsmen claimed there was no such thing as fortune, only invisible fingers sorting out demand and supply—the Southern Express needed guards who wouldn't ask for worker's comp. Bribe your way through a background check, and you were good to go.

So the woman behind the security glass waved them through, and, after a jog down twisting corridors too well-lit to inspire trust, and a longer elevator ride, they reached the guard trough atop the seventh car from the back. Techs sprayed them down, tested the seal, and locked the warding glass roof in place.

Gal sat cross-legged, back straight, and prayed. Raymet paced, glanced at Gal, paced more. At last she sat down beside Gal, legs crossed likewise. She closed her eyes, breathed, opened her eyes again. Gal didn't seem to have noticed. She shrugged then, and took out a book.

Ley removed her coverall and mask, double-checked her materials, and, satisfied, set up a chess game.

"That's it?" Zeddig said. She hadn't stopped pacing. "One review, and you're ready?"

Ley curled around two sides of the chess board like a cat, and propped her cheek on her fist. "I've reviewed past the point of nausea. At this point I'd rather trust my plans and wait."

"That's delving for you," Zeddig said. "Boredom punctuated by bursts of brief, near-fatal excitement."

Ley stretched her arm over her head until the shoulder popped. She sighed, as if she'd been waiting for that pop for weeks. "I prefer my industry. Art is constant near-fatal excitement—and if you win, you never have to wait for anything again. You pay other people to wait for you."

"Sounds selfish."

"It is—solipsism, creamy and rich, like burrata. I recommend it to everyone."

"Solipsism," Zeddig said, "would be a kind of hell, if you weren't perfect. Which you're not."

"Sit down, then." Ley slapped the floor across the board. "Play me. Show me different."

Zeddig was up a pawn when the train shuddered to motion and scattered their chess pieces. One, bouncing, landed in Raiment's book. She tossed it back overhand, and struck Ley on the skull.

They passed through the wall, and the sky changed.

The squid-certainty of Agdel Lex fell away, as if carved off by a knife. Sharp wind curled through the high places of their souls. Insulation churned and pumped and gurgled in the walls, and thin pipes of the stuff set into the foot-thick warding glass ceiling gushed green. Ice webbed the crystal. Wind shook the train on its tracks. A bird cried in the distance. Zeddig tried not to think about what birds might survive in the Waste, what they might eat, or how loud that cry must be to pierce the thick walls.

Zeddig and Ley drew their next game, and the next, and after that even Ley lost heart. She sat to wait, and watched her watch.

An hour passed. Two. An enormous hand made of ice and salt struck the ceiling, which shuddered, but held. Nails as broad across as Gal was tall scraped the roof, bent and splintered to powder as they failed to gain purchase. The hand slipped away, leaving streaks of melted rainbow ichor. The train rolled on. Gal had not moved. She sat cross-legged and gangly, praying. Raymet stared up into a sky green as old bone, and waited for the hand to come again. She breathed shallow and fast, like a rabbit.

Gal did not open her eyes, but she extended her hand, and Raymet accepted, squeezed it tight. Her breath stilled.

Zeddig checked her watch. "Ley?"

"It's time." They gathered close as she opened the blade, forming silver fractals. This time Zeddig was ready for the shift, as her mind came unmoored and Ley's web caught them all. The train steadied.

The wheeled access hatch to the cargo container below was locked tight, set to open only and automatically in the event of disaster below. Raymet pried up floor plates with a chisel, breathed deeply, and wriggled into the thrumming mechanisms. "Sapphire spanner," she called up, and Gal passed the tool down. "The other one." Gal got it right on the third try.

Ley packed her chess set and watched Raymet work, squeezed between pistons and gears and pumps circulating insulation sludge. A wrong move might cause a leak, or open the access hatch before vacuum pumps drained the insulation, venting godsludge into their cabin. They might survive, if that happened. There had been known cases.

Ley held her mask in one hand. "This is taking too long."

Zeddig agreed, but: "Give her time."

"Cutting torch."

Gal passed that down too.

Curses and the stench of burnt hair filled the silent room.

Gal leaned over the hatch. "Raymet, are you well?"

Below, something metal snapped. Zeddig's hand went to the club at her belt, for the small good it would do if the seals broke. Still, small good was better than none at all. "It's fine," said Raymet, or something possessing Raymet's body.

Pumps surged. The hatch light blinked from red to green. Gal tested the wheel, which moved. She glanced a question at Zeddig, who nodded: "Go."

The door opened, and they did not die.

"Phenomenal," Ley said, and dropped into the hatch before

Zeddig could stop her. Ley didn't bother with the ladder, just fell into the passage, landing with a clang on the wheel hatch beneath. It didn't give way, which was nice, as falling twenty feet down into the shipping container would be a bad way to start a mission. Ley shot a thumbs-up and a grin to Zeddig, who rolled her eyes. Ley shrugged, donned her mask, reddened her hair, straddled the hatch door, and cycled it open.

Light poured into the container. Their crew, their muscly crew, their cannon fodder, blinked up, shading faces with hands, save those that didn't have eyes as such. The armored lizard-shark-dude whose arm Gal had broken at their first meeting bared bright long teeth. A skinny man in torn jeans rolled over, grumbled, tried to sink back to sleep; his neighbor punched him in the ribs and he sat up, growling. Most observed professional silence. They knew the meaning of the light. The easy part of the trip was over, the part when discovery meant at worst a little time in jail. For those who signed up dreaming of riches only to spend the next week secretly hoping the plan would fall apart before they reached the fatal bit, Ley's arrival signaled that the time for secret hopes was over, and the time to pull their shit together had come.

Ley kicked the rope ladder down. "Good morning, friends. Time for work."

Chapter Forty-one

"WHAT THE HELLS," KAI said, inadvisedly, to break the silence, "are you doing here?"

"Enjoying a morning venture," Bescond replied. The Lieutenant sat next to Kai, leg crossed ankle on knee, one arm resting on the seat behind Kai's shoulders. Bescond flicked her pocket watch open, closed it again, turned it over in her fingers, and opened it once more. For all that opening and closing, Bescond never checked the time. "At the moment. Soon, I'll have work. I'm glad our investigations led to similar results, though this situation suggests we have a ways to go before we achieve true cooperation."

Kai glanced from Tara to Bescond and back. The Craftswoman set aside her newspaper, sipped her tea, and set the teacup down again. Outside, in the hall, Wreckers waited. Tentacles shifted under their dark robes. She thought she could hear them moan.

Had Tara betrayed her? Kai would have sworn the Craftswoman wasted no love on Bescond. Kai had felt her seething frustration with the Iskari, the tense mechanism of Tara's rage allowed, for that barest moment in the stairwell, to show—but the woman sat impassive as a mountain. Kai made a mental note, if they made it through this mess, to never play cards against Tara Abernathy. "Ms. Pohala was interested in our southern assets. I offered to escort her on a trip."

"Really." The circle of reflected light cast by Bescond's watch darted through the cabin: climbed the left wall, slipped across the ceiling, and vanished into the pane of smoked false day. "Over the last ten years I've built a list of languages I want to learn. My Talbeg serves, at best. Imperial, all the papers say, will dominate the world. Then there's Waldan and Zurish, setting aside the sub-Waste dialects. But I'm sad to say duty guides my hand. I learn what I must to do my job. There are only so many hours in a day, and we are accountable to our Lords for the use we make of them." She touched her shirt front, and Kai tried not to notice the writhing beneath. Bescond turned to Kai. "If this is, in fact, an exploratory mission, Ms. Pohala, perhaps it would interest you to know we are within minutes of apprehending your sister."

Green slushy insulation surged through the tank around the passenger car, protecting them from the Wastes. A tremor in the floorboards was Kai's only clue to the train's size and speed, the violence of its passage. She would have fought all the ghosts and gods outside for an instant of stopped time in which to scream, but she would not gratify Bescond. The Lieutenant expected a gambler's tell. No doubt she watched Kai's eyes, waited for them to dart to one side, seeking reassurance from Tara, or up, into the creative recesses of her brain.

Kai held her gaze level—though not too level. "Interest, yes. Why do you think my sister would be here?"

"Your sister," Bescond said, "has been betrayed."

Don't look at Abernathy. "I don't understand." The most powerful, and difficult, words in any language.

"She and her friends have been sold—at a reasonable price, by a gentleman seeking to insure his business venture. Now that you're along, I hope you'll help me bring her in, let's say, minimally impaired. I sent a Wrecker to your hotel room this morning, and was disappointed to find you gone. Now our collaboration can proceed apace. Ms. Abernathy—could you suspend your no doubt vital business to assist our endgame?"

Abernathy was a wall of cool. "The church will bill you for my time."

"Certainly. We must aid our allies, after all." Bescond tipped her hat.

Kai closed her eyes and breathed deep, relishing the privacy of her skull. When she opened her eyes again she found the compartment damnably unchanged. "I need to use the facilities. If that doesn't interfere with your master plan."

"Go ahead." Bescond opened the door. The Wreckers did not move. "You won't mind if one of my companions goes along? She'll wait outside. We have the situation in hand, but one can't be too careful."

When Kai stood, her train ticket slipped from her lap and floated down to the ornate rug. She stooped and caught it before Bescond could. She smoothed her skirt and straightened her lapels. "Not at all." She imagined her voice as a poison needle sliding into Bescond's ear, slick and sharp. Not fatal poison—just painful and debilitating. The Lieutenant's smile widened. Kai wondered if Bescond could hear her thoughts.

A Wrecker followed Kai down the hall. It did not walk so much as pour beside her, limbs churning under the robe. Kai glimpsed a face beneath the cowl: slick gray, ribbed, and moving. The shoulders, or what might have been the shoulders, slumped. "Early morning for you too, huh?"

The almost-face shifted like a mouth opening, though the movement didn't create a mouth so much as a shallow taut dish of skin like clay pinched into a bowl. The Wrecker's voice was the gurgling roar of surf in a narrow cleft.

Kai walked faster, slammed the restroom door shut behind her, locked it, and sagged against silk wallpaper. Ghostlight panels ringing the mirror shed the same fake daylight as the simulated windows. Staring into her own reflection, Kai allowed herself an instant's despair.

Sleep deprivation gouged the soul, made the world seem dubious and shitty. The face of the woman in the mirror grew strange in the way of faces in mirrors. In the blurring reflection Kai saw her sister on the seashore, willing her sand city whole as the tide rolled in. Ley stood against gods and sea and the breaking of the world, until she broke herself.

If Bescond caught Ley, she wouldn't submit. She'd fight those rubbery arms until there was nothing left of her but meat.

The Wrecker slapped the door. Of course—a wet slap was close as they could come to a knock.

"Privacy, please? Or patience?" She kicked the brass toilet handle, and the water ran.

Why was Ley doing this? What did she want from this train? Could she still, even now, be saved?

Kai read the note burned into her ticket—the ticket she'd never held, but which had, by Abernathy's Craft or simple sleight of hand, arrived in her lap. Not much help. She'd hoped for Craftwork glyphs, for magic to speed her way. She found a few scrawled words of advice.

Joss in second and seventh car, the note read. The Wreckers can't smell you in the ceiling.

Thanks ever so much, Kai thought, but it wasn't nothing.

She drew a sterile pin from her pocket, pricked her finger, squeezed a drop of blood into the washbasin, and prayed.

The Lady caught Kai's mind in Her blue spiral hands. Kai gasped and stumbled against the sink, lost in the pleasure and pain: razor wind howled between Kai and her Goddess. A hundred thousand voices screamed against the edges of her faith, a hundred thousand tiny fingers hooked her mind and pulled the Wastes, interfering with prayer. Kai ground her teeth and clenched every muscle in her body at once—only a small high sound escaped her throat.

The Wrecker slapped the door again, and Kai snapped. "A minute, I said."

Behind the door, the Wrecker made a seafoam grumbling noise, and flowed back against the opposite wall.

She prayed once more and felt, through the static of those screams, Izza straining against the train's speed, felt Izza's fear and awe and freezing metal beneath her fingertips.

The Wastes burned and froze and tore her mind to shreds.

It's a trap, she prayed as loud and clear as she could, and collapsed. Glass broke. She'd fallen forward in her swoon, and her skull cracked the mirror to a web of light. Blood leaked down her forehead. Fuck. The Wrecker rattled the door, but the latch held. "A minute, godsdammit!"

Kai scrambled up onto the toilet tank and the sink, pressed the ceiling panel, and, when it gave, pulled herself up into the train's guts. She smelled spent lightning and burned air. Cars seven and two—fore and aft. Fifty-fifty shot. Trust to luck. Reason hadn't done much for her so far.

She scrambled into darkness as, behind her and below, the Wrecker tore the washroom door from its hinges and found her gone.

Chapter Forty-two

EVERYTHING WAS GOING ACCORDING to plan, which really pissed Izza off.

When the security hatch opened overhead, she blinked against the sudden frozen Wasteland light, and stared up at the silhouette woman with the red hair and the mask, the woman who had to be Kai's sister in disguise. "Rise and shine," Ley said. "Many hands make light work."

The team swarmed up the rope ladder with pirates' ease, muttering jokes and curses and prayers. Isaak kissed the stone around his neck before he climbed, and Izza's stomach twisted as she followed him.

They donned hats and jackets, and woke elementals wired within—not enough heat to save them from the Wastes' cold, but they'd take the edge off so long as no one left the circle. While they suited up, Izza reviewed the delvers on whom their lives depended. Zeddig she liked: square, stern, strong, steady. "We'll form a perimeter. Stay inside, and you'll survive. Stray, and we won't save you. Watch the train. Don't look into the sky. Never look at the landscape. The things out there can sneak in through your eyes."

She did not know others' names: a tall inscrutable Camlaander, a young sharp Talbeg woman, bald and pacing, nervous, adjusting explosive bolts on the exterior hatch. And Ley.

Izza had seen Kai's sister in the meetings. There, Ley kept

still, watching the plan unfold. Now that stillness thawed to motion. She was everywhere, fast as a reflection, reviewing gear, correcting harnesses, circling, doubling back. "Young for this line of work," she said as she passed Izza, and set a hand on her shoulder, reassuring: Ley read her nerves as a first-timer's.

"Not really."

Nothing funny about that from Izza's angle, but then, she supposed Ley's laugh didn't have much humor. "Can you drink?"

"Better than you."

"We'll see, on the other side," she said, and hooked her thumb back toward Isaak. "Take care of that guy. He looks jumpy." Isaak, of course, looked like Isaak: six feet and change of sharp teeth and scales.

"I will." For the first time, she felt a pang of guilt. She was here to help Kai find her sister, but on the other hand—this was an adventure, they were in the shit together, Izza and Isaak and the goon squad and Ley and Zeddig so unconsciously regal, the kind of person Izza had wanted to be when she was a kid, before she'd lost those childhood dreams in the passage of a knife across a throat. In a few scared hours they'd emerge with fortunes to spend, or, if they were wiser, invest. (They weren't wiser, any of them, but a girl could always dream.) She was breaking the sacred fellowship of thieves. (Which was another lie you told yourself, that there was a sacred fellowship of thieves, that you weren't just a dangerous person who hung out with other dangerous people and hoped none of them would ever decide they liked your guts more on the outside. The Lady blunted that lie, created a real community, but then, none of these people worshipped the Lady save Isaak, and she already trusted him. Someday she'd find who invented this whole *adulthood* idea and kill them slow. You lost track of the lies you told. Speaking of which, Ley was lingering—she seemed to need one of those lies self-professed adults asked for from time to time. So.) "You don't have to worry about me."

The small bald woman burst the hatch and they emerged into the cold. Ten goons huddled between four women, they crept along the train, hair whipped and eyes stung by the wind. They jammed their boots against the steel, and looked at their feet, or, when they had to scurry across cables between the cars, at their hands. Never at the sky, never at the horizon, never at the Wastes.

Ice crackled in Izza's nose when she breathed, though she felt fierce equatorial sun against her skin. She'd heard sailors talk of northern cold, the chill of long dark nights and a shrinking distant sun. This was not that. This was Craftborn winter, cold that tore the soul, cold become insatiable hunger.

And the cold spoke.

There were voices, small and thousands, chittering, screaming, like a city's worth of rats stuffed in a hydraulic press. She did not hear them with her ears. They called to her as the Lady called, they spoke as She spoke, and Izza, priestess, back-alley queen, crouched low and focused on her hands and feet.

Save us, they called, and promised her riches and sex and glory if she would but kneel, and nausea wrenched her gut and she wanted so badly to look—

Ahead, she heard a prayer.

Isaak, head down, shoulder against the wind, clutched the Lady's stone in his claw, and he spoke, in his childhood Talbeg so close to Izza's own, Her words Lady shelter me. Guide my steps. Help me help myself, and help me help my friends.

She joined her voice to his. Her steps grew straight and firm, not by miracle, but by knowledge: there was a fellowship, not of thieves, but of the ignored and suffering, and she had built it. If she failed here, others would carry on the work. But she would not fail. Look how far she'd come.

She trusted to the Lady, opened to Her, and steadied. They reached the car behind the swollen locomotive. She prayed, huddled with the others, as the bald woman drew her tools and bent to open a hatch.

Izza sheltered in the Lady.

So when the Lady spoke, Her voice hit with the force of thunder, and Izza fell.

She struck the train's curved steel skin and her body scraped a broad trail through frost. Her stomach lurched. Honed reflexes and monkey instinct directed arms and legs abandoned by conscious mind. Fingertips snagged weld seams in steel plate, but her body's godsdamn weight tore her free again. Free and falling, falling—the world a whirl, one third train, one third sky, one third Wastes she could not allow herself to see. And as she fell the train sloped downward, and she fell faster, and thought failed beneath a chorus of uninventive curses.

Human minds being human minds, some grim fatalist tendency that really should have focused on survival still took the time to note: you can always trust Gods for shit timing.

She called to the Lady but there were too many screams, some of them hers, and she could not compose her soul. One last riveted line in the steel approached. Past it, no hope. She curled her fingers into claws, turned, caught.

Her numbed fingertips bit, tore, slipped. Arms jerked in their sockets. One hand bounced free. She anchored one boot against the train, but the other skidded against sheet ice. Tiny invisible fingers stroked her skin. The voices deafened in their chorus, in their promises. If she let go, they'd catch her. If she turned around, if she asked—

Izza pushed with her leg and pulled with her fingers, but the seam wasn't deep enough to give her the leverage she wanted. She kicked the ice, but it would not break, and the kick almost broke her grip on the seam. And she forced herself to think about the pain in her wrist and shoulder, about the slow loss of strength, about the cold, about falling, about anything but those whispers. One finger slipped. She strained with her free hand, couldn't quite get it over the seam, tried again—

Someone caught her wrist.

She tugged against the grip in those first few seconds—dumb and desperate, unable to control her instincts. She was screaming, she'd been screaming, and she looked up into Ley's eyes.

The woman still wore the mask. That unnatural red hair whispered loose from its braid. But the disaffection, the mockery, was gone. She held Izza over the abyss, teeth gritted, splayed spread-eagled against the steel, anchored by a rope at her belt tied to, gods, to Isaak, barely visible over the horizon of the train, and in that moment, despite all masks, Ley looked just like her sister.

Isaak dragged them up, one step, two. Izza's boots found traction. Her fingers hurt, her shoulder. Her lungs burned from the cold. She was babbling, she realized, speaking languages she didn't know. The Wastes played her like an instrument, and she spoke in their tongues.

Ley drew a glowing knife from her belt and rapped its blade against the train. Even that second's impact parted the steel, and green slush seeped out, twisting into weird tendrils and shapes. That would be a problem, Izza thought, with the idle calm of the almost dead. But, triggered by impact, Ley's knife opened like a flower, and Izza stared into its threading silver patterns, and the voices stilled, and she was, briefly—

Strong, and tall, and calm, and sad, watching the goons drop into the open hatch, and unaware of—

Tense and curled, tools in hand, and crushing, because it was superfluous to their purpose here, the ache that came when she glanced over at the tall strong calm woman by her side—

Rough and scared, anchoring Isaak with the muscles of her shoulder and back as she stared down, in love, afraid, at—

Pendant by a line through her belt, holding with slowly failing strength the girl who fell, utterly certain—

Trapped, blind, mute, deaf, compressed, furious, writhing in this warm nothing like a tadpole in syrup—

And was Izza herself again, and, scrambling, she pulled herself up and caught the line that held Ley's belt, anchoring them against the train's skin so the other woman could turn, kick off, and climb. Thin green tendrils coiled around their legs, but tore easily for now. Isaak strained, looking always and only down, never out at the Wastes; Zeddig held him with one arm and the open hatch with her other.

And in that grinding, panting confusion, they reached the top of the train, and Izza collapsed in the brilliant frost, panting steam.

Somewhere Zeddig shouted, not at Izza: "—of all the stupid selfish—" And Ley: "She's just a kid—" And Zeddig: "Venting insulation in the middle of the Wastes—" And Isaak, kneeling over Izza, arm around her shoulders, pulling her up, "Are you all right?"

She could use her voice again.

Below, green tendrils climbed the slick steel, inching and swelling, stretching out roots that were also fingers and hair and teeth, and Gal flowed forward clad in golden light to cast them back: a whirlwind, a fury, impossibly strong. Isaak bent over Izza as Zeddig and Ley argued. Raymet knelt by the hatch. Izza knew their names now. In that shared moment, sliding from body to body she had felt—ah, fuck it. She tried to use her voice, and she wasn't speaking tongues any more at least, but first she had to hack up a lungful of slush and phlegm and spit, hissing, onto the steel.

A green lasso of viscera launched toward Zeddig, but Ley's blade was faster; severed, the green slime froze and clattered to the surface of the train.

"Friends," Raymet said, "may I suggest we continue this inside?"

Izza found her voice in time to shout: "Trap!"

Ley turned to her first. "What?" Behind her, Gal and Zeddig fought the green.

"I had—" Isaak looked at her, and for the first time she saw questions spread throughout his body. Childhood trust only went so far. Had she betrayed them? Yes and no, but there was no time to sum up the complicated situation atop a moving train with who the hells knew what waiting down below. "I had a vision." Isaak's face filled with a wonder that left her sick. "There was a blue light, and I heard a voice, and"—Lady, she prayed, give me just a little help here—"She said there was a trap in the train. Someone's waiting for us."

A new light glinted off Isaak's scales, and the stone around his neck shimmered, and the world looked strange, charged with warm blue, pregnant with a Goddess's purpose. Izza realized her eyes were glowing. Unsubtle, but it would do.

"The Blue Lady." Isaak's voice filled with dumb adoration, and Izza wanted to be anywhere but here, with him looking at her any way but this. "She sent a miracle." Godsdammit. "The Lady spoke through her."

Ley raised an eyebrow. Zeddig, to Raymet: "What's going on down there?"

Raymet shook her head. "I can't see. But that means our team hasn't turned on the lights yet."

Gal: "I can't hold the slime much longer, friends." Her voice lacked stress. Something enormous roared, then screamed, then fell off the train.

Ley glanced from Izza, to Zeddig, then over to the blooming wall of green slush stretching rubbery fingers toward them.

Zeddig decided: "We go in. First sign of trouble, we run for the locomotive, pull the emergency hatch, head for the spire."

Raymet unfolded a warding circle and dropped it into the darkness. "That takes care of the landing zone, at least for a minute or two. You go first."

Izza rolled to her feet. Isaak scrambled to the hatch, breathed deep, and dropped straight down, landing in a crouch. Izza descended slower. Darkness wadded around them. Raymet followed, then, after a brief argument, Ley, then Zeddig, and finally Gal, clothes torn, pulling the hatch shut on a green pseudopod.

Raymet's hand torch cut the darkness, and Izza wished it hadn't.

The hall was full of tentacles.

They moved when light raked across them: dripping ropes of flesh. Snared within, beneath them, lay the advance team.

Twelve cloaked and hooded figures turned to face Zeddig's group.

Gal stepped forward, grim, Raymet by her side, and Zeddig. Ley, on the other hand, cleared her throat.

"Friends. I like a desperate last stand as much as anyone. But I suggest we run."

Chapter Forty-three

KAI DROPPED FROM THE air duct onto a metal grate above the locomotive's heart.

Machines surged under the floor and behind safety cage walls, and green insulating fluid rushed through translucent ducts. Recessed ghostlamps shed cold blue light that had nothing to do with the sun. Kai's shoes clanged on metal, which, considering she wasn't supposed to be here and didn't know who was listening, was a problem. She tucked her shoes under one arm, and ran down a staircase on stockinged feet. Pistons pistoned and gears turned and teeth met teeth and everything was wrong.

At least she'd made it this far. To cross the Wastes, the Iskari had built an Express like no other train: sealed and warded against the desert's half-dead gods, with its own air and heat supply, ventilation ducts and power lines strung from car to car. She'd shivered as she crawled between the cars, a few feet's insulation all that parted her from death.

Terror cleared the mind. The plan should still work. If she caught Ley before the Wreckers did, if she got the knife, Ley could escape. Bescond wouldn't chase her through the Wastes for spite. Probably.

As Kai ran toward the hatch, she wondered what she would tell her sister. She'd constructed five scripts to choose between, for a range of circumstances.

None of which included being thrust to one side when the hatch flung back to admit a clutch of desperate men and women—including Izza—the last of whom was red-haired, masked, and indubitably Ley.

Ley held the hatch open while a tall, blond, shining woman cut a tentacle off her wrist, then shouldered the door shut and struggled with the wheel lock. She finally noticed Kai when she helped her drive it home.

Their eyes met. The mask probably worked fine on people who didn't know her.

All Kai's memorized scripts caught fire.

An immense weight struck the other side of the hatch. The door dented, but did not break.

Ley's grin was a better mask than her mask. "Fancy meeting you here, dear sister. Thought you might travel south to see the damage our island's clients wreak? Tour the wreck of Alt Gehez or the Pridelands? I hear the ruins are lovely this time of year, if you don't mind ghouls. I know two vast and trunkless legs of stone you simply must visit while you're in the area."

"Take off the mask, Ley. And give me the knife."

"I'll meet you halfway." She peeled off the mask, and in a twist of warped rainbows her hair was short and dark again, and her features her own, though no more legible. She tucked the mask in a pocket; Wreckers struck the door again, and the metal buckled around hinges and latch. "As for the knife—that's mine." Kai reached for her, but Ley drew back snakelike, hands raised. In a moment, Kai knew, they could close to fists. Zeddig, behind Ley, watched, and the rest of the crew—except Izza, who Kai made herself ignore, refusing to give her away—waited, wondering what to do or where to run.

"If you give it to me, I can get them off your back."

"Earnest as an ingénue. You said you didn't want to get involved in my business. I thought I could trust that, at least."

"I want to help you!"

"You've handed us to our enemies."

"I did not."

"But somehow they found us."

"I'm sorry, Ley. For everything."

Ley grinned without humor. "We're long past the time for group therapy."

The Wreckers hammered the door again. Kai stumbled, caught the railing, and reached for Ley. Her sister drew back. Kai couldn't read her—not at this distance, not at any.

Kai turned to Zeddig, hoping for sympathy, for understanding. "This wasn't me. Whoever put this job together, he betrayed you. The train's full of Wreckers. I'm your only way out. The Iskari don't care about you. They just want that knife back. Give it to me, and I can make all this go away."

Booted feet marched toward the locked door. Kai heard a voice: Bescond. The Wreckers' monstrous scrambling stilled, and the wheel lock began to cycle open; the Camlaander ran past Kai and jammed the wheel with a wrench. The wheel turned anyway, just slower. The wrench bent. Zeddig said: "We have to go."

"I'm sorry, Kai."

"What is that knife worth to you?"

"A life," Ley said. "A city. A mistake."

From a side passage between boiler tanks, the bald woman called: "If you're as done with this as I am, our exit's ready."

"Sorry, sister," Ley said, and turned away.

Kai lunged for her, but Ley ducked under Kai's arms, caught the back of her jacket, and pushed her into the machine cage.

By the time Kai recovered, the six of them were gone—down the side passage through a security door already sliding closed, with Ley and Zeddig and Zeddig's accomplices, and Izza, on the other side.

The hatch behind her gave: tentacles pierced the steel, corkscrewed through the air. One caught Kai's arm. A razor of pleasure opened her from navel to sternum and she fell; her head hit metal and her teeth caught her lip. She tasted copper and fire and cursed, and screamed a scream that was a sigh—but before the Wrecker's joy could catch her once again, she followed the pain in her mouth back to her body, and tore herself free. She tried to rise, but her limbs were weak.

Bescond marched through the open door, in a tentacular halo, raising a small glass vial of blood. She met Zeddig's eyes through the safety glass.

Kai saw the world through a glorious afterglow. Outlines of Bescond and vial and surging engines melded into one another like cotton balls pulled thin.

The vial shattered in Bescond's hand.

Then the explosive bolts burst, and Zeddig and Ley and Izza and the rest tumbled into the Wastes.

Chapter Forty-four

IZZA LANDED IN COLD bright sand, and, breathless, rolled, until she came to rest face down. At first air would not come, she needed it too much, her lungs tight. She forced them still. Made herself breathe sharp air through grit, deep enough for the breath to take. She did not look up. A chorus screamed, and a monster roared, and roared, and roared again, a bellow pulse in her bones.

The roar faded.

She could not stand or raise her head. They'd warned her not to let the landscape slip in through her eyes. She heard voices. She prayed in spasms, memories: of Kavekana, of her friends, of beaches and stories, of a small dead bird on a pile of twigs, of freedom and of flight.

Those would not save her from the Wastes that folded people inside out and broke their minds and left them mad—the Lady could only do so much, even for her. You did not choose your death, but you could, sometimes, choose how to meet it. She'd heard people talk of promised afterlives, resurrection and the rest, she'd heard rescued drowners' tales of lights and dead lovers waiting, but she knew too much of gods to hope for afterlife. She knew too much of life to think you'd wish anything like it to last forever. People lasted as stories, as gods did. And people and gods alike told themselves stories as they died, because dying hurt, and stories helped.

This death, though, was taking longer than she expected. Then again, hells, she'd never died before. Maybe this was always how it felt.

A rough hand touched the back of her neck, and a human voice whispered, "Hold still."

Zeddig.

Thick goggles covered her closed eyes, and rubber slapped the back of her skull.

"You can look now. Look at me first."

Izza saw the world, and Zeddig, through a layer of smoke and shadow. The woman wore goggles of her own. Breath steam whirled from her nose and mouth like dragon smoke. She seemed sure. Everything had gone to shit, they'd lost their crew, but looking at Zeddig made Izza calm. Okay: the worst just happened. Now what? Izza wondered how you did that. She wondered if Zeddig felt as scared as she did sometimes, ever.

Izza stood, shaky, eyes on Zeddig.

"Good." Zeddig took her arm. "Look at the landscape now. I'll be right here. Ley's knife should keep you safe. What's out there can only hurt you if you let it. So, don't."

Izza nodded. Zeddig stood aside.

The brightness opened.

Bodies littered the Godwastes.

No. They did not litter the Godwastes—bodies *were* the Wastes, the salt flats framed in broken flesh. The swell on which they rested was an enormous arm, muscle tumbling into a rippled stomach that became a shoulder blade that became a sprouting wing. That hill was a clenched fist. Teeth lined the ridge. Claws arched, half faces contorted in pain fused to backs and sides and legs, frozen sculptures of salt and sand, long dead.

And yet they moved.

New tiny hands sprouted from the skin, reaching. The wing beat. The claw flexed. The mouth spoke. The nostrils breathed. That tongue twitched and rolled. And when Izza focused on each outline she saw smaller bodies, smaller arms and legs and faces, trying to tear free of the landscape.

She staggered. Zeddig caught her, held her. She heard Isaak retch.

She made herself look.

Her mind insisted the desert lay rolling and cold and brilliant white, reflecting noon sun in a colorless sky. But the land was made of bodies, and as she looked, they moved.

"Gods," she said.

"Yes." Zeddig glanced away: the others gathered on the hill. Isaak shook, and kept his eyes on his enormous feet. Gal held Raymet's arm. And Ley stood, scarved and ready, as if the fall from a train and the horror of the Wastes were all part of a day's work, and she didn't understand why they weren't yet moving. Behind her, miles away, atop a dune that was a skull, rose a structure not formed of god-flesh: a glass needle bridging pale heavens and deathly ground. "We have to go. But I'll explain on the way."

Chapter Forty-five

"INK AND CHALICE AND blood and beak." Bescond was not done cursing yet. The train rolled on. If the Wreckers minded their Lieutenant's language, they retained their usual rubbery candor. "You've ruined everything."

Kai found her voice with difficulty. A Wrecker's touch did not fade so much as dry like paint, leaving a stain on the soul. "No," she said. "I slowed them down for you to catch."

"Someone warned them. They were ready for our trap."

"I didn't know there was a trap until you told me. How could I have warned them?"

"You escaped my escort." Bescond, pacing, strangled her hat. "You ran."

The engines thrummed, and so did Kai's heart, and her rage. There was altogether too much thrumming going on. "I thought I could make her surrender."

"I could have used you as a hostage."

Kai snapped. The paint cracked, and flakes fell away as her edges cut through. "Do you think that would have made one damn bit of difference? Ley thinks I'm on your side. She has a goal, and we won't turn her from it. I had everything under control, but your mission creep is not helping."

"You don't know—"

"You want her knife. But you want the delvers she's with too, and you want her to suffer, and you want control. You want so many things they pull at one another, and you'd love to blame me for that, even though I'm the only person here with her eyes on the godsdamn target."

Bescond had crushed her hat into an accordion of felt. She stared down into the crumpled fabric, and, with visible effort, relaxed. The creases remained. "Fine. But your plan didn't work. Your sister is on foot in the Godwastes. Her only choice is to follow the train tracks back to the city. We'll pick up her up when she tries to sneak back through the gates."

"You won't," Kai said. "They'll get past you."

"Our borders are foolproof."

"You're not dealing with fools. You don't know my sister like I do. You won't get a second chance at her."

"We almost had her."

"Because you caught her in someone else's plan. She's on her own now."

Bescond set her crumpled hat back on her head. If she had an answer, she didn't say it. Silence expanded between them.

Kai was so focused on Bescond she didn't realize, at first, that silence meant the engines had stopped.

Tara Abernathy descended from the conductor's cabin, sliding her palms together as if brushing away dust. "I persuaded the conductor to stop the train."

Bescond swung to face her. "How?"

Abernathy shrugged off the question. "What's the plan?"

"The plan," Bescond said, "is for you to count yourselves fortunate I respect your pantheons' sovereignty, and our working relationship, too much to arrest you for obstruction of justice. I'm half tempted to give you to the Wreckers now."

Kai shivered with the memory of the Wrecker's touch. The paint hadn't all flaked off yet, and that had been a glancing blow from a single Wrecker. Ten robed figures gathered in the engine car, watching her, and watching Tara Abernathy.

Who raised one eyebrow, unconcerned. Her glyphwork slept beneath her suit. There was no starlight here, and the Courts of Craft held little claim on the Wastes. Yet Tara seemed at ease. Trusting—

Oh.

Trusting Kai.

Kai pondered her options.

First: leave—let Bescond chase Ley alone, and fail. At first. Ley was smart, but no one stayed smart forever. People slept. They drank. They trusted. They fell. If Ley ran to the corners of the globe, if she hid in some demon dimension, the Iskari would find her sooner or later, and the blade would fall.

So: option two.

A minor betrayal for a good cause.

Kai wanted to lick her lips, but did not. To sell, you projected confidence, and this was a kind of sale. "Lieutenant. You want Ley's knife."

"Yes."

"You want it more than you want her."

Bescond waited.

"I want to help Ley. I want you off her back."

"Why should I care?" Bescond asked.

Don't let your voice shake. Don't show weakness. You have to convince her you're an equal, dealing from a position of strength—not a woman alone in a desert, flanked by enemies.

"Because," Kai said, "I can lead you to her."

Chapter Forty-six

"GODS," ZEDDIG SAID AS Ley led them through the Wastes, "are stories people tell. The Hidden Schools claim gods evolved with us. We order the world in our minds, and our stories gather strength and power. Through them we become more than meat, and through us they become more than wind. Faiths are eyes through which we know the world. Gods and goddesses sing ourselves back to us through time."

They walked over bodies, and waded through slush rivers of rainbow blood. Ley, in the lead, consulted her maps and devices. The landscape twitched and rolled as she prodded it. They climbed the cleft between fingers of a giant hand, pitons gouging frozen flesh, and when they reached the summit the Altus tower had vanished; Ley knelt on a goddess's onyx brow, removed a stopper from a glass tube on her bandolier, and let one measured drop fall. The goddess's skin flushed and softened, the landscape quaked, and the tower emerged again from the sky, like clear glass immersed in water rendered visible by a shift in light. Ley stood. An eye the size of a hill blinked, and its tremor knocked Izza to the thawing skin; she regained her balance as the goddess froze again, her lashes icicles piercing skyward.

Isaak was praying. Zeddig glared at him. "Stop, please. We have enough trouble without drawing their attention."

Claw by claw, Isaak released the blue stone. Raymet,

crouched, stared through the icicle lashes into the depths of the eye. Gal set a hand on her shoulder; she reached up, about to push the hand away, but stopped.

Ley marched on, and they followed her.

• • •

Wreckers leapt from the train to land soundlessly in desert frost. They fanned out into a semicircle bordering train tracks. Tentacles lashed out from their robes, binding each to each, and within their perimeter and for some distance beyond, the ground stilled and settled and was only sand.

"Watch the sand," Bescond said. "It's safer. The things out there—" She shuddered. "Horrifying. And hungry. They'd like you."

"I'm used to gods," Kai said.

"That's exactly what I mean, Ms. Pohala. You're used to believing in many things at once. That's a bad habit. It makes room. If these things get inside you, they'll tear you to pieces. Watch the sand."

Kai glanced to Tara, but the Craftswoman hid any shock or awe or disgust behind a cool Craftswoman's façade. They must teach the art of that in the Hidden Schools—to see the world not as a wonder or a horror or even a place, but as a threat to manage and a resource to exploit. Glyphs burned beneath Tara's clothes. "We should get going."

"By all means." Bescond gestured. Long ropelike arms emerged from the robes of the Wreckers still aboard the train, wound together like vines, forming a ladder down to the sand.

Bescond stepped onto the ladder without checking to see if it would hold her. Her boots squelched on gray skin, and she gripped a tentacle railing with one gloved hand. She grinned. Showing off, Kai thought: demonstrating comfort with the impossible, challenging them to keep up. Bescond's afraid of Tara, afraid of the Wastes, maybe even afraid of me, but she can't let us know. Remember that. We can use it, maybe. Somehow.

"Come, Ms. Pohala. You claim you can lead us to your sister? Well, time's wasting."

I'm not betraying my friend, she told herself. I'm saving my sister. Izza knows the plan.

Kai took a breath, grabbed the wet length of—call it rope, that made it easier. She descended to the Wastes, and tried not to think about gods.

• • •

"In old Alikand," Zeddig said, "things worked differently. You've heard stories."

"The Angel's City." One epithet among many from childhood fireside tales.

"Two thousand years back, we had gods like any people. But we fought the Telomeri and their blood prophets, and they broke us. They shattered our palaces, burned our city, ate our gods. We scattered into the desert. We could not rebuild. What were we, without gods? When we prayed, the Telomeri smelled us, found us, killed us. They haunted our nights, and by day their soldiers came. So we wrote the names and stories down, and copied those books, and copied them again. A people, broken, will rebuild. Though a church is broken, faith remains. Souls hunger for order and direction. Reading stories, we found our gods again. But something strange happened."

They skidded down the inside of a thigh, passed beneath an arch of teeth, climbed an esophageal cave, and emerged from the eye socket of a bird that, wings spread, would have been larger than most buildings Izza'd seen. Flowers of ice grew from dunes and opened snapdragon mouths. Grass razors snapped against their boots. The wind bore voices. Izza ignored them. She felt the bond between herself, and Zeddig, and Gal, and Ley, and Raymet, and Isaak—that silver wheel turning in her mind, Ley's knife gathering and guarding them against the Wastes. She thought of her Lady, so far away. Was anything less like Kavekana than this emptiness?

She shivered.

Zeddig spoke as she walked, with a natural storyteller's ease, and Izza listened, because to listen was easier than to walk alone in the quiet of her own mind, with no company but fear and those mad half-heard voices that filled her soul when she thought of the Blue Lady.

"We found our gods again, but each of us found them differently. Texts speak different truths to every woman, and contemplation refines those truths, frames the reader into something less than god and more than human: beings sprung from the same family as gods, but tinted with individual faith. If gods were light, these were the rainbows a prism cast. Godlings. Angels. A scholar, contemplating tales, becomes one—for a moment. If you gathered faith from family and friends, you could spread your wings longer. We framed ourselves within the tales we read, and became beings more and less than human. We were heroes. We fought. We won."

Raymet snorted.

Zeddig glared at her, eyes glittering in the gap between her wool hat and her scarf. "I'm telling the truth."

Raymet waved her down. "No, it's cool. You're telling the rah-rah version, is all. And you're leaving the Iskari out."

. . .

"We," Bescond said, "should have let this place collapse."

Within the circle of the Wreckers' arms, desert sun burned the frost on the sand to steam. Within the Wrecker's arms, they walked, sweating, over salt flats, and climbed dunes. Within the Wrecker's arms, Tara glistened, and Kai carried her jacket over her shoulder, and Bescond's face turned a cancerous blotchy pink. They walked, and from time to time Kai corrected their course, tracing her bond with Izza across the Wastes.

Bescond continued: "We've had a close, long-lasting relationship. Our great-great-grand-et-ceteras, back in the mists of time, fought the Telomeri together—their empire pushed the old Iskari north to the Blightsea, killed our tribes one by one, flayed chieftains and hung them on trees for fuck's sake, until, on the most godsforsaken jut of barren nowhere, we called to the sea, and the star kraken heard us." She touched her chest, and no matter how used Kai had become to the sight of something wriggling beneath a believer's shirt, she still flinched.

A great hand burst out of the ice before them. Wreckers leaped onto the hand, lassoing fingers thick as columns and breaking them apart. A cage of bones caught the Wreckers, but they shattered it. They moved quickly, and knew their business.

"What happened next was awesome, in the old-fashioned sense. We still remember it, some of us—my older sister has the family Lord, but mine's only a tenth century bud, give or take, so I can't dream that far back. But it's a hell of a story: huge hairy blood-mad tribesmen swarming south, strangling the Telomeri in their own muck. We pushed them south, and south, allied with the real red-in-tooth-and-claw motherfuckers from Schwarzwald, the first Knights of Camlaan, and imagine our surprise when we found Alikand pushing the Telomeri north in turn, with their weird semi-divine militia. It wasn't a proper religion—I suppose you're the expert in this sort of thing, but I don't think theirs counts. Tribal shamanism, a regression to a pre-pantheon era they dressed up as something new. But, fuck, they helped us beat the bloodsuckers, and said in no uncertain terms that we should get out and let them mind their own business. Which we did. Until, centuries later, it all went to shit. You can't win for losing."

• • •

"Let's skip forward," Zeddig said, as they rappelled down a shoulder blade, "to Maestre Gerhardt."

"Oh," Raymet cut in from overhead, "so that's the plan. We gloss over, what, four different dynasties' attempts to reform the pantheon, two conquests, three empires, the rise of the Scholastic Senate and the Fifty Families."

"I'm trying to explain the Wastes."

"I get it. Just tell the girl what she needs to know. Which is why you started two fucking millennia back." Raymet let out her line, and skidded down past Zeddig to draw level with Izza. "Don't let Zeddig's *ancien régime* shit fool you. She and her family made out well in this story: if you had resources to gather a library, and train people who did nothing but study and pray and build souls all day, you had power, and used that power to get more. Interest compounds, when it has stable centuries to compound in. So, a hundred fifty years back, fifty families controlled the senate and university, and governed the rest of us on a don't-upset-the-rabble basis. You wanted power, you learned to kneel, minored in groveling, and if they let you in the front door, you were a good girl, because if you licked the right boots one of your grandkids would have someone grovel to them someday."

"Or," Zeddig said, "you stole books, and used them without basic safety precautions."

"See what I mean, kid? Three or four of your ancestors turn into giant city-smashing lizards, and the High Families never let you hear the end of it."

They landed. Gal coiled the ropes into her pack; she'd carried the gear without slowing a step. Ley took a needle from her belt and tossed it into the air. It hovered, glowed, and twirled; a ray of light emerged, pointing straight ahead. They followed.

After a while, Izza asked: "How does Gerhardt fit?"

• • •

A dragon reared before them, icicle teeth gleaming from its maw. Spread wings birthed eddies of dust and snow. Its roar buckled Kai's knees, but the Wreckers flowed forward and the dragon fell, melting, steaming, back to sand.

"Gerhardt spoiled everything," Bescond said. "Ruined our relationship with Agdel Lex, destabilized two continents, even before the wars began in earnest."

"Gerhardt," Tara explained, "came to study angels. He developed his theories of power transfer in the Schwarzwald, but no pantheon would let him experiment. Alikand had been a port of call for scholars and merchants for centuries. Everyone came here: it was stable, beautiful, peaceful, and cultured, with expat communities and immigrants hailing from Dresediel Lex to the Shining Empire. Gerhardt and his followers fit right in. They taught philosophy and mathematics and applied theology, compared notes on their explorations of the hells, made and squandered fortunes in research. And they learned about angels."

Bescond shook her head. "You're making it out like what happened here was some grand unforeseeable tragedy. Gerhardt came to overthrow the city. We have his records in his own hand. He and his disciples stole knowledge from the High Families, traded that knowledge for power, and when they were ready, began to perform miracles. They drained the earth, made buildings fly, raised the dead. But everything they did had a cost: it burned the land and sky and human souls. So the High Families brought out their angels, and did what you'd expect—"

"They killed him," Kai said. "I know this part."

• • •

The light guided them up a long, steep shin. Gal passed out crampons, and helped them strap the spikes to their boots. "Don't trip," she said, "or you'll slice your tendon and fall and die."

"Thanks," Izza said, without meaning it. Gal roped them together. Far up the cracked ledge, the tower waited. She felt seen. Of course: they were always watched here. "So," she said, to Zeddig. "You were getting to the gods."

"There was a fight. No one knows how it started."

"Some of us have theories," Raymet said, but stopped when Zeddig glared at her. "But no one really knows."

"There was a fight, soon after the Taifa resurrection. The High Families got involved. Gerhardt fought back, and the more he fought, the more he drained the land, the more he broke the sky, the more he tore from his victims' souls. The High Families sent flights of angels against Gerhardt's followers, but the angels shattered, wave after wave. Some foreign gods joined the fray. Domyel of the Zur was the first to fall, and then it got worse. Gerhardt's disciples scattered, fled to whatever universities and seminaries would harbor them, but their master stayed—and that was the beginning of the God Wars. Gerhardt slew gods and angels alike, but they don't die easily. Drained of power, torn from their faithful, they hid in dumb matter. Desperate, they fused sand to glass and stranger forms, built labyrinths to hide within. Matter is not so comfortable as a mind, to a god. But they tried to take the story matter tells itself—I am a stone, I am sand, I am a river—and shelter there. So, in his rage, Gerhardt broke even those simpler stories. And here we are."

• • •

"Gods," Kai said, "in the sand."

"Former gods," Tara corrected. "And angels. The last gasp of a drowning man, reaching for a rope."

Kai remembered her father, and sandcastles.

"These are . . . the nightmares of dying beings, feasting on one another, growing inside one another to burst from each others' chests. They war against themselves, in this world Gerhardt wrecked. In his hunger, Gerhardt scraped away the . . . there's a Waldan term for this, which in Kathic means *thing-ness*. He drained that from the Wastes—and when he began to die, he lost control." Tara shrugged. "The God Wars left bigger scars on the world, but nothing this weird. Every few years the Hidden Schools petition to send an expedition here, to cut these things up and find out how they work, but the Iskari have never been keen on the idea."

Bescond glanced back over her shoulder. "We've learned better than to let Craftsmen screw with Agdel Lex." She stopped walking. "Now," she said. "Kai. Which way?"

Kai listened, deeply, quietly. She did not look. She pointed, and they climbed.

• • •

One minute the spire towered atop the hill, and each step toward it bore them further back, as if they walked against a fierce current. Then, in a blink, Ley stood before a gate in a chain-link fence, and behind that fence lay a frost-crusted parking lot, a desiccated lawn, and a sixty-story glass needle that a sign identified as "Altus Industries, Beta Complex."

Ley slit the chain and padlock with her knife. Blinding sparks burst from severed links as she broke some Craft more durable than steel. She rolled the gate open.

"Frustrating," Ley said, "is how I'd sum up the whole story. Heroism, grim last stands against adversity, and what's left? A wasteland of orphan myths begging to serve anyone who will feed them—millions of voices that barely remember flesh, promising freedom and power and all sorts of things they think matter, if only you let them make you into something you aren't. Myth taints even warded ground. So, out here, every time you cross a threshold, you get caught in some damn story."

She demonstrated.

A frozen wind tore through the yard. Asphalt cracked and dirt flowed into a form. Dried grass twisted into hair. An abandoned rusted bench became teeth in a lion's mouth. Boulders of ice were eyeballs glaring down, and frost wings spread and scattered light.

"Kneel," the sphinx said in a voice so low Izza heard it in her stomach, "answer my riddles, and keep your lives."

"No thanks," Ley said, and reached for her belt.

The sphinx struck too fast for any of them to react. In one bite, she was gone.

Then the sphinx coughed, staggered, clutched its throat, and exploded into dust.

Ley landed on her feet.

She grinned to Zeddig. "I told you dragonheart was worth the trouble." She brushed ice off her jacket. "Come on. We have a lot of stairs to climb."

Chapter Forty-seven

SHE'S USING YOU.

Zeddig heard the knife's voice as she crossed the Wastes, beneath the tale she told to block it out, beneath the glacial creak and crumble of the shifting gods upon whose skin they walked, beneath the wind and the whispers that wind bore as near-dead beings begged her to believe.

She's using you.

Ley forged a path through the changing land, deployed her tricks and tools to find the Altus tower. She had never looked sexier than standing wind-bitten and defiant, consulting her map, one foot propped on snowbank, small gods' faces forming in the steam of her breath.

Zeddig wanted to believe. But she remembered Kai in the engine room back on the train, so fierce, so certain, so like the Ley she knew. What's that knife worth to you?

On the beach, Ley had begged Zeddig to back off, as earnest and as weak as she had ever been. Trust me.

If Vogel had sold them out to Bescond for protection, Ley's knife was worth more to the Wreckers than a train of joss, thirty crooks, and two delver teams. And Ley had promised it to Zeddig if she just got her to this tower. Which meant—what, exactly?

Zeddig hopped over puddles of sphinx blood, and caught up with Ley as she pondered the tower's front door locks. "Vogel must have given them my marker. They're chasing us right now. Hells, they could have broken me on the train."

Ley drew a narrow crystal prism from her belt and pressed it against the keyhole. The crystal deformed, some facets contracting while others stretched. "Which is why I swapped vials the night of the meeting."

When she'd come home drunk. "What? How?"

"Vogel has habits. I took advantage of them."

"Habits?"

Ley stared into the crystal as if through a kaleidoscope. "Do you really need details? Imagine he's a majiang enthusiast, or that he really likes eight-way chess, one of those games that get you, you know, tied up. Once I made the right friends it was easy to get into his apartment, find his stash, and leave again. I told you I'd take care of it."

"I can't believe you."

"Believe what you like." She tossed her a sliver of glass and red; Zeddig's stomach lurched, but she caught the vial, and as her hand closed around the glass she felt herself held too, as if in a giant's grip. At this level of pressure, it didn't feel so bad. She remembered vomiting on the floor of a bar, remembered pain curled like an ingrown nail around her spine. "Break it, if you want," Ley said. "You'll be fine."

Zeddig slid the vial into her pocket while Ley bent again to the door. Ley turned her crystal to the left, and with a click and a flare of light, the door opened. Warm stale air steamed out into the desert chill.

Gal entered first, her steps so soft that Zeddig heard only the wind. They waited outside. Raymet stroked her chin with her gloved hand. Ley counted seconds on her watch. Izza and Isaak watched. "Gal will be fine," Zeddig told them. "She does this sort of thing all the time." No one had ever done this sort of thing before—at least, no one had never done it and survived. They'd already more than doubled the unofficial world record for a delve, Ghazik's team's hour twenty. But Izza and Isaak needed calming. Zeddig liked the girl: a sharp little vector who looked at everything as if it might kill her, but if it didn't, she'd write a poem about it later. The armored seemed spooked. He knew the dead city: the place nightmares came from, and the twisted half things that jumped you mid-job when you took the wrong turn in an unmapped sewer. He knew to fear the Wastes.

They heard silence and breaking glass.

Raymet was half through the door before Gal said, "You can come in now."

A chandelier of mutlicolored glass hung from the high ceiling. Aluminum panels stamped with friezes of alien worlds lined the walls, and beneath those panels lay low uncomfortable leather couches. The receptionist's desk stood empty. The people who fled this building had little warning. Cardboard boxes of desk-stuff littered the floor. Paperwork spilled from multicolored folders. There should have been dust or spiderwebs, but there were no people here to shed skin, and gods must have killed the spiders.

Gal sat on top of what looked like a second, fallen chandelier. Thin cuts, already closing, lined her arms and face. She seemed at ease. Zeddig had seen illustrations in foreign books of boys sitting on pastel pastoral hills, wearing that same smile Gal was missing the straw hat and the blade of grass between her teeth, that was all.

"It was slow." She kicked one of the dead demon's many arms. "Shall we?"

Zeddig trailed them up the long concrete stair. Every few floors they emerged into a red-lit hall to wander past cubicles and display banks. Glowworms had consumed their protein substrate and spilled out to devour walls and floor, leaving a writhing multicolored carpet that crunched underfoot.

A chair squeaked, turning. Zeddig jumped. The chair swiveled all the way around, empty, and came to a stop facing away from its desk. Shifted by the draft of their passage? Simple entropy, rearranging the ruin?

They climbed.

"You owe me an explanation," Zeddig told Ley, when there was enough space between them and the others to talk without being overheard. "We're long past 'I don't want to get you into trouble.'"

More stairs. A security box Ley couldn't fix; Raymet pondered it, tiny probes in hand, ghostlamp burning on her forehead, loupe in her eye, lower lip between her teeth, while Gal knelt beside her and watched.

"Vogel sold us out," Zeddig said, upstairs, looking down. "He must have given them our names. There will be people after my family."

The multicolored light of Raymet's work played over Ley's high cheekbones, her thin lips. "When I'm gone, tell them: I only worked with her because she paid me."

"The Wreckers are chasing that knife. Did you plan on telling us? Or were we just the next patsies in line?"

"Ah," Raymet said. She took a lacquer box from her tool belt, opened the box with care, and removed a large cockroach from within. The roach's legs paddled the air frantically. Stasis box, probably. Raymet snapped the roach in half, and the door opened. "We're good."

They filed through.

"They want the knife," Ley said, "but they can't catch you while you have it. They can't stay in the dead city, only deny its existence. One delve with that thing, a suitcase of books from the Anaxmander Stacks, and you can buy your way out of any trouble. Or run off somewhere beyond Iskari law. You wouldn't be the first."

"And leave my city, and my people."

"Do you think either's so weak they can't get on without you?"

Zeddig watched the side of her face. "So, you give me the knife, and I draw every Wrecker in the city into a wild goose chase. What do you get out of this?"

"Time," she said.

In their winding ascent, the cubicles and offices gave way to smoother, sterile spaces, metal and bamboo and ultraviolet light. Lab coats hung on hooks. Specimens had grown to toxic forests in glass cabinets. Greenish-black tufts sprouted from black mugs that probably once held coffee with milk. The laboratories, in their turn, surrendered to halls unadorned save for countdown clocks. Gal cleared a half-open room they passed, in case a demon might be hiding there; she burst in, and Isaak, but found only large lockers full of bulky red suits like crude soft armor.

At last they reached a heavy door locked, like the train hatches, with a wheel. Ley tried to open it herself. Muscles strained beneath her jumpsuit. Zeddig couldn't budge the wheel either. Gal and Isaak managed it together. When the hatch hinged open, Zeddig saw it was two feet thick.

Beyond the door lay a cavern.

In the cavern's heart there stood a spear.

Beyond the door lay a cavern: for all the spire's size, it could not possibly contain a space this big, a hollow cylinder broad enough to hold the Southern Express, bridged by spiderwebs of silk and steel, ringed with catwalks and gantries, including the narrow metal bridge that extended from their hatch to—

In the cavern's heart there stood a spear: "spear" being the wrong word and the right at once. The shape was right: an object with haft and head, an impaling implement, yes. (Though the tip was blunted and knobbed; it would leave a grotesque wound.) But "spear" could not apply to anything this scale, made from acres of welded metal and bone; a God could throw such a thing, Zeddig thought, or a Goddess, and she wondered what sort of monster. They would need this spear to wound, or kill. All the suggestions her brain supplied were too horrible to contemplate, so she stopped herself wondering.

Good thing she was used to the dead city. She'd forced herself to stop thinking about so much, forced herself to see the world the way cops and teachers liked. She used that practice now, to remain upright.

Ley stepped onto the gantry, and turned back to face them. "Now. This is the tricky part. Follow me, stay close, but for the love of yourselves and your family, do nothing rash, or Crafty, and certainly nothing anyone would describe as 'springing into action.'"

Nods all around.

Ley marched onto the gantry. They followed her single file, gripping the rails with various degrees of terror. Their steps echoed into the cavern depths and back again. Someone hissed. Zeddig didn't think it was her. The hiss grew louder beneath the racket of their steps, until Zeddig realized it was too loud to be human.

She remembered there had been no spiderwebs elsewhere in the building.

Ley was looking up.

Zeddig followed her gaze.

The tip of the spear was moving.

What Zeddig had taken for ribs and bumps clicked up, and out, and were in fact angular, arched metal legs, clawtipped, fierce. Other distortions on the spearhead shifted, interlaced and spun, cables wired with other cables, fangs dripping acid.

Had the spider been a part of the cavern's initial design, weaving cables to protect the spear? Had some god crept through the walls and wards, a memory nestled in a spider's egg, and warped an arachnid embryo to feed on a cold metal world? Was this a security system, or had the buildings' planner just thought giant metal spiders were cool?

The spider glared down—an effective glare, given the many eyes it glared with. The hiss issued from somewhere within its maxillae.

"Don't worry about it," Ley said, and waved the spider off backhanded.

She marched to a door in the spear. The spider scuttled down from the spear-tip, leaving white trails where its claws touched. They were not, Zeddig realized after a moment's confusion, trails torn by the claws—rather, small pieces of claw rubbed off by the spear-tip, like chalk on slate.

"Shut up," Ley shouted.

The spider stilled.

"Just here for routine maintenance. In and out before you know it."

The spider drew back a step, and its red eyes swept each of them in turn. Zeddig felt that gaze heat her skin. She'd been watched by dying angels, in the dead city. This felt close to that—warmer, less ache, fewer tears.

Ley wrenched the door open.

Zeddig edged forward on the catwalk, to peer through.

In the heart of the spear lay a coffin.

That, at least, was built to a human scale. Past the door she saw a crawlspace studded with levers and controls, prayer wheels, dim glyphs, ghostlight paneling. But at its heart lay a simple coffin, open, facing up.

Zeddig knew it was a coffin, because there was a body inside.

The corpse was mummy-wrapped in cables, and a crown of needles lined its skull. Scraps of dark hair and leathered skin clung to bone. Here, at least, there was dust. The mouth was open, possibly screaming. Hard to tell, with tendons and ligaments rotted away. Whatever happened, it happened quick. One hand extended halfway to a Craftwork circle with a needle inside. What had she—Zeddig decided, arbitrarily—wanted to do? When the wards failed and the Wastes closed their fist, what could she want? Would that circle have helped her, or only killed her faster, cleaner?

She did not ask, but Ley spoke anyway: "She was bonded to the system. The wards failed during a launch test, and the Wastes rolled in, and the sensors fed the Waste-gods straight into her brain. She never had a chance. And all she wanted was to fly."

Ley took the skull by the teeth, and stared into its eye sockets. Dust rained down. Skin shook free. At last, wordless, she released the skull, and reached down through mummifying cables to a cold silver wheel-within-wheel pendant resting on the corpse's breastbone. The string that once supported it was long gone.

At least, Zeddig thought there must have been a string.

But Ley gripped the pendant with her right hand, the breastbone with her left, and pried. The silver came free with a dull boney crack. Tines sprouted from the pendant, long toothed lines that had spread through the corpse. Ley turned the pendant in the cold light of her hand torch, and the tines curled into a needle, like hermit crab legs seeing their shell. She nodded, and unzipped her jumpsuit.

Zeddig, still operating on the "don't-touch-anything" protocol, assumed Ley meant to slide the pendant into a pocket, to keep it safe.

Ley pulled down the neck of her tank top and slammed the pendant into her heart.

Zeddig tackled her, too late. Her skull clanged off the tomb's metal wall.

Ley smiled, then frowned, then touched her cheek as if she had never felt it before. Then she collapsed, curled into a fetal position beside the coffin. Spit leaked through her gritted teeth. Her eyes showed milk white between fluttering lids.

Above, the spider shuffled its feet.

Fuck this.

Zeddig wrapped one arm around Ley, and pulled her toward the door. Ley twitched. Her head struck the wall again, and Zeddig clutched her tighter; Ley's flailing elbow buried in Zeddig's stomach, and she winced, but held on.

"Let's go!" she called, as they reached the catwalk. Unnecessary. The others were moving already—Isaak to help with Ley, Gal toward the hatch. Lights burned on the side of the spear. Foul steam vented into the cavern. Cables burst loose from the spear's sides. The spider twitched, steadied itself, then set one tender, massive foot upon the gantry. Metal buckled under its weight.

All they had to do was cross the gantry before the spider got murderous, slam the door shut, and hope the thing couldn't squeeze—

A woman stepped through the open hatch. She was short, and strong-jawed, and she wore a badge and a small peaked hat.

"You're under arrest," Lieutenant Bescond said.

Then the Wreckers struck.

Chapter Forty-eight

REACHING THE SPIRE FELT like stepping from a raft to land. The Wreckers blunted the Wastes; Kai felt the cold only as a promise. They marched without hesitation over thin ice. If she flinched, if she ran from the Wreckers, she would drown and freeze at once. But when they passed through the fence around the spire, the yawning threat beneath her faded, and she felt, for a moment, safe.

She wasn't, but never mind.

Tara knelt by the sphinx, took what pulse she could despite the gaping hole where its head should be, then gloved her hands in shadow and shoved them into the monster's wounds up to the second knuckle. She frowned at the goo on her fingertips. "They're an hour ahead of us."

"Inside, then." Bescond stared into the sphinx's neck, down its collapsed gullet. "Funny, being back here." At first Kai thought she was talking about the sphinx. "It was a hell and a half, building this. Altus wanted to take advantage of the weaker rules in the Wastes; the wards to stabilize the desert enough for building cost a fortune. They planned an industrial park, a bridge between Agdel Lex and a better future . . . somewhere." She waved vaguely at the sky, then stood. "Shame."

"I'll go in first," Kai said. "You wait out here. Keep a cordon. They won't surrender the knife unless there's no way out."

"Not likely." Bescond raised one hand. "Wreckers in first."

The hooded figures flowed, bloomed, pulsed, into the tower. Before Kai could catch them they were all gone save Bescond's bodyguard, who followed the Lieutenant calmly across the yard.

Kai ran to block her path. "You said you would let me help her."

"Find her first, if you can," Bescond said. "You get that knife, I'll break off pursuit. I never said anything about waiting while you went in alone."

"You're cheating."

"Ms. Pohala, your sister will never give you what you want. You walk into that building, you're only handing her a hostage—and I'm done negotiating."

"You can't," she said, but did not finish that sentence. Bescond cocked her head to one side, skeptical. She was strong, with that wriggly thing on her chest, and bore weapons Kai could only imagine. Besides, the Wrecker stood behind her, tall and wet and cloaked. Kai remembered the touch of those arms, and her guts clenched, and her lungs felt small. She glared into the shadows of its face.

She could call on her gods; she'd never been a fighter, but she knew some tricks, and so did the Lady. But she would not win. Wreckers could descend the tower as quickly as they climbed.

She glanced past the Iskari to Tara, her not-quite ally. The Craftswoman said nothing, but she did look up, across the sands and vacant car park, to the tower. Kai didn't know Tara well enough to read her. Was that pity? Scorn? Compassion?

When Kai turned back to Bescond, the Lieutenant was waiting. Bescond stood with her knees softly bent, chin pointed, eyes level. Waste-wind ruffled her short dark hair. She carried no tension. She woke every morning with purpose. She lifted weights, and stretched, and when she visited a masseur, he probably complimented her on the looseness of her back and shoulders.

Bescond marched toward the tower, and the Wrecker followed.

Kai did not stop her. Some eight-year-old inside her railed at injustice. But she wasn't eight anymore, for better or for worse.

"Don't worry, Ms. Pohala," Bescond called from the door. "We'll find your sister soon."

She closed the door after.

• • •

Oh, Izza thought when she saw the Lieutenant. So this is how it goes to shit.

Then the Wreckers came.

Two rushed past Bescond. Tentacles uncoiled from their sleeves. Gods, they moved so fast.

But Gal was faster.

Raymet reached for the Camlaander's arm—"Don't!"—but not fast enough to catch her.

Izza knew street fights. She knew sharp quick blows and knives, seconds at most until someone died, or broke. You could walk away from one-on-two, if you were lucky, if some god loved you, if you had good insurance.

Once, in a Kavekanese back alley, she had seen a goddess's chosen fight: a flash of silver, a glory of wings, a terrible joyous purpose. She hoped she would never see that again, and sometimes prayed she would.

Gal, striding forward, smiled like a woman coming home. Light burned in jewel dots down her spine, tracing the tree roots of her nerves. A golden glow spread from them, from her heart, to her hands. One step, and she might have been a trick of candleflame and mirrors. Two steps, and her arms were clad in solid light. Three steps, and she was a halo.

When the first Wrecker lashed her, she caught its tentacles and threw it over the gantry edge. It fell, casting fleshy lines in all directions to catch itself and swing back. The metal spider tensed, and leapt. The gantry bent with the speed of the spider's departure; it caught the Wrecker in midair. Gal struck the second Wrecker in the chest with her elbow, so hard it tumbled back into the third that climbed up from below. Tentacles slipped off the light that clad her, and in a blink Gal held a blade like sunrise on an ocean's breast. The blade flashed out, and Izza heard a watery scream.

She heard softer sounds behind her: two damp thuds like wet leaves dropped from a height. She turned. Two Wreckers crouched by the spear, arms unspooling.

One jumped for her, but Isaak got there first. He went down, roaring as his scales bent in the Wrecker's grip; he tore one of its arms loose, then tried to sink his claws into its throat, only for it to snare him with more limbs. His knees buckled. Izza was there already, on the Wrecker's back, knife out. Her stomach turned as the blade slid into flesh. There were humans beings in these things, yes, but monsters outside. Her knife came out slick with purple, not red, and she did not know whether she felt relieved.

The fight got ugly. She saw the world in flashes, too godsdamn many things to hold in her head at once.

Two Wreckers held Gal's arms; she anchored herself on the

shaking gantry and swung one into the other and they went down in a squelch of flesh and crack of bone.

Zeddig, snared by a Wrecker from beneath, knelt, veins popped out against her skin, teeth gritted.

Zeddig screamed, drew a knife, cut the tentacle free.

Isaak slammed his Wrecker's head against the gantry, again and again and again. He tore rubbery flesh with his teeth.

More Wreckers joined the fray from both sides; Raymet tossed small dark spheres underhanded, and the spheres spoke with voices of curling chaos, and Wreckers fell, but others caught them before they fell too far.

Ley stared vacant into the fray, seeing visions. A tentacle caught her leg; she drew her knife automatically, slashed down—too late. Even through the pulse of blood in Izza's ears, she heard Ley's leg snap.

Izza moved as fast as the Lady could make her. Gal danced with monsters and blade: she was a woman of gold. Zeddig fought with her long knife, and Ley collapsed against the shuddering catwalk, and Isaak roared and tore and slammed and turned and broke, and Raymet threw weapons and dodged and fought, and still they were losing.

· · ·

"We have to do something."

Tara stared into the Wastes, unblinking. Kai followed her gaze, and flinched away from the pain of dying gods. Tara: "Hm?"

"My sister's in there."

Tara bared her teeth, not smiling. "I can't go against Bescond directly. No matter how much I'd like to. We have an agreement."

"There's more to life than godsdamn agreements," Kai said, and heard how she sounded, especially to a Craftswoman, for whom there wasn't.

"I know," Tara said, which surprised her. "That's why I'm thinking."

Kai blinked. Their alliance, if that's what it was, felt so tenuous: a few seconds' doubt and she shifted Tara from partner to enemy. Granted, Kai hadn't had the best run rate with trust recently, but even paranoia had its limits. "How can you help?"

Tara turned back to the tower, and closed her eyes—looking on the world as a Craftsman, seeing the reality behind reality, the realm of souls and faith. "They'll be fighting soon."

"What can you see?"

"Enough. I can't tell you the color of their hair, whether they're happy or sad. I can see deals they've made, geases and enhancements, all the ways they've sold themselves. I can see the building, too, its contracts and compromises. Points where its wards have frayed."

"Can you break those wards?"

"At this distance?" Tara frowned. "I think so. Can you still talk to your friend?"

"At this distance?"

Tara grinned. "I *thought* I liked you."

Kai reached into her jacket pocket, then cursed. "Out of pins."

"Bloodletting." Tara shook her head. "Old-fashioned."

"I'm a traditional girl. I have a knife in my purse."

The Craftswoman reached for her heart, and the world dimmed. "Here. Use mine."

• • •

Blue fire seared Izza's mind, and she fell. This, she thought, is not a good time. But the sweep of a Wrecker's tentacle overhead, where she had just been standing, excused the interruption.

This was you, she prayed. You fucked this up. You brought them here.

We need the knife.

Of all the godsdamn dumb ideas. I could have gotten the knife on my own.

Bescond promised—

You trusted the cop to keep her promises.

I'm sorry.

You sure talked a good game, about how much you learned from last time . . .

Can I make it up to you by getting you and your friends out of there?

What have you got?

A burst of images and emotion later, she forced herself off her knees, and ran to Zeddig. The woman stood with her back to the spear, one arm around Ley, the other stabbing Wrecker tentacles. "I can get us out," Izza shouted. "Down four floors and over. There's a hole in the security. I saw it." The wall near Zeddig blued. Fuck. Izza's eyes were glowing again. She'd have to talk to the Lady about that.

"Down?" Zeddig said. "How do you plan to—" And then she got it. "That's crazy. We'll die."

"Don't worry." Ley had recovered enough to show her teeth, not quite enough to grin. "If we fall, the Wreckers will catch us."

Zeddig tossed her a rope. "Can you tie this to the middle of the bridge?"

"Sure," Izza said, though she wasn't. "Isaak!" She didn't waste time on conversation, just charged onto the gantry, toward the cyclone of light that was Gal in action. Three tentacles had snared the Camlaander's left leg; they could not break her, but hold her, yes. She fought anyway, vicious and holy as the sun.

Isaak lurched beside Izza, growling prayers through his pain. He caught a Wrecker and heaved it over the side. A tentacle grazed her, but he clawed it off. She tied a rope to each gantry rail, tugged the knots to test them, and ran back toward the spear. One rope for Ley and Zeddig. ("Can you make it?" "I think I can spare us"—a grunt through gritted teeth as Ley tried her broken leg—"the shame of failure.") One for Raymet and Izza. Isaak and Gal could make the jump alone, unaided.

More wet thuds against the spear below the bridge. Izza stuck her neck out over the abyss, and saw two Wreckers climbing up. "We're out of time!"

"Gal!" Raymet cried.

Gal turned, and spent a second pondering the situation, during which she knocked one Wrecker to the side with a spinning kick, and cut her leg free. She ran—but Wreckers caught her again, and again she broke away. Three more snared her. Another cut, another break. Five, this time. Six, two on each leg, one on each arm. A Wrecker landed on her back, its arms and legs wrapping hers. Gal seemed, briefly, perplexed.

Then she grinned.

Not with the Wrecker's sick pleasure, no. She grinned like someone meeting a friend she long thought lost. "Go on," she said. "I'll catch up."

Zeddig nodded, mute, and wrapped the rope around her wrist. Izza reached for Raymet.

"She's not coming." Raymet's face was empty.

"Raymet," Zeddig said, "there's no time."

But what else exists save time? Heartbeats, breaths, intervals of decision: Izza saw Raymet look at Gal, at Zeddig, at the rope. She did not waste the time to shake her head. She ran onto the catwalk toward Gal, knife in one hand, wrench in the other.

Zeddig tried to catch her, but she was gone, into the coils and the light.

Izza hated herself for being the one who said: "We have to go!" A Wrecker landed on the underside of the catwalk and scuttled toward them, arms woven through holes in the grating.

Zeddig cursed and staggered onto the bridge, holding Ley. For a moment Izza thought she'd go too, after her friends, and they'd all fall together beneath layers of thrashing arms.

Then she jumped.

They tumbled, Ley's arms around Zeddig's shoulders, hers around her waist. Izza followed on her own rope, and prayed: Come on, Lady. I'm not asking much. Wind carved tears from her face. She swung through the dark and fell and rolled and landed and she was still alive, on a gantry four stories down. Isaak landed seconds later, covered in Wrecker goo. Ley screamed; she'd struck her leg in the fall.

Izza rolled, tripped, stumbled toward the door. It was ringed in reddish light; she pressed against it and it did not open. She cursed.

Then the light went blue, and it did.

• • •

"Forty feet?" Kai asked.

Tara shook her head. "Twenty-five. Blue door. No, green door. Three floors down after that. Don't try the knob—just hit it with her shoulder. Then, right, and down the first stair you see, far as you can"

"You're not sure if it's blue or green?"

"I can't see light like this, just contracts. The security system documentation's in Imperial, and their words for blue and green—"

"Green, okay." Pause. They circled the tower. "Bescond must have left a rear guard."

"Maybe," Abernathy said. "But she only has so many Wreckers, and Zeddig has a good team. Bescond's best chance was to hit them all at once. Besides, she didn't expect the building's security to fail. Wow."

"Wow?"

Tara said: "That's interesting."

"Interesting isn't good."

"I wish you could see this. I didn't know your sister had a Knight on her team."

"Really?"

"Oh yeah." Tara's nod: slow, exaggerated emphasis. "She's strong, too."

"I thought they were all out slaying dragons and committing atrocities."

"Guess not."

"How does chivalry square with a life of crime?"

"Maybe you can ask her, when the dust settles."

"Okay," Kai said. "They're down the stairs. What's next?"

• • •

Izza led them through the dark. Doors opened, doors closed. Zeddig and Ley made a lurching three-legged race of it, Ley supporting herself with one hand against the wall, teeth gritted as they ran. The tower swayed with the battle they'd left behind. Ceiling panels shook. Izza wondered who Gal was, and for what purpose she'd been made. She was not certain she wanted to know.

They ran. Kai spoke to her through the Lady—turn left, down those stairs, double back, third door on the right, trace the circle with your thumb, three times clockwise and one half counter-turn. Down again, down always and forever.

Isaak loped beside her, dark skin showing between his cracked armor plates. He did what she said, when she said it. Looked at her when he thought she wouldn't notice, and in his eyes she saw something that would have scared her, years ago. Now she knew it too well. That was how you looked at a priestess, a saint. That was not how you looked at a friend.

"She spoke to you," he said, awed, as they rattled down a flight of stairs. "She's speaking through you now."

There was too much to say, and she didn't want to say any of it, so she used running as an excuse not to. Gods. Lady, she did not sincerely pray, why don't you take this one for me, enlighten my friend as to what the fuck is going on. You and he are clearly on speaking terms. Or maybe you've kept quiet because you don't want him to know, because he might tip your hand to the squids about how you sneak through their arms, climb into the crevasses they can't reach. Maybe you don't want to spill all goods on the first date?

"What does it feel like?" he asked. "I've only ever—just a shadow. A touch. And you—"

"Right," she said, and they ran right, and "down," and they ran down. "Loading dock."

"Loading dock," Zeddig echoed.

Ley tried to speak, but groaned.

Izza could not hear the Wreckers following—but then, she would not hear them until it was too late, not under the noise of their running feet. Wreckers moved in silence, struck and darted, too fluid to track. She never thought she'd miss the Penitents at home—at least you could feel those monsters coming. The Wreckers might lurk around any corner, coiled hungry shadows, breathing their sick joy. Not around this turn, though. Not the next.

Ground floor. Throw a chair through the plate glass window into the stockroom, good, glass shards everywhere, just what we needed. Isaak helped Zeddig lever Ley over the windowsill, then vaulted through, his armored palms blunting the broken glass. He offered Izza a hand, which she accepted, though it meant she'd have to see that look on his face again.

Zeddig, panting, clutched Ley as if the woman held her upright, rather than the other way around.

"Straight shot through storage," Izza said. "There's a small door to the left of the big," she gestured, so vague with exhaustion she wasn't sure herself whether the movement described a box or a window or an arch or a, "garage door thing."

Zeddig nodded. She breathed too hard, too heavily. Her eyes slid past Izza without focusing. She'd run down the spire, carrying Ley and her gear, and she was human, as far as Izza'd been able to tell. In excellent shape, but only human.

"A brisk stroll," Ley said through gritted teeth. "Salutary for the constitution. Come on." She hopped on one foot down the hall, tugging Zeddig alongside. "Break a leg. It's your turn." Her gasps of pain didn't improve the joke, but Zeddig growled, and moved anyway.

High metal warehouse shelves made narrow halls in the vast chamber. A golem forklift loomed in one corner, flat prongs jutting like tusks, cabin empty. Izza ignored the cramp in her side, and wondered if there was still a demon trapped within that metal chassis, its wards unbroken after all this time, wondered if the mind within still wanted to go home.

She saw light—real sunlight, the pale Wasteland sky—through the open door. "There."

Something slithered over steel shelves. A goddess told her: duck.

A weight of coiled muscle tackled her, grasping, twitching. She fought free and stabbed, felt the goddess blunt the poison pleasure the Wrecker fed into her vein. "Go!" Zeddig and Ley hadn't broken stride. Of course. Every woman for herself now.

A coil tried to catch Izza's neck, but she ducked, wormed free and launched herself off the floor, running fast, so fucking fast, fastest thing on the islands with magic or without, no mainland Wrecker could catch her—even as Isaak, godsdamn Isaak, barreled unnecessarily to her rescue, grabbed the tentacles that had failed to snare her, lifted, slammed the Wrecker so hard into the shelves they toppled like tall slow dominos. Metal struts snapped, boxes fell, and Izza was still running, godsdammit, steal a page from those dumb hepcat meditation manuals the cabana bars back home left in toilet stalls for inspirational reading and *go toward the light—*

Behind her, Isaak screamed.

Behind her, Isaak fell.

Behind her, Isaak prayed for a miracle.

And she felt him pray, just like she felt Kai, like she felt the kids back home.

Ley and Zeddig tumbled out to freedom.

And Izza turned back.

Isaak fought, tangled in Wreckers' coils, scraping against the writhing limbs that slid into his armor's gaps and pried. He roared, coated in purple blood. He was losing.

The Lady's stone gleamed on his chest.

Izza cursed herself, and cursed the Lady, and ran back to help.

Behind her, the door swung shut.

Fucking typical.

Chapter Forty-nine

ZEDDIG STUMBLED INTO LIGHT and, blinking, exhausted, tripped down concrete steps to collapse with Ley in sand. Her heart battered her ribs. Her lungs filled and emptied on their own.

A short rest, that's all you can spare. Ten seconds. Count them. Nine. Eight. On one, you get up, pull Ley up after you, and run for the Wastes. Bend over. Breathe. Watch a point between your hands. Let the world spin.

"Zeddig," Ley said beside her.

Five. Four.

"Zeddig. We have guests."

She looked up.

Zeddig did not recognize the Craftswoman, but she saw Ley's sister by her side.

Zeddig tried to run, but the Craftswoman snapped her fingers, and her bones refused to cooperate.

"Fuck" was the only word adequate to the situation.

"Hello again, dear sister," Ley said, from the ground. She laughed through the pain.

"Talk fast," the Craftswoman told Kai. "They're coming."

Kai stepped forward. She looked at Ley, first, but she could not bear to hold her sister's gaze for long. What made her turn away? The pain? The weakness? What did she see? This was her moment—her triumph, after Zeddig had warned her away.

Was this Zeddig's fault? Had she fucked them over? "I need the knife," she said. "That's all. The knife, and you go free."

"My friends?"

"I can't promise anything," Kai said. "Bescond has them, and I can't bargain until I have the knife. I'll try to free them. But I don't know what she'll do. Give me the knife, and you go free. That's what I can offer now."

Ley's scornful laugh broke into a hiss. She pushed herself up, kneeling on one leg, the other straight behind her. "Nice fairy tale. If we run, they'll chase us."

Kai shook her head. "Bescond doesn't care about you. She wants the blade." Behind, in the spire, someone screamed. Zeddig wondered if it was the girl. Kai twitched. Closed her eyes. Her hand went to her brow. When she looked up again, she was hard and sharp and brittle as a glass splinter. "Give it to me, Ley. And get the hells out of here."

Zeddig remembered this woman in Hala's Fell, rich with smells of cardamom and butter, remembered warning her off, thinking: there was too much of Ley in Kai to let her get involved. Two of those would fight until they broke.

Behind Kai spread the Wastes, and freedom, or death.

And behind Zeddig rose a tower of fallen friends, caught in Iskari coils. She was their hope. If she stayed free.

"No," Ley said.

But Zeddig said, "That's not your choice to make."

Ley stared up at her.

"You promised me the knife."

"To use. Not to give my fucking sister."

"A promise is a promise," Zeddig said.

"You don't know what you're doing—"

"Saving us. And my friends." She reached for Ley's belt. Ley tried to fight her, but she had no strength—wrung out by their flight, by her wound, by fading adrenaline and the disaster in the tower.

Zeddig was almost as weak. Almost.

The knife felt weightless in her palm. The blood drop glittered in the blade. A voice cackled in triumph, but she did not listen or care.

"Break down the fence."

The Craftswoman shrugged, and the fence fell.

"Your word. We'll not be followed."

"Zeddig, you don't have any godsdamn idea what you're doing—"

"I do."

Zeddig looked down at the blade that was not a blade at all. So light a thing. She spat out a foul taste in her mouth, and tossed it across the sand to Kai.

The blade rolled to a stop at her feet.

Ley lunged for the knife, but her bad leg buckled. Zeddig caught her, wrapped her arm around Ley's shoulder, hoisted her to her feet.

"Come on," she said. She felt tired and firm—scoured as an abandoned building, all façade and polish worn away, until only the skeleton remained.

Ley sagged into her, and, arm in arm, shoulder to shoulder, they limped into the Wastes.

Chapter Fifty

THEY DRAGGED IZZA AND Isaak over broken glass and shattered concrete to the entrance hall. Izza bit and tore them with her nails, but the Wreckers' arms bound her tighter the harder she fought, and though they no longer tried to poison her with their sour joy, contentment spread like oil slick from their touch. Izza had never frozen to death, but she imagined that would feel like this, sensation fading until none remained to lose.

The Wreckers knelt them beneath the Altus logo, by the receptionists' desk. The one that held Izza bled purple from Izza's knife and Isaak's claws, limping, weak from its torn limbs. The second, which had surprised them as they made a break for the door, held Isaak, so tangled through him he was hardly visible save for his eyes. Beside them, the Wreckers held Gal and Raymet, Raymet unconscious, Gal supported by the mass of arms that bound her. The Camlaander was awake, pupils dilated, and she seemed vaguely disappointed.

Izza tugged against her Wrecker's arms, but they didn't give.

The Lieutenant paced before them, hands in the pockets of her overcoat, head down. "Hells do you mean, *lost*? They were together—" The Wrecker behind Izza gurgled, and Izza felt a stab of professional triumph. Someone made it, at least. "Follow them into the Wastes. They can't have gone far. Sedate these four, find the others, and come back."

A shadow impinged on the light streaming through the open door. "Lieutenant Bescond," Kai said. "May I interrupt?"

The Lieutenant turned, slowly.

Kai entered, with the Craftswoman at her side. "I have something you want." In her grip glittered a knife made of geometry, with a drop of blood at its heart. "My sister goes free."

"That," the Craftswoman confirmed, "was the deal."

Bescond stood vicious and sharp in silhouette, against Kai, against the Wastes outside, against the world. "I could take that from you right now."

The Craftswoman's voice remained casual, as if discussing weather. "If you do, you'll stand in material breach."

The shadows in the broken room darkened, and cold wind blew in from the Wastes. The Wrecker that held Izza twitched. The others shivered. Gal smiled like a war.

Bescond rolled her shoulders back, as if shedding a heavy cloak. "Fine. Give me the knife."

"Let the others go," Kai said.

"Our deal doesn't cover them. These two"—she pointed to Gal and Raymet—"are bound for the tower. These two"—to Izza and Isaak—"are thugs, juveniles. Jails for them. We dealt for your sister."

Kai glared at the Craftswoman, at Bescond. Then she reviewed the prisoners one by one, settling on Izza.

Izza's mind, sluggish, clicked into motion then. If Kai wanted wanted Izza free, all she had to do was make the case. Without their spy in the enemy ranks, Kai could not have traced Ley, could not have caught Zeddig and this godsdamn knife. Izza was an Iskari hero. Of course Bescond would let her go.

By her side, Isaak shouldered against his bonds, and snarled through sharp teeth. He glanced over to Izza. Blood streaked his face. Beneath all that fury and sharp teeth, he looked lost and scared.

Izza glared at Kai, and prayed with all the strength inside her: *Don't you fucking dare.*

Kai's knees buckled with the force of the prayer. The Craftswoman took her by the elbow—but the moment's weakness passed. Kai straightened, and offered Bescond the knife.

"Deal."

Bescond took the blade, and held it so the Waste light shone through. Izza knelt at the wrong angle to see how triumph looked on the woman's face.

Chapter Fifty-one

KAI STAYED NUMB THE whole trip home. Wreckers marched them back across the Wastes, their laced arms transmuting to sand dune stillness the slow anguished motion of the gods on whom they tread. After an hour's walk they found a waystation, a creepy ramshackle platform of rotten wood and cracked concrete guarded by the track wards. Bescond set a flag and they waited together and separately, each in her own head.

Tara did not look at Kai, or anyone else. She seemed far away—seeing and hearing other people, wishing she could make them real by sheer focus. Bescond marched along the platform, hands in coat pockets, shoulders back, self-assured and whole, situation in hand, that's what her body language said, all but the set of her jaw. She checked her watch three times each circuit of the track. Perhaps her watch held a step counter, and she wanted to hit her daily goal.

Then there were the prisoners.

Izza had not looked at Kai since that moment back in the tower. The boy, Isaak, kept his head down and did not move. The Camlaander sat cross-legged, bound fast by two Wreckers and gloriously composed, as if unprepared to admit the existence of the outside world. Not submissive—just submitting. The thin Gleblander by her side cursed everything nearby, and everyone, then asked for a cigarette.

They waited for the train.

Wind howled. Kai told herself it was wind. She did not look at the horizon. Too many hands rose to tear the sky, too many Beings forced themselves upright only to be pulled down once more by ropes of plasm.

Ley was out there.

She didn't think about that.

The Express returned. They felt its approach first as a stillness of the not-quite-gods. Against the world's curve, against physical and thaumaturgical law, against the bloody burden of its cargo, the engine worked. The train dawned to the south, an earthquake wrapped in steel. Insulating gel sloshed around cargo containers, around their vital weight of necromantic earths, of bones and oil. The Express was an enormous perfect vessel of trade, a weapon like the ball of knives in old Quechal tales, volleying between the Hero Twins and their opponents in a sacrificial game of ullamal, killing where it touched, rebounding to kill again. While the game endured, the blade-ball moved. The ball was the game, the game the ball.

But the Express stopped for them. They belonged to it. Mites, they crawled upon its back, eating the dust they found, and called that living.

Kai sat in the passenger car, not reading the newspaper by the fake light through the fake window, not looking at Bescond across from her, who did read the paper, not looking at Abernathy who stared, troubled, into her folded hands. Kai had seen art gallery collages of engraved black-and-white people scissored out from newsprint, pasted into backgrounds of glossy fashion magazine ballroom luxury. She felt like that, in the train, after the Wastes.

Ley was out there.

Somewhere.

Broken-legged and lost.

The world lacked a knife so subtle as Kai's heart. She bled within. Ley had glared at her through loose strands of hair, dark eyes sharp with fury. You should have listened. You never should have chased me. You should have let me go.

If not for Kai, Bescond would have hunted Ley and Zeddig across the Wastes, caught her for sure—two women on foot, one of whom could barely walk. Once she had the knife, Bescond would not have let Ley go, or even Zeddig for that matter. She would not pass up a chance for revenge against a woman who made her life piercing the Iskari shell.

There was no other way. But even so, Kai had played along. She gave Bescond the knife. Her mind was a cavern, and regret a bonfire, and she knelt in chains as memory cast distorted shadows on the wall.

Izza's rejection, her furious prayer to be left alone, had been easy to bear. But only by comparison.

The train reached its station. Bescond kept still. Abernathy waited. Venting the insulation slush took almost an hour. The conductor tapped the door with her knuckle, and said, in flawless Iskari, "It is now safe to descend."

Kai stumbled into her room at the Arms and shut the door with an exhausted slump. Behemoth curled, head tucked into belly, a roll of black fur on the windowsill lit slantwise by the last of the sun. The cat raised his head, blinked in suspicion at the general scheme of wakefulness, and lowered his head again.

Kai changed the food and water bowls, emptied the litter box, sunk twenty thaums into a tip for tomorrow's housekeeper. That, too, felt sick, after what she'd seen and done today. All of this did, this normalcy. She remembered Abernathy: Where do you think your pilgrims get the soulstuff they invest with you, the wealth they hope to hide from gods and men? Are they legitimate, really? Entrepreneurs? All of them?

What are you, if not a scavenger?

Descending sunlight stung tears from her eyes. The cat's purr echoed. So did his breath. There were no other sounds in the hotel room. Kai hated hotels. Should have found another place to stay. A corporate apartment. A bed and breakfast. She might have even asked to spend the night with her—

sister

Enough.

She took a saucer from the coffee service, drew a new supply of needles from her open luggage, sank to the floor, and let a drop of blood swell from her forefinger into the dish. Grace addicts collapsed veins this way. She needed a better solution. They really should reform the Blue Lady's theology to something less bloodthirsty, less pain-focused. Even if the Lady had been born from pain, even if Her followers had more pain in common than anything else.

Kai's heart pulsed as the blood struck porcelain. She watched a pattern form, watched shadows track across carpet as light changed and died. The bloodspatter was a tunnel into the depths, and she descended winding down to find at the world's heart a Lady radiant blue, her savior and salvation, perfect in her cleverness, a flash of the pads of running feet, a glint of horn and tail like a buck from the kind of woods they did not have on Kavekana—the Lady who chose Izza as her prophet—the Goddess who Izza, prophet, formed.

Kai's Goddess too.

Kai framed herself for each client, for each idol she served.

She was a killer, when their service called for death. Gods of pleasure, Ladies of love, required ecstasy and repose: you stripped yourself bare, you fit your being to requirements, you gave the idol what it needed to keep its story spinning. Queens of Heaven you met with submission or command, depending on the mythos. Such gods were masks, and she donned masks to meet them.

But the Blue Lady was a Goddess of ambush, subversion, and escape. She preached: outrun, outwit, endure.

Kai outran—some. Kai outwitted—occasionally. Kai endured—but in a different way from Izza, less hungry, more obstinant. She was not fast enough. She was too comfortable.

The Lady darted ahead through the minefield of her mind.

Ley would have been the Lady's better servant. She always was better at things, more kind and fierce at once. When Father died, Kai did not weep. Ley wept. When they read reports of war in Kho Khatang, when the body count rose, Kai did not rage like her sister raged. When the Kavekanese labor market teetered on the verge of collapse, when the shipping business failed, when idols became the island's main industry, when the choice came to stay or leave, Kai stayed, and Ley left.

Yes, Kai had her reasons: when Father died Kai planned dinner and breakfast, she cooked, she cleaned, because someone had to. When she read reports of war, there was more to be done than raging: she climbed the mountain to petition priests for aid. And when the choice came to desert your island, or to join its priesthood and stave off disaster serving pilgrims who, yes, might be in point of fact bad people, she stayed. But though she had her reasons, facts remained: She did not weep. She did not rage. She did not leave.

Kai had helped Bescond to save Ley. But the strength of

Ley's scorn, her anger as Zeddig dragged her into the Wastes . . .

The Lady ran, and Kai pursued. Why? Did Kai want to run, to evade, to step lightly and travel lighter, to break power's hold? Or did she pursue because, on a level she could not admit even to herself, she wanted to catch Her, and tie Her down, and stop Her running?

All those years ago, on distant Kavekana's shore, she tried to save her sister from the tide, from her single-minded vision, from the pain of the gallowglass at her ankle. She'd thought, today, that she was dragging Ley to safety once again—but no, that was Zeddig. Kai was not the sister, but the sea.

She called to Izza through the Lady's light.

Izza did not answer.

She ran through the dream, alone.

No.

Not alone.

She heard laughter.

Girl, said the deep voice in her head, said the hand on the back of her neck, the touch that slid away even as she reached for it, *there's more to crime than running. And there's more to running than escape. Don't just watch your feet. Look ahead.*

Her heartbeat steadied, and her breath, and her pace in the forest of her mind.

I saved her. I screwed up her plans, but I did save her. That was the idea, and if she'll never forgive me for it, I can live with that, because she's free, and safe.

I hope.

But Ley's not deranged. She's determined, and brilliant, and selfish by virtue of that brilliance, and strong enough to hurt herself and the world.

And so am I.

Ley thought Bescond's people should not, could not have that blade. While she was in danger, that didn't matter. Now she's safe—as safe as I can manage. (Don't think, *what if something goes wrong,* don't think, *what if she can't find a way back through the Wastes.*)

So, shift priorities.

Whatever Bescond wants with that knife, Ley didn't think she could stop it without a murder and a heist. So—fine. Ley was not a subtle human. She jumped first, thought after. That was not Kai's play. Kai helped the Wreckers, and they had swallowed her. Fine. Start from there. Be a hook in their gut.

Kai ran through the forest of her mind, and ran, and ran, and at last found the strength to turn—and there was light.

Her prayer flowered back into the world, where she found Behemoth nosing at the saucer and blood. His tail twitched.

Kai lifted the saucer before the cat could lick. Behemoth batted at her wrist, but missed; Kai scratched between his ears, then rinsed the saucer, grabbed her keys, and marched out into the night.

Chapter Fifty-two

ZEDDIG AND LEY LIMPED side by side into the Wastes.

For a long time they did not speak. Silence spoke loud enough for them both.

Ley placed all the weight she could bear—not much—on her broken leg. Or, Zeddig realized, reading facts less charitably and more true, she placed as little weight as possible on Zeddig.

They climbed dunes that were the spread of a broad slumped back, and skidded down a tricep. To control their fall, Zeddig dug her heels into skin, and tried to think of the grit sprayed in her face as sand. They found a flat ridge on the back of a massive snake, and limped along. Behind them, the tower receded, its peak still visible above the swell of half-dead bodies: a taunt, a memory that refused to fade.

Ley's ward held even without the knife—for now. Zeddig kept her delving gear ready just in case, but she opened the jacket and pushed back the hood and enjoyed the sweat. Heat pressed her, not the oven's weight of Agdel Lex, the breath of the conqueror squid, but the heat of heart and skin. She cooked herself with effort. Better that than freezing, or being torn by gods.

The snake held its shape as they crossed its back. Little else did. Landscape shifted, forms devouring forms to be devoured in turn. Small hands ripped plasmic gobs from giants, and stuffed them into tiny maws. A body became a forest, became a maze, became an undulating sea of limbs, became coral fronds, wove into a wicker basket in the shape of a man, burned glittering flames, melted back to skin.

Zeddig guided them north by the sun. They'd walked northwest to reach the tower. A day's hard walk, and a night's, and they'd reach Agdel Lex. They had water, and rations. If Ley's ward lasted, they'd make it.

That left only Ley's dead furious weight beside her.

"I made the right choice," Zeddig said.

"Dear Zeddig," with more venom than Zeddig had ever heard coat the word "dear," "I have nothing to say to you."

"Fuck you." She felt too tired to play their games any more—any of them. "This is your fault. We got that thing on your chest, and I listened to you when I shouldn't have. Now the Wreckers have my friends, and we have to get them back."

"*My* fault," she said. "What, among today's many disasters, is my fault? Diagram, please, how I contributed to your decision to throw our lot in with Vogel? Is it my fault you handed my sister, and the Wreckers, a tool I gave up more than you can imagine to keep from them?"

"A tool? You mean Vane?"

Ley stopped walking. "Don't bring her into this."

"You stuck a person inside that knife."

"She's not stuck," she said. "They can fix her. More's the pity."

"What the fuck is going on?"

"I asked you to trust me."

Zeddig turned to face Ley, as much as she could with one arm still draped over Ley's shoulders. Pain tightened Ley's features. She groaned. Zeddig had grown so used to seeing Ley masked that sunlight on her face looked strange. A spike of pity pierced her somewhere south of her heart, and she ignored it. "I won't give you up."

"We might have escaped without their help."

"Oh, yes. All we had to do was fight off a Craftswoman, you with a broken leg, and one piece of possessed silverware between us."

"They wanted to bargain. We could have lied, got close enough to hit Tara first. Kai couldn't stop us alone."

"Oh, so you're on a first-name basis with the Craftswoman now."

"You didn't even try."

"I was trying to save your life."

"Don't do me any more favors," Ley muttered, and ducked out from under Zeddig's arm. Zeddig caught her wrist; Ley tugged free, but in the shift and struggle her weight settled on her broken leg, and she screamed, high, sharp, short, and fell.

Zeddig caught her, and lowered her to the snake's scales. Ley snarled. Cords of muscle worked in her jaw, and stood out in her neck. Her lungs filled and emptied too fast for the breath to help.

Zeddig cradled Ley's head against her thighs. She slipped one hand free of its glove, and cupped the woman's cheek. "Do you need something to bite on?"

Ley shook her head, but kept her eyes screwed tight.

"I tried," Zeddig said. "I trusted your plan. But you would have thrown yourself to the Wreckers for the world's slimmest chance at escape. They'd take you, and break you. The dagger can't be worth that."

"It is."

"That's not your decision to make. Your life is my business."

Ley's eyes opened, tiny slits baring wet black beneath. "How do you figure?"

"I love you, you asshole."

Nothing lasted longer than that silence. The sky should have cracked. The world should have trembled. The Wastes should have become an enormous mouth to swallow them whole. Zeddig knelt, naked, above her, and any moment would come the scornful laugh, the joke, the deflection, the contempt.

"Oh," Ley said. Her jaw relaxed. A dark space opened between her teeth. Her tongue flicked her upper lip. Her lungs filled, all the way down into her belly, and she exhaled mist. "Shit."

Zeddig slumped to the sand. "That's a hell of an answer."

"I'm not talking about you," Ley said. Steam issued from her mouth with the words. "It's colder."

Zeddig felt it then: chill fingers of wind, the serpent's scales cold beneath her boots. She zipped her jacket, raised her hood. She cursed the sweat on her underlayers. "How long do we have?"

Ley breathed into her gloved palm, and watched the patterns in the mist. "The ward decays faster without the knife."

"You could have mentioned this before."

"Would you have listened?"

"Yes!" She was shouting. The cold insinuated through her coat—not unpleasant yet, just the first gentle pressure of a snake against skin, a promise of later tensing strength to come. Anger rose quick as ever to Zeddig's heart, and she felt the weight of all the choices made since she opened that window, and before then, even, when she saw this girl on a balcony, armored in her loneliness. None of this was fair. She should not have given up the knife—but there had been no choice. Ley should have told her—but she had not. "How long?"

"I don't know." And, before Zeddig could offer more than a preliminary growl in reply: "We never tested it for this. The ward's strong, we're far from the Wound, but the closer we get to Agdel Lex, the faster it will go."

"Ash." Zeddig could not swear to gods, not here, upon their bodies. "Okay. So we walk east, and follow the train tracks home. Their wards should help ours last longer."

Ley tried again to stand, perhaps hoping her leg had healed during her few minutes' lie-down. If she'd expected a miracle, she chose the wrong day. "Then what? We knock on the gates? Ask customs to let us through? We're not Wasteland monsters, honest?"

"The wall exists in the dead city, and in Agdel Lex. But there's no wall in Alikand."

"But the train tracks are in Agdel Lex. We can't get into Alikand while we walk them."

"So we walk away."

"Our wards will give out in minutes, that close to the city."

"So we walk fast."

"We'll die."

Zeddig recognized the brittle texture to Ley's voice—the broken pride, the self-inflicted wounds of failure. They couldn't afford that now. "I don't want to die. You don't, either. So we'll make this work." She pulled Ley into a seated position and worked her arm beneath her shoulders. "You want to be pissed at me, you want to scream and curse, you want to never see me again? Fine. But first, let's get home."

Ley nodded.

"Stand on three."

They stood—with a grunt, a hiss, and a weaving, wobbling

result, but still, they reached their feet. Ley sagged against Zeddig's shoulder. "Fair enough," she said. "I can—" She shivered, tried again. "I can curse you just as easily while walking."

Zeddig laughed at that, and they made their way three-legged through the Wastes.

Chapter Fifty-three

THE TRAIN, IT TURNED out, had cages. Izza, locked inside by Wreckers, tried not to ask herself what cargo the cages might carry during normal operation. The floors stank of reptile skin, and their bars were thick and silver-flashed. The Wreckers tossed Isaak in one cage, and she went in the other; Isaak drew back as far as he could from the bars, some kind of ward at work there no doubt, the fuckers. (Practical, she had to admit: the bars felt like iron, and Isaak could have bent them with his bare hands.) The Wreckers locked the cage with a big dumb padlock Izza could have slipped in seconds with the pin she kept in her braids, if the Wreckers weren't watching.

But that was the thing about Iskar. Someone was always watching.

She didn't talk to Isaak, and Isaak knew better than to talk to her. Anything they said would be monitored, passed along up the chain to the big squid-minds far away, and used against them. In Iskari clutches, talk as little as possible. They traded looks across the aisle between their cage doors: curiosity, fear, support. You learned to talk this way, when you weren't allowed words.

She refused to think about Kai. They could hash their issues out later. She had other priorities now.

She needed to free Isaak. She'd sought him out, used him to get into this godsdamn mess, to help Kai, and after all that, she would not let the Iskari have him.

Yes, she had a duty to her people, to the Lady back on Kavekana. But she'd come here to help a friend, and she'd stay to help another. And, much as the thought scared her, he *was* her people.

The car doors snapped open after an hour. Lieutenant Bescond marched in, hands pocketed, chin up.

"Here to gloat?"

"I don't gloat," Bescond said. "I review. There were reports, observations, of strange events connected with the pair of you: a god's touch, or a goddess's. Care to comment?"

Whatever you do, Izza told herself, do not look at Isaak—keep him so far from your mind that Bescond can't think of you at once, because Isaak can't hide how he watches you with those eager yellow eyes.

"Got no time for gods," Izza said. "Not yours or anyone's."

"It's a question of jurisdiction, M.—" The Lieutenant cocked her head to one side as if listening to a whisper. "Jalai. Iz Jalai." Izza tried to look as if it didn't hurt to hear her full name, so rarely used in the last seven years, in that alien order. "Last registration at High Sisters Thornside, age eleven. We did not have great hopes for you at the time, I'm afraid to say. But after that, you disappeared."

She tried to keep fear out of her voice. The Iskari liked their filing systems, and cultivated a fetish for data quality. "I kept out of trouble."

The Lieutenant did not smile. "Your friend, we understand. Several brief turns at High Sisters for minor infractions, suspicion of serious crimes, though no formal implication, illicit augmentation, known associations with the lower sort of criminal. He was obviously part of the train job crew—no delver, no true threat. But you." Bescond watched her like a bird, still and alien. "Tell me, Ms. Jalai. What do you know about foreign gods?"

In six years of running and hiding, Izza had never felt grateful for Kavekana's flesh-eating laws, for the people who hunted her and her Lady, who would have killed her Goddess and locked her in a statue until she became compliant if she slipped. She didn't feel grateful now—but all that fear and pain had some advantage: she'd become a master at staring grown-ups in the eye and spinning a tale she needed them to hear. "I don't like them, any more than I like you." The Lady chuckled in Izza's heart, and she ignored Her. "I left the city. I wasn't born here, had no ties, no reason to stay. But I was passing back through, needed a few thaums quick, and my friend"—not using his name, because Bescond hadn't—"offered me a job."

Bescond did not move when Izza finished, nor did she speak. She spun the silence out, built a space into which Izza was supposed to fall. But Izza had seen that trick before too.

"Courage," Bescond said at last, "I respect, even if it's misused. The Zur and the Imperials wouldn't employ so obviously tainted a vessel; you have too much spirit for an agent of King Clock, too little bearing for a follower of the throne-lords." The Lieutenant was firing into the dark, hoping her arrows struck warm meat. Izza wrapped herself in a foolish crook's bravado. "Very well. You'll learn to love the Lords, one way or another. You and your friend are still technically too young for our proper work-training programs, but High Sisters will care for you. Enjoy your stay."

And the Lieutenant marched out, with a nod to the Wrecker who lingered in the corner, watching wetly.

When the door closed, Izza sagged against the bars, and turned to Isaak, still seated in the center of his cage—but he wasn't looking at her.

No time to waste worrying about that.

She sat, and listened to the train, and tried to remember High Sisters Thornside. What scraps she could recall had been buried under seven years of willful forgetting, memories limned with stone and staring eyes, hardly any help at all.

The train stopped. Wreckers marched them to an armored wagon—two bound Isaak's arms, but they let Izza walk alone. They sat across from one another in the locked carriage, under Wrecker supervision, as the world rolled by unseen outside.

"I've never seen Her like that before," Isaak said.

She glared at him, did her best not to glance right at the Wrecker who watched them both. "I don't know what you mean." Subtext: shut the fuck up.

"In the escape. I saw it in your eyes. Miraculous."

Isaak, I know you think you're being clever, she thought but did not say. This is not clever. This is the kind of dumb that got us caught. "We almost got away, sure. But we didn't."

"Because I lacked—"

Don't say it, don't, Isaak, do not say the word, they can smell it even in your mind—

The Wrecker leaned forward in its seat.

That shift of rubbery flesh beneath coarse robes got through to Isaak just in time—or else her glare finally penetrated his reinforced skull.

"That is. I wasn't strong enough," he finished.

"Yeah," she said. "That makes two of us."

"You felt it, though. We—we almost made it."

"I don't want to talk about it."

She projected disdain until the wagon stopped, until someone unlocked the door from outside and the setting sun's light glinted red off the bare old bleak grounds she did, after all, remember, had seen in nightmares: the concrete towers and warden's balconies, the cells facing in. The High Sisters' turning lidless eyes glistened, affixed to every surface. Faceless ministers in tan jumpsuits fitted Isaak with his chainless manacles, and Izza with hers, and pulled them apart to the boys' and girls' sanitation zones. Isaak let himself be guided, at first; he turned back to her at the last moment—fought, the moron, against the hands that held him, scattered the ministers and ran toward her. "Izza, trust—"

She didn't look. She didn't have to. She heard the bass snap as the manacles engaged and slammed him down to concrete.

She felt lidless eyes upon her. She did not look back. She gave no sign she understood.

She prayed patience—not for herself, but for him.

Kai might come for her. But how? She'd have to navigate the justice system, find one juvenile facility among many, and if the Lieutenant hadn't sealed her file. She could pray—but the High Sisters would hear, and call the Wreckers. Isaak was praying loud enough for them both already.

No sense waiting for rescue.

The ministers escorted her to the showers, and locked the door behind. A jumpsuit, drab gray, vaguely her size, lay folded on a table bolted to the floor. "Disrobe," the eyes told her, "and bathe. In ten minutes, you will be led to your dormitory."

She shrugged, and undid her shirt.

The eyes watched her undress, passionless, unblinking, uninterested. She was just more meat.

Cold water rained on her shoulders and back. Shivering, she turned to the corner of the shower, where the eyes could not see her face.

Only then did she let herself smile.

It had been too long since her last jailbreak.

Chapter Fifty-four

KAI FOUND TARA ABERNATHY wrists deep in a corpse.

"I didn't expect to see you again," the Craftswoman said, her back to Kai, eyes on her incision. She'd unbuttoned her jacket's cuffs and rolled them up to keep her forearms bare; shadow gloved her skin from the elbows down, and when she drew her fingers from the body, blood rolled down the shadow's surface without sticking. "Your sister's free." She reached up to adjust one of the ghostlamps suspended from the ceiling on insectile metal arms. "And Bescond has what she wants. So, that's sorted." The dagger hung above Vane's corpse, at the heart of a silver wire lattice strung from pillars that ringed Tara's work table. "We've done the best we could."

"I want to know what's going on here."

Tara chuckled to herself, then said, wryly: "It's good to want things."

"Would you accept that answer?"

The Craftswoman did not speak.

Kai watched her work: the lengthening incision, the moonlit knife changing form, now thick and sharp, now serrated, now fine and slender as a needle, trailing translucent thread from a spool that hovered unsupported in midair. Tara moved with beautiful economy. Every incision, every binding, every ward she cast upon the corpse, she'd worked a thousand times before. She knew these procedures so well she didn't have to think about them. Maybe that was an advantage. But the woman bent over the table, the bed, practicing her art, was not the woman who planted seeds in the Temple of All Gods at dawn. She was more and less than that.

Frost blued Vane's skin. They must have stored her in a freezer.

Tara tried to pick up the conversation: "How did you get in here, anyway?"

"I told the squid at the desk that we had business. The building brought me." She did not shudder as she remembered the ripple of organic light that guided her down winding halls to this room at the tower's peak. Stars glimmered through the transparent membrane that served for a skylight. "I hope I haven't disturbed your plans."

"They're not my plans." But Tara cut herself off. "Keep going."

"I just want to know what it was all for."

"Nothing," Abernathy said.

"That's a lot of trouble for nothing."

"I mean, there's no one thing it was all for. Everyone here has her own goals—Bescond, me, her," tapping the slab, "even you. But all our goals required rescuing the knife, and waking this woman up."

Kai circled the table, and dug her thumbnail into her finger so she'd have something to focus on besides the gore. Craft-work made certain surgeries easier: death was the ultimate anesthetic. Abernathy took her time. With a twist of her fingers she knotted a stitch, then sutured a blood vessel, then slicked muscles back into their normal course and draped skin over them the way skin should drape. Glyphs on her forearms and back sparked, and Vane's skin bound once more to meat. Tara's brow furrowed as she worked.

"You're not happy with Bescond," Kai said. "Or with Vane, or this alliance. It must be hard, to be a Craftswoman working with gods."

"I've worked with gods before." Sweat froze on Tara's brow.

"Never the Iskari, though."

"No," she said. "Never them. And never here."

"Does it bother you?"

"What would bother me? Their mania for operant conditioning? The Wreckers? A society that grows minds like kittens in bottles? The propaganda and the brainwashing, this gross tower looming over a city that did not kneel to gods for two thousand years, to punish its people daily for the part they played in creating the Craft I practice? The fact that the Hidden Schools never came back here, that the courts look at Agdel Lex and see a situation well in hand, no need to intervene unless the wars down south impinge on the flow of natural resources? The fact that Alt Coulumb has played its own part here, as a trade partner who didn't ask too many questions? I don't know what about that could possibly bother me." She shook her head. "My . . . employers have worked with the Iskari for centuries. But this project was my idea. I came to see it through. I thought I knew what to expect. But. You don't need to know these streets well to see what's broken here. I told myself, this isn't your city. Just see things through and leave. Then your sister happened, and here I am. Implicated."

"You're trying to protect me," Kai said. "You want me to get out before this sticks to my fingers."

Tara did not reply.

"You wouldn't, in my place."

She stitched the incision above the breastbone closed. When she tied off the thread, it melted into skin. Tara removed her gloves, baring clean brown hands. She glanced at her watch. "It's time for you to leave."

"You're an only child."

Her eyes were dark and level. "What makes you say that?"

"My sister almost gave up everything to keep that knife from you. I have to know why."

"Turn that wheel to your left."

The iron wheel moved grudgingly at first, then faster. Kai heard a hiss and a knocking of pipes. A circle of floor beneath them began to rise.

The transparent membrane skylight unfolded like flower petals, and they passed through. Night plummeted above. Below, beyond, lay regimented Agdel Lex, its boulevard grids stretching from ridge to ridge, ghostlights aglitter, a geometer's city singing the lifeless music of the spheres.

The moon hung overhead.

Tara raised one hand, and the sphere-music stilled. Glyphs burned on her skin; a black curtain spread from the tower, carving the land from heaven. The Iskari city vanished.

And the stars returned.

They came tentatively at first, easing into the dark like swimmers into a pool at dawn. There had been stars before, but not so many millions as now, and everywhere she looked, in that blooming blackness, more. A galactic streak silvered the center of the sky.

Tara Abernathy was smiling.

The Craftswoman raised both hands, and spoke a word that fell upon them like a weight, a word that was bell peal and hammer blow, and the stars went out. All the light there was, gathered into the blade that hung above the corpse, into the drop of blood at its heart.

The blade opened, and the drop fell, so large it contained oceans. It struck the body's breast, splashed, and sank into the skin.

Blackness reigned, and silence.

A two-stroke rhythm sounded, and again.

Breath rasped through a dry throat.

Eyes of cold blue fire opened.

The stars came back, or else their faded remnants, and the city snapped to being below, its right angles and straight lines intact.

Alethea Vane lay on the slab. Her chest rose and fell. Her eyes, only blue now, not burning, stared up into the dark.

For a second, Kai thought Abernathy must have done it wrong. Vane was supposed to move, to swear, to speak. Kai had seen people woken from near-death before, and there was generally a lot of ugliness, flailing like a landed fish, cursing and spitting and crying. Vane's soul must not have meshed with the body right. Perhaps she was trapped within that skull even now, screaming without a mouth to scream.

Then Vane sat up, swung her legs over the side, stood, and said, "What took you so long?"

Chapter Fifty-five

THE QUAKE KNOCKED RAYMET out of a pleasantly intricate whips-and-chains-and-suspension sort of dream onto her cell floor in the Wrecker tower across the hall from Gal. Collapsed, cursing in Talbeg on the disturbingly warm chitin, she remembered that everything was quite fucked indeed. And not in the good way.

At least she wasn't alone.

Gal didn't seem concerned. She knelt behind bars in her own cell, radiant as ever, hands limp on her thighs, back straight, infuriatingly composed, serene, even, while this enormous stupid squid building trembled, as though debating whether to obey physics for once and collapse. Raymet rolled under her bunk for shelter, though that wouldn't help. At least the cell didn't have anything loose that might tumble down and kill her. No, if she died in a squidquake, it would be from a falling ceiling, from walls deciding they didn't want to be walls anymore and mashing her to pulp.

"No need to fear," Gal said. "It's not a real quake. Just Craftwork tremors—a resurrection, probably. Not nearly strong enough to hurt our host."

She stared at the underside of her bunk. Someone had scrawled a few lines of Imperial verse here, something about willows, as if willows grew anywhere near Agdel Lex. "Anything we can use?"

"I don't understand."

The tremor stilled. She rolled back to her feet and tested the cage bars—some kind of bone or horn. "To get out of here." The bars did not budge. She planted her feet and pulled until her shoulders hurt and her grip gave and she fell back to the floor, but the bars stood strong as any metal. "Escape while they're distracted. You don't have a lock pick or something, do you? If I can get this door open . . ."

"Why should we escape?"

There had to be loose metal somewhere. Raymet checked the bed—no springs. Checked corners, shelves, with as little luck. "What do you mean, why?"

"I have been taken in battle. Attempted escape would be dishonorable."

"What?"

Gal hadn't moved, but her eyes were open now. If she had been, in fact, a statue, one small enough to heft, Raymet would have thrown her across the room.

"This is a hell of a time to care about the law."

"This is the first time I have been taken in battle. They will contact my Queen for ransom, I expect, but she will disavow all knowledge of my activities, as is our custom. But, having been legitimately detained, I will not disgrace my order by attempting escape."

"The Wreckers will kill you. Or break you."

"They will not succeed at the second task," Gal said. If they succeed at the first, they will have honored my vow."

Raymet swore in Talbeg. She paced the cell. She kicked each wall twice, the first time because she wanted to, the second time because she still did. She glared across the aisle. "You get why we're in cells near one another, right? They want to play us against one another. They'll drag us out, one by one, and when they bring us back, we'll neither one know what the other said. Whether we broke."

"Reasonable strategy."

"That's a godsdamn strange perspective for someone about to be tortured."

"It is not the proper way to treat a prisoner of war," she said, "but, as I will be disavowed by the Queen, they have no reason to regard me as such."

"It's a fucked-up way to treat anyone," Raymet said. "Prisoner of war or not."

"Of course."

"So we should get out of here."

Gal said nothing.

"You won't even try?"

Still nothing.

"I came back for you, Gal."

"Why?"

Raymet, pacing, froze. Whirled on the woman in the cell across from her. Inhaled molten lead, and breathed out plasma. Gal knelt there, you could have gilded her and stuck her on a Camlaander cathedral just as is, the holy fool in her natural habitat. Pure curiosity on that perfect face, head cocked at angle. Like she'd sprung full-blown, navel-less, from some tyrant god's brow, innocent of everything.

The way she looked at life made tangles seem simple. In Raymet's head the world was four cats drowning in a sack, options and might-have-beens tearing each other bloody, ancient fears and unspoken needs and just-this-once ethical exceptions, and don't forget the lusts, all yowling in panic as black water seeped in. Against that, contrast Gal, who kept her code, who did what she could and never seemed to blame her-self when what she could wasn't good enough, who sat there as ready to meet torture and pain as she was to meet the dawn.

None of this was new. Gal lived this way even in the weeks when she never drew her sword. Raymet remembered her, holding her head over the toilet as she vomited out poison. Re-membered Gal's touch in fever dreams. Gal's hand extended as she climbed the ladder. Gal's weight beside her as she panted, scared, crushed by the horizon and the mass of open sky. Gal, fighting monsters in the dead city. Gal, who could shatter steel with a punch, and lived so gently. Gal, who needed nothing, while Raymet needed so much.

Why did she go back for Gal? Why run into certain arrest, into torture, into death? She knew. Of course she knew—she'd known every time Zeddig teased her about it. But when she tried to frame the answer, those drowning cats hooked claws into her eyes, teeth into her lip, and she could not speak.

The question hung between them.

Raymet couldn't bear to look anymore. She turned to face the wall, lay on her bunk, pulled the hairshirt blanket over her, and cursed herself to sleep.

Chapter Fifty-six

NAKEDNESS IS A STATE of mind, and states of mind differ from culture to culture, religion to religion—even from sibling to sibling. Hidden Schools sociologists survey this sort of thing, as they survey every sort of thing, and trace patterns of nudity across cities and classes. Some peoples have a kink of bare skin, though if we asked people from those groups they wouldn't likely accept the word "kink" in this context. "Complex" might raise fewer hackles: a nub of interrelated concepts, tying, say, nudity to vulnerability, and vulnerability to any number of other concerns depending on local constructs of power, gender, sexuality, and, more than most tend to admit, property and inheritance. Another person, in another place, might see nakedness as power: the greatest heroes stride into battle bare, and gods are depicted always in radiant nude.

The person stands unclothed, however we react. "Reality" does not change, but then, what's reality? Clearly not the information our limited senses report, subject to hallucination and mistake. One idea, with which philosophers would argue: we can regard something as real if perception of it does not vary—if, say, at least two independent observers perceive a phenomenon and agree on what they perceive. But to agree we must communicate. So, if our two observers differ about what nakedness means, how can they say whether someone is, really, naked?

Though Alethea Vane stood bare-skinned in starlight atop the Rectification Authority Tower, so pale her skin flushed blue, Kai could not call her naked. Vane glanced from Tara to Kai, waiting for an answer to her hanging question—what took you so long?—and, finding none, reviewed her limbs and scars, old and new, without concern, a general gauging battle-readiness without trace of sentimentality. Naked or not, she seemed more comfortable in her skin than anyone Kai had ever known.

"Good," Vane said, then struck her chest, bent over coughing, and spit over the platform edge onto the tower. "Good," her pitch higher now. "Fine." She sang a high pealing note that swept down to low registers. She touched her toes and bent her back. Kai expected pops and cracks, and heard none. "Thank you, Ms. Abernathy. Competently done, even absent a living will. I'm pleased to detect a heartbeat." The platform sank back into the tower. Membranes folded to close out the chill night air.

"You should be fully functional," Tara said. "We reached the body in time." Her tone of voice left some doubt as to whether this was a happy chance or a regrettable oversight. "Welcome back."

"I always wondered why more Craftswomen didn't shed their bodies altogether." Vane raised her hands and stood on tiptoe, as if being pulled up by an invisible rope. Muscles in her back lengthened. Stars and shadows and reddish tower light created an interesting topology on her skin. "Now I know. Damned impossible to get anything done without one. You have no idea the repetitive nonsense conversations I've sat through, the moralizing! I didn't even have a sense of time—had to borrow that from my interlocutors. Most would be driven mad. I have to say, I'm impressed with our Ley. I never thought she'd have it in her—but, hm." She turned back to Kai and examined her, utterly still, with raptor focus.

"The sister," she said.

Kai didn't see her move. Perhaps it was the stillness of that gaze, perhaps the evenness of the voice, perhaps the speed of the motion, but one second Kai was standing and the next she lay on her back on the dais, head ringing from impact, Vane's weight settling against her belly, forcing her breath shallow, Vane's hand on her throat, not squeezing, not crushing, just there, mastering her. Vane's teeth flashed white: Kai thought vampire for a panicked instant, as she brought her hands up to fight, tensed her legs to buck—

Black lightning split the red tower, and Vane flew back, spread-eagled in the air, still not precisely naked.

"Come on," Vane said. "I was mostly dead. Don't I get at least a taste of vengeance?"

"Kai," Tara replied, "is not liable for her sister's actions."

"Liability is beside the point, Ms. Abernathy. I want to hurt Ley, and her sister's available."

Kai sat up, feeling her neck, numb with disbelief. There had been no fangs in that mouth, and the woman hadn't moved with inhuman speed: she'd just decided she wanted to do the thing, then did it without hesitation. "Fuck you."

"Hardly."

"I saved your life," Kai said. "Ley would be happy if you hurt me."

"Would she?" Vane relaxed into the sorcerous bonds that held her, pleading, physically, no contest. "Kai, isn't it? You've never slept with your sister, I imagine."

"What?"

"You have no idea what sort of tight-wound spring you helped create there. She ran around the world to escape your shadow, because she couldn't make something worth you. Half her stories start with, one time, my sister. It makes a certain kind of funhouse mirror sense that you wouldn't know this. But never doubt: I could hurt her through you."

"Kai," Tara said, "helped steal you back. You're alive because of her. She's under Iskari protection, and mine."

Vane's blinked. "Really?"

"Without me," Kai said, feeling her throat, "you'd still be stuck inside that knife."

"Well." Drawn out like a cat's whine. She grinned. "That must have hurt her delightfully—you, too. Please let me down, Ms. Abernathy. I won't hurt Ms. Pohala any more than she's hurt herself. Swear to whatever you hold sacred. Choose a goddess or three, if it won't offend your sensibilities. But much as I'd like to hang around, I have work."

At Tara's glance, Kai nodded permission; the Craftswoman snapped her fingers. Vane landed bent-legged on the floor, stood, brushed off her arms as if the sorcerous manacles had left dust, then marched to the dais and snatched the dagger free of its wire mounts. She tossed the knife in the air, watched it spin, satisfied, and caught the handle as it fell past her, without apparent concern for the blade. "Good. I must say, in spite of the violence done my person, I appreciate dear sweet Ley's giving our project the ultimate test run."

Kai glanced at Tara, and back to Vane. "What do you mean? What is that thing?"

Surprise wrinkled Vane's forehead. "I would have thought she'd have told you, during her last-ditch play to buy the Concern out from under me."

"She didn't mention knives."

"It's not just a knife," she said. "It's a work of art." She marched past Kai and Abernathy to the door. A lab coat hung on a hook beside the door; she swept it on like a cloak, buttoned it up the front, and paused. "Are you coming?"

Chapter Fifty-seven

LEY COLLAPSED AFTER MIDNIGHT, so Zeddig dragged her the rest of the way: rigged a harness from cord and coat, and pulled her, sweating and shivering, across the frozen sand beside the train tracks.

As they neared the wall, the Wastes chilled. Barbed-wire winds cut Zeddig's cheeks. Her breath froze in tangles. In Agdel Lex, the tower loomed, imposing a dry reality, which at least would not try to kill them. But in Agdel Lex sentries waited on the wall, standing watch against invasion from the Wastes.

Whole, and alone, Zeddig could have gone around, risked the extra miles and a swim in the monster-swarmed Shield Sea. She could not take that route with Ley. And they didn't have time to circle and catch the Apophis Local, either—the wards wouldn't last the trip.

As they neared the wall, as its thousand-foot-high translucence loomed with Agdel Lex beyond, she stopped, knelt, and shook Ley's shoulder. "Wake up." Hungry ghosts and half gods gathered close; their hands played at Zeddig's coat, their teeth tested her boots. Ley groaned. "I need you."

Long lashes fluttered, and the eyes beneath, black, wet, beautiful, stared out. "What—" She couldn't finish the sentence.

"I need you to listen."

"You have—" She grunted. "A captive audience."

"I need more than that. I need you to pay attention."

"What do you mean?"

She'd spent the night thinking this through: pondering the knife, and the wall, and the rules of art and delving, but putting it all into words now left her feeling numb, imprecise. "The knife binds us together, you said. Without it, we fall apart, the ward fails, the Wastes roll in. If I tell you another story, if something else pulls us together, maybe the ward will last longer—long enough for us to slip into Alikand."

Speaking that name out loud, the name of her secret winding city without walls, the hidden streets where Wreckers could not go, was harder than she expected, even here.

Ley's eyes closed again, and Zeddig, afraid she'd gone back to sleep, reached for her again. "I'm still here," Ley said. "I'm thinking."

Cold wind blew.

"It might work," Ley said. As if she were pondering a chess move of unorthodox strategy. "But it won't last long."

"It doesn't have to. Just long enough."

"Okay," she said. "Let's try it. But when you start talking, don't stop."

"So long as you don't stop listening."

She grinned, or bared teeth. That would have to do for a yes, for now.

Zeddig set herself to harness, and took a breath, and marched away from the tracks, into the Wastes of her story.

"South of Alikand"—the name easier on her tongue the second time—"lie the flats travelers call the Fragrant Plain. Rain rarely falls here, but each year, at the death of the sun, the wind shifts to blow south from the Shield Sea, and carries an ocean's weight of water. Rain falls. Children run through the streets, gathering rain in bowls and dousing whoever they find, fearless: professors and Grand Senators carry their books wrapped in sealskin or waxed cotton during the Festival of Rains. But the children are not the season's greatest gift. When storms cross the Fragrant Plain, the ground floods, buried seeds sprout, and Alikander poppies bloom. You'll find many poppy fields in this world, but none to match these: red and yellow crowning hills and spilling down like skirts. Every poppy grows here; travelers gather seeds, bring them home, and cast them forth, and the bees the honey-makers keep wed strain to strain to make new colors. Not every poppy emerges each year. Some sleep centuries until they bloom. Each year the hills change cape, and each year their fragrance gains a new character, intoxicating, cinnamons and citrus and deep deep green. When the rains pass, we emerge from our homes to parade south, family by family, bearing baskets of food and wine, and spread on the hill, a million Alikanders, to sit in silence and hear the flowers bloom."

The air softened and warmed. She focused on the weight of her harness, on her feet and her step, and let the world blur. She smelled cinnamon and citrus, glimpsed reds and yellows to beggar dye. She knew too well what lay beneath her feet. There were no flowers anymore, and most who lived in Agdel Lex no longer remembered the winter rains, the poppy fields, the festival of silence. Little rain fell in Agdel Lex these days: it was a dry city, because it was a desert, because the Iskari believed it so. She had never known the rain herself.

But she could say the words, and Ley could hear them, and if they both believed, out here in the Wastes where belief could change the world, she could wrap them in the tale, in unwalled, ancient Alikand.

So long as she spoke.

There had been contests after the silence, of art and poetry and dance, attempts to catch the poppies' hillside splay and pass it down through centuries. They carved stone, and painted the patterns of the hills upon their walls, and visitors from the Archipelago wove those patterns into rugs, which became an industry and art all their own, though never approaching the firsthand sight.

Aman did not remember the hills either, but *her* grandmother had been young before the God Wars, and remembered the silent festival as a burden children bore after water-throwing antics—but her memory endured though the fields were gone, and she returned to it as she could not return to the hills themselves, and found the scents and silences waiting.

Zeddig's voice dried. Her legs ached, and her arms. She could not see, could not let herself see. Memory burned. If the tale stopped, if the world turned real, they'd be out in the Wastes again, or worse, within the wall, locked in stone, or dead.

She walked, and spoke, and pushed forward, blind, in hope, as the light changed, as the moon set. She told Ley about the Palatine Perfumer's Guild, who sent people each year to gather the poppies' scent, to bottle or fake it, and produced many symphonies in bottles but none that smelled so rich as the hillside in spring; she told of lovers' trysts in the red; she told every story she could remember save the story everyone knew, the story that ended in fire and in ice.

But she could not speak forever. She'd place her foot wrong, turn from the path, remember that this world was broken after all.

And at last, Zeddig stumbled, and the story slipped, and she cried out—

And they did not die.

Her knees struck cobblestones, hard, and her shoulders sagged. She knelt in an alley. Clotheslines wove a cat's cradle overhead. She breathed hot wet air. Her coat stifled her, and the harness cut her shoulders. She looked up, and over: a street vendor stood behind a cart, eyes wide beneath her scarf, ignoring the dough burning in her vat of hot oil.

And the woman, angels and saints love her, did not scream. Did not say, "Who are you?" Or "Where did you come from?" She knew.

She drew the dough from the oil, covered the vat, and knelt by Zeddig before her cart, and touched her arm, which steamed from the cold and the Wastes. "How can I help?"

Zeddig did not weep.

It felt good to be home.

Chapter Fifty-eight

IN VANE'S WAKE THE world seemed mad. She started and stopped suddenly, walked at a pace that would have been more comfortable as a jog, slammed doors, strangled knobs, stabbed buttons—but somehow she made her tempo seem ideal. Everyone, everywhere, and everything, should accept Alethea Vane's pace. Obviously hers was correct. If not, why would she have chosen it? A door's failure to open fast enough, a crowd's to ebb and flow in answer to her predictions, these were obstinacy at best, rebellion at worst, and what right-thinking person would tolerate rebellion?

Kai squeezed into an elevator as it closed, brushed past Authority cops who tried to interrupt their progress, shoved out into the chill purple night of Agdel Lex, and the whole time remembered Vane's fingers on her throat. And the whole time Vane kept talking.

"An interesting experience, to be trapped in one's own work. We didn't frame the project for such pedestrian use, though it's always pleasant to find general applications. You can find soulblades aplenty at your local murder hobo supply store; the present problem is far more general. The blade does not steal. It listens, aggressively, to the soul: it pulls people in. With an integrating sentience at the core, this effect creates a common frame of reference, lacking one, it draws its subjects until they're utterly incorporated."

Vane stepped into the street without looking. Oncoming carriages pulled up short. Horses reared and snorted; their hooves cycled in the air and plunged to the cobblestones where Vane would have been had she not turned at the last minute to check that Kai and Tara were keeping pace. A golem cart tipped on its side; piled lemons spilled across the intersection, yellow against the stone and muck. The golem driver cursed her with a ground glass screech.

"Still with me? Good."

Without pausing in case they answered no, Vane turned off the crosswalk and stepped into the street, picking her way through the traffic snarled around the upturned cart.

Kai glanced to Tara—she was fixed on the retreating lab coat. The Craftswoman looked like she was walking into a wind. Kai recognized that expression, had seen it on priests fresh from meeting with the kind of pilgrims who had come to Kavekana's shores with careful, deniable questions about extradition treaties and the extent to which the priesthood might cooperate with foreign clergy in the event of criminal prosecution. Kai had felt that way herself.

Tara Abernathy didn't like compromise. And working with Vane and the Iskari was all compromise.

Whatever. Kai didn't like Vane, but she didn't have to work with the woman. She just wanted to know what was going on.

So she ran out into traffic, after her.

• • •

Ley started babbling a block from the safe house. She tossed on the tarp, jerking Zeddig and the fried dough seller side to side; the dough seller fell, but Zeddig caught her, set her on her feet. "I can drag her the rest of the way."

"You're certain?"

"She's my responsibility." Zeddig put all the confidence she could fake into those words, and it must have worked. The dough seller nodded, hugged her, and left behind a cinnamon waft. After she was gone, Zeddig wondered if saying those words—*she's my responsibility*—had been a confession, or a decision, or the final acceptance of a decision she'd made long ago.

Ley twisted on the tarp, teeth gritted, sodden with pain. She grunted in Kavekanese, most of which Zeddig couldn't understand. Back when they first dated, she'd tried to learn the language, checked books out of the library, practiced flashcards, but she could never tell the tones apart. *No*, she understood, at least.

"Come on. A few more blocks."

She tried to slide her arms under Ley, but the woman did not keep still. She lashed out—struck Zeddig's face, her nails leaving stinging tracks on skin.

"Work with me. We're close."

A hiss. A name Zeddig did not recognize. Kai's, maybe, said in some odd case or irregular declension? Some other word, similar? "Sister"?

"Ley." She tried again to get one arm beneath Ley's back, but Ley, not quite awake, dug her nails into Zeddig's shoulder. Zeddig controlled her urge to pull away, to curse or push her off. There would be time for all that when they weren't wedged into an alley, hurting, hunted, and alone. "Ley, this won't take long. Work with me."

She wrapped the tarp around her to stop her thrashing, and lifted with her legs, and with her back and arms and heart. Ley fought. Zeddig would not have made it three blocks.

Good thing she only had to make it two.

. . .

"All nightmare telegraphic applications rely on a similar protocol: they exploit the tangency of human minds. The Craft uses the same principle, though your professors at the Hidden Schools, Ms. Abernathy, would warn that this analysis begs the question. A deal is a point of negotiated agreement, while the nightmare telegraph functions due to preexisting, nonnegotiated unities. Unfortunately, non-negotiated unities are few in number. We're forced to rely on deep evolutionary terrors, which burns out the communicating parties. Anyone can deploy the system safely from time to time, but the average tenure of a dedicated full-time nightmare operator hovers around eighteen months. The human filament can't bear any more. Even with postoccupational counseling, therapy, and hypnosis, that's a steep cost."

Vane had not slowed. Kai's feet complained that she'd been using them for a full day without a break. Scars pulled in her back and shoulders. Vane crossed roads and climbed stairs, still unshod. The pads of her feet flashed white beneath the lab coat's hem. She'd bound her hair back with a tie she'd stolen from a roadside stand. Abernathy followed, wreathed with lightning, keeping them safe. When Vane stepped into the street, Tara bound the cars around her, to stop another crash. When Vane made a sharp turn and shoved a thickset man off the curb into traffic, Tara righted him.

If Vane noticed this intervention, she said nothing. She tossed a lemon in one hand, and caught it.

"Art provides an alternative: a work becomes a touchpoint for its audience. The mind is never so vulnerable save when exposed to a story."

Tara's step hitched. Kai caught her arm; the lightning shocked her hand. Beneath the power that wreathed her, the Craftswoman looked—spooked.

"But art is a lossy medium. We need a work that is more than a static sensory touchpoint, a work that negotiates connectivity between its onlookers. The ideal work, for our purposes, would draw people in, and mirror them. It would serve as a vacuum, calling to individual audience members, and integrating them through an independent consciousness, creating negotiated agreement. The work itself would be a responsive second-order entity, mediating the audience's collective self through a single unifying viewpoint."

Kai recognized this street, and the building at which Vane stopped, and the Muerte Coffee across the way. She'd been here before.

Vane stood in front of the wall, which was blank one second, and the next second contained a revolving door. Vane searched the lab coat's pockets, frowning.

"And the Iskari sponsored this?" Kai didn't try to hide her skepticism. "Because this is constructive theology, just from an artistic angle. You're talking about building a god."

"Not at all." Vane slapped her forehead—actually slapped it, which Kai did not think was a thing people did in real life. "Sorry. The head's still jumbled." She stuck her hand in the revolving door, and before Kai or even Tara could respond, slammed it shut on her fingers.

The door sparked. Somewhere, a curtain tore. Space twisted.

Kai blinked. The door was turning clockwise now.

"There we go," Vane said. "Security system's built not to harm me or my employees. If you'd have tried that, you'd be missing a few fingers. Now, anyway, you said, right, building a god." She grinned. "Not exactly. But we built something *like* a god."

• • •

Zeddig set Ley down on the bare mattress. Streetlights filtered through thick dusty glass and glinted off the wet lines on her cheeks. Zeddig unwound her. She tensed when Ley's arms came free, in case she'd thrash, but she stayed limp. Black pupils darted between slit lids, surveying the room, no fixings, no furniture save the bed.

"Tell me," Zeddig said. "What's this all about?"

"I recognize this place."

"What did you steal from the tower?"

"That stupid door. I made that mark on the wall when I helped you move in."

"What were you running from when you found me? What had you done?"

"Did you bring me here on purpose? Did you, gods, did you move out when I left? Because it hurt too much to re-member?" Her voice twisted, sardonic, a hook in Zeddig's guts twisting upward to the heart. That was Ley trying to change the subject.

Zeddig let the rage come, and made it go. "Answer the question."

"The flat we shared back when we knew nothing about one another, back when you didn't ask and I didn't say, and we used each other to our hearts' content. Before I got too close, and you kicked me out."

"I trusted you," Zeddig said. "You used that trust to make a business. But nothing you say now will change what I said in the Wastes. No matter how much that scares you. I love you, and you owe me an explanation."

Ley closed her eyes. With her forearms as a prop, she pushed herself upright against the headboard, and hissed as her broken leg changed position. The mattress creaked beneath her weight, and the headboard, too. A dark stain climbed one bedroom wall. "The place looks grim without our stuff."

"Yes."

"It's not just the missing books and tapestries and furniture."

"Couldn't fit the bed out the door," Zeddig said. "I didn't want to leave the rest."

"It's us. We're not here anymore."

Zeddig did not answer with words. She could tell from how Ley's face changed that she had, in fact, spoken, on a level she could not control, by twitching or shifting weight or glancing down at floorboards or over at the stain on the wall.

Ley adjusted her leg and the angle of her back, untangled the knots of her neck and shoulders. Zeddig imagined her as a convalescent in some Iskari melodrama, seated on a porch, tea in hand, the axle of the stage. Her broken leg, her torn clothes, the dirt and sweat on her face, the matted hair, vanished beneath the shell of her composure.

Zeddig gave her the time she needed.

"They want—" Ley said. "That is, Vane, my old partner, wants—to destroy Alikand. And I was trying to stop them."

• • •

The Dreamspinner workshop, Vane explained, needed nothing from the outside world. Bioluminescent algae made its light, and while the building drew water off the mains it could, in a pinch, create that as well, through basic alchemy and recycling. A hydroponics lab grew food; in the event of demonic outbreak, the entire structure could submerge beneath the city and remain static until local authorities put the situation to rights. It was a white labyrinth of winding stairs, and as they passed various laboratories, Kai saw, behind glass, rats running mazes of their own.

"I'm no fan of gods," Vane said. "But they fascinate me—beings arising from interactions of human will. With that as our model, we built a vector to connect consciousness. An icon to draw the mind in, and a seed soul around which the network forms: a listening mind to serve as a bridge, a director and decider. Without that, the icon could inhale viewers' minds, separating them from physical substrate. That's what your sister did to me. Agdel Lex was an ideal first deployment. We could resolve its pesky indeterminacy once and for all. But of course the next step would be building a global dreamlayer. Instant communication, and a single source of truth, which would become, naturally, a single source of control."

Vane led them up three floors and down six, until, deep below what Kai thought was ground level, they arrived at an enormous wheel-locked door. Vane turned the wheel with a groan and the full weight of her resurrected body.

"What's my sister's part in all this?"

"I would have thought that was obvious." Vane pulled the door open. "She built the thing."

• • •

"You and I split up," Ley said, with a hitch even her self-possession could not hide, "after my show. I was so excited to share that work with you. You showed me Alikand, suspended between the Iskari and the wreckage. I wanted to show it back, the way I saw it."

"You stole my city. You used it. You had no right."

"Maybe I didn't," she said. "I wanted to capture this place. Praise it. Agdel Lex is a bridge over an abyss. The dead city is the abyss itself. And Alikand hangs between them. Everyone here lives in all three at once. If I could give people that vision, if I could tie the city together, then—"

"Then we would all be at the mercy of the Iskari."

Ley sighed. "That's what you said back then, too."

"Because it's true."

"But after we broke up, I found a partner who liked my ideas. Who saw my exhibit, and thought, yes, exactly: cities are acts of will. Cities are decisions people make, every day. They are artist and audience and art. If we could make a thing like that—if we could use my work on Alikand as a model to build new cities, with new bonds—we could do anything. Make new, better gods. We didn't know how to deal with the distribution issue at first—how do you get everyone in a city to stare at the same piece of art at once—but Altus solved that problem: we launch the knife into the sky, and unfold it over the city, drawing starlight for power. That was it. One weird trick, and we'd give Agdel Lex back its history."

"Agdel Lex," Zeddig said, "has no history."

"I know." She sounded tired. "I was excited. I was angry at you. And we had funding. Vane had a gift for finding investors.

412 • *Max Gladstone*

Millions of thaums rolled in. I made art. I wanted to show everyone, you most of all. And one day, Vane and I got into a fight over, I don't even remember, and I went, angry, into the files. And I learned where our funding came from."

"The Wreckers."

Ley's smile ran crooked. "Iskari Defense Ministry, not the Rectifiers. But, it amounts to the same thing. They wanted the system built—with their people running it. They wanted the Lords at the center of the web. Agdel Lex would be the first test: rectifying the city once and for all. They would stop its alleys from shifting, wall off the dead city and Alikand, too. They would make Agdel Lex a perfect, known place."

"No one would go along with that. The people would reject it."

"Fewer than you think," Ley said. "And those who didn't, those who turned away—the Authority wouldn't have to protect them anymore. The Wastes would roll in. They'd fall into the dead city."

There should have been a sound outside, a scream or a laugh, anything to relieve the silence between them, but the night was deep and solemn, and no birds woke to sing.

"I was an idiot."

Zeddig fought down anger, and fear. The walls of this room seemed so fragile now—they flexed with her breath. She did not scream. It hurt to look at Ley; she saw it hurt Ley to look at her. She gripped Ley's hand, and they clutched each other with lifeline strength.

"I tried to stop the project. I fought with Vane. I scrounged for funding. A few of the middleman investors the IDM channeled funds through didn't know who held their strings, so

I found some willing to sell their stake. If I added theirs to mine, I'd have enough control to wrest the concern from Vane. I needed a loan to buy the shares, and I needed sixteen million thaums as security for the loan. I looked everywhere. Vane must have found out—so she got there first. I was turned down again, and again, and at last by my own sister, with just days left before deployment. So, when all else failed—I stabbed Vane, and took the project, and ran."

· · ·

The door opened on heavy hinges, and Vane marched into a shadowless room. The light here issued from no single source, and there were no hard corners where shade might gather. Smooth eggshell walls enclosed them, matte white and glowing. Silver wires anchored to the walls coiled and snaked on the floor. Kai glanced back, nervous, to check the world outside still existed. The windowless sterile hallway seemed real and grubby by contrast with this self-complete space. Vane's feet left dirt prints on white as she padded to the center of the room.

"The knife," Kai said.

"This stupid knife," Vane acknowledged, raised the blade, and opened it, tine by tine, into a web. "It's made me rich, and it will save this city, and save the world, but I've spent my share of time inside it already. Still, needs must." The blade stuck in the air, and the walls rang.

· · ·

"You know the rest," Ley said. "Without Vane and me, they

couldn't build more knives. The initial design involved two blades: one on the ground, bonded to the Wrecker tower, and one in the Altus satellite payload, bonded to a human being. I had the Wrecker knife, but I couldn't get to the satellite—and they could launch with only one knife and a Lord-ridden squid. It might work. If I could reach the Altus launch site, I could break that knife, too, and save the city—and if I got this"—she touched the metal disk on her breastbone—"I could get into Altus. But to get there, I needed help. Which is why I came to you."

Zeddig could not trust herself to speak.

"I fucked everything up. Now they have the knife, and I'm useless, and your friends are stuck in the tower. So, there it is. I didn't change. I didn't try. I threw myself into more of the same godsdamn fix-everything nonsense that broke us up. I should have listened to you. But here I am. And I don't have any right to say it any more but—I love you too."

Those words passed between them, their own secret, carried by the air, by the lifeline tension in their hands, and Zeddig, who'd felt like a dry leaf in a hot wind, landed. The world was fucked, the city doomed. But there was this, at least and forever, in her hand. This, in her heart.

It was a small truth, against the travesty of the world. But it did not feel small. The fear did not leave, but she felt, at last and forever, anchored.

"You're not useless," Zeddig said. "What you did was wrong, and I don't—" Her voice shook. She felt hot and tense and sharp, and she breathed herself cool, and calm, and soft. "I don't know what to do." And easier than breathing, because more true: "I love you." There was so much else. She wanted to scream and weep and to march from that bare room into the street and never come back, and wanted to mash Ley's mouth with a kiss and break her, and break herself, in an embrace, and stain that bare mattress with their sweat, and topple the walls with their screams. "Can we stop them?"

Ley met her gaze, and for the first time since that rooftop night, Zeddig saw her lover unsure. "We can try."

. . .

Silver wires snaked from the eggshell floor, weaving through the web of the blade, unfolding it and unfolding again. Silver rubbed silver and drew it taut, guillotine strings vibrating with notes just below the edge of hearing. The system burned. Vane cocked her head back as the web grew, checking for damage, and knifelight made sharp edges on her teeth. "Your sister betrayed our work, and caught me in our trap. But now I'm back. So. Dear Ley has made herself an outlaw, turned down a fortune and a chance at something not unlike godhood, all to appease her memories of her ex-girlfriend. And even in that last-ditch effort, she's failed. You have my thanks. But, if you don't mind, I need you gone. We have two days to prepare for launch."

Vane had ceased to care about Kai, or Tara. She watched her glowing web, lit by the fleshless purity of angles.

Kai turned away.

Beside her, she saw Tara, looking sick.

Chapter Fifty-nine

DAWN AT HIGH SISTERS came early. A siren woke the children in their bunks, and they staggered out in long lines to present themselves for morning exercises and inspection. After that, gruel. After that, work. After that, classes.

No one liked High Sisters—not the sisters themselves, not the blank-faced guards, not the kids in featureless gray jumpsuits worn through at the knees from kneeling, each suit boiled to kill lice before it was passed to the next kid in line. Everyone here would rather be somewhere else, and the people who sent them would rather have sent them somewhere else too.

The Sisters themselves no doubt joined the corps imagining some humane assignment, in a war zone possibly, or a recent war zone, or even better, the aftermath of some unnatural disaster, the kind of thing where no one (certainly not the Iskari Demesne) was at fault, some skyquake or reactor meltdown in the wake of which they could comfort orphans, mend the sick, preach the glories of their Squiddy Lords to seekers abandoned by gods and people, human flotsam tossed on the wake of great events. They imagined comforting children who wept into their pillows at night. Instead they, the Sisters in flowing black, had been appointed guardians of ingrate kids, no three of whom spoke the same language. It stung. Street scum, clannish and suspicious, sad and angry and confused and above all, that greatest sin, ungrateful—would it kill these children just to thank them, even once? As if no one ever taught them to speak. The clerks and clerics who sent the Sisters to Thornside apologized when the Sisters sent sad letters home, and dispensed comfort in officially sanctioned increments: someone has to tend these lost children, but it won't be forever, we'll soon find you some position where you can be kind.

Izza had met many dangerous people, but few so mean as bruised idealists.

In any other situation the children would have been more or less all right—scared, alone, traumatized, hungry, but fine. They had come from across the Gleb, and spoke different languages, and cared about different things, and all were hurt and angry and sad and lost. Otha willowy and grim, Orolh with the mean twist to his lip and the scar above his eye, Egewe who gathered other girls to her like chicks to a mother hen and whose skin was a web of burns from before, and welts from now—they could have been friends, if they had time to hide and heal, to make peace with their dead gods and lost family. But they were fierce strangers here. They shared no language. They lacked any reason to live together save the Iskari desire to render them into citizens, like a cook rendering fat to oil. So, at High Sisters, they gathered into groups with those few others they could understand, and built petty empires when the Sisters weren't looking, of kids they could beat or cow into line.

The cops and Wreckers who sent those kids here would have rather seen them off to reeducation camps like proper adults, where their bodies might at least be put to use, or have kicked them out into the war, or drowned them in the bay. It would have been merciful. You only had to visit High Sisters to see how poorly these broken not-quite-children lived, what monsters the war had made them. If only the bleeding hearts back home, who filled newspaper column inches with tired quotes about the quality of mercy, could understand the futility of this nonsense, and give us permission to treat these not-quite-children the way they really should be treated. My Lords, did you see Sister Blanche last feastday? Bent at confession, sobbing? Her hand bandaged from where she'd broken one of the small bones in her palm swinging her switch too hard?

Izza didn't know much about the faceless guards, but she was pretty sure they'd rather be somewhere else too. Then again, you never knew. Some people liked not having faces.

Anyway, she herself would rather be gone. She had survived a brief stint in High Sisters before, played the good girl until they sent her and a few others to a factory by the shore, and, seeing her chance, she escaped. The Sisters would keep close watch on her, if they read her file. It might be fun to pit her will against theirs, to dismantle this gross institution from the inside—to shape the kids into a fighting force, strike back. But she needed out fast. Kai was out there, no doubt meshing herself deeper in this nonsense, rather than cutting and running like any decent person should. (Like Izza should herself.)

But she could not leave without Isaak.

At morning inspection, he hadn't looked tired by the exercises, so Sister Marthe told him to do more. He did, and after that looked no more tired than before. "Defiant," Sister Marthe said. "We can fix that."

He had the smarts not to talk back, at least. Poor bastard. Learning to survive outside left you unprepared for this sort of thing. Looking tough, here, meant you stood out, and standing out got you hurt. In the long run.

He knew who he was. Because of that, they'd try to make him something else.

After classes, more work. Her job was to pass sheets of metal to Otha, who ran the press, and scowled whenever Izza spoke to her. Otha did not know what they were building, and did not care. They repeated dumb slogans back to the supervising Sister while they worked.

Then, more gruel.

A body could get used to this sort of treatment. That was the idea, that was the problem.

So, after the gruel, when they were escorted out for a half hour of rec time on burning pavement under the sun's full heat, Izza started a fight.

She'd spent years avoiding this sort of shit, so it wasn't hard. All she had to do was the opposite of what came naturally. But first she had to get rid of Isaak.

He lumbered over to her as soon as the faceless men left them at liberty. The others gave them a wide berth. Natural: no sense tearing newcomers down so long as they stuck together. Too risky. Get them alone. At night, maybe, or in the small corners of the complex where the eyes on the walls sometimes shut from boredom.

"We need to get out of here," he said. "The Lady—"

"Don't, please." His eyes, shit, the pain in them—she wished she could get used to it, so it wouldn't hurt so much. But then she imagined the kind of person who could see that pain and not hurt, and she did not want to be that person, either. The prisons into which you locked yourself, you could not escape.

"She touched you. Izza, pray to Her. Try. She can get us out of here."

He sounded so excited: he could share this with her, if he could just make her understand. He deserved to know—when she could find a way to say it without changing a friend to a follower.

"We're getting out." She breathed deep, made her bones iron and her mind a blade. "But you have to give me space, okay? There's something I need to try first. Alone."

The armor on Isaak's face didn't convey subtle expressions well, but his confusion wasn't subtle. "Okay."

That would have to do.

She marched away from him, to Otha, who stood with a clutch of tall lanky dangerous kids, westerfolk, speaking a coast dialect that sounded to Izza like seashells scraped together—marched to Otha, who had power in this closed-in screwed-up world, who had put a kid in serious hospital one time, not even the infirmary.

Izza pushed Otha from behind, and said, "What the fuck is your problem?"

Otha fell. Her friends caught her, and she recovered, turned, hands raised, hair an angry halo. She made a fist. "We didn't have one," she said. "Until now."

And she lunged for Izza.

The scrap lasted seconds at most. Otha came for her, Izza hit her upside the head, Otha grabbed Izza's shirt and tossed her down. Izza got up, not quite fast enough to avoid the kick, and bowled into Otha, forcing the taller, leaner girl to the blacktop. Hands caught her, pulled her off—Otha's friends. Fists came. She heard faceless men whistle from the corners of the yard.

Good. Yes.

Fighting gets you solitary—just you and the eye of judgment. Perfect for her purposes. Once she was free, she could sneak Isaak out, and they'd escape together. This bit hurt—she doubled over a fist, gasped air, tore one arm free to protect her face—but the faceless men wouldn't let them fuck her up badly. The Sisters liked to pretend they cared.

Booted feet ran toward her.

And she heard a roar she'd hoped not to hear.

The hands that held her broke. Kids scattered. Izza fell without anything to fight against, hit pavement that seared her palms. She looked up, blinking. Isaak stood over her, hands clawed. He roared again, bared needle teeth, and the walls of High Sisters shook.

"No!" But she couldn't help him now.

The manacles triggered. Isaak slammed to the pavement, pressed down by an enormous weight. He forced himself to his feet anyway, straining against the magic of his bonds. To protect her. Beautiful idiot.

He didn't go down when the first faceless man hit him, or the fourth. He fell, finally, from their weight, and when he did, they kept hitting him.

"Stop!" She meant the cry for him, but he must have thought she was pleading with the faceless men, because he fought harder. This big dumb wonderful kid. Fighting for her.

Still the blows rained down.

She heard something break. She screamed. She didn't expect that. She didn't scream often. The cry slipped from her throat, drawn by its own weight, like a knife she hadn't felt enter.

They carried him limp from the yard. She didn't feel the faceless men's hands on her as they dragged her into the office. She didn't feel Sister Marthe's scorn, didn't hear her condescending speech, the blows that followed. She barely heard the cell door slam shut.

Chapter Sixty

KAI WANDERED ALIKAND BACK streets, and felt unreal. She bought coffees and asked directions, and though the answers she received bore little resemblance to the route Izza'd followed days before, her feet remembered the path. Blue sky peeked between the roofs of the too-close whitewashed houses, a deeper blue than the Iskari desert. Any moment Kai expected a great web to unfold in that sky, and draw them in.

Two days to launch, Vane said. The grand project almost complete.

She found Tara in the Temple, stripped to shirtsleeves, watering the dry plot. Two men were repairing the balcony above, patching a hole with fresh boards. They looked up as Kai passed through the gate, then returned to their work. Tara did not stop watering. "I missed yesterday," she said as Kai approached across the courtyard. The soil drank water. Leaves inhaled, flushed green. "The plants were thirsty."

"The tower said you didn't show up for work this morning."

"I don't work for them." The rain from the can's spout eased. Tara walked to the well and tossed the bucket down. It splashed far below. "Now Vane's back in action, I'm an observer again."

"They're going to kill this city."

"Not exactly," Tara said. "Right now the city's Alikand and Agdel Lex, woven through one another. Your sister's work will force the cities together, seal off the dead city forever. No more people dying as they fall through the cracks. Agdel Lex loses the wreckage of the God Wars, and the city makes a fresh start."

"And the Iskari control everything."

"That is," Tara said, "one issue. There are others." She worked the well rope to fill the bucket, and then started cranking. "Some parts of Alikand will resist incorporation. Those will be cast into the dead city, and lost. Reality papers over the wound." The rope creaked.

"You're okay with that."

"Of course not." The creaking stopped. Tara held the crank still. Light slicked over the muscles of her back and arms. In daylight, her glyphs looked like scars. "Every part of this hurts."

Kai joined Tara at the well. The crank was large, and her hands fit between the Craftswoman's. She didn't look at the other woman, just tried to help her. The rope creaked, the bucket rose. Water sloshed and fell. They worked, silent, together. On the balcony, the men hammered nails into board.

The sun burned, and she sweat through the shirt beneath her jacket. "I was in an accident," Kai said, "a while ago. I got hurt, badly. As I healed, they made me do all these exercises—hardly any weight, you know, they seemed so pointless. They hurt, and they helped. But while I was recovered, I thought, maybe this is all I'm good for now. Easy things that seem so hard." She stopped for breath. "But that's not true. We can do more."

The bucket reached the top. Tara unhooked it—two-thirds full, the excess slopped down in its violent rise— and filled the empty can. Sunlight made diamonds in falling water.

"You didn't know," Kai said. "Did you? What they were planning."

Tara set the bucket down and leaned against the well. Kai remembered how Tara leaned against the window at the bank, and wondered if this woman would ever learn how it felt to fall.

"No," Tara said. "When I was a kid I thought the Craft was the best tool for fixing the world: free intellect, unlimited potential, subtle and flexible. Anyone with will could learn. Smart people could run the world better than Gods. Gods chain people. Gods make you something you're not. Then, in Alt Coulumb, I started to think, maybe that was wrong. Gods emerge from human communities, working together to solve common problems. Nothing wrong with that."

"And then you came to Agdel Lex."

"And then," she said. "Yes. I knew the histories. But the histories don't include everything."

"They wouldn't."

"What happens when a city becomes its own problem?" She exhaled. "Alt Coulumb wanted—" She stopped, shook her head, tried again. "We needed to listen to the stars."

"I don't understand."

"We wanted to hear what was going on out there in the black beyond our world. We didn't know how. The Church of Kos has contacts in the Iskari Defense Ministry—and those contacts described your sister's project, in general terms, as an orbital listening device. It was built to hear people on the ground; if we expanded the project we could make it sensitive to subtler voices from beyond the stars. So we funded the project, and I came to watch it work."

"And now that you know what's going on here, you wish you hadn't."

"I'm bound," she said. "By our alliance. By my agreement—my mistake." She waved her hand, including the broken courtyard and the sky. "Alt Coulumb has been allied with Iskar for centuries. The Iskari call themselves saviors, but they've destroyed as much as saved here. More. And this whole scheme disgusts me. But we signed on to help them."

"They lied to you."

"They didn't lie. They just didn't tell us everything."

"The agreement can't hold."

"It does," Tara said.

"So you'll let them die."

"No," Tara said. "On launch day, I'll go to the wall and reject Agdel Lex. I'll hold off the Wastes as long as I can, give Alikand's people time to evacuate to the Iskari city before the Wastes roll in. I'll save everyone I can."

"By yourself?"

"If I have to," she said.

"Warn people first."

"I'm bound to confidentiality. I can discuss this with you, because Vane has—but I can't work against the project. If I did manage to break the bond, Bescond would kick me out of the city and launch anyway."

Kai always chose her words carefully, because you never knew who might be listening, or what they might want to hear. She sifted through everything she could have said next, like seeking the right piece of a jigsaw puzzle. "But I know about this. And I never signed anything."

An answer just as measured: "That's true."

"If something happened to the launch—"

"We'd lose the listening data."

"You're still worried about that, with everything else that's at stake?"

"I can worry about many things at once," Tara said. "That's basically my job."

"Even with a city at stake?"

Tara didn't answer. Her silence said too much. The morning closed warm around them, and Kai felt suddenly aware of just how much planet she stood upon, and how fit it was for human life: how good water tasted, how calm and comforting the weight of rock, and how much cold vastness lay above.

"Gods," Kai breathed. "What's up there?"

"We don't know for certain. Yet."

Chapter Sixty-one

THE LIGHT IN THIS godsforsaken place never changed, so Raymet counted heartbeats, breaths, and circuits of her cell. At what she thought was the end of the day, the door opened and the Wreckers dragged Gal back in.

She hung limp from their rubbery arms. The Wreckers bore the muscled length of her like dead weight. Gal's bare feet trailed over the chitin floor. Her head lolled from side to side like a newborn's no one cared to cradle.

"Gal!" Raymet ran from the corner of her room, where she'd crouched waiting for her own interrogators, scheming how to fight. All those plans, the games she'd play, the tricks she'd try—she cast those husks aside and thrust her arm through the bars. Her fingers rasped against a Wrecker's rough cloak, but the monster pulled away before Raymet could get a grip.

Gal's cell bars sheathed into the smooth white floor with the wet noise of retracting claws. The Wreckers tossed Gal in, like tossing trash, and the bars caged her again. The Wreckers sloughed out.

The door closed.

Gal lay still. She breathed.

"Gal?"

Breathed: her chest rose and fell, oxygen into the lungs, from lungs into the blood. Raymet had never seen the other woman sleep, she realized, only pray. She slept now. She was not so still, asleep, as when she prayed: she shuddered and twitched with memories of pain, or with the Wreckers' sharp sick ecstasy. Blood mixed with spit leaked between her lips and pooled on the floor. The pool shrank as Raymet watched. At first she thought the blood and spit were drying, but no residue remained. The floor was drinking her.

"Gal?"

Her eyelids fluttered, settled. She had long lashes, golden, with a slight curl like the tail of an exponential decay curve. Raymet did not often want to hurt people, rhetoric to the contrary. She wanted to hurt herself, now. She wanted to hurt the person who made Gal bleed.

"Gal."

She had thought of Gal as "the other woman." A technical descriptor, of course, there being the two of them in the room—but Gal had always seemed a creature of her own kind, divorced from gender. Thinking of her as being the same sort of being as Raymet required an exercise of imagination Raymet felt beyond her.

Gal woke. Her eyes were blue, beneath. Raymet rarely noticed eye color the way books made it seem people did. But Gal's eyes were pale, bright blue, and she noticed them now.

Gal pushed herself off the floor one-handed. She took her time, and reviewed her bones and joints like a clockmaker reviewing the naked guts of a watch. Tested one shoulder, then the other. Stood, slowly. Stretched. For the first time, Raymet heard cracks and pops from that well-oiled machine.

"Hi," Gal said. "What did I miss?"

Raymet's mouth opened and closed without help from her conscious mind. She made a few sputtering noises before sentences formed. "Nothing. They left me to think about you being tortured. Maybe they hoped imagination would soften me up."

"It could have been worse," Gal said.

"How?"

She wiggled her fingers: long and slender, blunt-nailed.

"I don't take your meaning," Raymet said. Then: "Oh."

"There are advantages and disadvantages to direct neural stimulus," Gal said. "On the one hand, stimulus can make you feel any amount of pain, or pleasure. Sufficiently advanced practitioners can control your sense of time, remove your ability to speak, make you think you're dead—you know, the usual."

"That's usual?"

She shrugged, though the motion made her wince. "In the long term, it can be debilitating. But if you remember it's not real, you deprive the interrogator of a primal tool: their ability to deprive you of options, to mark you forever."

"They could, though. I mean, if they wanted to start taking—" Raymet shuddered. "Fingers. Gods."

"They won't. As representatives of the Iskari church, they are bound by the Rift Accords, which detail interrogation techniques that may, and may not, be used on prisoners. Any violation would void my duty to comply with their custody."

"Which would change things?"

Gal shrugged.

"You're a foreign national, though. They might do it to me."

"It's unlikely," Gal said.

"How unlikely."

She didn't answer.

Raymet cursed. She paced the cell, kicked the wall. It discolored under the kick, then flushed white again. She cursed a second time, which did not help.

When she turned back, Gal was stretching.

"I've never done this before," Raymet said. "Any pointers?"

"You will talk," Gal said. "Find a truth you're comfortable telling. Stick to that."

"Truth?"

"Truth ensures consistency. I've known Knights who could spin elaborate stories under torture, but that's a high art. The risk, with a lie, is that if you lie to them they won't believe the truth when you do break—so they'll keep going. Then you'll start telling them anything they want to hear, to save yourself, and after that, you'll believe what you think they want you to believe."

"What did you tell them?"

Gal bent forward at the waist and hugged the back of her calves. Her white shirt fell down to expose the ridges of muscle that flanked her spine. "Why I came to Agdel Lex."

Raymet stared across the hall that separated their cells. Far beneath the floor, something like a heart beat.

Gal finished her waist bends. She stretched her obliques, and her hamstrings, and then noticed Raymet was staring at her. "Yes?"

"You never told me that story."

Confusion, on that golden mask. "You never asked."

"I thought you were just being private."

"I did not think you wanted to know. I stand with Zeddig, and with you. Does it matter what came before?"

"Does it matter?" How could she ask that question so calmly, as if of course it would not matter, as if nothing about her could possibly be of the slightest interest to Raymet. That quiet calm self-assured ignorance, that blindness. Breathe.

Count. Recite yourself a sonnet. Gal had not moved. "It matters."

"I'm the same person either way."

"It bothers me," Raymet said, choosing her words with tweezers, keeping close watch over the rising gauges of her anger. "It matters that the Wreckers know more about you than I do."

"Okay." Gal sank, sat. Touched her mouth with the back of her hand, and wiped away blood. She smiled, sadly. "I come from a noble family in Camlaan, about which the less said the better. I am the eldest daughter of my mother's house; I would have been an alliance-maker, perhaps with the new Deathless Kings, or I might have become a person of some importance in the church. But I wanted to be a Knight. I trained in secret, against the family's wishes. I made vows and pacts to my Order and to the gods. By the time my family found out, it was too late—and I went out to save the empire from its arrayéd foes."

Her voice changed when she said that last, as if quoting. Raymet did not recognize the reference.

"That did not go as I intended."

"What happened?"

"I—" Gal blinked. She blinked just like normal people did, but this one lasted long enough for Raymet to make note. Were her eyes brighter, wetter than usual when she opened them? "I did not think this would be harder to tell you than the Iskari."

She said, "You don't have to," but meant, I'm listening.

"The empire still exists, though it takes a different form now we have ceded sovereign rights to much of our old territory. Camlaan thrives through its bonds with Schwarzwald and Dhisthra and the Deathless Kings of the Northern Gleb.

On my first mission, I fought pirates and slavers on the Shield Sea, and that was a good fight, and they died in battle. My second mission, we traced the pirates' suppliers to an enclave south of Apophis, and fought them, and that was a good fight, and they died in battle. My third mission, we followed a lead from those suppliers to a group of what our questmasters claimed were rebel demon-summoners plotting to overthrow the Apophitan serpent congress. Yet I saw no demons, no plots. I saw scared people driven from their homes. I saw children. And my brother Knights hunted them. So I fought my brother Knights. They bested me, in the end, but before they did, many of those we had come to kill escaped. My—the Queen saw fit to offer me a kind of mercy. My missions had been secret, as are all Knights' missions these days, but my execution for treason would be public, because of my family, and they did not wish the scandal. So the Queen granted me a quest, from her mouth directly, a mission that could not be denied. I was to find an enemy who could best me, and die in honorable combat. I was banished from Camlaan, and I came to Agdel Lex, seeking my death."

"What," Raymet said, "the fuck."

"I survived. I have been surviving ever since."

"That's why—Gods. You've been trying to kill yourself."

"Not at all. My vow forbids suicide. Death at my own hand would embarrass the Queen. A prodigal daughter, dead on foreign sand, fighting for the crown, a tale to drum up vim and jingo—that's what my"—and again that slight pause—"the Queen prefers. Good press. I hoped the Wreckers might kill me, but they will not cooperate."

The only words Raymet could find were: "I don't want the Wreckers to kill you."

"Thank you," Gal said. "I don't want to die either. But the quest remains."

"That's fucked up. Your own Queen doing that to you."

"I have made mistakes," she said. "So did she."

"But you're the one paying for them."

"I saved her, in a small way, from herself. I stopped an atrocity that would have been committed in her name. I could not have done that if I stayed home." Gal cupped her palms in her lap. "It remains to be seen whether the Iskari will contact Camlaan, and if so whether Camlaan will acknowledge me—or let me disappear inside this cell. They cannot use my disappearance quite so well as they might use my sacrifice, but it will serve."

"Escape, then."

"There's no honor in escape from rightful imprisonment," Gal said. "And I must seek an honorable death."

All the words Raymet wanted to say were too sharp, too angry, too sad. Gal's tremors subsided, and she sat, perfect, this beautiful tall strong work of art some evil faraway Queen wanted to break, and because she was herself, she would let herself be broken. This was a gross world, and Raymet wanted to tear it apart with her hands, but here she was, small, weak, stuck behind bars Gal could have shattered in an instant. Because of a quest, because of honor, she'd let people who weren't worth the ground beneath her feet bind her.

She could not hurt the people she wanted to hurt, so she focused on her breath instead.

"Why did you come back for me?" Gal asked, after a while.

And still Raymet could not find the strength to answer.

Chapter Sixty-two

VOGEL DIDN'T BRING ANYONE home that night: no bed companions, not even a few easygoing philosophical kids to leave sleeping on the Telomeri leather sofa under the chrome-and-gold zodiac mobile in his living room. There had been so much work in the last few days, and little of it the work he loved, the taut messy human dance of dealmaking and strong-arming that led up to the big score. Vogel wasn't a hardworking guy, not even when alive. That made him a good crook: he took his time to plan sharp, sure things, and if he planned right, they came off with hardly any effort at all.

Cleanup, he could do without.

Big operation this time, the train job, and big operations left so many little loose ends to tie and braid and splice before a boss could sleep. For one thing, there was the actual score, the joss he'd employed good hardworking Zurish boys to convert to liquid soulstuff. Contracts got Krieg's team their twenty percent, and the toughs who escaped split thirty among their crew, leaving Vogel with a comfortable fifty—but you couldn't just bank that glistening glorious fifty, couldn't invest it in magesterium wood futures and Zurish oil, imprudent even to spread it around among your bed partners and your easygo-ing philosophical kids. You had protection fees to pay, not to mention all the little subcontractors: the forgers of papers, the guards on the southern gate who gave Krieg's wagons only the most cursory check when they arrived on the post road. Working with Bescond made some parts of the deal easy, but you could never be too sure.

And even after you did all that, you weren't done. Big jobs, and big flows of soulstuff, upset the social order—made overbosses worry you might be setting up to come for them, made underbosses see you as a target. When you won big at a casino, you bought drinks for the table, and tipped well; same principle here. Once your funds cleared you did the rounds, touched base with relevant entities, drank too many bad coffees and ate too many meals in sacrifice-dodge restaurants, and made sure you were well liked. All that niceness drained a body. At day's end you just wanted to stagger upstairs, leave your bodyguards at the door, stumble past the sofa and the chrome-and-gold zodiac mobile, into your bedroom, and kick off your shoes and drop face-first onto the fluffy white comforter, heedless of the flakes of dead skin or muck you shed onto the high-thread-count cotton. Who cares? You're rich. Anyway, that's what bleach is for.

So he wasn't at all ready for the hands that seized him, the tape that covered his mouth, the jacket pulled down to trap his arms. He wasn't ready for the steel cords with which they bound him, or the violence with which they threw him back against the headboard he'd paid a visiting Imperial artist to carve into a frieze of writhing dragons.

He tried to open his mouth despite the tape, but he felt the skin peel and break, and lips took forever to regrow.

There, in his bedroom, on his Skeld rug, heedless of the fact that she should be dead, stood Zeddig. Beside her stood a woman whose face he didn't know—but he recognized the body. Interesting.

If he had a heart these days, it would have beat faster.

"You sold us out." Zeddig loomed over him. There was a lot of power in those shoulders, and his limbs weren't well attached these days.

He tried to say some combination of, that was just business, and, I have no idea what you're talking about, without speaking. The message came out muffled.

"I have proof," she said. "A lot of people would like to know you sold their friends to the Wreckers. But I'm willing to cut a deal. I need twenty souls, free and clear, liquid, untraceable."

He kept still, thinking of outs and ins, and of the silent alarm across the room. If he could slip these cords without their noticing.

"I'm not giving you a choice," Zeddig said. "We have a deal, or I see how many pounds of flesh I can cut off before your guards break the locks on that door. You're a paranoid man. It might take them a while to get through."

Before he realized he had decided, he was already glancing left, to the closet.

The other woman crossed over, disabled the hidden catch that should have triggered the gas trap, parted the wall of clothes and leather gear, and found the safe. "It's locked."

"Combination?"

He mumbled something through the tape.

"If I take this off, and you scream, you're done."

He nodded. The tape coming off hurt worse than expected, and the sudden chill against his teeth told him she'd torn some of his lip off with it. "Gods" came out a bit lispy. "Diamond-sapphire-opal-quartz."

Pause. Zeddig glanced down at the tape, and the piece of lip stuck to it, disgusted.

"It's not working," the woman at the closet said.

"You hit the wrong opal."

The lock clicked, and gold light seeped into the room, gentle and slow as dawn.

"Are we good?" Zeddig asked.

"We are good." And the woman began shoveling joss, his beautiful golden joss, into a ratty backpack. "We are so good."

"This isn't done," Zeddig said. "If anything happens to me or mine, you're going down. For added security—" She folded the tape around the piece of his lip. "I'll keep this. It'll be nice to have a stick I can use to hit you, for a change."

"Pleasure doing business with you," he lisped, not meaning it.

"You're a loser, Vogel, and a bottom-feeder, and if we had time I'd give you a taste of what you've given me. But for now, you're not worth the effort."

He was about to come up with a witty comeback—he even opened his mouth—but before he could get the words out, there was more tape, and the lights died, and he lay alone and bound in bed.

At least this way, he thought, he would get a good night's sleep.

That was when the pain started.

Chapter Sixty-three

FONTAINE LEFT HER OFFICE late and stoned, red-eyed, swollen with a thousand half-had dreams. She staggered from the elevator, leaned against a small lacquer table on which a vase of artificial flowers rested, and waited for the room to steady, breathing the silk scent of a fake rose. The security guard waved good night. Fontaine had never learned her name—they blurred together, offices blending officeholders to one being diffracted through time, a Guard Who Watches All, male and female united in a single frame of care. Or else Fontaine once knew the guard's name, and forgot. Or never bothered.

Never mind. Scrape away hair sweat-plastered against scalp. Stumble through automatic doors into night. Stare up and see few stars. Smell dust and feel cool wind and the city's heat, grudgingly surrendered to a dark that harbored fewer stars than it should. A cab rolled up. She got in.

Kai sat, cross-legged, in the seat opposite.

"Hi," Fontaine said, lazily, and laughed at her own joke, because "Hi" sounded like, well.

"I wanted to talk," Kai said, "in private." She rapped the carriage window, and the horse started walking. The cab jostled, but Kai's gaze kept steady. Fontaine met those black eyes with her own. They were still as the center of the universe. They were, in fact, the center of a universe, unspooling always and forever, that universe's edges filigreed with other universes, smaller and smaller—places so minuscule no monstrosity could enter, territories so tiny light's touch would obliterate them, thus forever safe from the all-seeing tyrant eye. Fontaine raised her hand and watched it spin in the universe's revolutions around Kai's pupils. Her fingers shook.

She reached for her purse, but it was gone. Where? She patted around the seat, on the floor, searched her jacket pockets, underfoot, the seat cushions, gods, had she left it in the office, impossible—stolen? How could she have missed that theft, as easy to pickpocket her arm. "Purse," she said, then looked back to Kai, who, she realized, held it. "I need it."

"I need answers. And I need you sober enough to offer them."

"Sobriety," she said, "is overrated," and she lunged for the purse. Several moments in time unstitched from one another, and when entropy and consciousness commenced to fucking once again she lay on the bench seat Kai had recently evacuated, and Kai sat on the chair from which she had lunged, and her head hurt like some Quechal hell, and her hand stung as if she'd punched something solid. The carriage greened, and rocked, only it wasn't rocking really but spinning end over end, like she was strapped to the rim of an enormous wheel, which she was, she supposed, if you thought of gravity as an invisible strap. The spinning did not. Would not. Stop. "Help," she said.

Kai moved, this time in ways and at speeds Fontaine found almost comprehensible. The priestess kicked open the carriage door, lowered Fontaine into the footwell, and made sure she got as much of the vomit on the road as possible under the circumstances. When Fontaine tried to close her mouth, her teeth grit together, and she threw up again. The driver, at least, did not slow.

The lights of Agdel Lex seared her. She did not fall, because Kai held her jacket in one fist, and she did not fall, because Kai's other fist held her hair. Nonsense nonsense nonsense, was the churn of the carriage wheels against shock absorbers and Iskari cobblestones painted with Fontaine's dinner.

Fontaine wriggled, wormlike, back into the carriage footwell, and pulled the door shut behind her. Click was a nice sound for a latch to make. The wheeling sensation did not stop—odd how the trick of nerves could make you feel stretched out even curled into a ball on a dirty floor—sickness had that magic too, to transform a surface from which you'd recoil in disgust, sober, to a surface you could cuddle—she pillowed her cheek against her hand, and watching her reflection in Kai's shoe.

The woman tried to pull her upright. She slumped.

There wasn't much room in the footwell. When Kai joined her down there, they lay almost face to face. Fontaine knew what her breath smelled like; she tried to breathe through her nose. Her heart kept a running rabbit's pace. She listened. Kai spoke.

"No one else at your bank spends quite so much time quite so high. I've wandered the halls during business hours, and I pay attention. You can't have kept this up for long. You would have died. Your companion, your Lord—it feeds off your blood. You share the high, both minds at once. It's not human, and it's smaller than you—so it reels, shuts down, while you stay conscious, or close to it. Just blink once, if I'm right."

She blinked. Once. She wanted to say so much. Her Lord rested against her chest, His arms stilled, His mind reeling from the feed. Reflexively, He pushed antitoxins into her vein. She felt their weight on her bloodstream, tasted them bitter as angostura when she exhaled.

Kai sagged. Fontaine studied the skin between the follicles of her thick, black hair.

"You brought me here," she said. "I've wanted to approach the local artist's community for six, seven months, and your invitation came at just the right time. My sister approached you, didn't she? Explained the danger. Asked you for a loan. Maybe even asked you to set up a meeting with Jax. And you couldn't, because the squids didn't let you. They closed things down."

She blinked. Once.

"The Iskari Defense Ministry used your bank for their ends. You're a patriot. You believe in the system: free enterprise, development, the whole fairy tale. You're not naive. But you learned those stories deep down, before you learned to question stories. I knew a woman like you once." Kai sounded so sad. Fontaine wanted to touch her, and before she realized it, she was. "You went to your supervisor, and she said, it happens. The IDM uses us to hide their dirty work. We play along. You did. You turned Ley down. But she was desperate. And maybe you'd heard my name—maybe you'd browsed past my letter a few dozen times, thinking, someday. Why not now? So you took your drugs, and sent me a nightmare, and let Ley know I'd come. It would have worked, if I had listened."

Kai's arm, under her suit jacket: skin and muscle, bone and fat. Fontaine's fingertips explored cords of tension, dug in. Kai's features tightened. Pain? Pleasure? The woman felt warm.

"I can't change that now. But I can still help. I need to speak with Jax."

Plans, objections, words. The world's spinning slowed. Universes no longer birthed universes in her eyes. Some colors did not hurt anymore. She clawed at the purse Kai held. "It's waking up. If it hears—"

"I need you to remember this. I need Jax."

"Jax," Fontaine said, "Yes. Right. Good. Now." She was crying, when did she start crying. "Give me the godsdamn purse before you get us both killed."

Kai let go.

The pills tasted sharp and clear and rough as silk.

Chapter Sixty-four

SOLITARY.

There was an eye in the room.

There was a lidless eye in the room.

There was a lidless eye the size of Izza's head, in the room.

There was a lidless eye the size of Izza's head, in the room, and it watched her.

There was a lidless eye the size of Izza's head, in the room, and it watched her, and knew.

There was a lidless eye the size of Izza's head, in the room, and it watched her, and knew what was best, for her and for her friends, and for the world, because the eye was a bud of a greater mind, which knew truths too deep for any crawling, limping time-tethered mammal to comprehend. Eyes linked to other eyes, arms linked to other arms, throughout a city, throughout a globe.

There was a lidless eye the size of Izza's head, in the room, and it watched her, and knew her story to a point: knew the name of the village from which she'd come, knew the names of her parents and the face of her mother, knew the priestess, her teacher, whose throat was slit by raiders, by cultists, to feed their hungry Wastelands jackal-God, and to appease the Deathless Kings they had promised, on pain of greater pain and in exchange for sureties of protection, that they would pacify the narrow flat and fertile region foreigners called the

Imbar Valley, at the foot of the mountains foreigners called the Glain, after the Camlaander Knight who'd perished in battle with a local dragon there seven thousand years after the people who settled those slopes gave their rocks and rivers other names—for the slopes of the Glain were rich in ossuate, malevolite, and other necromantic earths.

There was a lidless eye the size of Izza's head, in the room, and it watched her, and knew that she fled the slaughter, to the train, to Agdel Lex, terrified—though it could not know what it meant to be "terrified," such experiences were beyond its ken—and it knew that as she walked the streets of Agdel Lex, a hungry kid, alone, she stole and fought and grew hard from fear, and even after the High Sisters wrapped her tight in their love, even though they granted her every advantage and every joy, she scorned their love, and left.

There was a lidless eye the size of Izza's head, in the room, and it watched her, and knew that in her wandering she had grown, and that she was wounded, broken, lost, that she fought because of her wounds, because of that break, because of that loss, and the eye knew it could help: the High Sisters offered all children their own Lord, a companion, a piece of the Being from whom the Eye took life, and if she accepted its love she would never lack again—might hunger, but not for meaning, might suffer, but not from loneliness, might stray, but not for ignorance of what paths there were in the world to walk, and all she need do to receive this blessing was extend her hand and open her heart, because the heart is a strange fortress, with portals and locks invulnerable to any assault but weak to an opening will within.

There was a lidless eye the size of Izza's head, in the room, and it watched her, and knew so much, wadded her round with the weight of its knowledge, and her every twitch, every word, every scream (for there was weight, and pain, in being the subject of such regard) added to its knowledge, as it learned the hidden paths of Izza, and how she could be encouraged to stretch out her hand, and open her heart.

There was a lidless eye the size of Izza's head, in the room, and it watched her, and knew her, and listened, and added to its model new certainties—it learned her stories, her tales of shore and surf, and of Smiling Jack, thin and tall, who lurked in dark alleys and caught kids in his bag full of knives facing in, and of the Lady Who Made Herself a Hummingbird and swift as swift unstitched the bottom of Jack's sack, so when he caught the kids and tossed them in they cut themselves on the knives, and screamed, but fell right out the other side and ran, until at last Jack asked himself why his sack would not catch, and climbed in himself, and the Lady Who Made Herself a Hummingbird, swift as swift, stitched the hole in the bottom of the sack to the sack's mouth, and Jack climbed further and further in, always seeking the hole that unmade him, and with each inch he climbed his skin came further off.

There was a lidless eye the size of Izza's head, in the room, and it watched her and watched her watching it and watched itself watching her and it knew her and knew there was a hole in her and knew it could fill the hole if it understood its depths, and so it modeled the hole, and modeled the story, and climbed into itself, and deeper in, and it knew her and through her knew Someone Else, a fleet Form within its mind, never wholly compassed by its gaze, always one step ahead, but the eye would catch Her, yes, would, must, know Her completely, must find Her where she hid, somewhere deep within this wood, somewhere down these dirty side streets, somewhere in this rain puddle, somewhere far down at the bottom of this bag of knives.

There was a lidless eye the size of Izza's head, in the room, and it closed, and a door opened.

Chapter Sixty-five

LIEUTENANT BESCOND COULD HAVE been the last woman in the world, for all she cared—she had her blood-streaked paperwork, reams and reams of it, she had her ruby port and high tower view of Agdel Lex in shining regular beauty, and she had the knife she spun, tip down, on her ink blotter while she reviewed the paperwork for errors. The blade's tip curled pig's tails of leather from the blotter, drilling toward the baseboard, and if she kept at this job long enough she'd eventually pierce into the wooden desktop. She would leave few marks on the world, but at least she'd leave this private scar.

There was a knock on the door.

Bescond felt her forehead wrinkle. Her Lord twitched against her chest, and its rubbery arms uncurled to caress her neck. Together, Bescond and her Lord searched their collective memory for the knock's pitch and volume, but before they could reach a conclusion, Kai Pohala opened the door.

A detective in one of the stories Bescond read when she was young could have deduced, no doubt, why Ms. Pohala had come, and even the path she'd taken, from the wrinkles on her skirt and stocking, from hairs out of place, from patterns of uncertainty in the track of her gaze through Bescond's office. Bescond sometimes missed the comfort that came from believing in those stories—the comfort of feeling, even if just in fiction, that a single mind might compass the world. If only there were some way to live effectively, she thought, without letting our ideals wither.

Her Lord shivered at her chest, and gave her certainty in the vein, and she reflected that, while no human mind could compass the whole world, this was only a sign that human minds needed help.

Kai wasted no time in greeting. "Why are you going ahead with the launch?"

"Ms. Pohala. The secretary let you in?"

"The building did."

Kai always sat oddly on Bescond's gaze, which bothered her. The bother lay in no particularity: so far as she could tell, Pohala's transformation was perfect, as were the alterations of all those remade in Kavekana's Pool. Even Bescond's Lord could find no flaw, no trace of Craftwork or divine grace. Kai Pohala had, quite simply, rewritten herself from first principles. No, the bother lay in the fact that she, Bescond, could not help searching for a sign. She believed there should be something to perceive, and so she insisted on perceiving.

The detective observes, but the detective also decides what to observe.

"I'm busy," Bescond said. She returned her pen to its stand, and tapped the stack of forms with the tip of her knife. "Our procedures aren't so different from those of standard police. Our forms must be properly formatted, to keep the squid from suffering indigestion."

"You actually feed the paperwork to the squid?"

"Paper goes into squid, the squid share fluids, and thus information propagates." Bescond signed the form with a flourish.

"Why are you going ahead with the launch?" Kai repeated.

"What do you know about that?"

"You want to collapse Alikand, and wall off the dead city."

Possibilities compressed to a single solution. "Vane told you."

"When she woke up. She thought it would piss me off. She was right."

Bescond sighed. "There is this problem with a certain sort of knowledge worker: since so much of their job involves following instinct—listening to hunches, chasing discovery, seeking the logic underlying personal misgivings—they can be too damn loyal to their baser urges."

"That's not an explanation."

"We proceed with the launch because it is in our best interests to do so."

"My sister thinks you're going to destroy the city."

"Your sister," Bescond replied, "has different views on the meaning of destroy, and save, than the Rectification Authority." She set down the knife, and stood, and took her glass of port to the windowsill. Music and light issued up from the city below; the air bore cooking smells and perfume and sewer-stink, but only the light reached her window, pure and clean. "We have fought for a century to build a lattice on which civilization can grow. Every year, the Authority expends untold souls maintaining this bastion against the pull of the wound at its heart. We should have abandoned Agdel Lex decades ago, let the Wastes take the whole city. Instead, we built a ruin of angels into a haven for man. Arts and culture and business thrive mere miles from the Wastes. I'm not foreign to this city, Ms. Pohala. My family has lived here for generations. I want my home safe."

"I've seen the figures. The Iskari get way too much out of Agdel Lex—resources, taxes, tactical advantage—to claim an altruistic motive."

"Does the Kavekanese priesthood give its services away?"

"We," Kai said, "don't oppress people." But Bescond could see that protest rang hollow, even for her.

"Are you certain? Show me your pilgrim rolls, tell me how morally your clients make their fortunes. I can see the truth on your face. Of course, *you also* is no fit moral argument—your errors do not make mine excusable: two failures at addition don't make math wrong. You don't like me? You find my methods grotesque?" The port in her glass looked like blood. "I agree. That's why I must take this step."

Kai said nothing. Bescond decided this was disbelief.

"I am destroying my job. I was ordered to do so: the Iskari Demesne wants to incorporate Agdel Lex directly, as soon as the city is no longer at constant risk. I could have dragged my feet. Many officers would. But I want the Rectifiers gone. We are brutal tools, necessary only because some locals do not recognize the need to use proper names for proper subjects. Once the world is whole again, once there are no more gaps through which a wanderer might fall, once people no longer risk their lives seeking useless trivia in an apocalypse, then Agdel Lex itself, its streets and architecture and bureaucracy, will do the Wreckers' work: it will impose limits, structure interaction, self-manage. Your sister's masterpiece will force everyone onto the same page. We can take it from there."

"People will die."

"Ask Vane about that. Or your sister. They proposed the approach. The church agreed. I am a tool of policy."

"You love to push responsibility onto other people, don't you."

"What do you think that is?" She nodded back to the paperwork. "Three hundred pages explaining why I let a fugitive escape. Because I promised you I would. I kept my bargain, and now I am taking responsibility. I could lose my job over this—or worse."

"Don't give me that," Kai said. "You wouldn't have let her go if I didn't force you. I still don't know she made it. She could be dead right now, in the Wastes. And if she's alive, she hates me."

"I do the best I can," Bescond said. "If you can undo history, if you know how to go back in time and force people to make better decisions so those of us left today aren't stuck making worse ones, please, do so. With my blessing. Failing that, I'll manage the present."

"You're a bully, and a thug."

"There are two kinds of people in this world, Ms. Pohala. Some build and maintain. Others destroy. I have never understood those who destroy. I build, and protect those who build."

"You're building over graves."

"Our planet is a tomb. I am building a system that will work. I am burying the skeletons of the past, so we can move on. I'm sorry you were drawn into this. Most people don't like to think about necessities."

"It's only necessary," Kai said, "because you want it to be."

And she walked out before Bescond could answer. Unfortunate. Bescond hated when emotions interfered with argument. Pohala couldn't see—perhaps something in her background blinded her. Bescond looked down into the ruby of her glass. I have never understood those who destroy.

I should learn.

This paperwork would not finish itself. And yet.

Bescond drained the last of her port, and prayed for a prisoner to be delivered to interrogation.

Chapter Sixty-six

WHEN THE WRECKERS CAME for Raymet, she fought. They'd been ready for Gal, but they didn't expect much from a tiny lapsed academic, an underestimation Raymet had relied on to see her through many a back-alley scrap. She grabbed the first Wrecker by the cloak and struck it in the face with her forehead, slipped past while it reeled, almost reached the door before a tentacle caught her. She tripped and sprawled onto the bone floor; with clawed fingers she caught a door jamb, pulled herself upright, kicked free of the tentacle, made it to the hall. She got to the lifts before they tackled her, and even then she did not go quietly—never would while she had teeth.

It took three of them to drag her to the small bone-white room, sit her in a chair that grew from the floor, and chain her. That Lieutenant from the Wastes, Bescond, watched from the shadows. Raymet felt the bruises she'd have tomorrow.

Tell them a story, Gal said. Tell them the truth.

"Doctor Haaz," Bescond said. "This is a purely informal interview, preliminary to questioning."

"I know exactly what this is."

"We're attempting to fill in a few gaps in your résumé, so to speak."

"Fuck you."

"This isn't an adversarial proceeding."

Raymet glared at the Lieutenant and imagined strangling

her, imagined wrestling her to the ground and breaking her arm, imagined knocking out those perfect teeth with a stiff elbow to the face. She imagined the blood and spray, the crack as bone gave, and hoped all that translated, somehow, through her eyes.

"In fact, this interview may lead to a job. We're always looking for new talent."

She imagined the arm breaking: Bescond's bone in her grip, her shoulder straining, and—

"When did you start to delve?"

The vision faded.

"Was it before you defended your dissertation, or after?"

If they knew that, they would have an excuse: lean on professors and student clubs and drinking circles, civilly at first, pardon me, fellow students, but has anyone in this vicinity been engaged in seditious thought? They knew already, of course. The Wreckers built lists, in this obscene tower, of people identified in confession, of friends sold out by friends. They used the lists when it pleased them, or when they were bored.

"It's a simple question."

"No question's simple."

Bescond sighed, and stood. She removed her jacket, and rolled up her sleeve. "Was it a funding issue? I know it's difficult to make ends meet on a graduate stipend. The funding collapse, plus your own lack of family resources, must have hit hard. You went to a prestigious school. Many of your peers came from families of means. Might have driven even the most law-abiding individuals to ends they'd never consider under normal circumstances. Or was it simply a knowledge issue? You studied languages, culture, architecture—hard to resist the temptation to see what was lost, despite the danger. There's no shame in being drawn out of your depth. In making a mistake. I just want to understand."

"Get it over with," Raymet said, before the knuckles met her cheek.

Minutes later, spitting blood, stars dancing in her vision, she heard Bescond's voice, unchanged. "When did you start to delve?"

She'd counted on the woman to break. To get angry and dumb. It was easy to clam up and spit insults, to meet rage with rage. But Bescond didn't sweat, didn't fight her, just asked, in an even, measured voice, without even the fucking decency to lose her breath. Her arms moved, and her body, but the mind seemed cut out of the mix. Not a passenger, even, but an advisor, a central authority directing distant hirelings to take unpleasant actions, like a slur-voiced crime boss in a mystery play.

"What about your companions? Tell me about them."

She glared through blood.

Eventually Bescond brought in Wreckers. Raymet's heart rushed when she saw them, and she fought against her cuffs. When they started feeding her pleasure she dug her nails into her palms to edge that joy with pain, to anchor herself to herself. That worked, until they saw what she was doing and straightened her hands for her. She almost bit through her cheek before they forced her jaw open. And the whole time, that infuriating level voice asked: "Why?"

She was fucking fed up, is why: fed up with being poor, fed up with walking the line, fed up with Zeddig's folks and the High Families and all the other godsdamn great-grandchildren of Senators who had retreated to their enclaves to mourn

Iskari rule rather than fight back, who pretended they could live a closed life out of the occupier's eye. Raymet never had that luxury. So why not break into the dead city and steal the High Families' history out from under them? Why not learn and plunder, and make those Senators' kids come to her? Why not fight the Iskari direct—not by building dreams of pleasant imaginary pasts, of perfect worlds that never were, but by burrowing straight through the illusion they called Agdel Lex into the slaughter on which that illusion was made?

But she would not give the Lieutenant satisfaction of an answer.

Gal's advice: tell them a true story. You will in the end. But Gal had been trained for this, and given up everyone she cared about already. She came to Agdel Lex to die. Certainly not to love.

Fuck the wracking waves of pleasure, fuck the pain they tried when that didn't work, fuck that level voice. She had wadded-up animosity aplenty from thirty years of life in Agdel Lex, and did not owe Bescond an ounce of truth about her, her people, her self.

"Why?"

When individual Wreckers didn't work, they dragged her to a wall niche and plugged her in, wadded her with squid things that tried to convince her she belonged. They were all in this together, they all wanted the same things, they only had to communicate, to recognize the problem. The squid was mother, the squid was father, yes you've been abandoned by your people, yes your dad's a drunk working a third-rate steamer in Kho Khatang and Grandma took you back from Mom for a reason, yes you're in so far over your head you can't see sunlight, but we're all Iskari together, we're all Agdel Lex.

Fuck you.

You want me to belong? Same as wanting me to know my place. I'm making my place, and I'm making my people, I'm making a godsforsaken nation of people who want nothing to do with you. Why do I delve? For fortune, for fame, for thrills, to get laid, and because when I delve, I delve into a world I know for damn sure isn't any part of yours.

But she didn't say any of that.

She just grinned through the blood.

It went on longer than she expected. They moved her again. They tried techniques.

And at last, when even Bescond's polite queries began to sour, they dragged her back to her cell and left her in a heap. The bars snapped shut. Her jaw ached from being so long clenched. She tried to move. Couldn't. Maybe she was broken. Maybe she just lacked the will.

"Raymet."

Gal's voice.

"Raymet, are you there?"

She was. She tried to say so; it came out as a groan.

Eyes, blue, shone beyond the bone bars.

"Raymet," Gal said, as if someone else was there to hear. Her name sounded heavy in Gal's mouth, as if it hurt to say, as if the name was a splinter that drawing forth exposed a wound. "Why did you come back for me?"

And still she did not, could not, answer.

Chapter Sixty-seven

THE TELEGRAPH WAS WAITING for Kai when she woke the day before the launch: come home.

Home. What a concept.

She hit the gym first. The Arms was enough of an overaccommodating piece of tourist fluff to have a full gym, benches and bar and even a squat rack, so Kai spent the better part of an hour destroying herself. No spots—the only other person in the gym this early was a centipede-looking individual in a tank top blazoned with the Zodograd 30K logo, skittering on the treadmill, and so far as she could see, it didn't have arms. No help there. No sweat. Just don't go overboard on weight, and mind your form.

So of course she got herself in trouble on the bench, couldn't make the last rep, arms shivering stuck halfway as breath ripped through her nostrils, overcome with clarity of failure. You can do it, godsdammit. Worthless. Useless. One last push, just three inches, bare your teeth, press your traps into the bench. Make it happen.

She did.

There was this thing people didn't tend to understand about the way Kai psyched herself up in the gym, something her exes, especially Claude, never quite got: she wasn't cursing herself. She was cursing the self she fought to overcome.

When she stumbled back to her room, muscles singing, to

shower, the telegram still lay on the table by the window, and Behemoth lay on the telegram, staring out at the waves, and past the waves to the Altus tower.

Come home.

Showered, Kai walked downstairs in sweatpants, slippers, and a T-shirt, piled a plate with fruit and yogurt and eggs from the buffet, gulped a mug of not entirely terrible coffee (everywhere's coffee was bad compared to Kavekana's, but you couldn't hold that against them, most places didn't have volcanic soil), refilled the mug, and returned to her room, her desk, the paperwork the business center forwarded from the nightmare telegraph office. She spent an hour signing off and signing off, jotting memos, shifting investments. Then, she prayed.

She worked her idols in groups, based on the type of worship: no sense shifting from ritual contortion to bloodletting to ecstasy and back to contortion again. Shifting, in the same pose, from contemplating the infinitude of one God to contemplating the infinitude of Another, required a peculiar frame of mind. That was why her pilgrims hired a professional. Kai's idols were fine—slightly overexposed to the Imperial housing market, she should rebalance that, but, for the most part, healthy.

After her ritual rounds, she prayed to the Blue Lady, to the figure dancing just out of reach in the woods of her soul. Izza, she prayed. I need you. Harder to admit: I miss you.

She felt, echoed, confinement, tension, a grotesque smell. *I'm a bit busy at the moment.*

Izza! Izza, you're all right!

Wouldn't go that far. And I can't pray much. They'll hear me.

Izza, I need your help. The Iskari want to— *Want to what?*

They want to fix the city. Destroy Alikand for good.

Pause. *This isn't our problem.*

They'll feed Alikand to the Wastes, and Ley wanted to stop them, and we stopped her—

How long do we have?

The launch is tomorrow morning.

Silence, at first. *I can make it. Have to wait for nightfall here, but once that happens I can get Isaak out to a ship. We don't have documents, but the Lady will provide.*

Izza, I don't—

Shit, from the other side of the prayer, and *Sorry,* and Kai was alone in her skin again. She had knelt, without realizing it, before the small table by the window, where the telegram lay.

Come home.

What was home, anyway? She didn't belong in Agdel Lex, in Alikand. These streets were not her streets, this pain was not her pain, this fight was not her fight. Her sister did not belong here either—but her sister clearly, painfully, loved a woman who did. Ley had betrayed Zeddig; she would give up everything to save her now.

Kavekana was Kai's home, with its cool evening breeze, its warm wet air, its smells of citrus and green, its beaches and bad poets. Kavekana, island among islands, which thrived by its ties to other lands across the sea, a hoop with an empty center. Without those bonds, without the sea and the winds and the ships, Kavekana was nothing.

Kavekana was home, because it cared for her and she cared for it in turn: her gods, her calling, her friends, her family. Those, she could defend. And so, though Ley told her to run, she stayed, to grab her sister, hold her close, and drag her from the dark. To save her.

But could you save someone by destroying what they would die to defend?

What would a woman be, if you broke her world around her?

And if that woman was your true home: What then? You could destroy yourself trying to save yourself. You could hold people so tight you might strangle parts of them you did not understand.

Whitecapped waves rolled on a sea darker than her sea.

She slid the telegram out from under Behemoth. The cat rumbled discontent, stood, paced, jumped into Kai's lap, and dug in his claws.

The window only opened a few inches, just enough to let the outside in. She watched the water, which no Iskari hand had shaped, and breathed in, and smelled the faintest trace of Alikand.

Some blood remained in the silver bowl. She hoped it would be enough. She prayed out, and through, to Izza:

I'm not leaving. I have to help.

She heard no reply.

Kai stood, spilling Behemoth from her lap. The cat yowled, hissed. Kai stroked her under her chin.

Then she left. She had work to do.

Chapter Sixty-eight

ZEDDIG AND LEY STAYED in, the day before the launch. They didn't wake until noon, having spent the night preparing. When noon came, they didn't rise together—Zeddig rolled from bed, leaving Ley to sleep, cheek pillowed on clenched fist, while she made breakfast: eggs and flapjacks on the two-burner gas stove, sliced fruit, percolator coffee. They ate in silence, weighed down by the day.

Aman knocked on the door at two, and entered, escorted. "Your brother's waiting outside." She walked surefooted in the bare room, in these Alikand back streets, far from the Agdel Lex she could no longer see. Ley pushed herself upright in bed, shifting aside tray, setting down her coffee cup. Aman waved her back. "We don't have time for formality."

"We can stop this," Ley said.

"Maybe." Aman nodded. "I bore your message to the other Archivists."

"And?"

"It is complicated." Aman did not look at either of them. Zeddig felt the scorn in that silence, the reluctance to share her difficulty. "We all take care. We keep faith. But some fear setting ourselves against Iskar. Some say, if you fail, it would be best for us to harbor our knowledge and hand it down, so at least our children will remember what's lost, than resist and lose it all."

"No," Zeddig said, and Ley at the same time—but Ley closed her mouth and let Zeddig talk. Zeddig knew how the conversation must have moved between Aman and the other Archivists, their habits of preservation and secret-keeping, the need of generations under rule. "Aman, they want to take it all. If we—if the Families mean anything, we have to stand now. For everyone."

She stopped when she saw Aman was smiling.

"What?"

"You remind me of your grandfather."

"Aman."

"I told the others, child. They agreed. Some faster, others with more reluctance—but if it comes to that, we'll fly." Simple words, simply spoken, seemed to have no weight at all. If Aman wanted to give them the force they deserved, she would have to scream, to sing. They did what had to be done. "Is that leg still giving you trouble?"

Zeddig saw Ley consider lying. "A bit," she said at last. "Here." And drew her leg from beneath the sheets. Aman's touch had straightened the bone, bound torn muscles, but a bruise still cuffed Ley's shin.

"You haven't come up with a better plan?" Aman said when the work was done, before she left.

Zeddig answered: "None that works."

"I love you," she said.

They embraced. Zeddig breathed in, and wished she were a Craftswoman, to arrest her body's function so she need never breathe out again. Then Aman released her, and left, and when the door closed Zeddig let her go.

When she returned to the bedroom she found Ley in underwear and T-shirt by the window, coffee in hand, watching the sky. Light painted her half-gold, half-dark. Ley rose onto the balls of her feet, settled again, testing ankle and shinbone with the smile of a pleased operator. The movement changed the curl of her calf, carved lines of muscle into the side of her leg.

The world held other angels than those of old Alikand.

Zeddig wrapped her arms around her, and bent her head to rest her temple against Ley's. Her fingers slid beneath her shirt. Zeddig must have been colder than she felt: Ley tensed and drew a short, sharp breath through her teeth. Ley ran hot, like an engine strained to melting. There was such a thing, Zeddig knew, as a friction weld. To bond two pieces of metal, you set them touching and rubbed them back and forth, faster and faster, until their walls softened and melted. Once the pieces stopped moving, they could not start again. You had to be careful, making two things one.

"I missed you," she said.

Ley turned against Zeddig's chest, and kissed her for the first time, because every time felt like the first.

Zeddig turned her and lifted her. Ley squawked—"Coffee!"—leaned away, the gap between them momentary, unbearable, set the coffee down. Zeddig pressed her against the wall. Fingernails carved tracks on Zeddig's back as Ley peeled off her shirt. Their skin met. Ley's legs bound Zeddig's sides. They stumbled to the bed.

Time passed.

"Your leg—"

"It's fine."

"I—"

"Don't. Stop."

Breath and sweat and sweetness.

"I missed you too."

Time is weird. It runs faster or slower on different worlds, at different speeds, or so the Hidden Schools claim, and people, especially lovers, create new worlds constantly: realms of play, torment, consequence, abandon. If time changes pace from world to world, and if lovers build new worlds together, might not one of those worlds be—

"Purple!"

"Oh. Sorry. Damn."

"No, it's—" Breath. "I'm okay."

"You're sure."

"Give me a second." A nod. "Yes. Good. Yesss."

Even if we saw time like gods, divorced from petty sequence, moments webbed to moments in jeweled space, still the webbing would endure. No matter how memories trail back (to their first time together, in a dorm bed they'd now think barely broad enough for one, but which seemed palatial once; to their last before the breakup, angry and sullen and hungry in each other's arms for assurances that would never come, to that night after Ley's first delve, the party Raymet threw, making out in the laundry room), circling through memories evoked by Iskari pastries or other tastes, more bitter, deep, and sweet, we would still find ourselves moving toward the future, the godsdamn subsequent moment when—

"Oh. Shit. Don't we have to, um. You know. Save the world?"

They were still laughing when they entered the carriage, weighed down with gear.

• • •

Even with Fontaine's introduction, Kai still had to argue, wheedle, duck, and at last fight past one doorman, a second, more elite doorman, three personal assistants, and someone she assumed was a bodyguard, before she reached Eberhardt Jax's suite. Izza would have snuck through, no doubt, and Ley would have swanned past security with a toss of her head and a projection of authority so complete no one would dare challenge her, but one used the tools to one's hand, and if one happened to be priestess of half a hundred idols, all of which were, on some level, masks for a still greater Being, well, one's tools were miracles.

After all that work, Kai found herself before a closed door. She checked her hair and makeup in a compact mirror, clicked it shut, and returned it to her handbag with the other still-burning religious equipment. Waiting would not make this easier. Behind the door, she heard loud music, labored breath, and the sharp clash of metal.

She knocked. No answer. The music did not stop. Ordinarily she would retreated to wait, but she doubted the miracles that had brought her here could hold out much longer.

So she opened the door.

Within, Jax fought for his life against a black glass demon: four arms and scalpel fingers, six banks of red eyes glaring from a fused face, every corner a spike, every edge a blade, always moving, its carapace rippled with broken reflections. Jax dodged cuts and blows, blocked and counterpunched from a boxer's guard, his skin slick with sweat; silver light clad his hands and climbed his arms, and a sharp spinning Craft circle burned on his back, running down his spine. The demon kicked; Jax stepped aside, caught the leg, tried to break it, but the demon slid out of his grip, its bladed leg drawing sparks against the wards on Jax's hands. They fought without words. The conversation of scraped wood, struck flesh, rung glass left words superfluous.

Then the demon saw Kai.

It opened a previously invisible mouth, beared razor fangs, and boiled toward her.

The window of decision opens briefly. Boozing coworkers can talk a good game about about the heroics they'd commit if threatened, but all they're really saying is that they hope they would respond that way. Perhaps they would. Perhaps not. Nothing's true 'til experiment unearths it.

Kai, if pressed, tended to assume the answer to what she'd do faced with a demon was, *run*. She was as surprised as anyone to discover the answer was, in fact, to hit it with her purse.

The force of Kai's blow spun the demon's head all the way around, but the demon didn't seem to mind. It reached for her anyway, fast and vicious and sharp, and then—

"Stop."

All that movement stilled in the instant of Jax's command.

Kai did not need to open her eyes, because they were not closed. Another surprise. You found out so much about yourself, when faced with new experiences. She blinked, and the demon's claws feathered her eyelashes.

Jax stood in the center of the room, panting, radiant with sweat; he wore a sleeveless shirt and black pants and leather shoes, and looked embarrassed, as if she'd surprised him in the middle of something far more compromising than, well, whatever this was. "Are you all right, Ms. Pohala?"

"That," she said, straightening first her stance, and then her jacket, "is an interesting way to exercise."

He shrugged, and reached for a towel. "Fear of death is a

great motivator. Just ask the Craftsmen."

"Just a moment." The demon's mass and its outstretched arms blocked her passage into the room. She squeezed under one armpit, though her jacket snagged on a projecting hip spine, and she had to back up to extricate without tearing fabric. By the time she managed, he stood by the water cooler near the window, filling a bottle. "I see two problems with that statement."

He shrugged.

"First, did you actually ask this—" She remembered R'ok, and did not say *thing*. "Demon" was a weak substitute, but worked. "Did you actually ask her to kill you?"

"To fight until she could kill me, and then stop. It's the only way to be certain my training has practical application. I can last almost four minutes now."

"What if she forgets you asked her to stop?"

Jax raised a finger, begging delay, and drank half his bottle of water, then refilled it. "That, I suppose, will be my final exam. What's the second problem you see?"

"Craftsfolk don't fear death."

His laugh was deep and guttural, and held no humor she recognized. "Of course they do. They fear it more than anything."

"They don't die."

"They've built our whole world from their desperation not to die. And they—we—are wrecking the planet to satisfy that desire. I understand the resistance: who wants to die? Your whole subjective world vanishes at once. The universe goes away. The smarter and more powerful you believe yourself to be, the more terrifying that evaporation. All this can't be for nothing. So you trap yourself. You don't trust your friends, your family, your world to carry on without you. That's what happened to this city. Gerhardt lost, for all his power, and could not accept his death. He stands on a rooftop in the dead city where that obscene tower rises today, delaying forever his final passing, and destroying the world around him to do it. If he'd just die, the whole world would be better off."

"I wanted to talk about that," Kai said.

Jax wiped his face and arms with a towel. His breath had almost returned to normal, and Kai could no longer see his heart throbbing in his throat. All the Craftwork enhancements had faded. He looked almost human again.

"Do you know what you're launching tomorrow?"

"In general outline: an observation platform. Something to stabilize the city. The contents are classified. That was the deal. Sponsorship, investment, and access to the ... topological oddities around Agdel Lex, which were helpful to our research. Commerce makes strange bedfellows."

"It's more than an observation platform," she said. "They want to wall off the dead city, and the shifting spaces between them, where the Wreckers can't go. They want to lock it all away."

"That seems reasonable."

"People will die. Their history will be shut away forever. Not even the ruins will remain."

Jax tossed the towel into a bin in the corner of the room, and said nothing. He looked out over the city, as still as the frozen monster behind them.

"It's true."

"I don't doubt you."

"You have to stop the launch."

"I can't."

"It's a complicated system. Something could go wrong."

"Oh, yes. Something can always go wrong. You do not, I think, comprehend just how much has gone wrong with this project in the last ten years. We built a launch center, and the desert swallowed it. I made fortunes, spent them, made others, spent those, all to save humanity and pry us off this doomed rock. If something *goes wrong* with a launch this high profile, this close to success—Ms. Pohala. My side of the operation has to go forward without a hitch. Nothing can compromise it." Jax's speech began slow, and grew faster, fiercer, as if with each comma and breath he felt with renewed weight the long slow push of decades that had brought him here.

"Agdel Lex has fought longer than you have," she said, "and they've lost more." She wished someone else were here to make this case. It did not belong to her. Ley would make it better, but really it was Zeddig's case, or Fontaine's, or Izza's. But she was here, and they were not. The world was built to stop them from making this kind of case.

He drummed his fingers on the glass, once, twice. Kai recognized the way he held himself, poised, locked: he had spent his life in his own kind of Penitent—or locked in some other sort of armor, like Bescond's Wreckers, his joys twisted to chains. "The launch must go forward," he said, and could not face her even then.

He could not face her, nor speak the words he wanted. She felt their outline, and her own inadequacy, and his, for all his wealth, for all the curve and line of his muscle. There should have been a storm to batter at the windows of this grand hotel. The sun burned instead, in an Iskari sky. "You didn't know about your payload," she observed.

"No."

"You can't possibly be liable for whether it works, then. No Craftswoman would let you sign a contract with that stipulation."

Even then, he did not turn.

"Bring me to the launch," she said. "And give me time alone."

He stood in silhouette. An elevator dinged; doors rolled back. Footsteps marched nearer, nearer down the hall. They paused at the door, two broad men and an equally broad woman, all in black suits, all discreetly, politely armed. If not for the frozen demon in the doorway, Kai figured she would already be on the floor, arm on the verge of dislocation, with a blade pressing into her back.

Jax turned from the window, and the only parts of his face visible in shadow were his teeth. "It's all right, friends." The hesitant, locked man had vanished behind the mask. "It's all right. Ms. Pohala is a guest of mine. A guest," he repeated, special emphasis, drawing close. He smelled beautiful. "My guest, for tomorrow's launch."

Chapter Sixty-nine

ZEDDIG AND LEY REACHED the shore at sunset. Sauga's glittered on the Shield Sea as its first diners arrived for the night, in slim-cut suits and trailing gowns, in tuxedoes and frock coats, robes and masks, arrayed in shadows, jewel-bedecked: they strode onto the water, straight-backed and proud, and the maître d' welcomed them home. Blushed sky curved to the horizon where the Altus Spire stood, lit against the coming dark.

"I'd hoped," Ley said, "we could eat at Sauga's together, when this was all over."

Zeddig caught her arm, and squeezed. "We will."

They wore delvers' coveralls, heating elements quiet, for now. They had changed in the cab.

"You're sure about this," Ley asked her.

"No going back."

"There's always a way back."

Zeddig kissed her again. "I'll distract them, and keep you safe. Don't try to talk me out of it."

Ley kissed her back. "I love you."

"Have you ever said that first?"

"I'll say it more, if we get out of this."

"When."

She nodded once. "When."

Zeddig checked her watch, though she already knew the

time. The watch assured, like the sand, like the waves, like the whole unconscious world around them, that would not care if they survived. "Seven fifteen."

Ley adjusted her own watch to match. "Give me half an hour. Then get to safety."

"I'll give you forty-five minutes."

"Be careful."

"I'll be better than careful." Zeddig squeezed her shoulder. "I'll be fast."

Ley looked at her, then turned away as if she had been looking at the sun—and, as if she had been looking at the sun, her eyes were wet and bright. She fixed her gaze on the horizon, and bent, a woman become an arrow knocked to fly.

"Let's go," she said.

Together, they fell into the dead city.

Frozen waves stretched north. Metal monsters crawled a beach strewn with bone shards and barbed wire. Behind them, the skeleton of the dead city towered, sick, frozen, and aflame.

Ley ran toward the water, Zeddig toward the necropolis.

Back in Agdel Lex, sirens wailed.

• • •

Raymet woke to the alarms. A rotting sock stuffed her mouth—no, that was her tongue. It obeyed commands, a pleasant surprise, and with its tip she explored her teeth. Still there, mostly, which reassured. She realized her eyes were closed, then realized how bad a sign it was that she had to realize her eyes were closed.

She opened them. Gummy mucus had stitched her lashes shut. Through eyelash interstices she saw the bone ceiling painted a warning red. Her arms moved by puppetry: her wrist raked across her lips, pulling cuts there. Blood flaked and fell. She tried to rise, couldn't quite, but rolled onto her stomach and told herself that was a good start.

Booted feet ran down the hall outside the closed door, and she heard the poured-syrup sound of Wreckers running too, their limbs slapping walls and floor.

"You're awake," Gal said. "I was worried."

She rolled sideways. Her cheek pooled against the chitin, and from the pattern of pressure she deduced her face had swollen to an unfamiliar topology of bruise. "Alarms," she said, the word slurred. Water would be nice. There was a sink in here, if she could do the impossible and rise.

Gal knelt by her bars, mottled from her own session with the Wreckers, but she didn't look nearly so bad as Raymet felt.

"You didn't talk?"

"Fuck 'em" turned out to be easier to say than "Alarms," or "What's happening," which she tried next. She had a lot of practice cursing.

"I've never been inside the tower during an alert," Gal said, "but this sounds like delvers. Lots of delvers. Or just one, being very stupid." She looked so calm, so godsdamn perfect. Maybe they taught you how to do that in Knight school—to seem glorious when bruised, battered, and behind bars. "You should have talked. They would have stopped."

"Not giving them satisfaction." She had to choose between breathing and speaking a complete sentence; her lungs told her she chose right. With the aid of the bars she levered herself up into a sitting position, conscious of torn muscles, tension. "Maybe we can get out of here now. They're all—" *Distracted* was a tall order, vocal-production-wise, but she tried anyway.

"Distracted." Almost. B-minus, even on a post-torture curve.

"Escape," Gal said, "is dishonorable. I was bested. I surrendered."

Raymet hit the bars with her balled fists. The bone, or teeth, or whatever, made a wooden sound when struck.

"That won't work."

"Shut up."

"I'm sorry," she said, and sounded it. "I didn't mean to make this harder for you."

"You're not worried—well, good for you." Talking hurt, but there was too much she'd kept inside, and when she started she could not stop. "You trained for this. You're not from here. On some level, whatever happens, if they start at you with pliers and a crowbar, it will all be just one more move in your honor game, part of the adventure you wanted when you were a girl. You're still kneeling there, playing with dolls. And the squids will play along with you, because your game fits theirs. I don't get to play. I'm the fucking *field*. I'm the dollhouse. I'm the board. I hate the people who make the rules, and I hate the people who made you so you'd want to play by the rules they set, so when they told you to find a hill to die on, you did. I just want to be out of this godsdamn cell. I just want us both to live."

"Why," Gal asked, "did you come back for me?"

• • •

The sirens required a change of plan. Izza, prone between the drop ceiling and the rafters where she'd hidden after she gave the lidless eye the slip, had expected to escape under darkness, but Camlaanders had that weird saying about plans and mice and gley.

Izza's original plan had been sheer elegance in its simplicity: the Sisters wouldn't check on her until lunchtime the next day. They'd expected to find a young woman weeping, contrite, broken by the eye. When they found an empty cell instead, there would be trouble. By that point, Izza and Isaak would be far away, toasting their success, and figuring out how to deal with Kai's prophecies of doom.

But the alarm changed everything. Once the sirens stopped the Sisters would check their charges, even the ones in solitary. Don't want the poor dears terrified in a way we don't intend. Terror is a resource, after all. And the Sisters had to be shown in control.

So the sun was just setting when she removed a ceiling tile and dropped into the infirmary.

Two beds were curtained off. Izza ignored the gurgling wet sounds within. Isaak lay propped on pillows near the back, sleeping, a mound of muscle and armored flesh under a thin white sheet. Splints held his arms and legs together.

She would have sworn she made no sound when she approached, but he snapped awake anyway. He tried to focus on her face, couldn't without his glasses, but he still knew her. "Izza."

A hero, in her place, would snap back something witty, make him laugh, get his arm over her shoulder so they could limp to escape. In a mystery play the whole complex would blow up behind them for no reason, without apparent concern for the kids still trapped inside. Another sort of hero would have said nothing, just got them both the hells out of here. She wasn't any kind of hero, so she said, "Hey."

"Go," he said. Drawing breath seemed to hurt. That would be the ribs. "I can't. I'm beat up too bad."

"We're leaving together."

"Take care of yourself." He breathed slow. "Trust the Lady. She likes you. Stay smart, pray to Her, She'll help you out."

That was when the other half of her plan failed.

In the crawlspace, she'd imagined faking another miraculous episode: pretending to be overcome by inspiration, blue eyes and burning hands, to save him and escape High Sisters without any confessions or hard conversations, with this friend she did not want to be her worshipper.

Her friend, to whom she'd lied, and kept lying.

Gods, she prayed. Maybe someday You'll stop getting me into trouble.

Sirens wailed. Did they have ten minutes? Less?

Not enough for this. She might as well get over with it now. She held his hand, and said, "No."

. . .

Zeddig did everything wrong.

And the wrongs felt glorious.

When you delved, you honored simple rules: only when nobody's watching. Only in places you know intimately, in the living cities and the dead. Exit where you entered. Proceed with plausible deniability. Everyone knows the dead city exists, everyone knows it waits behind the curtain of Agdel Lex, hungry to drag us all down into its maw—we just ignore it when we can.

The rules were for everyone's protection. The city would crumble if people remembered where they really lived. The delver was at risk, too: she carried the dead city's stench, an aura of blood and gunmetal and wrong names.

You played safe, you did not offend the sensibilities of the mass, because if you didn't, the Wreckers would smell you. The Wreckers stood guard against incursions from the dead city—so all Zeddig had to do was cause an incursion.

She ran down the Boulevard Pragmatique in Agdel Lex, and fell onto the road that in the dead city was called La'at, half as broad and bounded with structures twice as high, their façades tile mosaics twined with burnt vines. A library tower stood here, caved in by a fallen angel. Running, she stitched between worlds. Half-dead once-human beings, limbs contorted by phage-curses, metal bugs writhing in their minds, light leaking from their eyes, leapt out of the wreckage, and Zeddig danced back into Agdel Lex, running once more down the Boulevard Pragmatique, against traffic. She dove from street to sidewalk. Phages chased her, clawing against the world-skin. Behind Zeddig, a man almost saw them, and screamed, remembering for one instant the pit beneath his feet.

Good. She ran.

She stitched across the boundary in plain sight. The more witnesses the better. Sirens followed her. She sprinted down side alleys, uphill into the Bite, and fell into the dead city for the few seconds she could bear so close to the Wound. Frost crystallized on goggles as a golem made from buildings wrestled an angel whose wings cut pavement. When she emerged, the frost on her goggles burst into steam, and she heard more sirens.

The Wreckers closed in, sniffing the night. They swung from building to building, wriggling along walls to fight the incursion she, Zeddig, faked—and ignored, in the commotion, Ley's sprint across the frozen ocean to the Altus Spire.

That was the idea. Distract and outrun. Spread chaos and trail a city's worth of salarymen and tourists, artists and husbands, mothers and daughters who remembered, in the moment of her passing, what lay beneath them. So, when she cut across a trolley track into the Bite's orgiastic thrumming bar streets, and saw the Wrecker perched atop an ancient observatory tower converted forty years back to a beer garden—actually saw it—she felt relieved.

But the Wrecker didn't see her yet.

So she waded into a fountain, climbed the naked Iskari cherub in the center, and, straddling its shoulders, waved her hands in the air, and shouted, "Hey! Ugly!"

The hood turned her way.

She raised both middle fingers, and dove into the dead city again.

• • •

Raymet forced herself to her feet. "Why the hells do you keep asking me that question?"

Gal waited.

"I would have answered it already, you know, if I wanted. I would have said something before."

The sirens wailed outside, but the running feet had passed. Most of the assholes must have run off to wherever they were running to.

"I'm not scared of answering. I just—"

The cuts on her face pulled.

Gal waited. She looked so calm Raymet wanted to smash her, and wanted to weep.

"It's not like I wanted to. It's not like I thought to myself, oh, you know what's a good idea, I should throw myself against Wreckers I can't possibly fight, to save someone who doesn't need saving, that's an excellent idea, let's try it."

One more passing set of boots. Late.

Blue eyes. Breath, in that body.

"It's not love, dammit."

She did not move.

"I don't know what it is. Maybe it's just sex, the old monkey-brain fucking with me again. Maybe it's the godsdamn seasons. I don't understand you. I don't understand this. Your head's full of all this worthless godsdamn honor and duty that's done more to break our world than save it. And you're so certain, and so steady, and so—so—Gods!"

The way Gal did everything made it seem like the most natural and beautiful thing in the world. Now, she stood.

"It can't be love. Love is something two people do when they know each other, and trust each other. Love's what Ley and Zeddig had. Damn if I grew up around any of it. This is, I don't know, whatever it is people have in those dumb dragon-killing stories you must have mainlined back when you were a kid, two people get their wires crossed in a crowded room and turn dumb. It's madness. As if I have anything to offer you—I'm just some colony punk who's never put on a damn ball gown, let alone, what, courted a Knight? Neither of us makes the slightest bit of sense."

She didn't speak. She panted, furious, raw, in her cell.

"I dream about you. I know what I'd do if you were any other girl. But you're not. You're so damn sure. I wish I could be that. I wish I could be as honest about this, about anything, as you are just standing there."

She felt empty.

"Call it love. If you want. I came back for you because I couldn't leave."

. . .

"Hold still," Izza said, "and shut up." She set her hands on Isaak's scaled and armored skin, and prayed.

I know we don't usually do the laying-on-hands thing. But he's a friend, and I'd say you owe me at least a double handful of favors, for all the trouble I've pulled you out of. A sickbed is a kind of prison—and healing's an escape.

The Lady was a streetlit smile.

Izza felt her hands warm.

"Izza," he said, "what are you—"

Then he could not speak. The sirens wailed. Five minutes, Izza bet, before anyone looked in on them. You didn't worry about escape from the infirmary, or even theft. They didn't keep the good drugs here.

She should open her eyes. She owed him this much at least. The Lady worked him from head to toe, meticulous: wounds knit shut, bones wriggled into proper alignment, the body a lock the Lady learned to pick. However imprecisely.

Are there really supposed to be two bones in the arm beneath the elbow?

Yes.

And one above?

Yes!

I can think of better ways to do it.

Just put him back like he was, okay?

Before or after the augments?

After!

The process did not look pleasant. Isaak moaned through grit jagged teeth and screamed once. But it did end, eventually, and left him whole and gasping on the sheets. Tears looked different on his armored scales than they had on the skin she remembered.

And for my next trick, the Lady said, and the manacles fell from Isaak's arms and legs.

Isaak stared at her with awe and wonder, and when he said, "Izza," it did not sound like her name at all, but a title.

Might as well get this over with. "I didn't tell you the truth. The Lady comes from Kavekana, where I live these days. I told Her stories when She was young. People tried to kill Her, and I saved Her life. And now, we're . . . close." Faster, because she couldn't bear it if he tried to get a word in edgewise here: "We work together. I didn't tell you, because—you were devoted, loyal, faithful, and I just wanted to see my friend again. So I lied. That was wrong. I'm sorry. But we need to get out of here, so maybe if you're going to be mad at me could we deal with that later?"

"You're the Prophet Thief," Isaak said.

Yes—and no. That was one name the kids whispered, one of many she asked them to stop calling her, so they said it behind her back, this name like a Penitent itself, armor and chain at once. But it meant something to him, and to deny it would be to let him down, to break the hope in his eyes.

"I—this is my life now. I love it, but it's a lot to swallow at once, so can we please stick to Izza? Friend Izza, who wants to break out of jail while everyone's still distracted?"

Two minutes, maybe.

One.

And Isaak, however uncertain, nodded. "Okay," he said.

"Friend Izza." He cradled one fist in the other. A salute? A bow?

No. He cracked his knuckles.

"What took you so long?"

She had a retort ready, but then a Sister entered the infirmary, and they had important screaming and running to attend to. The witty comeback could wait.

• • •

Zeddig, running, thought of Ley, running.

She'd been afoot for twenty minutes by the watch. Ley ought to be halfway across the frozen sea by now, guiding herself to the Altus Spire. Ley had never liked running, especially not in Agdel Lex. She took to the road, laced up her sneakers, because she hated her body and herself, and running was a fit punishment for existing. Back in the early days, broke and in love, she and Zeddig had run by the beach until stitches in their sides doubled them on the sand, and Zeddig would be happy for the run, and Ley would be happy the damn run was over.

Zeddig loved running, loved feeling muscles coil as her feet met pavement; it pleased her, as she ran her alarms across town, to imagine Ley unfurling into the solitude of the ice. There was packed snow on the frozen waves, good traction; she could make decent time, maybe even better than Zeddig's run through the Bite and Wings. Maybe, in these last moments as Ley fought toward the spire, in that expanse of razor wind and dead sky, she would find peace.

She might as well. There would be no peace left in Agdel Lex once Zeddig was done.

She mapped the city in her mind's hot core. There were forty Wreckers on duty at once, spread across the city and standing guard at the wall. They patrolled territory: some the Bite, others the Wings, a few the Iron Coast, though everyone Zeddig knew laughed at the notion any of those foreign hipsters might delve. Zeddig had laughed too, before Ley managed.

Delving attracted local Wreckers. To seize the collective's attention, to get everyone so focused on you they wouldn't notice your—call her *girlfriend,* she can't hear inside your head—your girlfriend sprinting north, you had to run between the districts, dance across them and back, you had to be everyone's problem, had to use back alley shortcuts to stay uncaught for another—glance at the watch—say, twenty minutes.

Tick, tock.

Zeddig ran down an alley; two Wreckers fell from the sky to cut off her escape, while two more pursued behind, swinging from lampposts and scuttling over walls. (That's good: figure twenty percent of total available squidpower, minus the ones they won't pull off the wall.) She dove into the same alley, a hundred fifty years and a heartbeat ago—shattered timbers towered above, a door hung off its hinges to her left. Her breath cut her throat.

At least it was a dry cold.

Bad joke. No laugh.

She ran through the broken door, past the table where a family of burned-out skeletons sat at breakfast, through the wreckage of the library. Zeddig remained professional, even after running so fast, so far: her gut twisted to see the books destroyed. Burnt scraps of vellum and cream paper tossed like flower petals in the breeze of her passing. The South Bite had never been rich; the family whose tomb this house became must have accumulated these over generations, volumes added to volumes at marriage, duplicates bartered for new texts or copied by hand, first editions set down against the dowries of children. All lost, now, that wealth of ink and paper broken forever into carbon.

Angels writhed impaled in the thorn tree sky.

Shamblers woke in the ashes, drawn by her heat, the demon bugs in their brains writhing. They sprang for her, and she was slow, too slow. One caught her leg.

She kicked, fell. Claws tore her boot, snapped heating filaments. Cold entered through the wound. She struck the shambler's hand with her other boot, broke off its thumb, pushed herself to her feet and out, through the ash heap of the cloakroom into the narrow street, and surfaced.

Light, heat, pain, noise smothered her. Carriages rolled and water-sellers cried and she heard a busker playing sax, and before she could recover a Wrecker landed in her path.

No, this was wrong—the Wreckers of the South Bite shouldn't be here yet, she'd just verged on their territory—she spun away, running by the wall, tripping over a trash can. Rotten garbage spewed into the street.

Wet limbs snared her and set the world right.

She could not pull away. Why would she? This was her place, her moment. She was a limb out of joint, guided by sure hands back to its socket.

She remembered that wrecked library, remembered the world she'd lost, and dove.

It hurt. The Wrecker told her where she was, where she belonged. Denying that, with its arms around her, felt like sawing off her own arm.

This is good. Trust us, because we made the word, and we're the ones who should know.

Zeddig ground her teeth, focused on the pain, and dove.

The Wrecker was a monster, from a city of monsters. It belonged down here, with her.

She felt the cold, and grinned.

Ice claimed the Wrecker's limbs. It thrashed under the broken sky, tentacles recoiling from icy pavement. Zeddig slipped from sluggish arms. Her brain hurt. She saw doubled, tripled.

A carpet of metal spiders boiled from cracks in the pavement and covered the Wrecker, biting, climbing, spinning sharp wire nets.

When a Wrecker screamed, the scream was wet.

Zeddig surfaced, alone, and ran.

• • •

Raymet panted. She felt naked in her cell, and not in a good way. The godsdamn squid had been listening all along. It knew, now, how she felt about Gal, and could use that to use her. "Well?" she said. "I answered your damn question. What the fuck do you have to say?"

Gal smiled. "That," she said, "changes everything." She touched the bars, tested them.

"What does it change, precisely? Seems to me we're just as screwed as we were before, only now I've embarrassed myself."

"Not embarrassed," Gal said. "Never." She nodded, satisfied with whatever she'd felt in the bars.

And she looked at Raymet.

Not for the first time. They were partners, colleagues, they knew one another well. Of course she'd looked at her before.

But Raymet had never felt this seen.

"We will have to talk," Gal said. "I have apologies to make. Zeddig told me I should speak with you, but I expected—no, that would be a lie. I thought to spare you entanglement with my condition, with my quest. I was wrong."

"Gal—"

"There are forms for such an affair, and proper ceremonies. The shortest, for now, is: I share your esteem."

Raymet blinked. "What."

Gal looked unshakeable as ever, behind those bars. "I do not understand you. But neither do I understand fire, or starlight, or storms, and I love them. I have no land, I have no title. I come from a world you hate. I did not want to trouble you with my affection. You are fierce and beautiful and clever, and I should have told you all this before. It is cowardice that I have not."

"Well." Raymet released the bars of her cell. Without their support, she swayed. "Um. I. That's. Great?" Stupid, stupid. After all that, after the fucking heart-wrenching confession, to hear this and be unable to speak—but she couldn't say anything like that, about storms and fire and shit, and—"I'm, I mean, I'm glad."

Gal tightened her grip on the bars.

Raymet paced. Pressed her hands to her temples. Laughed, and couldn't stop. She felt the good sort of naked now.

"What's so funny?"

"This would be a lot more convenient," Raymet said, "if we weren't in prison."

Gal laughed too, but only once, and without the hysterical edge even Raymet could hear in her own voice.

"Same question," Raymet said. "Back at you."

"I do not understand."

"What's so funny? We're stuck here, the world's out there, and I'm glad I told you, and gods, I mean, you have no idea, or maybe you do, what it feels like to hear you say you feel the same way, it's, I don't know, I was never good at all this poetry shit, it's spring, it's a bath and clean sheets and a journal letter that says 'accepted without revisions,' but *you* are on the other *side* of two layers of cell bars."

"Details," Gal said.

"Are those details? They seem like a critical component of our situation."

"The critical components of our situation," Gal said, "have changed."

"Really."

She licked her lips once, and took a cell bar in each hand. "My vows forbid escape, once I have been subdued by adversaries in honorable combat." Golden light seeped from her skin and hardened to a glassy sheen. "But a Knight may rescue her lady from a tower. That is practically what Knights are for."

She broke the bars of her cell like twigs. Then she stepped over the splintered bones, crossed the hall, and broke the bars of Raymet's, too.

"Wow," Raymet said.

"Shall we?"

She hesitated, only for a heartbeat. Then she took her hand.

• • •

Forty minutes. Time.

Zeddig ducked away from an angel's flailing arm and surfaced on the Boulevard Corrigé, skidding down the centerline.

Horses reared, carriages rocked on two wheels, bicycles swerved; she found her footing and ran. Wreckers ringed the rooftops, closing in. She counted ten. Others nearby, no doubt. If Ley kept a good pace, she'd have reached Altus, with plenty of time to sneak through security.

Now, Zeddig's job was to escape—if she could.

She scrambled to a manhole cover and lifted it, though muscles in her back and legs screamed. She slipped down, landed in muck, and dove.

The storm drains and sewers of Agdel Lex were grotesque, but the sewers of the dead city . . . She looked around as little as possible, found her footing, and fled. On the plus side, the cold reduced the stench. On the minus side, these tunnels were even more full of things that wanted to kill her.

A razor-edged serpent fell from the tunnel roof to wrap around her neck, but she tore it off her and threw it down to the ice. Her shoes crunched things like bugs that vented poison gas—she stopped breathing and ran. (Another advantage of the cold: gas diffused slowly.) She skidded through frozen shit between the legs of a scorpion tank, and bluffed her way past a killing curse.

She'd delved more tonight than she'd ever delved before. If this had been another, better era, someone would have made a ballad of her exploits, something with good scansion even. She'd settle for a few stories whispered at the graduate department meetings, the kind that started, I know you won't believe this, but I heard . . .

Of course, the department meetings would stress the wrong part of the story: Zeddig's previous delves had been peripheral affairs, lasting a few seconds at the outside. This run, near the core, through sewers toward the Wreckers' tower and the

Anaxmander Stacks, toward the Wound where Gerhardt hovered, always dying, never dead—this was a fucking masterwork. This was record-book.

Ice spread up her leg from the cut in the suit. She lost sensation, slowing. Some of that skin was probably frozen solid by now. Might lose the leg. If she survived, she could get a Craftswoman to make her a spare. If any of them survived. If Ley saved them.

Forget all that. You're running uphill into terror and cold, through sewer tunnels that don't exist anymore, skidding past monsters, and tracking all the while, on the map inside your mind, the points where the dead city's sewers overlap Alikand's.

The nearer Zeddig drew to the tower, the less the Wreckers could smell her when she emerged. If she came out close enough, she could escape through the Agdel Lex steam tunnels. She'd used this path before, once. She could make it.

Left, straight a hundred meters, through the sewer arch with the grapevine decoration, into a side tunnel that, halfway down its length, in another world, was a half-built subway station, abandoned when the Wreckers decided underground transit was too hard to oversee.

Her leg felt leaden beneath the knee. She could not breathe. The suit's heat was gone. Seconds left. Almost there.

Spots danced on the edges of her vision.

Her numb foot struck—something. She stumbled. Fell. This would have to do.

She tried to surface. Couldn't. Too tired to panic. There was something in Agdel Lex where she stood. Roll left, or roll right?

She chose right, and surfaced, panting, against a ticket

stand. Her suit lights cast bright circles on the subway station's mosaic wall: on Dame Progress wreathed in the halo of her arms.

Her leg hurt. Breathing hurt. Everything hurt.

She commanded her arms to do the work of legs. Reached her knees, easy, planted on all fours. Focus on the ground. Don't throw up. One more push after this, use the ticket stand to force yourself upright, get blood into that frozen leg.

Up. Go.

On the bright side, she came up easier than she expected.

Of course, she had help.

She stared up into the face of Lieutenant Bescond.

"Hi there," the Lieutenant said, and hit her.

Chapter Seventy

KAI SHELTERED IN PLACE when the sirens came, and when they stopped she spent an hour hunting for a cab. When she finally tracked one down the horse informed her, with a whinny, that the fare would be twice normal. Fine. She expensed it, locked the carriage doors from inside, and watched life leak back into the city as her carriage bounced down streets emptier than she'd ever seen in Agdel Lex. She passed a melting patch of frost, which a sidewalk vendor covered with her cart.

Kai's heart ran fast. She thought of incursions, and the Wastes, and Ley, and tomorrow's launch. Had the dead city tried to break through one last time, sensing the Iskari plot? Where was Ley in all this mess?

Bescond waited for her in the lobby of the Arms, seated, hat pushed low to shade her eyes against the light of the chandelier. She held a newspaper open, unread; when she stood, she moved stiffly. She must have been waiting for Kai longer than she would prefer. A bandage wrapped the knuckles of her right hand, and she favored her right leg.

"Lieutenant." Kai forced herself calm: relaxed her shoulders, breathed deep into her belly. There were too many ways this could go wrong. "Sounds like you've had a long day."

Bescond folded the newspaper, and folded it again. "Ms. Pohala. You're home late yourself."

"Meetings," she said, which was not false.

Bescond rolled the newspaper into a cylinder. A bit of dried blood stuck to her fingers. Her lips curved. Kai could not tell whether her smile was real. "I'd like to show you something."

Am I under arrest, would be an imprudent response—signaling she had something to hide, forcing Bescond to make the conversation formal. "Are you here in your professional capacity?"

Bescond gripped the newspaper roll in both hands, and her forearms tensed, but the paper, tightly wound, did not crumple. "I was not fair, in my office. Family matters are difficult to square with affairs of state. I deal with the latter. You are torn between them. But you have split the difference well."

What did Bescond know? "Thank you." She did not add: I think.

"I have a peace offering," she said. "Come to the tower."

"I've had bad luck in that tower before."

"I promise, on my Lord, you will leave tonight unharmed, in full possession of your faculties." She frowned. Her shoulder pads could not disguise her disappointment. "I'm sorry we've reached the point you feel you need those assurances. I appreciate the help you've given us."

In a better world, Kai often thought, one would have a sort of scale with which to weigh the voices in one's head. Others—Izza, for example—seemed to hear fewer voices, or at least tended to have one clear conscious favorite. Such minds must be easier to navigate. In Kai's head, there tended to be many voices, all deafening.

Should she give herself to Bescond, and trust the promise? Beg off and play it safe, so Bescond would not deduce Kai's plans? But if she refused, would Bescond, olive branch rejected, turn a more suspicious gaze on Kai? Or, and or, and or, and here the particular skills Kai's profession, of addressing each new idol with utter conviction, cut against her: she argued each option against herself, and the next, in strobe succession while Bescond waited.

She was tired, and scared, and when she was tired and scared she erred on the side of curiosity. Things you knew couldn't surprise you later.

"Show me," she said.

"Thank you." Bescond clapped Kai wincingly hard on the shoulder. "You won't regret this." She marched from the lobby, newspaper tucked under her arm like a marshal's baton.

Bescond's carriage, Wrecker-escorted, led them to the tower. Kai was used, by now, to the certainty she felt in the Wreckers' presence: how permanent the world seemed, how perfect and how calm. She thought she knew what to expect on entering the tower itself, but there she found herself surprised.

"What happened?"

"Hm?" Bescond raised one eyebrow.

"That big white scar in the tower's side."

"Oh." She waved the newspaper dismissively. "Prison break. Rare, but we'll track the fugitives down. They can't run forever."

"That," Kai said, "looks pretty bad."

"We have difficult prisoners at times." They entered the garage, and the carriage stopped. Kai followed Bescond to the lift. "Though I can't remember a surprise on this scale. Fortunately the tower, being biological, can heal itself—in time. You too, the process has already begun. In a month there will be no trace the breach. Meanwhile, scar tissue will suffice."

The doors rolled back on the twenty-first floor. The halls

were a color Kai had never seen. Not a color she had never seen in the building—a color she had never seen, period. "Did the escape cause the alarm?"

Bescond counted doors. Kai felt the tower's heartbeat through the soles of her shoes. They must be close. "Hardly," Bescond said. "The alarm prompted the escape, rather than the other way around. Tonight, we experienced our most complex incursion in years; the Wreckers were spread thin containing the damage. Our system worked, as ever."

"Was the dead city trying to break in?"

Bescond arrived at a door larger than the rest, emblazoned with a seven-pointed star. "That's what we thought at first, but no. It was a delver breach—a noteworthy event for a few reasons. First, for its scale: a dozen punctures in twenty minutes, in five different districts. Second, for the size of the delver crew."

"How many?"

Bescond touched the star, and the door irised open.

"One," she said, louder, over the beating of the enormous heart.

Thigh-thick vessels of cobalt blood snaked along the walls of the chamber beyond, pulsing with the heartbeat. No—the chamber was the heart, an enormous hollow heart at the city's core: its walls vibrated, channeling the tower's phosphorescent blood. Blood lit the chamber with a light deeper than blue; Bescond's teeth glittered, and the whites of her eyes, and her cufflinks.

An enormous twisted column of gray flesh descended from the dome's apex to its floor, or rose from floor to apex, the spongy trunk of an immense tree whose branches wept down like a baobab's to become roots again. Sparks and rainbow colors danced through the gray in domino cascade. Kai tried to trace the light's path, but it moved too fast. She imagined dominos that, falling, knocked other dominos upright again, to be struck in turn by still other dominos, ripples adding to ripples, waves adding to waves.

She did not tremble. She did not kneel.

She entered the tower core, warily.

The heartbeat receded, or the parts of her that could register such a low pervasive sound grew numb.

As the horror and size of the space sank in, Kai's mind made room for details.

Like: a human figure bound to the trunk of the nerve tree.

Zeddig.

"I cannot prove that your sister lives," Bescond said. "If I could, I would have caught her already, to remand into your custody."

The room was larger than it looked, or else geometry behaved wrong here. It took a long time for Bescond to walk Kai toward Zeddig, and the tree.

"But I can prove the next best thing: she did escape the Wastes. Her death is not on your hand, or mine."

Kai controlled her breath, her stomach, her stride, and remembered the woman bound to the brain, in a different time. Remembered her warning Kai away, in the hallway of her grandmother's house; remembered her imperious on the train, remembered how she held Ley close and held her up at the foot of the tower in the Wastes, remembered her trapped animal glare, her body thrust forward by instinct to protect Kai's sister from Kai herself.

Half Zeddig's face swelled purple with a bruise. Bonds of flesh grew over her arms and legs and mouth. She breathed heavily through her nose. Her eyes were blank.

"Trust me, Ms. Pohala. You don't know Hala'Zeddig like I do. If she came out of the Wastes, your sister did as well. She would have died out there rather than let your sister perish. So, Ley's in the city. We haven't yet forced out of Zeddig her reasons for tonight's mad delve—that will come once the tower has had time to make her comfortable. She lacks faith in our Lords, so we must build it within her. She's long been an outsider in Agdel Lex."

At that name, Zeddig's eyes narrowed, and Kai retreated a step at the hatred that burned there. Zeddig's bonds tightened; her body shook, and she sagged again.

"Your sister," Bescond said, "is alive. Zeddig may have hidden her with her family. Likely, Ley resides in a part of the city our agents cannot reach—a part I will not name, which will face extreme sanction after tomorrow's launch." Bescond peeled back the strip of flesh over Zeddig's lips. The woman panted through her teeth. "Kai wants to save her sister, Zeddig. Can you tell her where she is?"

Zeddig forced her head up. She glared into Kai's eyes. They watched one another for a time that could not have been longer than seconds.

Don't say anything, Kai thought. Don't tell me. If I know, she knows.

"I want to help," she said, to give Bescond the impression she was playing along. "If you can give me anything." She didn't dare stress the "me." "Please."

Zeddig's eyes rolled up into her skull. Her lips moved. The tower's heartbeat echoed. Kai moved forward to catch the whisper. Bescond leaned close too.

Zeddig's teeth flashed brilliant blue, and snapped shut just shy of Kai's car. Kai fell back. Dimly, she saw Bescond bind Zeddig again. The Lieutenant took Kai's arm, helped her to her feet. "My apologies, Ms. Pohala. I hoped we could get something out of her."

"No." Kai brushed mucus off her skirt, tried to ignore the wet warmth of the floor beneath her hands. "That's fine. I—I didn't expect."

Bescond escorted her from the room. "The launch will be at dawn tomorrow," Bescond said, when the door closed. "That's all the time I can offer Ley, I'm afraid."

Kai stammered thanks, and let Bescond walk her to the cab.

"I know how you feel," Bescond said. "It's a sad affair. But I'm trying to help, to the extent possible."

"I know," Kai said, "thank you," and closed the door.

On the ride back to her hotel, she pondered Zeddig's skyward gaze, and the word she'd whispered: "spear."

Chapter Seventy-one

"IT'S COMPLICATED," IZZA TRIED TO EXPLAIN, panting, as they ran from High Sisters through the shipyard, dodging spotlights and guards.

"I figured that out," Isaak said, as he choked out a guard who had made the simple mistake of diligence on his rounds. "Around the moment my friend turned out to be a prophet."

They could make better time over the rooftops, and they'd only have a minute, at most, before the guard woke and sounded the alarm, so she climbed a fire escape, Isaak clanging behind her. For the next minute of roofs, gantries, jumps, and sudden drops, they were running too fast to talk.

Sprawled on another roof, they caught their breath as watchmen and undead dogs ran past below. The fallen guard must have recovered enough to sound the alarm. Izza prayed thanks for that—Isaak was good, but knocking someone out without killing them always involved a bit of luck. She mopped sweat from her brow with her jumpsuit sleeve. Once they made it to the city, she'd have to steal some clothes. "The Iskari want to break the city. Tomorrow, they'll launch something that will force everyone into Agdel Lex. No more in-betweeners, no more Alikand. Just the Iskari city, and the dead one. My friend's trying to fight it, but even if she wins, it won't be clean. The Wastes will rush in, and eat people. We can help—the Lady can help. We just need to get to the Temple of

All Gods. The priests there should be working on a defense."

"How do you know all this?"

She tapped her heart. "The Lady passed along the details. And—" She should stop, but she owed him truth. "Kai told me."

"Kai?"

"The woman from the train. Ley's sister."

Isaak's eyes flashed gold in the shipyard lights. "You knew her."

"I—" Gods. They didn't have time for this. There wouldn't ever be time for this. Best to do it quick. "I came because of her. She was in trouble with the Wreckers. So was her sister. I wanted to help them."

"And you knew the underground. You knew me."

His lips curled open, and his teeth were very sharp. There was a wall behind his eyes.

"Yes," she said. "I didn't think it would go this far. I hoped—"

"You sold us out."

"That wasn't the plan." She was talking faster than her mind could keep up. "I just wanted to get her on the train, so she could talk to Ley."

"Lady." He looked sick. Disappointed.

"Vogel's the one who sold us out to the Wreckers. Not Kai."

"Whose word do we have for that? Hers?" Her silence was all the answer she could give. "Gods, Izza."

"Freeze!"

Izza swore. The last few days had worn on them both. No personal conversations on the job, that was way down around rule zero. Personal talk left you arguing while guards crept up behind.

"Stand slowly. Hands up." One man's voice. Three more behind them, judging from the footsteps.

They stood slowly. Hands up.

Two pairs of feet approached.

"Trust me," Izza said. "You have no idea what Kai's been through—for me, and for the Lady. Torture doesn't begin to cover it. She's on our side. She prays like you do. Like we do."

"Shut up!" The guard's voice, not Isaak's.

Isaak was still, and angry. And when the guards drew close, he moved.

A crossbow plucked an ugly note. Izza dropped, kicked the legs out from under the guard behind her, and tossed him down onto the fire escape. By the time she turned around, most of the screaming and snapping had stopped, and Isaak stood in the center of the roof. Blood dripped from his fists. The guards were still breathing, shallowly.

Reinforcements came soon, and there wasn't time to talk. There was more hitting, and running after the hitting, and a brief enthusiastic fence climb—Izza called on the Lady to snip the barbed wire atop the fence, while Isaak just vaulted over and down, trusting the scales on his palms—and they escaped into the shadows of Agdel Lex and Alikand, and betrayal and secrets and gods and years fell away and they were just kids running side by side through the night.

Until Izza glanced back over her shoulder and found she was running alone.

She skidded to a stop between a trash can and a wall. The alley stood empty, and smelled of garbage. He must have climbed the wall, or cut down a side street.

"Isaak!" she called.

No answer.

She called again. Still nothing. "I know you're angry." He could hear her. His hearing had always been excellent. "I'm sorry. I should have told you sooner." Silence, but a different silence. Or else the difference was only wishful thinking. "I wanted to help her. And I wanted to stay your friend."

Fuck.

"I'm going to the Temple," she said. "Find me. I need your help. I need all the help I can get."

Tin cans shifted behind her. She turned, fast, heart swollen. A scarred ugly cat crouched in the shadows, judging her.

Fine, she thought. That makes two of us.

She ran.

She did not cry. Crying slowed you down. You needed breath to cry, and time. You needed room in your heart to feel. So she ran and hurt, and stole clothes, and snuck upslope, and came back to herself limping, exhausted, sweat-soaked and in pain, at the door of the Temple of All Gods.

She knocked. More or less. To knock on a thing was to strike it, and she definitely struck the door as she collapsed.

She started to cry, then, a bit. A bit more.

The door opened. She staggered into a thin-boned man in a scratchy robe. "I suppose," Doctor Hasim said, "some experiences are habit-forming."

She needed to laugh and blow her nose and weep, and instead of doing any of those things, she punched him, and let him bring her inside.

Chapter Seventy-two

DAWN THREATENED.

Across the city, people woke or slept, or slumped home from graveyard shifts, or lived, or died in hospital beds or in stupid accidents, or sent rats to tell their bosses they were sick before they snuck back to lovers' beds, or counted the night's take twice, three times, in case their dealers had stiffed them, or fried breakfast, or jogged along the coast, or worked their businesses, or failed at same. They lived their stories as if no one else's would ever intervene.

Tara Abernathy worked the garden before her shower. Doctor Hasim and Umar circled the grounds to check the wards they had built against a day they'd hoped would never come. They prayed, which was not unusual. She prayed, which was.

Tara thought about why she had come to Agdel Lex, and what she had done here, and what she might have done instead, and what she could do now. Then she showered, armored herself in suit and boots and sorcery, and a touch of lip gloss because why not, and set out for the wall.

In Hala's Fell, Aman heard a knock on the front door. She navigated the halls by memory and smell, by darkness and light and the touch of her cane. The Iskari city, Agdel Lex, crept in everywhere, like sand blown from the desert the Iskari thought all deserts were: it covered even her own home, smudged it to her gaze. She guided herself by the light of old familiar things: by this rug, woven a century and a half ago by a woman whose family died in the wars, which Aman's grandmother bought in a market where an Iskari office building now stood. By that shallow bowl on a table by the door, with water for guests to wet their hands, which she refilled each morning if she could reach it before her daughters and sons. By the pattern of tiles around the door, which Zeddig had seen in a delve to the shattered palace that was once their family home, and taken the time, though beset by monsters, to sketch. When Aman became Archivist, long ago, she had pledged to live in her city. She saw by its light.

She opened the door.

The women waiting on the stoop shone brighter than all the suns Aman had left behind. Ko'Adal, frail and bowed but fierce. Zel'Hojah, half her face burned, the other half a mass of wrinkles, perpetually smiling, first to laugh at jokes others did not intend, appalling punster, linguist, mother of eight. Lai'Basbeg, stern and tall, who outlived six husbands, ran a butcher shop for twenty years, and in retirement made wooden puzzles for children. Jol'Haskei, willowy and gorgeous and white-haired, and broad-faced Tosg'Homain, her hair still deep black as nights never were in the Iskari city—whose marriage, and more to the point, the joining of whose libraries, had caused such furor four decades before. She had known them all her life. They were old, and beautiful. They were Archivists.

She invited them inside. The dawn was cool, and none of them were so young as they once were. Hojah observed that this was true of everyone. They all knew this joke, but they laughed, because it felt good to laugh. The morning had left them cool and damp, but tea warmed. The children, grandnieces, grandnephews who had brought them ate and drank in the kitchen as they sat in the courtyard, and when the tea was done they all climbed the winding stair to Aman's roof.

Across town in the Bite, Fontaine shivered in her kitchen, knees pulled up to her chest beneath her nightgown. Coffee steamed on the table, and three pills lay on the napkin, side by side by side, next to a glass of cool water. She had slept little that night. She did not know what would happen today. She knew enough to scare her. That was fine. She had drugs for the fear. She had drugs for all occasions.

The kitchen smelled of coffee and stale water. The faucet dripped. Should get the landlord to look at that. She wanted to call her dad, her mom, her college roommates. She wanted to write a letter right now, run down to the post office in hope her note could make the morning mail to anywhere else. Nothing grand: no warning, no confession. Just reaching out to mark a world that did not much care for that sort of thing. Fontaine had made her life in stories and fortunes, and those bore as little trace of those through whom they passed as did the surf.

She wanted her drugs.

The pills lay red and green and white against the brown paper, printed with glyphs that meant something, she supposed, to somebody.

She gathered the pills in the napkin, in her fist, and threw them down the sink, to the monster that lived in the pipes and ate her garbage. She ran the water as it chewed. Footsteps behind her. Her husband's arm settled around her waist. He bent to press his cheek against her cheek. She reached up and back, and clutched the tight coils of his hair.

"Long night?"

"Yes," she said, and "I love you."

The sky blued, and the Shield Sea with it, and Kai, on the pier, wished she'd packed a thicker coat. She turned her collar up against the breeze, and reviewed herself: her linen suit, her little black prayer book in the inside pocket, her purse heavy with religious paraphernalia. No glyphs. No weapons. No deep magic from before the dawn of time. The Altus Spire stood, a bare splinter on the horizon, half in sea and half in sky.

She heard Eberhardt Jax's lighter, and smelled his tobacco, before he joined her on the pier. Jax wore boating shoes and checked trousers and an ascot, and a blue blazer draped over his shoulders, and must have used a razor to part his hair. He smelled of sandalwood and pomade. She liked those smells, even as the tobacco eroded them. "I'm sorry," he said, drawing the cigarette from between his teeth. "Bad habit, but it calms the nerves. Big day." His eyes flicked left. They were very blue. "You want me to put it out. You think I should put it out?" He shrugged, dropped the cigarette, crushed it with the toe of his boater. "I should have quit years ago. But we only have so much willpower, and every decision we make, we spend some. I conserve mine, to spend it in the right places, at the right times."

"Where's your boat?"

"Oh," he said. "That." He raised his right hand, and made a gesture almost like a conductor beating six-four time. A ring on his index finger trailed ruby light, and one on his ring finger trailed sapphire.

Space lurched at the end of the pier, and there was a ship where none had been before: a tall white yacht built like a teardrop, contoured for speed, save for the bristling nightmare antennae on the cabin roof. Kai blinked. "I expected something more practical."

"If you have nice things, why not use them?"

"I thought the whole point of owning a Iokapi 2300 was to show it off. Hard to do if it's invisible."

"You know boats?"

"My mother runs a small repair Concern. I don't think she's ever worked on something this fancy, though."

A sailor with a metal arm lowered the gangplank.

"I find observation tiring," Jax said. "It is good to be seen. But sometimes it is more comfortable to go without." He stepped onto the ramp and extended his hand with self-conscious goofy gallantry she played into by accepting. "Take us home," he told the sailor when they stood aboard; she raised the gangplank, shouted an order, and took the wheel.

Jax, one hand pocketed, strode to the bow. The way he stood, moved, spoke was all assumption: he expected the world would bend to his wishes, because it so often did. But Kai knew tyrants, and he lacked their scorn. Eberhardt Jax was a machine more than a man, a system of ideas, a rumor and a fortune and a set of contracts dedicated to building that fortune. Eberhardt Jax, the meat, the person who once was born and might one day die, was incidental to that machine. He guided it, built some parts and directed others, but the machine did not need the man. Many of Kai's pilgrims, no matter how great their wealth, no matter how vast their power, never grasped this truth. Jax cultivated carelessness, and let his machine carry him.

She joined him at the bow. The boat gained speed. He clutched the rail and grinned. A gust tore his blazer from his shoulders. Kai caught the blazer one-handed before it went over the side, and passed it back. He grinned his thanks.

The Altus Spire grew on the horizon. The yacht sailed

smooth for all its speed, so the spire seemed to grow from the waves, an architectural obscenity—but as they neared, its scale crossed from grotesque back to glorious. Crystal and glass and steel facets broke sky and surf into a thousand seamed reflections, some inhumanly perfect as a demon's painting, some mere washes of color. The spire did not belong here, would not belong anywhere, did not care. It was not built for this world.

Somewhere within, Kai's sister hid.

The sun cracked the horizon, and the spire took flame.

Kai gripped the rail, and told herself she was ready.

Chapter Seventy-three

TARA CLIMBED THE WALL.

Stone pulsed underfoot. Hollow tunnels ran beneath the wall's rock shell, strung with nerve and muscle and vein, extensions of the squiddy Wrecker Tower. Below and to the north, four-story apartments grew in the shadow of the wall, and laundry waved on rooftops. Old men and women walked in public parks, or danced to the bands of dawn, lifted weights in public gyms, played shuttlecock by the Express tracks. Long ago, when the Iskari made Agdel Lex, they'd judged this wall a good limit for their city. Someday, they imagined, the godlings beyond would kill each other, and the plains could be settled again. Until then, they would station Wreckers on the wall, to guard against the monsters of the Wastes.

Someday had not happened yet.

But today the Iskari would force the issue—unfurl their web in the sky, make the Wastes flower again, and save the world. With a minor, forgiveable human cost.

The long climb winded her. She waited atop the wall. To her left, far away, stood a Wrecker, and to her right another. The Wastes were a smudge of roiling gray, save where the Express tracks printed a clear line through chaos. Or printed a clear line of chaos through . . . something else.

Tara gripped the rampart, and felt nervous. A city behind her, a city that wasn't hers, a city she'd done more to hurt than help, while trying to solve another problem altogether. She had not pondered second-order effects, let alone third. She wondered what her old teacher Ms. Kevarian would think. Had she ever found herself in a mess like this, a catastrophe she'd helped shape, beyond her power to control?

Probably.

Tara wished she knew what Ms. Kevarian had done.

Then she cracked her knuckles.

. . .

Take an anthill, marble its tunnels, polish them glistening white, limn each surface in silver, and you'd come near the Altus Spire. Ants included. Scientists and techs quick-marched through the halls, intent, carrying clipboards, arguing, men and women and golems with a mission. At every corner Kai turned, she saw a clock counting down. Loudspeakers announced: launch in one hour. Fifty minutes. She tapped down the halls, keeping pace with Jax, because he was her host, and because the crowd parted when he neared.

Questions dogged them down the white corridors; Jax brushed most of them off with one raised hand. His assistant paced at his right, Kai at his left, which frustrated Kai, who was nobody's assistant.

"Sir, the Imperial Mark—"

"It's a blip, not a proper correction. Hold through. Draft a quote for the *Times.*"

"Dhisthra's high council—"

"Next week."

"Seventy—"

"Ask for another ten percent. If they don't, dump our stake."

"Grimwald—"

"Next week, if they have room. Anything else?"

The assistant displayed his clipboard. They'd barely cleared the first page, and Kai counted ten more.

"Karl. Please. Deal with it? We have history to make."

The elevator doors closed, leaving Karl on the other side.

Jax did not press a button. He turned a key, and the elevator thrummed up in silence, smooth, and so fast blood gathered in Kai's feet. They did not talk for most of the elevator's rise. "History," he said, wistfully.

The floor onto which they emerged was busier than the ones they'd left. Kai could tell, because the halls were empty. Windows opened onto a dizzy height, the sea and the continent so far down Kai might have been flying. She would have been more comfortable if they were. If they'd been flying there would have been good dependable magic keeping them aloft, or a dragon's wings; in this case someone had just stacked things on top of one another until they were so high the fall would kill her before the ground could manage.

Jax burst through double doors into a room walled with glowworm monitors. Techs and acolytes and Craftsmen worked sigils and prayer wheels and thaumaturgical implements. A squat woman in a V-neck sweater stood in front of the monitors, hands behind her back. When the door burst open, she turned. "Sir—I didn't expect you for another half hour."

"I came early, Doreen. Wanted to show my guest around."

"Of course."

The woman in the sweater frowned at Kai, and Kai tried her best to look like someone who might be shown around high-magic installations during a critical operation. Girlfriend was the obvious choice, so she settled for *consultant,* which more suited her skill set. She suspected Jax's girlfriends might tend toward simpering, and she'd never been able to fake a simper.

Jax glanced at his watch. "Everything in shape?"

"Slight echo on the passenger telemetry"—she nodded over her shoulder to a station where a man and a woman frowned at a spinning planchette—"but we're fixing it."

"Could we have the room for five minutes?"

Doreen blinked. "Sir." Kai knew that tone of voice. She'd used it herself, when supervisors turned idiot.

"Or three. I want to show our guest around without getting in anyone's way."

"So you'll get in everyone's way at once."

Jax grinned, or at least bared his narrow white teeth, which was close.

"Okay, people." Doreen clapped her hands. "Coffee break. Out in the hall. The old man wants the room. Three minutes. Go."

Grumbling, arguing, furious, the techs shuffled out. Doreen had to pry one from her seat. And that left Kai and Jax lit by glowworm monitors in a maze of equipment Kai did not understand, before windows overlooking an enormous metal spear, which she did.

"History," Jax said, staring at the monitor. "That was the plan."

"You'll still have your history. Only now you won't go down as a mass murderer in the bargain. Sounds like a good deal to me." Kai sat at the telemetry station. "Does this give you a read on the pilot's location?"

"Not precise enough to pinpoint someone within the building." Jax turned to her. "I thought that didn't matter. You just wanted to—"

"There's been a change of plan."

"A change of plan." He echoed her words in the tone of voice people used to describe kinks they didn't share.

"I know." She struck the side of the telemetry station. One pilot marker glowed in the prep room. "That's Vane?" They'd gone over this the night before, but a review never hurt.

"Yes. According to the schedule."

"Who's this?" She tapped the screen, where a second pilot marker glowed.

"Tracking glitch."

"What's supposed to be in that room?"

"Spare suits."

"Okay." Kai stood, and rolled her shoulders. No matter how deeply she breathed, she could not make her diaphragm relax. She thought about surf, about beaches, about cities made of sand. "It's time."

She turned, and kissed him on the cheek. She didn't know why. She needed to kiss someone.

Glowworms writhed on the wall, and in their writhing made pictures.

In his office, the night before, they had debated whether she should knock him out. For all the theatrical appeal, that would draw the wrong kind of attention. Better to open the door, invite the techs back in, and slip out in the fuss.

Then the door swung shut, and Kai stood alone.

• • •

Izza, Hasim, and Umar paced the Refuge. "We can't stop the launch," Hasim said, as he finished the salt circle. "But we know how the system works. The Iskari wish impose the squid's vision on reality. We will offer a different perspective—and protect as many people as we can. As the Iskari withdraw their protection, the half-gods of the Wastes will rush in, and flock to us, to devour our faith."

"So we will strangle them," Umar said, as he lifted an enormous iron bar and settled it across the doors. "Cast them back. And the Fifty Families will do what they can."

Izza traced mazes in the salt with a stick. A small part of her couldn't believe she was still here, trying to help, asi f she hadnt' tried to convince Kai they should both run, as if this city had ever been kind to her. Agdel Lex hadn't—neither had Alikand. But Hasim, and Umar, and Isaak had. "How long can we last?"

"Long enough," Hasim said. "We must hope."

She prayed. How can we help?

We'll think of something, the Lady replied.

For a Goddess, You're not particularly reassuring.

A grin, slender as the edge of broken glass. *I like to improvise.*

· · ·

Kai's watch ticked. She crept down the hall past the room marked "Prep," to an unmarked door with a lock she prayed open. She turned the knob slowly, and closed the door behind her in a way that made no sound.

Dim ghostlights illuminated row after row of standing almost-human forms, like empty suits of old-fashioned armor without plating, helmets with transparent visors that wrapped the head. Decapitated Knights, shoulders blazoned with the Altus up-arrow insignia, they waited, watching.

She heard a muffled curse from behind a row of suits.

She stepped around the corner.

Ley looked up.

She'd been trying to lock a gauntlet in place with her teeth, having, apparently, given up on using her other, already gloved, hand for the task. Kai stared into her sister's eyes in the dim.

Neither moved, for longer than either could afford.

Kai's goals dried in her mouth.

Slowly, she approached to within arm's reach. She caught Ley by the shoulders. Before her sister could draw back, or fight, she pulled her into an embrace.

"I'm sorry," she said. Nearby, clocks counted down.

Ley froze, at first, then softened. Even through the layers of armor, Kai felt her sister's arms circle her, hold her.

"I—" Ley broke off. "Can you help me get this glove on?"

"I love you."

"I love you too." Said automatically, but then, again, with thought: "I love you. What the hells are you doing here?"

"They got Zeddig."

For her sister, one sharp indrawn breath took the place of tears. Kai felt the muscle of Ley's jaw twitch against her cheek. "She knew that might happen."

"Bescond chained her to the tower."

Ley drew back. She looked down.

"Go. Save her."

"And give up—" The dim light glinted on Ley's cheek as she turned away. In a minute, her voice was steady. "We planned this. She made the run, distracted them, let me sneak in here. They'll be telling stories about that run for years. And if I do this, no one remembers my name. There's a neat balance to it. Almost art." She drew a wet breath through her nose. Dragged her armored forearm across her face. "You made me get snot on my spacesuit."

"Save her." Kai took her black book from her pocket. "Here. A simple prayer—lets you walk on water. There's an Iokapi 2300 idling offshore. A sailor and a mate on board. Try not to hurt them—I'm sure they can swim. Once you make land, you're on your own."

Ley did not reply.

"Let me do this for you."

"This isn't your fault."

"It's not yours, either. It's not even Bescond's. It's just a bunch of people doing things history told them to." She drew back. "Besides. If I let you go up in that thing, Mom would kill me."

Ley turned back to face her. She looked so tired. She was cut, somewhere it did not show, and bled need. Kai wondered what it felt like, to feel that way about someone else. Then she realized that she knew.

"Do you trust me?" she said.

Ley looked into her eyes. "Yes."

"Then go save your girlfriend. Let me save the world."

"You never let me do anything fun."

"Older sister's prerogative."

Ley smiled. "How long have you been thinking about that saving-the-world line?"

"Twelve hours."

"Twelve hours and that's the best you could do?"

Kai scuffed Ley's hair, and Ley batted her hand away.

"Come on, I'll help you put on the suit."

"Can I have one without snot all over it?"

"Try that one on your right. It's more your size." Ley unhooked her gauntlet, undid the clasps around her waist, and shucked off the top half of the suit, and the body stocking beneath. Under that, she wore a tank top; a piece of glistening gold clockwork ticked above her heart. She tapped the gold gears with her middle finger. "First, though, I have to stab you in the chest."

Chapter Seventy-four

VANE WAITED IN THE white room, alone, helmet off, elbows against her thighs. When the door opened, she glanced toward it, and saw the suit, visor down. "I was starting to think you wouldn't come." She examined the space between her boots. "I'm glad you escaped the Wastes. The good Lieutenant thought you were looking for a weapon out there, some way to break the ship. You did not, of course, want to stop the launch. You wanted to hijack it, use its power, like one of your pirate foerbears, paddling out in a canoe to steal a treasure ship. You couldn't stand to see your work bent to another's service—the Iskari's, or my own. You didn't need a weapon—just a key." She tapped her chest. "I could have told her. But I'd rather wait for you."

The suit creaked as Vane stood. If she cared about the approaching footsteps, she didn't let on.

"Or am I wrong? Was it all for love? Did you try to ruin our lives for the sake of a woman who never understood you, who never could have understood, trapped in her broken city and sad traditions, a woman who can't even conceive of a horizon, let alone advance against it? Someone who cast you to the curb for trying to describe her world? Compare that to what we had: we were equals, Ley, a pair of bonfires. We would make millions, pose on the cover of every magazine. Jealous cocks around the planet would look at the losers they work beside and wish they were us. You couldn't have thrown me over for some delver."

The footsteps stopped.

"Well. Bescond has her now. You know, back in the days of empire we used to parade conquests through the streets in triumph. You ever wonder what that would have been like? To be in the chariot, or behind the bars? Perhaps we should revive the practice."

She bent, hooked her helmet with her fingers, and examined her reflection in the glass.

"You came to stop me. But you can't. Darling, I have years of you back home—strands of hair, bits of skin, your spit sealed in vials. I know all your secret names; I know the way you breathe in bed, and what makes you weep. I'm careful, you see, with lovers. I've had months to build traps for you. I hired very reputable disreputable people. Spent tens of thousands. You can't stop me now. You can't even move." She turned. The tinted helmet bent the white room: the benches, the lockers, the clock on the wall, the ghostlights in the ceiling, her own teeth. "Try."

The suit stopped.

The clock on the wall ticked. Vane's smile widened. The minute hand advanced. A siren wailed.

"You should have known better," she said, when she was ready. "You killed me once, when I wasn't ready. Did you think I'd let you stop me again? You wait here. I'll be back before you know it. Then we can talk about our future."

She leaned in to kiss the glass. The angle changed. So did her expression, when she saw the face within.

Then Kai punched her.

Vane fell, more from shock than pain, but Kai didn't wait.

Before Vane could recover, she grabbed her with both arms, lifted her, shoved her into a locker, and slammed the door closed. Vane cursed, and pushed against the latch; Kai searched for a proper lock, found nothing, and wedged the door shut with her shoulder. Something hard, thin—

There was a weird oblong pen clipped to the suit. Thread that into the latch, and easy going. Vane hammered the door from the inside, roaring in frustration, but the pen didn't give, the locker didn't dent, and her voice was lost in the launch countdown. Kai wondered what, exactly, you were supposed to do with mad installation artists, decided this was as good a solution as any, and turned toward the door.

She stepped through the hatch, out onto the gantry that led to the spear.

She'd worked in shorter buildings. She'd climbed shorter mountains, for that matter. Denuded of fuel hoses and diagnostic tools, it stood; glyphs burned blue on its side, the spear Altus would throw to wound the heavens. And Kai, for her sins, would ride it.

Don't look down, had been Jax's advice when they discussed the approach. You're not used to drops like this. It'll make you sick, and scared. Kai pointed out that she was used to diving into a bottomless pit.

Jax's answer: this one has a bottom.

So she stared straight ahead at the capsule door. Within, banks of switches and glowing Craftwork equipment menaced her. The chair did not look comfortable. She remembered the archives back home, the thorn couches that let a priestess see all her gods all at once. Just take it step by step. She didn't have a part to play at this stage, just a monkey along for the ride. Once the web unfurled, that would be her chance to—well.

Shine, hopefully, though not in a burning-up sort of way.

Eyes in the chamber's walls watched her, feeding images back to the ops room's glowworm screens. She shot Jax an okay sign with her left hand, as agreed.

Then she stepped into the capsule, and settled back in the coffin.

The capsule closed on its own. There was a seatbelt here—what she'd heard dragon jockeys call a five-point restraint. Good. Fine. She clicked the straps together.

The capsule felt small. The tiny windows did not help. She heard her own breath. Vane probably had more room in that locker.

She laughed. None of this was funny, so she laughed harder. The clock ticked down. One minute.

Lines of blue and white cracked the gray dim silo. The spear, the ship, rumbled, but Kai felt none of the weight Jax warned her about, none of the pressure. The ship did not move. The building opened around it. Silo walls split, unfurled. Sunlight and sky spilled through the gaps. Kai stared up into blue.

This was a bad idea.

Scratch that. This was a horrible idea.

But Ley was safe. She'd save Zeddig. And maybe, if this worked, Kai could save the rest.

The system needed a focus—a mind to bridge the minds below. All Kai had to do was get up there, and refuse, under any circumstances, to be that focus. Don't let the machine make you one. And, while you're up there, listen to the stars.

Glowworms in the control panel writhed green.

Somewhere, a loud voice said, ten.

Lightning danced between the spire's petals.

Eight.

There was a roll of thunder.

Six.

Coils of shadow rose overhead, fast as a whip crack, sapping blue from the sky.

Four.

The lightning settled into steady arcs between the spire petals.

Two.

Light bridged earth and sky.

Kai felt heavy, and yet she rose.

Chapter Seventy-five

LIGHT PIERCED THE SKY.

Aman saw it from her rooftop in Hala's Fell, where she gathered with the other Archivists. The city spread below in haze and shadow save for rare oases where a street, a building, stood in perfect outline, crisp as the texts upon their laps, unchanged in a hundred fifty years. The sharp light splayed their shadows open. Aman reached out with her hands, and found her friends reaching with theirs. Together, the Archivists bent to read.

Tara, on the rampart, glanced over her shoulder, saw the light, and nodded. Her watch must be a minute slow. She closed her eyes and laid bare the world's convoluted spiderwebs of Craft, all pale before the mass of power Eberhardt Jax cast toward the sky. Then she turned back to the Wastes, and counted heartbeats.

In the Temple of All Gods, Izza saw the light and prayed. Doctor Hasim and Umar stood beside her, facing south toward the Wastes beyond the walls. Izza prayed Kai's plan worked. She prayed Kai made it home. She prayed there would be a home left to come back to. She fixed the city in her mind, Alikand of winding passages, its coffee and parks and chess boards and its old men singing. She did not love it like she should. It was not her city. But it was Isaak's, and she would fight for it, regardless of how he felt. That didn't hurt, much.

She called for the Lady, and She came.

In the Rectification Authority Tower, Bescond paced, and checked her watch, and paced more. She could not see the light, or the launch. She had told herself, that morning, it would be better to remain below, tending the tower's needs in case anything went wrong. She felt the change through her Lord, through the web of Wreckers across the city. Tentacles pressed her neck, soothed, like a mother cat gathering her kitten in her fangs. "On schedule." Bescond flipped her watch shut and tucked it in the pocket of her vest. "Not long now. Then we can turn our attention to better things." Her audience hung limp in her restraints. "I'd hoped for some conversation, at least, while we wait. I admire your determination, Zeddig. I think we might like one another, if we met under different circumstances." Zeddig rolled her head around, and stared up through the blood. "Then again," Bescond said, "perhaps not."

Across Agdel Lex, the light drew them: artists and Craftsfolk and rubberneckers, locals and foreigners. Enthusiasts who'd flocked to the seashore to watch the launch cheered, and toasted with beers; some popped bottles of sparkling wine, corks vaulted skyward chased by spray. They donned sunglasses so they could stare into the light and watch the spear rise, a black sliver at the column's heart, moving slowly, it seemed, because they had nothing against which to judge its scale, or the speed of its ascent. They watched while the sun quailed beneath the weight of the Altus Craft, and stars emerged from the blushed purple of dawn.

• • •

Raymet would have slept through the whole thing if not for the knock on the door.

She blinked, found her eyes gummed shut, tried to wipe them with her wrist, found said wrist otherwise occupied beneath a weight, tried the other one. Sore all over, and not the good kind. Her lips stung when she licked them. The knock didn't fucking *stop*, might as well have been hammering her skull as the door. She tried to tell whoever it was to lay off for a moment, but her voice was a growl—what had she been up to last night, anyway?

Oh.

She did not recognize the room, because it wasn't hers. Of course not. She sacrificed to the squids, for all the good it did her. She had a mortgage, like a good girl. So they knew where she lived, which meant they couldn't sneak off to her place. They'd gone to Gal's instead. Gal barely existed so far as the official system was concerned—a foreign ghost, a rat in the walls.

Raymet's memories of the night before lay scattered like notescards on a scholar's desk. There had been running, and fighting, and screaming, and more running, more than even Raymet was used to. And then.

She turned to see what, exactly, kept her arm still.

Gal stretched beside her, tall and strong and gold and naked. She glowed. She radiated heat.

The door burst open, and Ley stumbled in and scanned the room. Her gaze hitched on the bed, and she turned right around to face the wall. "Sorry!"

Raymet pulled her arm free, stood, and tossed the sheets over Gal, just waking. "What the hells are you doing here?"

"They got Zeddig. We don't have time to talk. I need your help."

"What? Who's *they*? Where are we going?"

"The tower," Ley said.

"Fuck!" Raymet punched the wall. She realized she was also naked, which didn't help. Her skin was a mottle of bruises, but nothing felt broken. Another memory from the haze of the night before: Gal's shining hands smoothing her skin closed, her bones straight. The glorious godsdamn pain of healing. "We just broke out of that place. They'll have double the guards, triple the alert."

"We can delve in."

"Into the tower? We'd last maybe ten seconds, even if we had equipment, which, in case you didn't notice, is a bit lacking at this point. Do you have the knife?"

"Lost it."

"Great."

"In a few minutes, the dead city won't matter." Ley turned around. Raymet had seen her serious before. This looked different. "Zeddig is in the tower. I can't get her out alone. Will you help me?"

"Yes," Gal said, before Raymet could reply.

"Dammit!"

"Did you intend to turn her down?"

"No, but I wanted to work my way up to it."

"Get clothes," Ley said. "Shoes. Weapons, if you have them." She checked her watch. "We have ten minutes before the city goes weird."

• • •

Kai rose.

An invisible giant's hand pressed her against the couch. She tried to lift her head, and could, but her stomach lurched. She settled back and dragged deep breaths, forcing her reluctant diaphragm to do its job. So far, so good. She wasn't dead yet.

Dials counted altitude and speed. Others angled her ascent. The glowworm screen writhed to convey messages from the ground: stage timing, operation progressions, all systems go. She could do nothing with this information, barely understood most of it, but she felt better knowing someone, somewhere, knew what all of this meant, and anyway all the lights were green.

Aside from the air around the capsule, of course, which burned red and orange and gold and blue. As did the capsule itself—its exterior, thankfully. Kai wondered if the glass in the windows was really glass, and if so, whether it would melt. Probably not. Jax had far too many smart people working for him to slip up on something like that. Then again, she'd worked with smart people—hells, she *was* smart people—and she never ceased to be amazed by how smart people could fuck up, given opportunity and time.

A crack echoed through the capsule. She glanced out the window, and saw the building-tall spear shaft fall away and drift, spinning, down.

That was probably supposed to happen. At this point, if anything happened that wasn't supposed to, she'd be too dead to care.

The shaking stopped. The fire died. Outside her window shone stars, and the black between, and there, big and bright and clear, the moon.

The giant uncurled her fingers and let Kai go. She raised her arm, experimentally. The movement felt too slow and too fast at once—buoyant as if in water, but without water's weight.

Lights blinked. Dials clicked. She heard a low grinding

sound like surf, but not. Her weight shifted. The stars spun. Below her, above, dawned an enormous blue green sphere, scored with swirls of white cloud and lines of mountain gray. Categories she'd only ever applied to maps wrapped themselves around an object in space: an enormous object, yes, in a space all the more enormous, but an object nonetheless, a shape that held her, that she could hold. That oval down there was the Shield Sea, and that other smaller oval the Ebon, and there the forked prongs of Telomere, Isarki swells and Camlaan, and west across the ocean, lost among the blue, a green dot of home.

I can see my house from here, she thought, and laughed, and realized when she laughed that she was crying.

She flew, or fell, above the world.

The glowworms writhed. *Deploying Payload.*

Fixed on the world above, on the enormous smallness of sky and sea, of everything she'd ever loved, she almost missed it when the silver net began to spread.

But she still screamed when its claws carved her mind.

Chapter Seventy-six

IN THE HEAVENS THERE was a seed, and from that seed grew a silver web.

In the city, they saw it grow. The Altus Spire sapped blue from the sky and left stars and purpling black above. Men and women, demons and children, born abroad or with roots straight back to Telomere, they watched great lines unfold and birth smaller ones, each pattern echoing the whole.

Watching, in awe and fear, they were many. Watching, in awe and fear, they became one. Gendarmes of Agdel Lex and grand dames of Alikand's secret alleys, Craftsmen and bankers and grad students and refugees and thieves, they stood together. Even those who hid from the web in the sky existed in some relationship to it, defined themselves against it. For an instant, the whole city lay tangent to itself.

An instant was all the web required.

The world slid past itself and began to change.

• • •

Raymet, running between Gal and Ley, felt the change. She'd spent years studying the topology of belief upon which Agdel Lex was founded; she'd built her life around exploiting it. And now it changed. Uncertainties meshed with uncertainties, and grew certain.

The ground quaked. Alleys stretched to give birth to city blocks. The skyline revolved on hidden axes, as the dead city's broken spires twisted into daylight. Air spasmed: now blew the dry desert wind of Agdel Lex, now Alikand's wet Shield Sea breeze, now the dead city's razor chill. The clash kicked up dust devils and whirlwinds. Each streetcorner birthed a storm.

When they reached the Rectification Authority Tower, the barricades were up. Someone, Bescond perhaps, had weighed the risk of uprising during broad-spectrum universal realignment, and didn't like their odds. Wreckers waited there, and conventional troops, some wearing exoskeletons of glyph-glistening steel, others shouldering blast rods. A net cannon swiveled toward them, spoke.

Ley shouted, "Delve!" and they did, and landed in the dead city, skidding through hoarfrost on broken pavement, in a university quadrangle studded with decapitated statuary. Before them, where that gross tower stood in Agdel Lex, rose a wave of stone and gold and mosaic and light: the Anaxmander Stacks.

They sprawled before a gate that never knew a door. The ancient scholars and Queens who threw off the yoke of Telomere's blood-mad legions had decreed the mother of the mother of the mother of this palace would have no door, and their children honored their decree. Beyond that tall portal, beneath stained glass, rose shelves carved centuries ago from the wood of trees long gone, some killed in the wars when they fought Craftsmen, others harvested to extinction. The Anaxmander Stacks, the greatest library in the world.

The architect Hala'Koselli, ten centuries before, and of fucking *course* Zeddig's great-great-great-something-or-other, had built a masterpiece. Its lines drew the eye skyward to the summit, where life and world went wrong: the Wound in the dead city's heart, where Gerhardt hovered always dying, never dead.

They scrambled to their feet, and sprinted toward the gate.

"We should be dead already," Raymet said. "This close without gear—"

"We don't need gear," Ley replied, "anymore."

"But we don't have the knife, either, so—"

"We all have the knife, now. Up there, in the sky."

The barricade remained in vaguest outline, like a fog bank. Gal ran through it without slowing, and up the stairs toward the gate. Police pointed; a blasting rod flashed, and a wave of mist passed through Raymet before she could flinch. If she'd been back in Agdel Lex, her guts would be splattered across the library stairs. "They can see me. In the dead city."

"It's all coming together," Ley said. "Like a deck of cards. This is the shuffle. The next part's the bridge."

"Do I want to know what that means?"

"You'd probably rather run."

In a better world there would have been time to mark the first entry to the Anaxmander Stacks in generations. A ceremony would serve. A prayer, perhaps. But this was not a better world, so a curse would have to do, and the sound of running feet.

• • •

Kai was ten thousand feet across and growing.

This was the plan. Ride the system, don't use it. It wants to give you power. It wants to let you decide what the world is. Resist.

The web unfurled, she hovered weightless at its center, falling and staring down. Silver wire spun from the capsule, filament by filament built against the stars. And the web was part of her, as if some surgeon had stripped her skin, cut free her nerves, rolled them like a stick of glass above a flame until they glowed, then spun them to fine thread.

She heard.

How many voices, in Agdel Lex and Alikand? Ten million? Eleven? Present, wondering, tired, scared, eleven million of them to one of her, each staring up, seeking truth from this extravagance in the sky. Kai heard them all. Some of their languages she knew. (Iskari: never seen anything like that befo— Talbeg: please, just come here and look out the godsdamn windo— Schwazwalden: pondering in perpetual expanse— Kavekanese, to her horror: a children's song.) The words were shards, signals, footprints. The voices mattered, the voices and the selves behind.

What were they? Who were they? So *many*. They were not her people, they were not one another's people, they were together and they tore apart. Hearing them, holding them all in her mind at once, broke her. Who was she? The fisherman's daughter, the banker, the woman screaming pleasure, the sister, the artist, the wanderer, the priest, the thief, the lover, who? Who, to look out from so many eyes? Who, to hear with so many ears? What did her one body matter, when she could be both sides at once of a screaming orgasm in the Bite, when she could hold an infant to her breast and suck, when she threw burning bottles at cops and trampled herself underfoot and felt her own ribs break?

They were scattered shards on a floor.

She was one among so many, and she was coming to pieces.

No.

She fought to remain herself in the flood. A reflex, the oldest battle: she knew who she was, she knew her body, knew her past and her home and her family and her soul. She clung to them.

And the web heard her, and began to change.

• • •

From her rooftop, Aman heard the screams. More worrying, she saw their source. The city tightened into focus in pieces, striations of Alikand forced to union with the Iskari city. Structures unfolded from the sky like cut paper models. Streets unzipped between buildings. Worlds that did not admit other worlds existed scraped sides.

They were not one city yet, but many cities striped through one another. The clarity of Alikand, its colors and draped rugs and fluttering flags, pressed against the plaster and gray steel of Agdel Lex. Pressure built. The clarity gave way in places, held fast in others. And, on the borders, the dead city's monsters boiled through.

They were half things. Skeletal torsos webbed with metal crawled on their forearms, spitting spring-loaded poison tongues. Spider walkers scuttled up buildings, pierced onlookers, infected them with whirling bugs that made them turn, hungry, to devour. A shell long frozen in another world detonated in a market square, tossed shrapnel and wood splinters and bodies—but the explosion inverted, warped, twisted itself back, and shaped all that debris to a lumbering almost-human form of fire, triple-jawed, full of eyes and diamond teeth.

The war kept clear, she noticed, of the Iskari sectors. They did not have such memories.

Aman did not remember the God Wars. Her grandmother had been a girl when the city broke. Adda never spoke of it, and Aman, who spent long hours with her in the courtyard learning backgammon and chess, learning about Adda's childhood, about the school where she taught and the girls and boys who studied there, about everything but the war, found her silence carried more than speech could bear.

These monsters were echoes of a blast Aman felt happy she never heard. How horrible it would be to watch all this from a rooftop, unable to help.

"It's time," she said, and each finished what each had already begun. Adal set her hand upon her book, and glared into its paper and the labyrinth printed there. Hojah turned a page, grinned, chuckled, and began to change. Basbeg ran a finger down a margin as she read, and her skin shimmered. Haskei's thin lips twitched as she scanned her text—she made no sound, but loved the shape of words in her mouth—and wings slipped from her back, and she was tall and dark and lustrous as a statue three thousand years old. Homain touched her with a hand deep black as the night, and her hair was a nebula, and she was huge and strong, and sacred words glistened on her skin. Aman read her acrostic, and spread her wings.

They were not themselves anymore. Adal was Ko, and Hojah was Zel, and Basbeg Lai. They were the angels of their families, last links of a chain passed back and back. The libraries fed them, gave them light and life and strength: volume after volume, gathered, cared for, shelved and shared, loved, read, stained by coffee and by ink, wrinkled with tears and rain.

They looked at one another, and at the world.

And for the first time in a hundred fifty years, the angels of Alikand took flight.

• • •

Tara, on the wall, saw the Wastes flicker. The twisted self-devouring mess of almost-gods writhed as the web spread in the sky, and then they were gone, and desert, blasted here and there to glass, spread to the horizon. Then the Wastes flickered back, only to vanish again.

The web was working—for now.

Tara wished she knew how long Kai needed her to last. She wished she knew the other woman had made it—that this would be anything more than a last stand.

But then, nothing was ever easy.

The Wastes could not be part of Agdel Lex, Iskari city. There was no room for dead half gods and war damage in the Demesne. Before the web, the Iskari could only wall out the Wastes—now, with ten million citizens' negotiated faith, they could seal them over entirely. Of course, the Wastes' half gods would not go without a fight. But as consensus pressed down against them, they found another realm lay free: Alikand.

Wet gray beasts made from braided snakes roused themselves from the divine slush. Great skulls rolled toward the wall; a hundred enormous hands, claws, paws, assembled into a centipede with fingers and talons for legs. They advanced in strobe-light flicker as the Wastes faded in and out: barely present, trickling forth, and now a wave, a flood.

She could stand aside, and let them pass over her, through her. She belonged to Agdel Lex. The visa in her pocket, with its tentacled seal, said as much. She stood under the squids' protection.

She raised the visa before the godflood, and tore it down the middle.

The seal flared. She let the two halves of parchment fall, burning. A pair of winged fangs bubbled up from the flood to eat them.

She fell into the dead city, into Alikand. She stood on a wall. Then the wall was gone, and she stood on air. The flood came for her.

Fucking *finally*.

Tara Abernathy drew her knife.

Ready? she prayed.

Across the city, Hasim and Umar answered, *Ready,* and another voice, too, a girl's.

Good. The more the merrier.

Far away, Tara felt the moon smile.

They had that in common. This, at least, at last, felt right.

The flood reared, cobra-like and vast, slavering mouths and crooked claws and burning eyes, and struck.

And Tara cast it back.

· · ·

Izza stood, hand in hand in hand, with Hasim and Umar, in a ring in the salt circle, facing out. They prayed. Izza felt the Lady inside her, lending strength from the congregation back across the waves in Kavekana, and she listened to Hasim's chant in a Talbeg dialect she barely understood, felt him do things with faith that she had not known possible. He found tangent points of belief, he bridged the gap between his weird bird-headed knowledge god, Umar's massive sharp white river, and the Lady—did not combine them so much as braid them, and pass that cord of faith to Tara on the wall, to the Craftswoman who was a priestess, for use as a lash.

But when the Wastes struck, they struck hard. Hasim staggered first. His hand twisted in hers. He buckled, and Umar held him up. Izza felt the impact like a fist in her gut, like a knife in her arm, like a broken leg or a coal in her grip. She'd borne all those before, so she kept still, and fought.

Silver monsters and corpse-snakes and things no language Izza knew could name climbed into their courtyard: the dead city's demons, drawn by the smell of faith. Umar's grip tightened, his focus shifted, and one of the courtyard's chunks of masonry flew to bash in a corpse-snake's skull, then struck a six-armed silver gorilla-scorpion thing in the chest. Izza heard a series of sharp pops, like a firework string, and fléchettes appeared, arrested, hovering, in a globe around them, stopped by the salt. One tiny razor hovered at eye level, burning red-hot as it tried to cross the enormous space the salt maze created. Momentum spent, it fell harmless to the courtyard stone.

The rope of faith pulled, and this time Izza had no yardstick for the agony.

In the cramping, aching wash, she almost missed a voice calling her name.

She knew that voice. Isaak.

Isaak, not distant, not praying, but Isaak *here,* banging on the door Umar barred.

"That's my friend," she said, through gritted teeth.

Umar: "A trick."

Sweat ran down her temple. She could barely speak through the agony. "Bullshit a trick. That's my friend. He's here."

"It's not safe," Hasim said. A spider-walker dawned over the eastern wall, huge and globular. Talon limbs tore roofing tiles free.

"I think we're a long way past safe." No answer. Only pain. "If I go, can you hold up until I get back?"

"I—" Hasim said.

Umar said, "Yes."

And before Hasim could convince Umar otherwise, Izza slipped from their hands and jumped across the salt.

The pain, instantly, got worse. The world outside the salt line rolled like a ship in a storm, and Izza's experience of ships in storm tended to be from the shittiest part of the vessel. She kept her stomach, barely. Kept her footing at first, then didn't. Tumbled. Some sort of revenant with turning blue gears in its eyes jumped her; she stabbed it in the side. It did not seem to mind, but at least the knife gave her a handle with which to shove it off. "Izza!" from behind the door, scared. Sounds of a struggle. She slipped out from under the revenant; a line of fléchettes tore through space in front of her; close one, she thought, diving into the shelter of the doorway, before she realized her cheek lay open and there was quite a lot of blood.

Fuck it. Scream later.

Grab the iron bar. Lift. Come on, Lady. I know You're busy, but opening doors, this is what You're for.

"Izza?"

"I'm coming!"

The Lady tried to grip the iron bar, but it was iron, and iron didn't like gods. She tried to make Izza strong, but some damn thing happened on the wall and all Her power slid out into Tara Abernathy. Behind the doors, screaming.

Then the Lady laughed like Kai did when solving a puzzle, and popped the hinges.

Izza danced back as the door fell in. Beyond, she saw Isaak, breaking the neck of a mantis wolf sort of thing three times his size.

He landed in the dust, on his feet, bleeding. The mantis wolf fell beside him.

Had they been alone, there would have been time for an apology, an embrace maybe, a joke.

But they were not alone.

The alley before the Temple of All Gods was full.

Most were children. Street kids in rags, youngest around seven. Bruised, some. Some missing limbs, one or two blind, led by others. Among them, at their lead, in a rush of vertigo, she recognized the boy with the flowers, from the pier, with the scar on his cheek. He wore her blue disk around his neck, on a thin leather thong. And once she saw that, she saw the blue the others bore: a bead at the wrist, a shirt, a ring in ear or nose, a flash of tattoo on skin.

Some were older: toughs and shy slender kids she recognized from the bars they crawled after Vogel's meetings. They, too, wore the blue, and they were fighting, against the monsters of the old war.

And the Lady was with them.

She did not know what showed on her face. Something hot and wet stung her cheek, aside from, of course, the blood.

"Did you think I was the only one?" Isaak asked.

"They're all—" She lost her voice.

The kid with the blue stone around his neck knelt. To her. And others started.

And she felt them join her: awe and faith, strength, loyalty. Joy.

She caught the flower boy by the arm, and pulled him to his feet. "No. We don't kneel." He rose, awed. "Get inside. Jump across the ring of salt—don't touch it. Go!"

The kids ran past them, and Izza caught Isaak in her arms.

He was covered with ichor. Izza didn't care.

"Thank you," they said at once, and, as something exploded in the background, there was time for a smile.

Then they ran.

• • •

Zeddig hung from the squid's heart, beaten, bloody, and fought to care.

Some damn chemist could probably name the drug cocktails flowing through her, but chemistry was less than half the game. Sounds below the edge of hearing worked inside her brain and told her to relax. The mask piped mother-smells, triggering instincts of receptivity and information acquisition ontologically prior to more developed notions like judgment. Accept us, they did not command. Never command. Only suggest. Offer. Present a framework for thought, fix a maze for the rats to run where every end is one you want, and you won't even have to train them.

She tried to hate the squid, the tower, but could not muster the will to hate. This did not hurt, exactly. She had been hurt, in the rush, in the fight. She had hurt herself, been hurt by others who wanted to protect the city and its people. She fought for her faction. The squid tried to keep all factions safe. A clear hierarchy applied. And at this moment, the squid fought harder than ever. Something was happening. Zeddig thought she remembered it being important.

She tried to hate Bescond, pacing the chamber of the heart, flanked by Wreckers, barking orders. Bescond, who hurt her, Bescond, who chased Ley through the city, Bescond, instrument of empire. Bescond, who herself inherited a system, Bescond, who did the best she could with the world in which she lived, Bescond, who saw chaos and wanted order. She was a zealot in pursuit of that order, Zeddig's jaw proved that, but—no, she could not hate Bescond.

Could she love her? the squid asked.

Zeddig refused to answer.

She dreamed, and in her dream, the door burst open.

Three women ran through.

Gal, ten feet tall and shining, for Camlaan and glory. She loved Gal.

Raymet, too, bleeding and short and fierce, knife and blasting rod drawn, at Gal's side. She loved Raymet.

And there, beside them, in black: Ley.

Gods.

Zeddig realized she was crying.

Wreckers launched themselves at Gal; she swung one into the next, and drew her sword. She brandished it, trailing rainbows, and the world sang.

Raymet and Ley ran across the room toward Zeddig, but Bescond stood in their way: tripped Raymet, and punched Ley in the face. Raymet rolled forward, came up, scrambling toward Zeddig, but Ley grabbed Bescond's arm and tried to break it.

Ley knew how to fight. She took classes, at university, and kept in shape. But Bescond had made her stripes enforcing arrest warrants in the Wings. She broke Ley's hold, and buried an elbow in Ley's stomach. When Ley folded, Bescond kneed her in the head. Ley stumbled, blinked, blocked the follow-up jab, and the cross, but she took the uppercut below her ribs. She staggered. Bescond moved in, but the stagger was a feint, and Ley caught her by the shoulders and they went down together.

Good instinct. Dumb move. Bescond was stronger, more compact. She wriggled under Ley like an eel; Ley grabbed her jacket, pulled it back to trap the woman's arms, but when Bescond flexed, the jacket split. The Lieutenant reached back over her shoulder and jabbed her thumbs for Ley's eyes, and Ley head-butted her in the back of the skull, and they rolled.

Ley was bleeding. Bescond almost caught her in an arm lock, then did. Pulled. Ley pulled back. Raymet had reached the squid, struggled with Zeddig's bonds; one Wrecker lay at Gal's feet, and Gal fought the second now, blade flashing—but more arms sprouted from the chamber walls to snare her.

Bescond tugged harder. Ley's arm gave.

Zeddig could not hear the crack, but she felt it, as if the arm were hers.

And she screamed.

This was good, the squid told her. Painful, but good. We have priorities, in this world. Hierarchy. Some may suffer, briefly, to keep the city safe.

Bullshit.

Bescond moved her grip from Ley's arm to her neck.

This was wrong. Zeddig would not accept. She would die first. She would kill.

A space opened between her and the squid, and in that space, Zeddig dove.

She fell into the dead city as the squid's world tore, and she dragged the others with her.

She sprawled on a checkerboard tile rooftop. She should

feel cold. Delving inside the tower—she should have died at once. The knife must be working, in the sky. No time to think. Zeddig scrambled across tiles. Everything hurt. Her leg did not work. How many broken bones? She didn't care. Didn't care about Gal, or the Wrecker she'd dragged through into the dead city, or Raymet.

She forced herself to stand, and scraped across cracked marble to Bescond, who straddled Ley's back, struggling with both arms against Ley's one to crush her windpipe, break her neck. The Lieutenant had not noticed their fall. Her teeth were bare and bloody, and her hat had fallen. The squid-god at her neck pulsed joy into her blood.

Zeddig hit her, with her full weight and her closed fist. A bone in her hand snapped. Something in Bescond's face did too. Zeddig liked that. Balance.

Bescond fell, and Zeddig fell atop her, and kept hitting her until she went limp.

She collapsed, barely able to breathe, staring at Ley, who cradled her broken arm and clenched her teeth against the pain. Or was that smiling?

"Don't you have somewhere to be?" Zeddig asked.

"I love you," Ley said. "I had to come back."

"Yeah. But." She pointed up, to the web in the broken sky.

She slumped against the checkerboard tile. "My sister's up there," she said. "She can do it."

• • •

Kai was losing it.

There were too many voices. Scared, sad, loving, furious, resigned, they warred, these visions of the world. They were tearing her apart. She could not let them break her. She had to forge them to a single truth.

To live was to decide. Each path killed worlds. Which to choose? Who to break?

I have a few suggestions, a squid said.

• • •

On the beach of Alikand, ancient glass beasts from the God Wars charged onlookers gathered to see the Altus launch. A man screamed. Blood sprayed sand. But the glass beasts shattered as Aman flew among them, the angel of Hala, full in glory.

In the Bite, where rambling alleys sheltered pockets of Alikand, a spider walker tore through an apartment block, until Haskei struck it in a cyclone, tearing limbs asunder.

Where the dead city rushed into Alikand, angels flew to meet it. Lai toppled a tower of glass and eyes and teeth; Ko swept down into rippling streets to rescue a young man almost crushed by falling buildings. But they could not be everywhere at once. The Craftwork monstrosities Gerhardt called to being, they knew how to fight angels. Lai suffered the first great wound, as the wreckage golem gathered her into its flame, and exploded; she flew free, skin cracked, victorious and bleeding light. But each victory slowed them, and there were too many to save.

They tried. Down generations they had saved themselves, gathered texts and argued timing and tactics. They feared the right moment would never come. They feared it would. And now, they fought, and soared, and spent themselves to save their people.

And still, people began to die.

. . .

Kai lacked a Lord herself, so the voice was not in her mind—but it remained in the web all the same, a burbling immensity turning in the depths of this crafted nightmare, a rubbery ground of being.

You see the chaos they create, it said. You see what happens when we let them work their will. People scream and die. They suffer—they cannot help but suffer. They cannot agree on names for roads. How could they agree on the foundations of a world? Only we can fix them. Only we can braid them whole.

Hear the screams. Smell that child's sweat as she flees the many-limbed horror of her history. Feel the heartbeat: a man runs home, fears his children lost. They all knew this day would come. The dead city would break through; the world would fail. They know, deep down, that this is what freedom looks like—and so, though they claim to yearn for it, they truly yearn for us.

They're tempest-tossed. They have made their own storm, and when the flood takes them, they drown.

You cannot stop this. Let me.

Fuck you, Kai told the squid. I can save them myself.

She took the voices, and looked down upon the city, and began to decide.

. . .

Pain split Tara's skull, and she staggered in midair as the world changed beneath.

She let a screaming godlet's body fall, but two more caught

her from behind. Their talons skittered off the thin glyphs dyed into her suit in place of pinstripes. Coming back to herself, she cast the godlings off and shredded them, exploiting a weakness in their strange loops. A wave of gray struck her shield—and some splashed through.

The shield hadn't broken. Power still flowed from the Temple of All Gods. She was winning, dammit! This wasn't fair.

What else was new?

What had happened, what (jaws formed of a god's ribs snapped shut around her, but she splintered them offhand)—oh. The shield stood, in Alikand. But now the wards of Agdel Lex were breaking.

We have a problem, she prayed.

• • •

On the roof of the Anaxmander Stacks Raymet saw Zeddig fall, and Ley, and Bescond, together. She knelt, herself, beneath an obscenity.

A cold wind blew from the Wound. She did not, at first, look up. She kept her eyes to the ground, and would have prayed if she had any god to hear her.

Across the rooftop, Gal tossed the Wrecker into space. She radiated glory. Smiled like a storm front. She was not looking at Raymet.

She was looking up.

Where the gray flesh pillar of the tower's heart had been, in a wrongness in the sky, there stood a man. He was dark-skinned and white of hair and beard. He wore a gray suit, and there were no eyes in his sockets, but fire. His teeth were bare, and he clutched one hand to his side.

Maestre Gerhardt. The first master of the Craft, who had destroyed half a continent in the infancy of his power. Always dying, never dead.

Broken angels and impaled gods and snapped girders and chips of stone orbited him. Space warped and rippled, and time ran strange.

Another shape shared the center of the chaos: a woman in a suit, holding a blade driven to its hilt through the man's ribs, piercing his heart.

But Gerhardt would not let himself fall. He would fight forever. He would kill all who came before him. And Gal's Queen had sent her into the world to die.

Gal was already running, blade raised, toward the Craftsman. Who stood, crazed in his dying moment, unable after a hundred fifty years to let himself fail. Who could kill Gal in a heartbeat, and she would die happy, quest fulfilled.

And Raymet would lose her.

No.

She threw herself into the dying Craftsman's storm.

• • •

Izza's mind was a mess of prayer.

—*Just bottle the Waste-gods somewhere else*—

We can't, Hasim shot back. *There's no other choke point.*

I'll fight them. Umar.

Bullshit, Tara prayed; her limbs ached with her struggle, and her focus was slipping. Some teeth got through her wards, and a gray god-stain spread across her arm. *I can handle this. There's no sense in all of us dying.*

We will fight together.

Adults, dammit. Izza held Isaak's hand, and the faithful, her Lady's faithful, gathered in the circle, each linked to each. She felt the Lady's frustration: She had power, She lent power, but She *was* a story, and this story was not Hers. The Lady didn't make last stands.

The Lady ran.

Izza squeezed Isaak's hand, and slipped from it, and vaulted over the salt circle. She was in her limbs: the Blue Lady of Kavekana and Agdel Lex and Alikand, and gods alone knew where else around the world by now, as the faith spread shipboard from poor kids and thieves to poor kids and thieves. Izza crested the wall in a running jump and sprinted south through the unfolding metropolis: a leap carried her from a dead city siege spire to an Alikander market, and with a slip she found herself running through an Iskari office, between cubicles, as scared clerks sheltered under desks, only to dive out the window into a bomb-blasted crater, because the Blue Lady scorned all borders. Izza sprinted, climbed, scrambled along clotheslines, vaulted from lamppost to lamppost, toward the gray tide flowing into Agdel Lex. Toward Tara Abernathy, who fought that grayness back with lightning and razors and will.

What, Tara prayed, *the hells*—she stabbed a thing that did not have a face in its face—*are you doing?*

What I can, Izza answered.

The gods of the Waste towered above her, inchoate. They were knives in the dark, they were fire, they were Penitents' eyes and stale beer breath and everything Izza ever feared.

She stood atop the tallest building she could find—it had been an observatory, once—and spread her arms, and let the Lady burn through her: all that faith, all that meaning, the tastiest target in the world, theirs to seize if they could just catch her fleshy shell.

"Come get me," she said.

The gray roared, roped itself into a mile-high serpent, and lunged for her.

And she fled.

. . .

Kai cursed and swore and screamed. So much pain, down there. She could fix it. She could fix everything, if they would all just listen to her. There would be no storms, and the sea would never take them. No pain. No death. No bodies, no mourning white, no pallbearers bringing fathers home. She'd fought so hard to make the world obey—to take her life into her hands, to force fate down proper courses. And here she held the reins of the world, but they were hooked through her hands, and other reins pierced her arms, other bits tore her mouth, and she and they were all just puppets moved by hooks that tore their flesh, but if she fought hard enough, if she bled long enough, she could save it—

. . .

Ley stared up into the sky. Somewhere, there was a war. Somehow, people fought. Around her the city twisted and coiled, an injured octopus, a gallowglass in tangles. She could barely move. Her shoulder and arm, her ribs, were masses of agony. Zeddig sprawled beside her, and Bescond beside *her*. Alikand and Agdel Lex were burning. Angels flashed, fought, died.

The web spread in the sky.

She stared up. The strands drew her in. The web listened to her, molded to her.

She spoke her sister's name.

• • •

Izza ran.

The Blue Lady sprinted like a shadow through the trees, and she was the Lady's prophet. There were no trees here, but Agdel Lex and Alikand and the dead city were forests, after a fashion—different layers of the same forest, and she sprang from canopy to trunk to root and back.

The gray followed her. It wanted her. She tempted and tantalized. All that faith, all that meaning, all that soul, out of reach. The gray had no form—lacked believers save its need, lacked dogma save expedience. She ran? Fine. The gray would make itself run faster.

She sprinted over rooftops in the Wings, darted down mazelike Alikand alleys, guided by the knowledge of the kids she'd left behind in the Temple of All Gods. No need to ask directions. She knew these streets as if born to them. Doubled back, ran loops, cut across the great Iskari boulevards, stitched the city to the city. The gray could not touch her. Could not keep pace.

It wanted her, though. All the little godlings bled together as they tried to solve the problem of Izza. The gray saw the Lady, felt the shape of her story, and changed to match her. The smoke of godlets became a cascade of footfalls, thousands of Izza echoes, running.

She had left this city long ago, hungry, furious, sad, and

never thought to return. She never expected to save it. Or to sacrifice herself in the process.

She leapt over the walls of the train station, darting past cranes, over cargo containers, through warehouses, and the flood of Izzas scrambled after.

. . .

Gal was a poem. Lightning struck her, but she cast it aside with her burning sword. Space crumpled around her, but she was not there to crumple with it. She fought toward Gerhardt, singing.

Raymet, on the other hand, lurched, dodged, tumbled, fell. The air around her thickened, and she could barely breathe. Time ran slow in the center of that bubble. Gerhardt, within, had aged ten seconds in a century and a half. "Stop it," Raymet cried. Choked, as a tongue of thick air wriggled into her mouth, but she bit that tongue off and spit it out, then fell through a cloud of razors that cut her skin. "Stop, dammit."

She did not die. Vines of iron thorns sprouted to spear Gal, who danced past, grinning.

"It's over," Raymet shouted against the torrent of time. "You won. You won a hundred godsdamn years ago. Stop fighting."

Gal cut through the thorns, but some had caught her. She bled. She slowed.

Raymet lost all words for the battle between Gal and the Craftsman. The Craft sent against her were thorns, so she was a flower growing from the thorns; the Craft a hand to pluck the flower, and she a bird to fly from the hand, and the Craft a net to catch the bird, and she a seed to slip the net.

Gerhardt's lip, Raymet saw, twisted up just slightly. Cruel. Amused.

"You think this is a fucking game?" She reached for him. Her fingers numbed. Chilled. She couldn't feel them anymore.

Gal fought on behind her, beautiful and doomed.

Raymet caught Gerhardt's lapel. Her fingers were ice. They would not close. She did not care.

"You have the whole fucking world," she said. "Just die, and leave me her."

The smile faded. Like a glacier receding, his eyes tracked left.

The woman who had stabbed him held her arm across his neck. There was a ring on the finger of the hand that held the knife. Tears glittered, frozen to her cheeks.

• • •

"Kai," her sister said.

In the silence of space, in the maelstrom of her mind, she heard the voice. She felt a hand on her shoulders.

"I can do this," she growled. "I can fix it. I can—"

"I know." She felt her cheek against her cheek. "That's how it gets you. You want to fix everything, so badly. You want to prove you can make it work. We both do. It's okay. We can't. The world's not ours to fix. Things change. Dad's gone. And I love you."

• • •

Izza vaulted to the roof of the train, jumped onto the station, and dove off—landed, with a roll and a skid, in the plaza before Gavreaux Junction.

Fitting. Agdel Lex ended here, for her, years ago, in fire. Might as well end here again, in ice. If the plan didn't work.

The gray landed behind her, skidded exactly like, and came, in perfect time, to their feet. An army of Izzas, they were, an army of Ladies optimized to sprint and chase and flee. Desperate in their hunger, the gray did good work. They made fantastic copies.

And, with stories, a copy always flows back to the tale that gave it form.

The gray realized what was happening, too late.

They tried to scramble, scatter, flee. But as they ran, they blued, and changed, and the Lady closed Her hand and made them Hers.

. . .

Kai let go.

The voices called to her, in their millions. They were not hers to shape, but she could not stop up the ears of her mind. So she let them speak.

There were so many cities, below. How strange, to try to force them into one. A city was a prism. Hold it up and look one way, and you saw one image; hold it another way, and another formed. She listened to the tension; she heard the squid railing for its vision, and the other voices hungry, so hungry, for theirs.

Looking down, she saw Agdel Lex and Alikand.

Good.

Let them be.

Kai had a promise to keep.

"Kai," her sister said, at first. "What are you—"

Her voice faded, with the others.

Gyroscopes within the capsule shifted. The web tangled, re-aligned. The world wheeled beneath her, and set. The moon remained. Stars filled the porthole overhead.

She kept silence, and listened.

• • •

On the roof of the Anaxmander Stacks, the wind stopped.

Many things died at once.

In the center of the space, on a raised platform, where once astronomers sought the stars for truth, crumbled two skeletons in suits of bloodstained wool. They both wore rings.

As they fell, as they died at last, so too did the dead city's war machines, its spiders and its revenant monsters and the Craft loosed on Alikand. The Wound slipped shut and, healing, left a scar in space.

Raymet collapsed. Her hand struck stone, and shattered.

She was too numb to scream. But she could breathe, and when warm arms wrapped her, she could speak the name of the woman to whom they belonged.

Gal looked beautiful. And not entirely disappointed. "Your hand."

"It's—" Her voice was hoarse with the cold. "I'll get another one." To distract herself from the pain, she caught the front of Gal's shirt with her remaining hand, and pulled her down, and kissed her.

• • •

Angels gathered in the silence above the city. Ragged, hurt, and shining, they watched the new world unfurl: broken glass and broken alleys, burned towers, palaces unseen in a hundred fifty years, bomb craters and broken windows filling with people as they explored the fresh and long-hidden damage. Prayer flags fluttered in market squares. The angels hovered above a city they did not understand, a city they recognized from maps and memory but had never known in life. They saw it clear and crisp as new type.

They had not won. They had fought, expecting death, hoping for survival, but they did not know what to do when death failed to oblige them.

A blue spark rose from the city below, and stood before them. A Talbeg girl, barefoot, proud, her clothes torn and dirty, no kind of Queen at all, her eyes were blue from lid to lid, and when she moved blue light trailed her limbs. She was larger than the limits of her skin. Before her, the angels fell back.

"Do we know you?" asked the angel of House Hala.

The girl seemed to find that funny, but the angels did not laugh. She said, when she recovered: "You should. I'm the people who don't fit. I'm refugees and migrants and street kids who've never been anything like legal, caught between the lines of your long slow war. I saved you. So now let's build a future that leaves no one out."

"There have been no gods in Alikand for two thousand years," said the angel of House Lai.

"Then we have a lot of catching up to do," said Izza.

• • •

Bescond woke to find herself on some godsdamn rooftop, blinking into sunlight. No way she had been out that long. She could not breathe through her nose. Her ribs hurt like hell. Several knuckles broken on the other hand. Something fucked with her ankle?

She sat up. The world swam.

She stood.

This was not her tower. This was not her city.

Beyond the building's edge—she could not make it all sit side by side in her mind. *War zone,* she thought first, and there was that: craters and corpses, shattered markets, ruins she'd only ever glimpsed before through the little breaches her Rectifiers sealed. She could not be seeing it now: she would be dead. And yet it lay beneath her, and living people stood among the craters, tiny at this distance, but wondering, and scared, prisoners with their blindfolds removed. Prayer flags fluttered on the wind. Talbeg calligraphy climbed crumbling proud walls, and made them poems.

But not all the city was dead. Dense winding alleys ran like webs, like cracks in ceramic glaze, between plaster buildings, up and down the Wings, along the Bite. The shore was bare of factories and hotels, the port of container ships, the jetty where High Sisters should have stood was wind-washed rock again, but the fishing wharf remained, small boats bobbing at anchor. She recognized these places, though she'd never thought to know them: small corners not worth her notice. And they were woven through the dead city now, and no one was dying.

Impossible.

And, since impossible, she had no need to understand.

She looked down.

Zeddig and Ley sprawled on the ground at her feet, side by side, breathing slow. Exhausted. Hand in fucking hand.

Lords.

She reached into her jacket for her knife.

An enormous shadow blocked out the sun, and the wind of wings blew her hat from her head.

The angels landed in a semicircle around her. They were too big to be human, and their wings glimmered deep gold.

The one at the circle's apex said, "This is not your place anymore. It never was. You have built your own. Go back to it."

And then she fell.

• • •

Kai hung above the world.

She did not know what was supposed to happen now.

She felt light, in more ways than one.

There were systems, Jax had said, to bring her back. Would they still work? Maybe. She hoped.

She listened.

After a long time, the capsule woke with silver.

There was a woman outside, framed by the moon, though the moon had set long since.

"Tara?"

The woman smiled. *Not exactly.* She looked behind her, at the sky. *It's nice out here, isn't it?*

"Yes."

I don't think about space this way, She admitted, a bit embarrassed. *This is not how they told the story of the world when I was young. That may sound odd, I guess.*

"Not really," Kai said. "I've met You before."

Once or twice. Seril sighed. *I wouldn't blame you if you wanted to stay. It's peaceful out here. There are so many places to go.*

"Someday, maybe. For now, I have work."

The Goddess smiled halfway. *You need a vacation.* But She reached out, through the window and the capsule's skin.

Kai took Her hand.

Epilogue

LEY WAITED ON THE beach as the sun sank and the sea grew dark.

Behind her, cities sorted themselves out. Her shoes sank into the sand. Shooting stars fell above, and the moon claimed the sky.

A shadow marred—or perfected, depending on one's point of view—the silver disk. Was it a face? A woman reclined beneath a tree? A rabbit? If Ley had a lover in another country, she would see what she was raised to see, and so would Ley, yet they both watched the same moon.

The air rippled, and Kai stepped out as through a curtain. She looked . . . like Kai. There was more to say, but there were no words. She landed gently, but sagged when gravity took hold. Ley caught her before she fell, with the arm she had to spare. Kai's weight hurt, but she did not let on.

"I would have thought," Ley said, "the Goddess could have found you a tailor."

"I'm trendsetting," she replied. "Rags are in this season." Laughing seemed to hurt. "Zeddig? Abernathy?"

"Busy. There's been something like a revolution."

"I heard."

"You saved my life. I saved yours."

"Cancelled the debt."

"I'd rather not think of it like that," Ley said.

"How would you rather think of it?"

She helped her up the beach. "Miracles. Not only is Sauga's still open, but I got a reservation. I'm loopy on painkillers, but I can't think of a better way to spend the next few hours than to hallucinate while you drink wine, and talk about anything but business."

"I'm not dressed for Sauga's."

"I thought you were trendsetting. Just be yourself. It'll be fine."

Kai laughed. "I think I can manage."

Arm in arm, they made their way.

"Do you know," Kai said, "I still have your cat?"

• • •

Women waited on the water. Some stood upon its surface, as if on a marble floor. Some hovered over it, wings spread. Zeddig sat in a boat, and wondered why she was here.

The water went glassy at first, then bubbled and surged. An immense eye breached, star-pupiled and red and ringed in rubbery flesh. A robed man took shape over the pupil's center—his form and figure clear, but the sea visible through him, as if he were a trick of the light. "You betrayed us," he said.

"No," an angel answered. "We defended our city. We did not harm yours." Which is more, she did not continue, than you can say in return.

"Ms. Abernathy," the man continued, as if the angel had not spoken. "You are in breach of our agreement."

"Let's set aside," Tara Abernathy said, "the force majeure question. Neither I, nor Alt Coulumb, has harmed Agdel Lex, or Iskar generally. We even protected your territory, when we were under no obligation to do so." Her skin glistened a mottled metallic gray beneath her shirt collar. "We have, however, formed a separate agreement with the interim clericy of the sovereign state of Alikand."

"Leaving us a city of roads and temples, and no people."

"Now you're exaggerating," Tara said. "The cities split. The split is stable. Alikand has its territory. You have yours. Many stayed on your side of the line. Others will come."

"You will starve Agdel Lex of trade."

"That is not our intent," the angel said. "But if the cities of the South would rather trade with Alikand than Agdel Lex, they're free to decide. Competition and free trade are your bywords, not ours—but we will hew to them."

The great eye blinked. The man disappeared, and reappeared when the eyelid opened. "Those you have seduced to your banner will find your yoke as harsh as ours. We will pry them from you." The calm sea boiled with great limbs.

"I don't think so," said a new voice, younger. A girl stepped forth from among the angels. She glowed from within, and swirls of blue light rose where she set her feet. "This isn't just the old guard talking. The city stands, or falls, through its people. All of them. And the Fifty Families will listen." Izza looked uncomfortable in the center of so much attention, uncomfortable with the way space warped around her. But she stood anyway. "I don't know what we'll build. We'll sit down: the old families, my people, the folks at the Temple of All Gods, the guilds and the gangs and the folk who don't belong. But whatever we make, it won't be about you."

"Who are you?" asked the man who wasn't there.

"I'm the woman who ate the Wastes," Izza said. "Now get lost, before we spit in your eye."

• • •

Three days later, Tara met Kai on the top floor of Iskari First Imperial. "I love this," Kai said, looking down at the city: at its towers, and the gaps between them. "It looks so *weird*."

Agdel Lex lay massive, and in pieces. The great boulevards remained, and the waterfront, and much of the Bite. But the territory beyond—

"I've seen worse," Tara said. "There's room for development now."

"Thank gods." Kai pointed at the papers on the conference table. "If I have to commit a few million thaums of Kavekanese capital into the local economy, construction seems like a good bet."

"Better in Alikand."

"Well, yes. But this way Fontaine gets her chunk, and I get mine. And Jax, through me, gets privileged access to Alikand's new capital markets, which was a cheap enough price, considering he let me interfere with a twenty-million-soul project."

"The capsule landed."

"It was on fire."

"The fire is normal. Happens on reentry."

"I've lost track of which of us owes the other," Kai said, after a while.

"Or who was playing whom."

"Does that hurt?"

Tara stroked the smooth mercury skin on the side of her neck. "It—somethings."

"Thank you," Kai said. And: "I listened, while I was up there. I almost died, but I did listen." She produced a crystal from her purse: a recording of heaven.

"That was the deal." Tara accepted the crystal. She did not look embarrassed, but something close. They had both gone too far for deals. "What did you hear?"

"Stars."

"Yes."

"They . . . sing." She licked her lips.

But Abernathy was too much a Craftswoman to be put off by that. "And."

"I heard—legs. Skittering closer. Whispers older than time. They speak in the pulses of distant suns. They're so, so hungry. And they smell us."

"It's okay," Tara said, and took her hand. "We'll think of something."

Kai squeezed Tara's hand back. She wasn't reassured. But she smiled anyway.

• • •

Raymet heard the metronome tick of a heart monitor, and opened her eyes to an unfamiliar ceiling. She found Gal waiting. She had taken enough drugs to recognize their effects: opiates, laced with dreamdust, some analgesic Craft, with something she didn't know to round out the soporific edge. She didn't feel nearly paranoid enough. Maybe almost dying had something to do with that.

She tried to push herself upright, and fell when her left hand passed through the railing around the bed, because the hand, of course, wasn't there. A smooth steel socket capped the limb where the wrist should have been.

There were things she was supposed to feel now, she knew, from watching plays, and reading books, but none of those felt right. She cast about the room and settled again on Gal, who knelt beside the bed, calm.

"I guess I fucked things up for you," Raymet said.

She wanted an anchor for the grief beneath her surface, she wanted an excuse to pour it out onto someone else, spewing rage like pus from a sore, only to make the infection worse. But Gal said, "You made it." And she sounded glad.

"You wanted to die. Wasn't that the point? You'll never get a better chance."

"There are many kinds of battle. This is one."

She did not say anything. Gal hugged her, and kissed her on the ear.

That, of all the damn things, made her lose it.

When she could gather words again, she said, "I guess I'll get a hook."

"They have hands."

"Do they?"

"I thought I'd wait, and let you choose. I don't have an eye for this sort of thing."

"Maybe I can get one with flames. To make it go faster."

Whatever Gal thought about that, she kept to herself. But she rang the bell, and before long the doctor came with the case of hands.

. . .

Zeddig almost missed them in the throng before the wall. She had to climb a statue and scan drifting heads, waving banners, sprinting children, cameldancers, street carts selling fried dough and coffee, mothers with picnic baskets, for the two Kavekanese women hand in hand, looking lost: Ley in a white linen suit and straw hat, Kai in a sundress and big red sunglasses, carrying her picnic basket.

Zeddig somersaulted down, danced through the crowd, and rescued them from a barker marketing some newfangled variety of meat on a stick.

"Busy," Ley said, after they kissed.

"First time we've done one of these in a while. I didn't expect this many people."

"No way it's safe out there," Kai said, grim, as the gate opened and the desert light rolled in.

"Of course not. But we'll be careful."

Beyond the wall, the plains spread: scrubland and brown grass, hard earth erupting sometimes in thorn. Silicate crystal god-bones formed cathedral arches through which children ran, screaming laughter. A human flood, they moved uphill, touching and seeing, shying from places where geometry grew too strange. The Fragrant Plain smelled of carbon, dust, and glass. But it was a start.

They climbed. Someone chanted in a Talbeg dialect Zeddig could barely place—a home-song from a long time gone.

They each moved at their own pace, and Ley's pace, for all her arm in a sling, was fast; it was not hard for Zeddig to find a moment with Kai alone. "I'm sorry."

Kai glanced sideways, past her glasses. "I'm listening."

"I didn't mean—" But she had. "I didn't trust you, when we first met. I had my reasons. But I was an asshole."

"I didn't give you much cause to like me, either."

"So." She found her lower lip between her teeth, and worked it out. "Why?"

"Why did I help? Why did I introduce your mother to Abernathy?"

"Why any of it? This isn't your city. It wasn't your fight."

Kai closed her eyes, but she kept walking, and did not trip, as if she knew the path unseen. "Why do you think Ley did all this? Why stab Vane and run? Why almost kill herself trying to stop everything she'd put into motion?"

"Because she was responsible," Zeddig said. "Because she wanted to save the city."

"I don't know," Kai said. "Maybe you're right. You know her better than I do, these days. But cities are big, messy things. I think she did it all to save a person."

Ley crested the hill and waved back to them, in silhouette against the sky.

"Go on," Kai said. "I'll catch up."

She did, eventually, and spread the tablecloth from her basket over the cracked ground while Ley poured the wine. They touched glasses. Zeddig tasted red, and felt Ley's heat beside her. Below, far away, they saw Alikand and the dead city rolled to one, the towers topless, streets littered with a century and a half of wreckage, pitted and webbed with empty space where Iskari boulevards once ran. Cranes rose and fell; the city lived, and built. Above it, and around, Iskari ghosts remained.

"It won't last," Zeddig said.

"Not on its own." Ley nestled beside her, and watched the world through the ruby prism of her wine. "We have to help it grow."

Wind whispered toward them, bearing promises of rain.

"Hey," Kai said, pointing: "have you ever seen a poppy like that before?"

Acknowledgments

Sixth time's the charm, they say. Some of them, at any rate. Probably.

Thanks as always to the fantastic team at Tor and my new gracious and excellent hosts at Tor.com: my editor Marco Palmieri, Irene Gallo art director (and now publisher!) most fantastic, to Mordicai Knode and Katharine Duckett for intrepid marketing and publicity support, and of course to Goñi Montes for this brilliant, fiery cover.

Family and friends and fellow travelers have been, as ever, steadfast and insightful in their criticism, analysis, response, inspiration, and raw emotional support: John Chu, Anne Cross, Gillian Daniels, Seth Dickinson, Amy Sarah Eastment, Amal El-Mohtar, Matt Michaelson, Stephanie Neely, and Marshall Weir most especially this time around, but really if we've talked about cities, startup culture, space, surveillance, histories, philosophy, academia, or anything at all in the last six years or so, you're probably in this book in some way, and thank you.

Also, thank *you*. If you're new here, fantastic, and welcome. If you're an old hand, thank you so much for supporting these books. They're strange, fun, and they give me room to talk about things that are important, and hard, to discuss head-on. These books travel from hand to hand; what they've done, they've done through your offering them to friends, to family, giving them and talking about them and drawing art. I'm so grateful.

The world, right now, needs delvers, and angels, thieves and heroes, and Craftswomen. It needs us. It needs stories, but it needs praxis, too: the acts that make ideas real. Keep fighting, loving, speaking, standing up for one another and for a liberated world of guests and friends. Work. So will I.

About the Author

Photograph by Nina Subin

MAX GLADSTONE has been thrown from a horse in Mongolia, wrecked a bicycle in Angkor Wat, and sung in Carnegie Hall. In addition to the Craft Sequence, Max is lead writer for the eBook serial *Bookburners*. He has also written several short stories for Tor.com, as well as the interactive story games *Choice of the Deathless* and *The City's Thirst*, both set in the world of the Craft Sequence. Max was nominated for a Lambda Literary Award and is two-time finalist for the John W. Campbell Award. He lives near Boston, Massachusetts.

www.maxgladstone.com

TOR·COM

Science fiction. Fantasy. The universe.

And related subjects.

*

More than just a publisher's website, *Tor.com* is a venue for **original fiction, comics,** and **discussion** of the entire field of SF and fantasy, in all media and from all sources. Visit our site today—and join the conversation yourself.